NOT YET DEAD NEARLY

1.

Crack.

The half-light of a dying flare fell to earth, illuminating the sack of flesh and bones that crumpled to the ground. He had only been sent out to fix the wire.

The man on watch straightened up, eyes searching for the source of the gunshot, his person as grey as the scene he surveyed. Dirt stained his face and hands which scrubbing could not remove and the hair beneath his soldier's cap was thick with it. A raised line ran halfway across his face; a souvenir gained during his first shift at the front. He had since seen shrapnel do much worse. The disfiguration to his face was the least of his worries. French mud was thick and deep and stuck his boots to his feet, and the lice that found their way into the men's clothing ensured they never rested.

And of course, there was the ever looming presence of Death. He sat at his post, rifle in hand, keeping the reaper at bay for the moment, his blue-grey eyes alert and watching through the periscope for anything that moved in the vast wire graveyard.

A flicker of light made him jump, but this was small and came from the British side of the field. Another idiot with a cigarette no doubt, lighting up at night despite the warnings that this may be the last thing you ever did. He held his breath. He could have hoped not to hear the piercing sound of gunfire, but prayers were rarely answered this side of the channel. Instead, he kept his focus ahead of him, determined to pinpoint the shooter this time.

Sure enough, the light went out, coupled with two bursts in the dark. So there were two of them. He fired a shot in their direction, ducking as the invisible enemy returned the favour. His heart pounded, but he had learned quickly not to let that affect his head. Another flare tore through the sky and he raised his eyes just a little over the parapet, searching for any movement. He checked his rifle and fired again, this time hearing a cry as he hit home. There was no time to celebrate; a bullet flew past his ear and he slipped down onto the firestep.

One down, he told himself. *One to go.*

He pulled himself back up, keeping pace with the other man who was firing faster now – he hoped out of desperation rather than confidence. He ducked again and shot blindly, waiting for the return bullet. It never came. He kept a wary eye above the trench for a few minutes, then let his head drop with relief and leant against his rifle. He breathed heavily, adrenalin coursing through his body.

It was an odd feeling, killing; like you had won a great victory but lost something precious at the same time, and he wasn't sure he would ever get used to it. There was something exciting about it though, something that made him feel alive, though he would only admit this to himself. Taking a deep breath, he returned to his watching.

The faintest sliver of moonlight cast an eerie grey shadow across the miles upon miles of barbed wire and blood that held the land its hostage. Reflections in the murky pools of debris showed only the wire and the wreckage and the diseased moon; no summer trees to grace the water with greenery and shade. Here was only grey and brown and red. Every splash of colour had long since deserted, fleeing the flank of skeletal horses that pulled the big guns.

He remembered when the horses were seen often; a final image of fleeting life, a sign of hope for the glory-hungry men fresh off the boats. They had seen the cavalry pass as they marched, the horses' heads held high like their riders, snorting and prancing like true warriors.

They still saw horses now. They were lying twisted and grotesque in the wire, bellowing as they fell down in the mud, unable to pull anymore. Their flaming white eyes reeled until a merciful bullet put them out forever. Gone were the horses with the high heads and pounding hooves. Like the men, they put down their heavy heads, or had them shot down.

"Private Stack."

After one last swift glance across No Man's Land, he turned his eyes to look down the trench. Second Lieutenant Sandford marched briskly towards him, his blonde hair also dusty beneath his cap but looking considerably cleaner than Private Stack.

He was a young man, much younger than Stack, and walked much like a schoolboy trying to impress his parents. There was an air of false authority about him; a kind boy thrown into an unkind place and forced to grow into a man before the mud swallowed him. He was a strong believer in duty, loyal to the platoon he commanded and friendly enough until somebody proved unlikeable. For Second Lieutenant Sandford, this meant cowardly. Despite seeing just as much of the war as the rest of them, he still couldn't understand why a man would not want to give his life for King and Country.

"Your watch is relieved," he spoke sharply, like he thought an officer should, gesturing to a man behind him. "You may find somewhere to rest."

Stack stretched his stiff legs and stepped onto the rough duckboard that ran through the trench. Sandford's face softened and his voice slipped back into the smoother tones of the young man he had been just months before.

"Get some sleep man, you look done in."

"If I can sir."

Sandford patted him on the shoulder as he walked past. "Good man."

He supposed he was tired. He had been alert and focussed on watch, but now it washed over him like molten lead. His eyelids drooped and would have closed had they not been interrupted by a familiar utterance of mirth; Private Daniel Captain, the only man who could find so much to laugh about on the front line.

Like Stack, he was in his early thirties, and the two had become close friends since enlisting, despite Captain being able to hold a lot more drink and survive on a lot less sleep. He was a handsome man and accustomed to being the centre of attention, his black curls brushed just right even now. His smile made him look younger than he was and he wore it often, defying the German guns with a grin. While everybody else crouched and cowered under fire, he would punch the air and curse loudly, daring them to hit him. Sometimes Stack wondered if he actually believed he was invincible.

Unsurprisingly, that smile was plastered across his face yet again as Stack turned the corner. Trenches were full of corners; the sharp change of direction allowing for a grenade blast to be contained within one bay. Captain was perched jauntily on the firestep, watching as others from their section went about the maintenance work he was no doubt supposed to be helping with - Albie Rigby, little Tommy Miller and Stack's brother Edward. Watching them sweat, Stack was almost glad he had drawn watch duty that night; it allowed him to skip the fatigues at least.

"Budge over there Cap," he nudged his friend and collapsed gratefully against the wall.

"Benji!" Captain looked up with delight. "Going to sleep already?"

Stack grunted.

"Germans," Captain sighed, pulling a face. "They suck the fun out of everything."

"Not that I can see any fun here in the first place for them to suck."

Captain chuckled. "Now that is where you're wrong my friend. Where there are uptight people there is always fun to be had. Take tonight. Young Tommy and I were just discussing the likelihood of us getting away with putting a rat in Bollock's hat while he's sleeping."

"How about none?" Stack raised a thick eyebrow but couldn't help being amused. "You're a sick man, you know that Cap? Poor bastard's got enough chance of waking up with a rat in his hat without you getting involved!"

"Oh but he deserves it so much," Captain dismissed him. "Though not half as much as Kent, maybe we should do him instead."

Captain Kent was a wiry man with little patience and even less humour. He was a textbook officer; always well-presented and formal, in a much harsher and authoritative way than Second Lieutenant Sandford. If any of the men put a toe out of line he took it as a personal insult, and he had taken an instant dislike to the jokes and frivolities of Dan Captain, a hatred which was gleefully returned.

It had taken Sergeant Pollock a little longer to gain Captain's aversion, but the bumbling man had soon found a place under Kent's wing and could at times be even worse. Of course it had been Captain who first started calling him Bollock behind his back – much to Stack's amusement and Tommy's admiration – and the name had spread through most of the company.

Tonight however, Stack was too tired for his friend's foolery and Captain could tell. He shrugged and admitted that it wasn't the best plan; he could do better later. Tommy Miller looked humorously relieved. His hair was uneven in places where it was starting to grow back, making him look comical along with his reddened face and round cheeks. Headlice had persuaded them all to shave their heads at first, but after being plagued by every other louse anyway, only Tommy and a few others bothered to continue. The rest simply kept tidy enough for Kent.

"Alright fellers," the curly haired man sighed, leaning back against the wall. "Unfortunately Ben's a mortal and needs his sleep, so we'd better shut it."

"They should put you on sentry duty every night if you're such an insomniac," moaned Rigby, a tall auburn man with heavy eyelids.

"We all know Cap's only awake so long because he can't get to sleep without his sister tucking him in at night," Stack teased, pulling off his overcoat to use it as a blanket.

"I wouldn't mind her tucking me in neither," Tommy Miller smiled, getting a kick from Captain's muddy boot.

Stack pulled his coat over his head, blocking out the sounds of men working and focusing instead on the ringing in his ears that had never really left him since his first taste of war. There was a constant supply of work to be done at night, when poorer visibility made it safer to move. As soon as any repairs were done the Germans would blow them to bits, the sandbags were forever being dislodged and the water had to be kept under control, and the digging of new latrines was always greatly needed, not to mention men constantly on guard.

Edward took these duties very seriously, as he took most things in life, and Captain's light-heartedness had driven a further wedge between the two brothers. Despite living on the same farm, Ben Stack had never felt as close to Edward as he thought he should be. In fact, he tended to prefer the company of his brother's sons to the man himself. Being the middle boy of three, Edward had always been the one with the most weight on his shoulders – even if he did put it all there himself – and it drained him.

His older brother, Thomas, and Edward were only two years apart and had competed fiercely for supremacy since they could walk. By the time their youngest brother came along six years later there was no space for him in their quarrels. Ben learned from an early age that there was no point in trying to be the best when there were already too many people sitting in this position. He slotted casually into life, good-natured and laid back but without much ambition. When Thomas moved away to pursue engineering Ben had stayed on to help Edward deal with a farm, a wife and a growing family, without reaching for any of that himself.

Their differences had followed them into war; Thomas with the engineers and his brothers with the infantry. Edward tired himself out with the struggle to constantly improve and control his battling emotions following the news of Thomas' death. Ben put his head down, laughed with Captain and got on with what life they had.

"Rise and shine sleepyhead!"

A sharp whisper from Captain clipped his dreams like wire cutters and his eyes snapped open; there was no time to wake slowly on the front line. His friend was already immaculate; clean-shaven with his hair combed neatly and his uniform brushed. They washed in small basins and their own hats, only Captain managing the results he did. It was highly likely that he had been awake all night, but his eyes were still as bright as they had been on the first day of training.

Stack didn't care to think what his own eyes looked like above his scar; probably lined and bagged beyond all recognition.

"Is the captain here already?" Stack blinked, running his hand roughly through his hair and replacing his cap.

"I am the captain," he winked, taking pride in his surname as if the word actually increased his rank.

"You keep believing that," Stack smiled. "Though if they made you a captain I think we could safely say there is no hope for the British army."

"True," Captain paused and looked thoughtful. "They would be much more sensible to bump me straight to field marshal."

The stand-to was no different to that of yesterday or the day before. They stepped up onto the firestep, pointing their bayonets out towards No Man's Land, saying nothing and moving only their eyes as they scanned the mist for signs of life. Every now and then an elbow slipped or a weapon had to be re-adjusted, but Captain Kent's stern and watchful eyes kept such movement to a minimum. No shadows slunk through the fog that dawn, and as light started to take hold the first machine gun fire of the morning shouted into the wire from both sides. With this, and the inevitable wailing of shells, the silence was broken, rifle shots tearing across the terrain in the usual morning hate.

After a measly portion of canned beef, bread and biscuits – which made up most meals, but this time was called breakfast – they reported for inspection, while they waited for the relief troops to file through the communications trench and take their places at the front.

They had been looking forward to this part of the trench cycle; making the anticipated journey back through the lines and passing the torch to replacement troops fresh from rest. All battalions were expected to rotate between the front line, support trenches and reserve trenches, with a spell of rest in between. Depending on conditions and how desperate the need for soldiers was at the front, the length of such cycles would vary. Having been a quiet stint, this was their eighth day.

The section marched through the communications trench in an orderly queue, talking of home and ways of killing rats, while occasionally ducking mud and debris kicked up by shells that landed too close for comfort. The smell of cordite was ever present, as was the smell of the people who would not be joining them again behind the front line. A good day was one where you didn't have to walk over the dead.

"Where do you think we'll be next?" Captain asked. "I really hope we get rest somewhere more interesting this time. A town with a nice pub close enough that walking in a straight line isn't a problem."

"Anywhere with living people would be nice," Rigby said dully.

"Anywhere with a cowshed and you'd be happy," Captain joked, making Stack snort a laugh. Captain and Rigby were constantly arguing about women. Rigby was devoted to the point of obsession with a girl from home and carried her picture everywhere; a picture that Captain was quick to point out would never match up to the many women he had loved. "Or a kennel perhaps."

"Anywhere with a brothel and we wouldn't see you for days," Rigby retorted.

"I'm insulted!" Captain pulled a face. "You don't honestly think I need to pay for these things?"

He was cut off by a huge explosion that shook the earth, showering them with wet mud and knocking many down, blasting somebody into the side of the trench. They watched him drop to the floor with a thud, a large piece of metal protruding from the bloody mess at the bottom of his neck.

Stack pushed himself back to his feet, looking around frantically for his friends. Captain had been thrown back into Edward and was bleeding slightly from his head, and Rigby and Miller were coughing on the floor.

He clambered hurriedly over his fellows, keeping low but unable to avoid the splatter of mud thrown up by another shell. He slipped on somebody's arm but reached the man slouched against the mud wall. Covering himself with one arm, he tried to stem the bleeding with the cloth he kept to clean his rifle, but it did no good. People around him yelled for the stretchers, but it didn't look good. A shattered collarbone protruded through the tangle of skin and muscle ripped open by the lump of shrapnel embedded in him, tearing him further as he tried to move. He spluttered blood and gasped for air through a ruined windpipe, his eyes wide with shock; open but not seeing anything.

"Where's the bloody stretchers?" Stack yelled over the gargling and coughing. "We need help!"

He fought a gag reflex as he felt warm blood over the bare flesh beneath his fingers. Flecks jumped at his face and he wiped them off quickly with his shoulder only to be covered again in seconds. The man tried to push himself up and wailed in pain, life spilling from his mouth and the gaping hole in his chest. Stack forced himself not to look away; taking in the exposed ribs and muscle contorted around them. He took his arm away from his face to grasp the dying man's hand. It shook uncontrollably as his body convulsed then went still.

His gasping stopped, the only movement now the flow of blood across broken skin, bone and tissues, running over fingers and cloth and soaking into his uniform. Stack closed his eyes and let the boy drop. Feet squelched through the mud behind him and Captain knelt to place a hand on his quivering shoulder. Nineteen year old Charlie Pepper had trained with them, travelled to France alongside them, sang of glory and returning home to marry his sweetheart.

Now he was dead.

****

"I hope they sent a message to his family," Rigby said for the hundredth time, dropping his cards wearily onto the box-table and pulling on his cigarette with little enthusiasm.

"They will have, don't worry."

"His poor mother," Edward mused. "He always said how upset she had been when he left."

"Mm," Stack agreed. "He was so excited about getting home and proving her wrong."

"Stupid boy."

"I wish you'd all stop talking about it," Captain said from the corner of the crowded rundown outbuilding, where he sat counting the small flasks of rum that had somehow found their way out of Corporal Marshall's possession and into his. They were camped for rest at barracks hastily converted from a boarding school, looking a lot worse for wear now infantry took the place of children. "We're at war, soldiers die – it happens. You can't let it take over your minds or you'll be next. He was a cheery lad for the best part; he wouldn't want to see you lot like this."

He flicked ashes into the grass that grew through the cracks in the floor and let the smoke escape his mouth in a thin wisp.

"We won't be at rest forever, let's make the bloody most of it."

"He's right," Private Jack MacDonald – known to the men as Mackie – nodded. He was a quiet man of twenty-three and spoke very little, usually agreeing with somebody else when he did so. He was nothing remarkable to look at, but training had shown he had probably the best aim in the regiment. He was quick and alert too, with stamina gained from a love of athletics; something that Stack had often thought would be to his advantage one day.

"You didn't see his face Cap," Stack muttered. "You can't tell us to stop talking-"

"I saw it," Captain cut across him. "I saw it plain as you, and I'm forgetting it. We'll see worse things still I bet; got to be ready for them when they come."

He took another puff of his cigarette and stubbed it out on the floor before getting to his feet.

"I'm going to the tubs," he said, stopping at the table where Stack and Rigby sat with their abandoned card game. "Might as well take a break from washing out of shrapnel while I can. Come with me Ben, you're filthy."

"Maybe later," Stack grunted, with the forced hint of a smile. "I'm not a pansy like you."

"Suit yourself," Captain grinned. "I'm planning on sneaking out there as many times as I can before we go back to the mudbath."

He bent down and spoke into his ear in a low whisper.

"You'd better snap out of this one," he said, his voice soft but firm. "You're a strong bloke; you get on with things and you don't complain. The young ones look up to you, Ben. Don't go scaring them with talk of dead men's faces."

"Don't be daft," Stack dismissed him. "It's you they follow around like you're their mother."

"They may find me amusing," Captain agreed, his face serious for once. "But it's you they reckon's going to get them through this war alive. You just remember that when you're feeling like you could've done more – because I know that's what you're thinking. You were there with Pepper; he died knowing that somebody in this goddamned world cared about him and that eventually he was going to be alright. That's enough."

Stack and Rigby attempted to continue their card game, but to no avail, Rigby deciding instead to write a letter to his sweetheart and Stack following Captain's advice and heading to the tubs.

"Feeling better?" Captain looked around at him.

"I guess not everyone can smile as much as you Cap."

"And for the grumpy bastards, God invented rum," he finished splashing his bare shoulders and lowered his voice. "You know I have a secret stash of the stuff for times such as these. What do you say Benji, just a little bit tonight? It'll make you feel better. Just don't tell Rigby."

A 'little bit' for Captain was more than enough for Stack. Night found him leaning against a tent pole, doubled over with his head reeling. Judgement blurred by the first few swigs, he had allowed his friend to coax him into more and more, while Captain had at least two gulps for ever sip he took. Annoyingly, the other man seemed fine, laying happily on his back and singing at the stars. Stack followed his gaze, a memory stirring in the back of his mind; a rare thing from a world before shellfire.

"I watched the stars before," he said groggily. "With a girl from back home."

"*You* and a *girl*?" Captain exclaimed, looking like somebody had just told him the war was over. "I don't believe it!"

"Thanks a lot," Stack scoffed.

"Well I guessed you knew a few, but I never saw you as a romantic."

"Don't worry," he smiled despite the growing ache squeezing his brain. "It wasn't romantic. We were drunk too."

"Good," Captain turned back to the stars, satisfied. "You keep being the sensible bastard I know; I'll get all the ladies."

Stack went to make a sarcastic remark, but his stomach heaved and he retched at the floor.

"And you better keep my rum down."

"Private!"

Captain raised his head to see the dark silhouette of the platoon sergeant making his way over to them. A huge grin spread across his face and he jumped to his feet. Stack's heart sank – though it may have been the contents of his stomach – and he reached out a hand to try to stop his friend.

"Sergeant Bollock!" Captain reached out his arms in mock friendliness. "Or would you prefer Pollock? Is it true, what they say?"

"What do they say, Private?" the sergeant asked icily; though Captain seemed to take no notice, still beaming from ear to ear.

"About you only having one-"

"That's enough," Pollock cut across him. "You're a disgrace, both of you." He leant over and pulled Stack roughly to his feet. "You two will report to Corporal Butterfield tomorrow; I want you helping with the transport of supplies to the front."

"We've only just come back from the front!" Captain complained. "Come on, it's only a little bit of rum! The second lieutenant would understand."

Pollock didn't look impressed. The sergeant was teetotal and had often tried to persuade Kent to disallow rum rations altogether. "We will speak to Sandford now; ensure he knows that you are undisciplined and your punishment is not to be softened."

He led them both away from the tent; Stack with his head down and Captain deliberately walking in the wobbliest line possible. He caught his friend's eye in the moonlight and winked.

"You know what," he whispered. "I bet your girl was better than Rigby's."

****

Tomorrow found Stack and Captain sitting on opposite sides of a broken cart on the outskirts of the camp, waiting for the group of unlucky soldiers charged with heading back towards the fighting with crates of supplies. Still lively as ever, Captain had been singing to himself and cheering every man who walked past, while Stack kept his head back and tried to convince himself he was alert. A large group passed by with a football and joined in Captain's cheering.

"Shut up," Stack moaned. "This is the last time I ever listen to you."

"Is it also the last time you say that? Cheer up; we're not too far from the lines here." Captain leant back against the cart as if enjoying the view. "I've heard of people marching for days to deliver supplies, only to get shot at the end of it all."

A groan came from the other side of the cart. "I hate you."

"Well good day to you chaps."

"Get stuffed Rigby," Captain greeted him affectionately.

"That's not very nice now is it?" Rigby leaned up against the cart and started to pick out the dirt from under his fingernails. "Ben, tell him not to be so rude. I only came to say hello."

Stack chuckled and said nothing.

"You would not bother walking over here just to say hello," Captain pointed out, scowling like a child. "You came here to laugh at us and that's a fact."

"Well you are quite funny," Rigby grinned, enjoying the look of disgust on the man's face. "Didn't you ask the sergeant if he only had one bollock?"

His black curls bounced as he let out a laugh. "Yes I did, didn't I. I suppose the whole battalion knows by now."

"Possibly. I can tell them if you like," Rigby pulled a cigarette from his pocket and held it between his lips to light it. "I would offer you one, but there's no way I'm getting thrown in with you two."

He puffed smoke teasingly in Captain's face and patted him on the arm, a mischievous grin playing about his mouth.

"Well I'll see you boys later," he flicked his cap in a mock salute and headed back towards the tents. "By the way Cap, lovely singing."

"You know what," Captain said through gritted teeth. "If he survives this war, I'm going to kill him."

The road was long, the journey not helped by the sweat running down their foreheads and the heavy packs they carried along with their own rifles – even more being pulled by horses for the first leg.

The nearer they got to the front the louder the shellfire came, splitting their heads into thousands of pieces with every explosion. They had been lucky to rotate out when they did; the poor men in the lines now, Butterfield told them, had had no rest from the constant barrage since the previous day.

They knew they had reached their destination when they were met by chaos. Mud flew about the hoard of men bleeding and screaming on the floor barely out of the firing line, many with limbs incomplete or missing altogether.

"Shit," Captain voiced Stack's feelings.

They made their way slowly down a communications trench, hindered by the bodies they stumbled over and the need to shield themselves from debris. They gritted their teeth and pressed on, knowing they had a few more trips down this tunnel of hell to deposit the entirety of their cargo. They had reached a junction into a further trench when a shell exploded a few feet away, forcing them all to the ground and scattering the contents of Captain's crate into the mud.

"Leave them!"

Stack picked him up and helped him carry what remained to a hole dug into the side of the trench, where an exhausted sergeant was helping them unload. They dropped off their cargo and turned back for more, running crouched along the boards as another explosion sent dirt and men falling about them. They pulled each other back to their feet and spied the sergeant lying face down in a puddle, having strayed at the wrong time from his hole. Two men with a stretcher rushed forward, but they had misjudged the tell-tale wailing and both were taken down, thick blood spilling from the holes in their faces.

"Shit!" Captain wrung his hands before ducking again, pulling Stack down with him. "Shit!"

The supplies sergeant rolled over, clutching his stomach with one hand attempting to pull himself along the ground with the other. Stack glanced about for Butterfield, but the corporal was nowhere to be seen. He made a split second decision; there was no point in them returning back down the communications trench empty handed.

"Come on!" he shouted to Captain, rolling one of the stretcher men away and taking hold of the poles on one end of the stained white hammock. His friend followed suit at the other end and they ran back to the sergeant, heaving him out of the puddle. A sharp sting brought Stack's hand to his cheek, but it was only a light cut.

They lifted the stretcher with difficulty and picked their way back as fast as they could with the added weight between them. He was lighter than the crates and packs they had been carrying, but having to keep pace with each other while keeping their heads below the parapet and their feet away from the wounded proved harder than they had anticipated. They pushed past a few of their party already returning with the second wave of supplies, bouncing the poor sergeant as they rushed and ducked, slowing only when they returned to their starting point.

"Privates!"

They left him moaning on the ground and turned to Corporal Butterfield, who was collecting another crate from the pile.

"Get more of this down the line, go, go, go!"

"Yes sir!" Stack replied sharply, heaving a pack onto his back and finding handholds on the side of a fresh crate. They ran back into the fray, arms aching and ringing in their ears, eyes blinded by the dust thrown up by the blasts.

A well aimed shell brought down a group of their companions and they stopped to pull Butterfield free from under them, leaving the smashed crates where they fell with the broken bodies. There were no more stretcher men to be seen, and more of their own party joined them on the way back in lugging dying men back to the daylight.

It felt like days before they finally regrouped and returned to camp, where Second Lieutenant Sandford came to release them. Though Captain had sobered up at the first sound of shellfire, he was now lively as ever once out of harm's way. Stack envied his ability to drown out the screams and the stench with happier thoughts of a job well done.

The young officer approached them with his head held high in the usual manner, though he seemed to be fighting the urge to lower it due to something similar to embarrassment or guilt.

"That's it for today," Sandford looked almost as relieved as Stack felt, and not for the first time he had to admire the love this man bore his troops. "You're both to return to your section; please report to Corporal Marshall immediately. And may I suggest no more rum tonight."

Captain snorted a laugh. "I couldn't even if I wanted to, sir. He's drank me out of every sip I had."

"Well that's a blessing."

****

Captain awoke a few nights later to the booming shouts of Sergeant Pollock mixed in with sharper barks of orders from Captain Kent. His friends were still asleep so he woke them each in turn, knowing they would hate him for it. It was time for the gloomy walk back to the trenches; hundreds of feet stamping down the same dark dirt road down which he and Stack had lugged supplies, the occasional low singing cut short as they neared the firing range.

They carried heavy equipment and tried not to think of how much heavier their boots would soon become when filled with mud and rot. Stack marched between Captain and Rigby, head held high, following the progress of those in front.

He tried to see the road ahead, attempting to paint a picture of a landscape before guns, but it was too dark and signs of war were not easily forgotten. They passed abandoned machinery and people, the rumble of their feet penetrated by the occasional wail of an invalid left at the side of the road for the next passing ambulance to pick up. It was eerie in the dark, but Stack was grateful for the cover all the same; the enemy couldn't see them, and they were spared the view of any bloodied faces staring back from the roadside.

Corporal Marshall, their section's NCO, walked ahead of them. He was an odd man whose constant ill-hidden fear drove Sandford to distraction and caused the second lieutenant to take special interest in the section; some form of compensation for giving them such a poor leader. Marshall fixed his eyes firmly on the man in front, shivering at Captain's deliberately loud comments on ghosts and dead men on the road. Stack and Rigby shared a disapproving look and they walked on through the night.

****

Despite being behind the front line, the support and reserve trenches did not in any way guarantee safety from the falling of shells or sniper fire. What they did offer however, was a greater opportunity to work; something Captain Kent was not going to waste. After the daily routine of pumping out water and building up walls of sandbags that would soon be broken down again, Stack was exhausted. He left Tommy Miller to Captain's jokes and made his way along the trench to their small dugout. He had meant to use the privacy to finally respond to a letter, but his tiredness took hold and he let his eyes lose focus and his mind wander. He almost didn't notice Edward entering until his brother was shaking him, his eyes bright with excitement.

"Violet!"

"No, I'm Ben," Stack said groggily, pulling his mind back to the present.

"Violet," Edward repeated. "My daughter, she's walking!"

"That's great Ed!" Stack got up to clap his brother on the back, looking over his shoulder to read the letter he held in his shaking hands. He recognised Sylvie Stack's smooth handwriting and bad spelling, spilling out the details of how the girl had taken her first step when her brother Rob had teased her by holding a toy out of her reach. The step she had taken had been only one, as she had then fallen down and Sylvie had had to scold Rob for laughing instead of helping. It seemed the baby was persistent, however, as she had since walked the full length of the table. Edward swelled with pride.

"Have you told the others?" Stack asked.

"No," Edward gulped a breath. "I wanted you to be the first."

Stack smiled. He knew that were Thomas alive it would have been him receiving this honour, but it pleased him anyway. Perhaps now the older man could put his rivalries aside, they might finally start to connect as brothers. That thought made him very happy indeed.

"Come on," he made for the exit of the dugout, holding out his hand encouragingly. "We can tell them together."

He heard the explosion seconds before he was plunged into darkness, his arm crushed under the weight of the mud and his back bent at an odd angle. One of the planks of wood that had held up the simple structure had struck his head and was now pressing down against his skull. He tried to move and felt the dirt pushing into his nostrils.

Not thinking, he gasped for breath and his mouth filled too, stifling a vain cry for help. He tensed his arm against the pressure, hoping that he could somehow swim through the mud, but the only movement was the shift of dirt between his fingers. He wriggled his leg and the mud fell heavier on his back, making him clench his teeth around the mud in his mouth to stop him crying out and swallowing more.

At least it moved though.

There was some hope. He tried to get his bearings, though his head was swimming from the pressure and lack of oxygen. He thought of Thomas, crushed to death in the tunnel he had built beneath the German lines.

No, he was not going to drown in the mud. He was an infantryman; if he had to die it would be a bullet, or a shell, not mud. He kept his eyes clenched shut and tried to focus. He must have fallen forwards, so his legs were near the exit, where the collapsed trench wall had fallen less heavily. If he kicked hard enough he might be able to dislodge enough to pull himself out. He moved his foot but his strength was quickly failing; he needed air.

I am not going to die, he told himself angrily, forcing all his might into his legs and kicking out.

A foot moved sharply, though his limbs were going numb and he couldn't tell if he had reached air or just moved more mud. He needed to breathe now; the small supply of air left in his compressed lungs had been exhausted. His leg moved feebly, but couldn't seem to do any more. It might have been wind that brushed his calf, or it might have been dirt. It didn't make a difference though; he had no more strength to pull himself back even if he had found air.

He stretched him arm, feeling about for Edward, but his fingers found nothing. He couldn't stop himself. His mouth opened, desperately gasping for oxygen, and he swallowed the soil as he blacked out.

2.

South-East England, Summer 1914

"Aedan!"she whispered loudly across the grand hall, finally catching the footman's attention. He made his way over to the door from which she was peeping. "Are they gone?"

He nodded.

"Excellent," she grinned and straightened up, emerging from her hiding place.

He could see why she had been avoiding her sister; the older woman wouldn't have been particularly pleased with the girl's choice of clothing. She had a plain grey hat rammed tightly over her curls and a shabby overcoat that made her almost unrecognisable as the sister of Mrs Peter Gale.

"Can you take me down to the village tonight please?"

"How?" he gave her a suspicious look. "Mr Brian's with your sister."

"Oh you don't have to act all innocent with me," she flicked a hand dismissively. "You can drive the carriage perfectly well yourself."

"No," he said firmly. "They would murder me!"

"I don't think so. Besides, I'm the lady of the house when Eliza's gone, so you have to do as I say." She smiled sweetly, but his expression didn't change so she switched to begging. "Please! All these weeks smiling at pompous old fools, I need to see something interesting! Don't you want to go to the fair?"

"I'll take you milady," he frowned. "On one condition; we aren't seen, and we get back hours before Mr Gale."

"Yes!" she grabbed his hand in excitement. "Thank you so much! That's two conditions though, and I'm not a milady."

"You are whatever your sister tells me you are, and that's final."

The carriage slunk out between the great gates of the Gale estate, wheels giggling over the gravel like the girl who ran this way years before. Despite the darkness of the hour, people still lit up the square, like the light erupting from the windows of the public house. A boy was juggling balls of something that was on fire, to the delight of a swooning group of young girls. There were stalls still open too, attracting little crowds that jostled and gossiped – a much more pleasant sight than a room full of stuffy landowners.

"Come on Aedan!" she hopped down from the carriage, running over to the group around the fire boy.

A jolly looking man with a flushed face handed her one of his tankards and she took it, grinning widely at the thought of how much her sister would squirm at the thought. She had been the picture of obedience all week; it was time for a little rebellion.

Aedan had not yet reached her side when a loud bang scattered the crowd as the pub door flew open. A man staggered out backwards, tripped on a flowerpot and fell hard on his back. A few people laughed from within.

"You never touch her again, you got that?"

The boy who followed him out couldn't be over sixteen – she could see his young face clearly in the light – but he stood tall and well-built, fists clenched. The girl beside him was much smaller and looked at him with great admiration on her face; a look that was quickly wiped off as the man on the floor got up and swung, missing his assailant and hitting her instead. This enraged the young man and he flew at him, punching him hard in the stomach so he doubled over to a height where knee could connect harshly with chin. It wasn't a fair fight; he may have been older and possibly taller, but it was obvious that his wits were heavily doused with alcohol while the boy was quick and alert.

"Rob!" a voice called from inside the pub. "Give it up, he's learned his lesson."

The boy kicked him one more time then turned to go back into the building. One of the juggler's watchers muttered about him having an awful temper.

"Oi, Stack!" the crowd went quiet as two boys of about twenty pushed their way through. "You think you're finished?"

A pained look crossed his face, but he tightened his fists and stepped over the man on the floor. The silent onlookers sensed the tension, backing away slightly to create a half circle about them. Only the girl stayed with Rob, standing uncertainly with one hand holding her face and the other reaching tentatively towards him, unsure whether to stop him or not.

"Looks like the party's over milady," Aedan put a hand on her shoulder and tried to steer her away, but her feet would not move.

One of the older boys landed a direct hit in Rob's jaw, sending him reeling backwards. The girl stepped between them, but she was thrown aside like a sack of potatoes.

"Let's go!" Aedan pulled more firmly.

"No."

She ran in the opposite direction, pulling the girl back before she could get herself more hurt.

Rob was struggling now, on the floor with both men pummelling him clumsily. The girl started to cry, sobbing that it was all her fault. He jerked his head out of the way and the fist hit hard floor, bringing the man down on top of him. Taking his chance, he brought his head up to meet him, butting him in the nose so blood ran freely into his hair. He got his knee up too, landing a blow in his opponent's stomach, forcing him backwards.

The second man made a lunge at him, but he caught his arm and forced him over onto his back. Rob rolled aside and sprung to his feet, pushing the man to the ground and attempting to dodge the attack of his companion, but failing.

He was saved by the appearance of a man from inside the pub who, with Aedan's help, managed to pull the three apart.

"Get out of here," he snarled. "Or your father'll be giving you a worse beating than this."

"You wouldn't."

"I would," he glared at them and they slunk away, no longer so tall and threatening. "You okay Rob?"

"Thanks Uncle," the boy spat blood and wiped the cut above his eye. "But I could've handled them."

"Good," he put an arm around his shoulders. "Because we're going home now and you can handle your mother."

"You can't tell her!"

"You think she won't notice this?" he gestured at the boy's battered face.

"He was only protecting me," the girl spoke timidly.

"I know that," Rob's uncle looked troubled, thick brows furrowing over eyes that looked strikingly familiar. "But I don't expect Sylvie to see it so simply. Daisy, can you get home?"

"I can take her," the woman in the grey hat spoke up. "She can ride in Mr Gale's carriage."

"Thanks," he looked her in the eye and she was certain she knew him. "Come on Rob, we're going. Now."

The boy groaned but followed his uncle, casting a look back to Daisy as she mouth a quick 'thank you'.

"And thank you too miss," she added. "For taking me home. You're really kind. I'm Daisy Lane."

"Who's that?" she squinted at the shrinking backs.

"Rob Stack," Daisy sighed dreamily. "I want to marry him."

"No, his uncle, I'm sure-" she cut herself off, raising her voice excitedly. "Ben Stack!"

He stopped and turned.

"It is you!" she waved, ignoring Aedan's prompts that they really should go. "It's me! Harriet Redmond!"

"Really?"

She couldn't see his face in the dark, but his voice told her that he did remember. Aedan was pulling her now, and she noticed for the first time that she had blood on her coat. That would have to be hidden, for Aedan's sake.

"What are you doing here?"

"Eliza got married!" she shouted back, stumbling backwards to the carriage. "To Peter Gale! I have to go, but I'll come back! I'll see you then!"

She jumped up beside Daisy, who was telling Aedan excitedly that she had never been in a carriage before, and watched their backs until the dark swallowed them. She leaned her head contentedly against the curtain. Perhaps this new life was not so dull after all.

****

Harriet Redmond frowned at the mirror, swishing the borrowed dress about her legs. She looked like a fool, she decided, as she did every time Eliza hosted a dinner. She had never been as shapely as her sister – skinny in all the wrong places with wider shoulders and larger feet – and where the fabric would complement the older girl it fell limp and lifeless around Harriet's frame. Her own boots peeped out below the hem, reminding her just how scuffed there were in comparison. They had looked fine when she wore them under her nurse's uniform, back in her father's hospital in London, but everything about her seemed out of place in this dress.

"Oh do stop fussing," Eliza smiled from where she lounged on the bed. "You looked beautiful at dinner today."

"I'm sure I looked bored," she corrected her, flopping down a lot less elegantly beside her.

Eliza raised a perfectly shaped eyebrow. "You seemed entertained enough by the footman."

"I wanted intelligent conversation, and you were at the opposite side of the table."

Eliza laughed. Harriet was glad; there were occasions these days when she wasn't quite sure if she would amuse or offend her. Back in London, it was often Eliza who had kept her sane; the two of them would joke about their mother's pretentious associates and even played pranks when they were younger. Now, Harriet feared that her sister was becoming just the same as the mother they had ridiculed.

"If you wanted intelligent conversation, Hattie, you should have listened to the men!"

"Aedan's a man."

"No, really," she propped herself up on a gloved hand. "Peter thinks there's a *war* coming. He's bought a munitions factory in preparation, and he's going to make a fortune!"

"A war?" Harriet looked alarmed. "There isn't going to be a war."

"Oh don't be scared," Eliza flicked her sister playfully with one end of her elaborate shawl. "In fact, father has written and expressly forbid you to return to the hospital if there is a war. You'll stay with me, no need to treat wounded soldiers; we'll keep you safe from all that."

"And what about those wounded soldiers? Doesn't somebody need to keep them safe too?" she set her face firmly. "There isn't going to be a war, Liza. There isn't."

It felt good to remove the borrowed dress and pull on her own nightgown when her sister left for bed. She let her hair tumble loose over her shoulders and rested her forehead against the window, watching her breath fog up the glass. She blew out across the pane, creating an uneven square of fog covering the fields beyond the estate. She brought up a finger and ran it over the length of the road, smearing a line in the fog. Smiling faintly, she drew a house at the side of the road; small enough and cosy with a fenced garden, just like she remembered.

This was the Kent she had wanted to return to; the one she had grown up in and still loved, even as the memories faded in the bustle of London. The rolling hills and small farms, and woods with little streams running through them that drew all sorts of wildlife, and paddocks of horses to sneak apples for.

They had moved into the little house by the road when they were just girls, before their father ran the hospital. He was already renowned in certain circles as a competent doctor, and had been summoned by the widowed lady of the old estate to care personally for her sickly son, George. Eliza had said it was a waste giving such a nice house to a boy too feeble to enjoy it, but Harriet had always felt sorry for him. She could run through the fields and climb trees and play with her friends at the farm, but he was stuck in his house with no friends and no fresh air. She thought it was no wonder he was always ill.

In retrospect she should have expected it all along, but the death of the little boy had shocked her all the same. She supposed she had thought things would always be as they were; her father constantly at the big house, her mother constantly complaining, and Harriet and Eliza free to roam the land.

Even when Eliza became too old and dignified for climbing trees and chasing rabbits, she would still accompany them on picnics, especially if Edward would be there. Harriet chuckled, remembering the way her sister would watch him work and gaze dreamily at his arms. He was the sort of man Eliza should have married. She needed somebody strong and brave, who could look after himself without a large pile of money to do it for him. Not Peter Gale.

She smiled wider as she sketched the shape of a man in the window fog. Ben Stack was still here, and perhaps Edward too. Maybe so much hadn't changed after all.

****

The morning was beautiful, rays of sunlight bursting through her window and following her as she scuttled down the grand staircase, not stopping for a coat or more suitable walking shoes. She ran down the gravel path, stopping only to pet the groundsman's hound before slipping through the gates and onto the road. A cart passed and she moved to the verge, slipping her feet out of her boots to feel the wet grass between her toes. She had never felt so liberated.

After climbing her fifth fence, she was beginning to lose certainty in her sense of direction. Her face was flushed, her feet filthy, and the hem of her dress had snagged on fence number two, but she was not deterred. In fact, the idea of being lost in the countryside she loved was rather exciting.

A loud crack made her jump, dropping her boots. She calmed herself quickly, reaching up a hand to brush back her loose hair and smearing dirt across her forehead. It was probably only a farmer scaring rabbits away from his crops; hopefully a farmer who knew his way better than she did. She picked up her boots and rammed them back onto dirty feet – better not to look completely deranged – and hurried in the direction of the shot, trying to rub the dirt from her face as she went.

She heard the voices before she could make out their owners; one man with two boys, one about fifteen and the other roughly ten or eleven. The younger was running towards her, a cross look on his skinny face.

"I will not kill a rabbit!" he exclaimed, turning his head to shout back at his companions and nearly losing his footing. "I *like* rabbits!"

"Don't be a coward Matthew!" the older boy yelled at him and she recognised Rob Stack, holding the gun that had drawn her attention. "You're just scared of the noise!"

"Am not!" he shouted back, before noticing Harriet and slowing to a halt.

"Umm, Uncle Ben," he called hesitantly. "There's a lady coming."

Harriet certainly didn't feel like a lady, and the term made her laugh. She picked her way through the corn, raising a hand in timid greeting as she approached the small party. The little boy called Matthew had returned to his family and was currently standing behind his uncle's legs, regarding her with great caution. She couldn't blame him really; she must have looked like a madwoman. The older boy stepped forward boldly.

"Hello," he said, in the uneven voice of a boy halfway through achieving manhood. "I'm Rob. What are you doing on my land?"

"Your land?" Ben chuckled. "Is my brother dead? Please excuse my nephew; he thinks he's a little lord. Rob, this is Harriet. She saw you getting your face kicked in the other night."

She looked at him nervously, not wanting to stare too long. All of those years of following him through the woods, sneaking onto the land of the estate to try to catch a glimpse of little George, laying in the hay barn for hours talking about things she had been scared would make her seem foolish, and she hadn't even known him in the dark a few nights ago. He had grown, of course; he was taller and his shoulders were broader, with a layer of stubble covering his chin, but he had the same kind eyes and rough smile as the youth he had been.

"Hello, sorry," Harriet smiled apologetically. "You probably don't want me remembering that."

Rob laughed. "That's fine lady, I remember you now. You took Daisy home; thanks for that."

"I'm not a lady," she shook her head sheepishly. "Look at the state of me. The way from the estate has changed a lot since Gale bought it."

"You've walked all the way from the estate?" Ben looked amused. "Why?"

"Something like nostalgia I suppose," she shrugged. "I don't regret it. Eliza will probably murder me and have me scrubbed like a naughty child, but I can handle it. I wanted to see you again; life in the big house is hardly riveting, and since the fair it's seemed even duller."

"That sort of night is normal for us," Rob grinned, leaning confidently on his gun. "You'll never be bored this side of the gates."

"Normal for you perhaps," Ben rolled his eyes and cuffed him affectionately about the head. "Rob, take your brother back to the house, and mind you don't shoot him or it'll be me giving you your next beating."

"Do we have to?" Matthew asked timidly. "Thomas is here; they'll be yelling again."

"Go find a tree to play in then, just watch the gun or it'll be me in trouble."

"Gotcha Uncle Ben."

Rob slung the gun over his shoulder and took hold of his brother's hand, pulling him away through the field. Harriet watched them go for a while before turning back to her old friend, remembering how they had run similarly through the fields years ago.

"God," he scratched the back of his neck. "It doesn't seem real, you and Liza living up at the big house. We used to spend our lives getting chased away from there; how things change."

"Not too many things," she smiled, pulling off a boot and showing him the mud and grass stains on her foot. "I'm still the same old Hattie."

That made him laugh. "You haven't changed, have you? Only you could survive London."

"Oh, London's not so bad," she fell into step with him as they began to walk to nowhere in particular. "Too many people and not enough space for them all, but you learn to live with it. I've been working with my father; he's head of a fancy hospital now. Eliza doesn't work of course," she grinned. "Her job is enticing rich men."

"Well she's done well at that," Ben commented.

"Maybe," she sighed, before flashing him a mischievous smile. "I always wanted her to marry Edward."

"A bit late for that, sorry. The boys are his; Matthew and Rob, and he's got another on the way."

"Wow," she shook her head. She should have guessed really, with both calling Ben 'uncle', but it still came as a shock. "Edward has children. Last time I saw him he couldn't even grow a beard! And you? You haven't got ten tucked away somewhere?"

"None for me," he smiled, looking so much like the boy she used to know, behind the weather-lines and stubble. "It's hard work enough looking after his two; they're little rascals. You're lucky I recognised you or Rob might have actually shot you."

"Well I'm glad you have a good memory!" she laughed.

"Be glad you're as scruffy-looking as ever or I might not have," he teased.

"Excuse me!" she exclaimed in mock offence, delighted that they could still play like this after all those years. "I'll have you know I have been quite the lady since I came here."

"I'll believe that when I see it."

"Well, you'll probably never believe it then," she giggled. "I still don't."

Still, she was at least clean the next time she visited, and wearing her shoes – something Ben was quick to point out. She even managed the carriage a few times, encouraging Aedan to join them and get some fresh air when Eliza was out with Peter on business. She accompanied him everywhere; something his friends found endearing, and Harriet found incredibly dull.

Harriet had asked if she could join Rob's shooting lessons, partly out of want for company and partly from a reawakened fascination which she had felt as a girl watching Edward firing at birds. She liked spending the summer days shooting with the boys, or watching them work the farm, before returning to the cosy little house where Sylvie would make them tea and ask her about Eliza and the big house while she played with baby Violet.

She didn't jump at the gunshots anymore, watching more in admiration as Rob aimed perfectly again and again. A pheasant rose from a nearby hedgerow and he took it down, pressing the gun proudly into Harriet's hand and picking up a basket.

"You'll be better than me soon," Ben congratulated him.

"I already am," Rob grinned cheekily. "That doesn't matter though. I'm better than my father, and I'm good enough to join the army. There'll be a war soon – everyone's saying it – and then I'll show him."

"Good enough, but not old enough," Ben ruffled his nephew's hair, before he shook him off. "If there's a war in four years, I'd be proud to fight with you. For now, you can stick with shooting pheasants."

Rob shrugged, smiling like he knew something they didn't.

"Come on Matthew," he beckoned. "Whoever gets to it first gets the biggest portion."

They hopped the stile and Harriet rearranged her hands on the barrel, trying to aim at the tree stump a few fields away. A barking laugh from Ben told her she was doing it all wrong and she lowered her hands, pointing it instead at the floor.

"How can you still forget?" he shook his head with fond amusement. "You're utterly useless, you know that?"

"Ben," she said quietly. "I don't want there to be a war. Do you really think there will be?"

"I don't know about these things," he replied, his face softening. "Maybe there will, maybe there won't."

"I'm scared," she admitted. "My father saw such awful things in the Boer; I don't want that happening again."

"There won't be a war," he told her comfortingly. "But just in case there is, you might need to know how to lift a gun."

"I can *lift* it," she protested. "I'm not that bad."

"Like that time you tried to shoot the weathervane at Holler's farm?"

Harriet giggled, remembering the day that Edward had managed it and won a penny, and she had sworn she could do the same. "You remember that?"

"I remember everything," he grinned playfully.

"Oh dear," Harriet grinned sheepishly. "That's going to come back and bite me isn't it?"

"The things I could tell your Mr Gale, you'd be out of that house in seconds."

"You wouldn't," she set down the gun and bent clumsily to pick up a large stick, holding it how she thought one should wield a sword. "I'd kill you before Eliza could!"

"Put it down," he warned her. "You could never beat me before, and your hands have gone all soft and ladylike."

"Try me," she stared him down, burrowing her toes into the grass for a better foothold. He reached down for another stick, then dropped it and charged at her, ducking under the 'sword' and sweeping her off the ground. She shrieked and kicked as he carried her over to the fence and sat her on it triumphantly.

"That," she scowled. "Is cheating."

She spied the boys coming back over the stile at the bottom of the field; they were also carrying sticks, Rob's with the dead pheasant impaled on the end.

"Rob! Matthew!" she called to them, waving her stick in the air. "Your uncle is a cheater! Get him!"

They grinned at each other before sprinting up the hill, shouting war cries. Ben shrugged at her in defeat and let them bring him to the ground, stabbing at him like a wild boar. Harriet watched the three of them rolling around in the grass, Ben and Rob now turning on Matthew and trying to tickle him into submission. She remembered doing something similar with her father and Eliza many years ago, their mother watching with icy disapproval. Yes, this was a real family; not a fancy house and perfect manners.

"Alright you two," he pushed them off, Rob straightening up immediately as if suddenly remembering to act his age. "Time to go home."

"Do we have to?" Matthew complained, crossing his arms over his scruffy shirt. "We want more pheasants."

"Come on," Ben said encouragingly. "You can ride on my back if you like."

****

They were interrupted one morning in early August by a shout from the road, turning to see the shape of Rob's friend Billy Wayson vaulting over the fence, almost tripping over he was travelling so fast.

"Rob!" he shouted, waving his cap at him. "Rob! Ben, Miss Harriet. Rob, there's a war, there's really a war!"

He stopped in front of them, panting, Harriet and Ben looking at him with concern.

"There's a sergeant in the village, he's been telling everyone they need more men. He's an inspiration, Rob, we have to go!"

He looked at Rob, and his friend met his eyes with something more than boyish excitement. He puffed out his chest and drew himself up to his full height, turning to his uncle.

"I'm going to enlist."

"You're too young," Ben put a hand on his shoulder, looking troubled. "They wouldn't want a fifteen year old who can barely shoot straight."

"I won't be fifteen forever, and I'm a better shot than any other boy in the village, and nearly every man too I'd wager."

Ben leaned down and looked at him sternly. "You're fifteen. Don't go giving your parents nightmares."

Rob gave him a sour look. "Well you can't stop me going to hear him talk at least."

He didn't wait for a response, sprinting off ahead of Billy in the direction of the village.

"He won't really sign up will he?" Harriet asked, her eyes wide as she watched the two disappear up the road. "Everybody knows him; they know he's too young."

"I have to go," Ben said quietly, also looking towards the village.

"What?" Harriet felt like somebody had punched her in the stomach. She stared at him as if seeing him for the first time, yet knowing every line on his face better than her own. "Why?"

"Why?" he looked at her like she had asked the strangest question in the world. "Why does any man join the army? To protect his home and family."

"But the Germans are nowhere near your home and family," she gulped back the lump rising in her throat. "They're in Belgium and they're going to stay there."

"And who do you think's going to keep them there?" he put his hands on her shoulder and held them gently. "To be honest, I've been thinking about it for a while. Edward can handle the farm on his own, I'm as much use here as a lame plough horse. If I go I can do my bit and be home before anyone misses me. It'll be an adventure."

She wanted to scream at him that he was being stupid, that he was much more useful than a team of plough horses and they would all miss him every day, but it wouldn't come out. It was too much for her, and she knew she had to get back to her bedroom before the tears came spilling out. She said the only thing she could think of without wanting to shout. "You're very brave."

****

Eliza had not been able to control herself when her husband told her he would be leaving with the cavalry. She had bragged to everybody who came near of how brave he was, and how dashing he looked in his uniform, until Harriet was absolutely sick of it. She thought she must be worried really, somewhere beneath that proud exterior, but she was certainly hiding it well.

The party had been Eliza's idea; a farewell to all the brave men of the village and nearby estates, celebrated in marvellous fashion with a band and the gardens decorated to perfection. Harriet made her way through the growing crowd, nervously trying to look elegant for her sister while searching for a familiar face

She let out a breath of relief as she caught sight of Aedan, standing under an open tent and holding a tray of wine and brandy. She took a glass enthusiastically and threw it down her throat, grimacing at the taste. She had seen her father drink often enough when he needed to calm his nerves, and today her own nerves felt like bolting thoroughbreds.

"Steady on," Aedan warned her as she reached immediately for another. "That's strong stuff."

"Good," she prepared her taste buds and took another big gulp. "I need strong stuff or I'm going to cry."

"I daresay you won't be the only one, don't worry," he looked out at the sea of women clutching their uniformed husbands and sons. He too had forsaken his footman's garb tonight and was dressed as the soldier he was soon to become.

"You look very handsome," she remarked, taking another glass but sipping this one slowly; her head was starting to feel odd. "And I though nothing would suit you more than your black and whites."

"I hope to return to them once the war is done, if Mr Gale will still have me," he motioned to the man striding through the guests, stopping to talk to anybody in proper tails or officer uniform. "You don't look too bad yourself milady."

"I'm not a milady," she reminded him for the thousandth time. "You really shouldn't be serving us, not tonight. You're a soldier now; this party's more for you than it is for me. I should be holding the drinks."

He eyed her disapprovingly. "Beg your pardon, but if you were holding the wine nobody else would be getting any."

She laughed. "I have to admit, you've got me there. But there's a perfectly good table over there and if you don't set down your tray I shall have to drink every drop until you have nothing to hold anyway. You're leaving tomorrow, who could possibly tell you off?"

"You have a point," he hesitated, then put the tray down triumphantly. "So now I'm a soldier, could I ask a pretty girl for a dance?"

"I don't know about any pretty girls, but you could ask me," she swallowed the last of her third glass and let him lead her to the perfectly trimmed grass by the rostrum, where the band had begun to play. The wine had taken a hold of her head and she let it, feeling the music wash over her senses as she rested her head on his shoulder.

"You'd better look after yourself, okay?" she murmured, watching a man in uniform comforting his crying daughter. "I wouldn't like it if you died."

He didn't say anything and the tune changed to a happier melody, allowing her to pick up her feet and return the feeling to her brain. She wasn't sure how long they had been dancing when she spotted a familiar figure making his way up the path, carrying Matthew on his shoulders, the boy wearing his uncle's cap. His uniform really did suit him, she decided, set off by the smile that filled his eyes as he talked animatedly to the boy on his shoulders. Aedan must have noticed her face light up, because he loosened his grip on her waist and gave a gentle push in the direction of her gaze.

"Go on," he told her. "Don't worry about me." She pulled her hand away from his shoulder, her blurry mind only half hearing him. "You're a strange one milady. I'm going to miss you."

"And I'm going to miss you too!" she flung her arms around him and gave him a tight squeeze before bounding across the grounds to greet Ben and the others.

She caught Matthew as he was heaved from his mount and he thrust the cap back at Ben before running off to join the other children in their tent. Sylvie kissed her on the cheek and apologised that they couldn't stay too long – they had left Violet with a friend – before leading Edward away for a dance. Harriet couldn't help but notice how the woman's eyes swum with moisture behind that strong smile.

"Can I wear the cap?" she asked, pulling it over her hair. It was too big for her and fell almost into her eyes, but she liked the idea of wearing it.

"Only if you dance with me," Rob took her hands and pulled her towards his parents. "They say I'm too young to be a soldier and too young to drink, but I can at least dance with all the women tonight."

Harriet laughed and let him guide her. She didn't think all the women would particularly mind dancing with Rob; he was tall and attractive in a young way, and a lot better at the dance than she had expected. She was glad he was only fifteen. He had plenty of life ahead to enjoy and all the traits to enjoy it well; it would have been an awful waste to send him to war.

After a while he spun Harriet away and was immediately gobbled up by one of the post boy's young sisters. Ben caught her and they continued the dance, Rob flashing his uncle a teasing smile every now and then as she buried her cheek in the rough fabric of his tunic. The boy moved effortlessly from girl to girl – and sneaked glasses of brandy when his parents' backs were turned almost as effortlessly – until they were interrupted by Mr Gale rising to the rostrum. His cavalry uniform was different to the plain infantry-wear of most of the other men. Eliza thought it made him look like their valiant hero. Harriet thought it made him look like a snob.

"This is it boys," he spoke clearly, moving his eyes so it seemed that he addressed each man personally. "This is the moment we have all been waiting for. I leave in the morning to join the finest regiment of the British cavalry." A spatter of clapping interjected. "And you will all be leaving too, to add valour to your own regiments." A lot more clapping followed, and a large cheer from a group of red faced boys who had had a bit to drink.

"I would like to thank you personally, on behalf of the country, for giving yourselves so willingly to the cause. I hope you all know that whatever your fate, from this day on you are forever heroes, and people will speak your names with awe and gratitude. We are fighting for our lands, for our freedom, for our women!"

He cast a glance at Eliza – a glance that would have been loving if he wasn't Peter Gale.

"We will cross the channel and Fritz won't know what hit him! We are the strength of the British Empire, and they will rue the day they decided to mess with us! Arm yourselves, brothers, this is our war!"

He punched the air and the crowd followed, cheering and whooping. Harriet saw Rob at the front, cheering louder than any of them. She scowled and turned her back on her brother-in-law, storming across the grounds and stopping to kick the bottom of a perfectly pruned tree.

"What an absolute *grr!*" she struggled to find a word strong enough to describe him. "Standing there talking about heroes and brainwashing young boys, when I'm sure he won't even fight! He'll give orders and sit back at headquarters with a cup of tea and a biscuit!" She turned to look at Ben, tears forming in her eyes. "Let's get out of here."

He took her hand, squeezing it gently. "Do you remember the weeping hill, past Holler's place?"

"The one where I thought it always rained?"

"That's the one. You can see the channel from there, remember. If it's really clear, sometimes you can even see France. It's not that far away, when you think about it."

"Show me," she said, her voice coming in a squeak. "I want to see where you're all going."

She wasn't sure how long they walked – it could have been hours, but with the wine in her head it felt like half a second before they were seated in the long grass at the top of the hill. She squinted into the distance, trying to make out a difference between black and black.

"So that's France?" she asked. "It doesn't seem that far away."

"Not too far," he agreed, twisting the cap from her head and putting it back on his own. "Not even far enough to get seasick on the way."

"I hope so," she leaned back, slotting her head between his chin and shoulder. "I'll come up here every night, just to watch."

She paused, a memory returning that was lost a long time ago. "There was a clock tower in London, when we first moved back. Eliza told me you could see the whole world from the top of that tower, and there were steps to climb too. I promised myself I'd climb it every day and watch Kent, and try to find a way back." Her voice choked in her throat. "I never climbed it once."

"You're back now," he pointed out. "And living in the big house you were always trying to get into."

"Yes, but you're leaving," she replied sadly.

The long grass rustled in the night breeze and she imagined that she could see grass just like it on the shores of France; strong and tall and alive. A drop of water fell onto her nose, another running down her forehead. She laughed, brushing away a tear.

"It really is always raining here."

"Not always," he gave her back the cap, positioning it to protect her face from the rain. "I'll be back before you know it. See if you can learn how to shoot before I'm home."

"I'll try."

She turned and buried her head into his chest. It felt safe here, despite being in the rain in the dead of night, with war on the horizon. She had always felt safe with him, even as a girl when he had scared her with ghost stories in the hay barn.

"Nothing's changed really," she murmured. "Edward and Thomas still fighting, Eliza still trying to impress mother, us out in the rain trying to escape it all. Only difference is it's you leaving this time, not me."

"I'll be back," he promised. "And you'd best be getting back too; your sister will be worried."

"Okay," she sighed and got to her feet. "I trust you."

3.

"Near miss!" Captain yelled above the noise, back pressed hard against the wall of the trench as the ground lurched towards him. "Ten points!"

"I am not playing your game!" Stack slammed into the wall next to him, clutching his rifle to his chest.

"Pity!" Captain shouted back. "You'd be on fifty already!"

"Really?" he pulled himself up onto the firestep and took the quickest of glances at the battered terrain between them and the enemy.

"How many are you on?"

He slid back down and something sharp-looking whizzed through the air where his head had been moments before.

Captain jerked his leg back, out of the way of somebody who fell right in front of him. He grimaced and prodded the man with his toe to bare his face.

"Don't recognise him."

He breathed a sigh of relief, covering his face as more dirt was thrown up.

"And I'm on thirty," he grinned slyly at his friend. "But not for long."

"Oh no you don't!"

Stack read his mind and reched to grab hold of his tunic, but he was too slow. Captain jumped to his feet and sprayed a round of bullets blindly into the fray, bellowing and whooping, before throwing himself back down again – out of breath and grinning like a maniac.

"You bloody idiot!"

"That's worth fifty points I'd say," he winked and ducked Stack's fist. "So I'm on eighty now and you're losing."

"Eighty?" he pulled a face. "That's nowhere near enough. Move!"

He yanked his friend quickly around the corner into the next bay, out of the way of the explosion that shattered the wall they had been leaning against, throwing trench and men alike into the air.

"Close one, ten points!" He caught his breath before continuing. "They'll need at least a hundred before they can take me down!"

"You'll get more than that if you stick your head over one more time!"

"Trust me," Captain grinned. "I'm invincible."

A smaller blast caught the dirt beyond the parapet, showering it down upon them. Captain paused, his handsome – and now very muddy – face not looking impressed.

****

Working parties did not begin that evening. The bombs had stopped, but something didn't feel right, as if the night was trying to tell them something, sending dust clouds still unsettled to float like ghosts over the British lines. The moans of the wounded could be heard clearly now as the stretchers finally managed to reach them, and the silence of those beyond reach was clearer still.

Even Captain kept quiet as they sat along the firestep, watching the skyline with trepidation. They kept their rifles in their hands and their eyes unsteady, flickering from the sky to the floor to their fellows then back to the sky.

Bang. The rat exploded, black guts spilling into the mud and across the face of the man it had been devouring. Tommy Miller jumped a foot in the air, clutching at Marshall who looked no less afraid. Stack glared at his victim down the barrel of the gun, but made no attempt to retrieve it. He sat with shoulders hunched, the only movement a soft heaving of his chest and the occasional blink.

He spotted the flick of another tail hurrying up the dead man's leg and swung his rifle quickly to follow it. His finger closed around the trigger, but was stopped by Captain's hand.

"Stop it Ben, you'll need those bullets later." Stack scowled but lowered his hands. "Nice shot though."

Stack wasn't sure what time it was when the signal came from Rigby to send a hot vein of adrenalin to freeze their blood. He had been struggling to stay awake and the ringing in his ears had been lulling him into a fuzzy state of grey, where sights and sounds alike spiralled together like ripples in water. The rippled shattered at the alert and his eyes snapped back to life, filling with the sharp picture of the swarm of rats on the body in the ground and the dirt upon his rifle.

He sprung to his feet, sensing rather than seeing the men on either side of him follow suit. He heard Marshall whispering a repeated prayer as he often did, and somebody slip as they stood – probably Tommy Miller.

"Up, up, up, get yourselves ready men," Sandford hurried down the line at a brisk walk, blue eyes scanning for anybody asleep or moving too slowly.

"Sir," Stack caught his attention before lowering his voice, eyes on the terrified Tommy Miller. "Are they coming?"

"The watchers spotted something," Sandford replied in a similar tone. "The men should be prepared for anything. How are they?"

"Well enough," he looked them over, searching for any word other than 'scared'.

"I'm sure you'll all do me proud," Sandford patted his arm and continued down the trench.

They lined up along the firestep, bayonets fixed and aimed into the night. Captain stood on Stack's left side, his dark curly hair bursting out from under the recently issued steel helmet – a welcome replacement for the fairly useless caps worn previously. Tommy Miller shivered to his right, clutching his rifle too tightly, wide eyes staring.

"If I kill more than you," Captain whispered. "You're buying all the drinks next time we're on leave."

"I don't want to kill anyone," Tommy's voice came quiet and and shaky. "Not this close. I've never seen a German's face."

"They look just the same as anyone else," Stack told him, keeping his own voice calm for the boy's sake.

"That's what I'm scared of."

"*Where* are they?" Captain hissed, grinding his teeth in frustration. "If Rigby's got us all worked up for nothing I'm sticking this bayonet in him."

"Keep your eyes on the wire," Stack told them, keeping his own frustration at bay by attempting to quell theirs. "Spot them in time and you might not have to see their faces."

"My eyes are on the wire," Captain replied through gritted teeth. "But I'm not seeing anything."

A crack sounded from further down the line, somebody losing his nerve and shooting too early. Stack glanced sideways at the others, noticing the shine of sweat on Miller's forehead and wondering if he looked the same. He flicked his eyes to the other side and Captain met him with a resigned half-smile.

A shadow moved beyond the wire and he pulled the trigger, imagining a faceless man exploding like the rat he had targeted earlier. He wasn't sure if the thought made him feel victorious or sick. He felt Tommy Miller jump at the noise, his own clammy fingers slipping on the rifle he held.

"Don't shoot yet," Marshall whispered, barely loud enough to call it a command. "Wait for the signal."

Stack wasn't aware there was to be a signal, but held his fire anyway; no use wasting blind shots in the dark. He cursed the thought of all those convenient shell holes; perfect for hiding patrols, especially on a night like this. He kept his eyes fixed on the spot where he had seen the movement, breathing slowly and straining his ears beyond the white noise for any scuffle or whispered order.

The explosion made them all jump, contained a few bays further down the line, followed by a wave of shouts. Men started peeling themselves from the wall and diving down onto the duckboard, heading for the stricken bay. Stack saw Marshall rushing past and was about to follow when the glint of something metallic caught his eye a few feet away.

"Wait!" he called after their backs. Captain was the only one who paid him any heed. "It's only a distraction – we're leaving this whole bay unguarded! Corporal!"

"You think they're coming here instead?" Captain hesitated, legs still poised to run.

"We need somebody to hold it, or they will be!"

"Right," Captain nodded and climbed back onto the firestep.

Shots began to sound from the grenade site; a full raid or a noisy distraction – either was possible. Stack could only hope that the other sections had NCOs with more sense, or it would be up to himself and Captain to hold what felt like the whole front line.

Something thrown with force glanced off his helmet and he fell backwards, trying to stop the world swirling into blackness. The man who vaulted into the trench after him came with almost as much force, but this was to be his downfall as he threw himself onto Captain's bayonet, ripping open his torso as he fell. Stack threw him off before the wounded man could get his bearings, fumbling in the dark for his rifle. The German found it at the same time and their eyes met over the sliver of cold moonlight, held there for a second before they began to grapple for this lifeline.

Captain watched them out of the corner of his eye, but was unable to offer assistance as two more came running, wire cutters still in hand. He shot one down, but the other arrived too soon and threw the cutters at his face, distracting him long enough to slip past, knocking his rifle aside. Captain caught his arms and twisted him onto the ground, stamping hard on his hand and hearing the sickening crunch of bone as the man cried out.

It wasn't enough. Four more leapt into the trench, running unhindered into the next bay. They could come up on unsuspecting troops from behind and cause serious damage before they were apprehended, or else find some sort of important information to carry back to the enemy. Captain seized his rifle and fired after their backs but caught nothing but mud. Stack's hands were starting to lose grip on the slippery barrel of the rifle, his foe having caught hold of the butt. The German yanked it free, but had no chance to use it as his head was blown backwards, blood rather than bullets raining down on Stack from the mutilated neck.

"Private Stack, Captain!"

Sandford made his way down the trench, officer's pistol held out hot and ready, his overcoat billowing behind him and making him look a lot more threatening than the boy lieutenant they were used to. Stack pushed the dead man backwards and scrambled to his feet, snatching his rifle back from the German's bloody hands.

He swayed a little as he stood, but didn't risk removing his helmet to inspect the bruise. Captain's man lay moaning on the ground, battered and bleeding, until a quick bullet from the private put him out of his misery. Captain panted, blood running from a cut in his head and matting his hair, the helmet having been knocked into the mud in the scrap.

"There's more," he gasped, pointing down the trench, hand shaking with adrenaline. "Four of them, I couldn't stop them. God knows if any more got through in other places."

Sandford was scanning the significantly empty stretch of trench, his eyes narrowing in disapproval. "Why are you the only two here? Where's Corporal Marshall?"

"He led the others to where they threw their bomb," Stack explained, bending to pick up Captain's helmet for him.

"And you disobeyed his orders?"

"He didn't order anything, sir," Captain spoke up, wiping his hand across the blood on his face in disgust. "Just ran off. Ben thought we needed to stay to hold the line here."

"I'm glad you did," Sandford looked darkly down the trench. "I'll be having words with the corporal after this. Can you stay here and stop any more? I need to see what's happening over there that requires so many of my men."

"We can try," Captain gave a grim smile and Stack nodded in agreement. The second lieutenant hurried off in the direction of the shooting.

"Reckon there will be more?" he asked Stack when Sandford was gone.

"Maybe," he replied gruffly, still struggling to hold his head upright. "Better safe than sorry. Look out for those others too; if they make it out with anything important we're better off shooting it into the mud than letting their officers get at it."

"They're raiding the wrong place," Captain said, fixing his sights back on the barren wastes of No Man's Land. "If our leaders have trusted important strategies to Kent they're even stupider than they look. Sandford's the only half decent officer we've got and he's only a second lieutenant."

"I may have to agree with you there," Stack managed a hardened smile before turning his full attention back to the positioning of his rifle.

A scuffling behind them alerted them to the reappearance of two of the four surviving raiders, making their way back along the trench. Perhaps they had expected the two English soldiers to be dead by the time they returned, as they faltered at the sight of them, their faces a picture of shock. Stack and Captain swung and fired in unison and they fell to the ground before they could even raise their guns, crumpling like sticks in a fire. The Englishmen looked at each other, not entirely sure what to do with them now they had stopped them.

"Would they have found anything?" Captain asked dubiously.

"I don't think so," Stack frowned. It was hard to think straight when his head felt like it was trying to rip itself apart. "We should check just in case. You search them, I'll cover you."

Captain jumped down from the firestep and quickly rummaged through the pockets in their tunics, pulling out a few collections of papers. Some he discarded immediately – a photograph of a woman and two children and a letter written in German – and others he gathered together and flicked through, opening a thick letter and beginning to read.

"Do you think they can even read English?" he asked, pulling a face. "This is just something from Kent's wife."

"Stop reading it and get yourself back up here then," Stack ordered.

Captain pushed the papers back together and stuffed them into his pockets, ducking instinctively as a shot rang over his head. Stack reloaded without taking his eyes off the man who had rounded the corner, dragging something or somebody behind him. He had fired too hastily and hit nothing but the man's courage. He cowered in the shadows, screaming something in German. It sounded like pleas.

Stack got down from the firestep and walked slowly over to him, rifle loaded and aimed straight at the man's chest. He could make out what it was he had been heaving down the trench now; the body of a person, wearing the grey uniform of the Germans. He was bleeding heavily and his eyes were closed but twitching unnaturally. His comrade babbled faster as Stack approached, backing away with fear but keeping himself in front of the wounded man.

"He's not going to make it," Stack told him, but the man just cowered further at the sound of his voice and broke into a full stream of rapid German.

"Don't talk to it!" Captain shouted at him. "You'd be dead if it was the other way round."

Stack shook his head, hearing the man whimper pitifully. He took a step forward and the German fell to the floor, hands over his head, repeating the same phrase over and over. Stack turned back to Captain.

"What's 'surrender' in German?"

"Probably that," his friend replied, advancing behind him with his own rifle in case the man tried to run for it. "Besides," he smiled cheekily beneath the blood still drying on his face. "I think a surrender is worth an extra rum ration, don't you?"

****

The hall was a sea of khaki, blue and brown, packed full with the soldiers of D Company along with other British, French and Canadian troops. It had been a theatre before the war – the large curtained platform and ornate walls paid homage to this – but now there were rough wooden tables covering stage and floor, and the bar staff were rushed off their feet catering to a crowd with a much greater thirst than those who used to grace the room.

A few nights ago a Canadian band had played with a local French singer for the soldiers, but they had moved back to the trenches and tonight the only songs were sung by grizzled men merry from drink and rest. A couple of tables beneath the stage had been pushed together and were now home to a large card tournament, guarded by a bristly looking lance-corporal ready to alert the gamblers at any sign of the military police. The table next to this was in danger of overturning as two men strained against it in an arm wrestle.

Stack and Rigby had managed to pull Captain away from the cards – he had already lost a large chunk of his wages to a sergeant from another platoon – and had settled around a long table under the balcony with a few others from the platoon, pints in hand and beaming for the most part.

"I killed *so* many Germans!" Tommy Miller boasted, standing on the table and lifting his drink into the air like a conquering hero. "Right up close too, I swear I'll never be scared again!"

"You shot two," Rigby picked at a splinter; he hadn't been impressed the first twenty times the story had been told. "They might not have even died."

"Oh, let him have his glory," Captain rubbed the boy's back a little too enthusiastically, making him spill his beer. He was in a particularly good mood, helped a lot by the chance of real leave and an excuse to celebrate. "Tommy boy, you are a true warrior."

"Can I talk to your sister now?" he asked eagerly.

Captain ran a hand through his hair; clean and shining after managing to charm his way into a real bath courtesy of one of the locals. His uniform was cleaned and buttoned up immaculately, ignoring the fade of colour caused by exposure to the elements. Rigby too was looking dapper today, and Stack had managed to bring himself to shave and have a proper wash.

"I suppose writing to her would do no harm," Captain shrugged happily. "I'll even lend you the paper if you like."

"More importantly," Rigby clinked his empty glass with Stack's. "Someone needs to get me a refill."

Captain opened his mouth to tell him to get his own, but the words changed halfway out and he let them willingly. "I'll get you. It is your birthday after all."

Stack snorted a laugh at the surprised look on Rigby's face. Captain spied a barmaid crossing the hall and waved at her.

"Excusey moi, madmaselle!" She turned and he held up his cup and pointed at it. "More beer, sivvou play."

The girl came over with a large jug that looked too large for her to carry and began to pour into the separate glasses. She was a pretty little thing; high cheekbones and large brown eyes that spent too long fixed on Captain's face to be good for his ego.

"You speak good," she smiled shyly.

"Pah!" Stack almost spat beer all over the table. "No he doesn't!"

Rigby joined in. "He's got a pretty face, but you don't want him opening that mouth of his."

The girl's brow furrowed a little in confusion, but she seemed to get the gist of what they were saying. She looked back at Captain.

"You don't listen them Tommy," she told him. "You speak good."

"Hey, he's not Tommy!" Miller's round red face looked indignant. "I am!"

Captain dismissed him with a flick of his hand. "I'm Dan, madmaselle, Dan Captain."

She giggled at his pronunciation, her cheeks turning a healthy pink. "A captain? You must be brave."

"I am," Captain swelled with pride, ignoring how Stack's shoulders were shaking with silent laughter. Rigby was staring at him with a look somewhere between disgust and admiration, shared by Johnny Pritchard and Jim Collingwood – known as Collie – from Butterfield's section.

"Hey, miss," Miller butted in, still screwing up his face in confused offence. "*I'm* Tommy."

"Hello Tommy," she said kindly. "More drink?"

"I don't think he'll be needing more of that," Captain laughed, casting a glance at the boy tottering about on the table. "Look at him!"

She finished distributing drink to the rabble around the table and straightened up, eyes still on Captain.

"Excuse moi," she shrugged apologetically. "More men, more beer."

"Of course," Captain handed her more than enough money and leant forward to give her a quick kiss. She turned a shade of beetroot and scuttled off across the hall, stumbling over a bench on her way.

"You," Rigby said incredulously. "Are an awful human being."

"He's a bloody excellent human being," Stack gasped for breath, his whole body still shaking. "She thinks you're an officer!"

"It's not that funny," Captain raised an eyebrow. "This is just what happens to me. Rigby, why is it only you and I who can hold our drink? Maybe I should start being nicer to you." The men looked at each other then spoke at the same time. "Nah."

A crash and a wave of laughter signalled that Tommy Miller had fallen off the table. Seizing the opportunity, Captain leapt onto the rickety old thing and pulled Stack up with him to propose a toast to Rigby's birthday – one more year of boring the world. Rigby scoffed and climbed up between them, attempting to make a real speech but getting interrupted by so many heckles from Collie and the others that he gave up.

The three of them thrust their drinks together with a loud clink and Captain began a song. Collie and Pritchard joined him, along with a few men who had already been singing at nearby tables. Stack and Rigby swallowed the rest of their drinks, put their arms around each other's shoulders and followed suit. Before long half the hall was belting out "It's a long, long way to Tipperary", led by the three on the table for whom some had even bought more drink. Captain grinned widely and stamped out a beat, greatly enjoying all the attention. Tommy Miller was lying passed out contently on the floor and the barmaid had to step over him to get near enough to catch Captain's eye.

"Captain!" she called, large eyes shining. "You sing good!"

Captain thrust his beer into Stack's hand and leant down to pull her onto the table with them, while she shrieked with delight. He left the rest of the room to continue with the singing and wrapped his arms around her instead, leading her up and down the table in a jaunty foxtrot. She was out of breath by the time he flung her at Rigby and went back to stamping his feet and clapping in time with the song. He sped it up until neither Rigby nor the girl could keep up and they stopped dancing, the girl flocking immediately back to Captain's side.

"You Tommies are fun," she puffed, holding her side but looking very happy.

"You hear that?" Captain addressed the hall. "She says us British are fun!"

A cheer went up, interjected with a few shouts of "You should see the Canadians!"

Captain waved a hand to silence them, taking his glass back from Stack and swigging deeply. "So folks, I'm your captain tonight."

"Bollucks!" Collie shouted. Captain ignored him.

"Some of you may know my good friend Albie Rigby. Well it's his birthday today, the lucky bastard! Who thinks that's fair? He picks the day we're singing and drinking – the rest of us get nothing but shells and trenchfoot!"

People laughed, and one man shouted that he had shot his first German on his birthday.

"Good for you!" Captain continued. "But despite it being horrendously unfair I do love him, when he's being decent. So you'd better all wish him a happy birthday! Twenty-six years, who the hell let you live that long, ey?"

The listening soldiers cheered again and started up another song, this time accompanied by a trumpet brought out by a French infantryman.

"Yes French!" Captain applauded, giving the girl a squeeze before leaving her to link arms with Stack and Rigby in a clumsy cancan.

Collie was quick to snatch her up, bringing her down to dance with him between the tables. He was almost as handsome as Captain, with bright blue eyes and yellow-blonde hair, and the girl didn't seem unhappy to be dancing with him, though her eyes did slide back to the man on the table more than once.

Nobody noticed the door swing open and the form of Captain Kent step inside the crowded hall. He looked tired, with dark rings beneath his hard eyes and an expression on his face that clearly said he was not in the mood for nonsense. The scenes of frivolity that met him as he entered did nothing but sour his mood further.

"D company!" he shouted.

Nobody heard, or paid him any attention.

"D COMPANY!" he bellowed, firing a blank into the air. The singing stopped instantly and the Frenchman hurriedly put away his trumpet, giving the British a sympathetic look.

"Reporting for duty," Captain saluted cheerfully.

Kent glared at him.

"Next patrol I hear of, private, you'll be on it," he snarled and turned his attention back to the rest of his company. "We're moving back to reserves; there's suspected trouble at the front and they need as much backup as possible. We leave in six hours. I suggest you all head back to barracks and get some sleep before the march."

Rigby grumbled. "I thought we were meant to have two more days."

He hadn't grumbled quietly enough.

"No complaints," Kent barked. "Private Rigby, you'll be on patrol with Private Captain."

Stack and Captain opened their mouths to protest, but closed them again as Kent added Stack's name to the list. The whole hall was silent now, and Collie's snort of laughter was not easily hidden. Kent turned on him.

"You think it's funny, do you?" He shook his head. "What's your name, private?"

"Collingwood, sir," he dropped the barmaid and tried to look regimental.

"One of Corporal Butterfield's section, yes?" He nodded. "Well I expect to see you with these men on the next patrol! Does anyone else think that this is funny?"

"Captain Kent," Butterfield stood up from the table he shared with another corporal and some Canadians. "Could I have a word please?"

"No corporal, you cannot persuade me to change my mind. If you have anything important to say then yes, you can have a word."

"Sir, he's a good soldier and he's done nothing wrong. He'd be wasted on a patrol-"

"Then maybe you would like to go along too and protect him?" This shut him up, and he sank back into his seat, anger clear on his face. Stack couldn't help but notice that Marshall made no such show for them. "Any more volunteers? We're building up quite an army."

"Something's really ruffled his feathers," Captain muttered. "I reckon he was planning on visiting the brothel tonight and this move has scuppered his fun. Poor bloke would only have been disappointed; nobody would sleep with him no matter how much he paid them."

"Private Captain!" Kent screamed. "How many patrols do you want to be on!? All of you, back to the barracks. Now."

He spun on his heel and slammed the door behind him. Rigby kicked the table. The hall started to empty as the majority of the British soldiers made their way out. The Frenchman started to play his trumpet again but no singing accompanied him this time, the hum of chatter considerably quieter than before.

"Well I'm not going back yet," Captain jumped down from the table and picked up a jug that somebody else had left behind. "I don't need sleep."

"That's alright for you," Rigby followed him down and went over to Tommy Miller – still asleep on the floor. "Some of us do need to. Someone help me with him."

Mackie made his way over from where he had been sitting on his own with a book, so silent that nobody had even noticed he was there. The two of them took one of Tommy's arms each and half dragged him out into the night. A Canadian leaned over from a nearby table and addressed Captain.

"You'd better get out of here pal; he really didn't seem happy with you."

"He never is," he rolled his eyes. "Which is why I'm waiting at least an hour before I go back – can't have them thinking I'd actually follow his orders."

The other man grinned. "Well good luck to you. It's been a good night."

"And here's to many more," Captain raised his jug and touched it against the Canadian's glass. "May you return to your friends and family alive and well."

"Who knows," he shrugged. "But you too, Tommy, you too."

****

Captain Kent was true to his word. Stack, Captain, Rigby and Collingwood were grouped under the command of Corporal Butterfield on a cool spring night, along with two others from Butterfield's section. There had been an increase in patrols recently – if the talk was to be believed – with more prisoners being taken, the higher the rank the better. It was obvious, the men said, that something big was being planned.

More and more new recruits were being flung across the channel - most with too little ammunition and equipment, many far too young and inexperienced to call themselves soldiers. Thorough training seemed to have been forsaken in favour of fast delivery. They could only hope that arms would be delivered just as quickly, but of much better quality; something they all knew was unlikely.

"Do you all understand your instructions?"

Nine months in the trenches had slowly started to wipe the inexperience from Sandford's face. He looked older now and surer of himself, though his eyes would never be as hard as Kent's and the looks of empathy he gave his men were still as genuine as ever. The face of a strong leader, Stack thought.

"Get over there quickly and quietly, observe their defences, take a prisoner if you can. Most importantly, get yourselves back here just as quickly. I'm losing seven men tonight; I expect to see all seven returned to me."

"Yes sir," they replied.

"I have faith in you corporal," he clasped Butterfield's shoulder.

"I'll do my best," Butterfield nodded and turned to his companions. "Ready men?"

They nodded stiffly.

"Heads down, helmets on, let's see how far we can make it before they spot us. Nobody gets their heads blown off tonight, understood?"

"What about a leg?" Captain joked.

"None of those either. Okay? Let's go."

Sandford stood back as they scrambled over the top, watching until their silhouettes became one with the night. The weather had been kind at least; heavy cloud cover and no moonlight to give them away. He glanced towards the clouds, hoping that the rain would hold off for a little while longer, before returning back along the duckboard.

"No flares tonight?" Collie asked quietly, crawling beside Butterfield. The two had known each other before the war and there had always been a sort of fellowship between them.

"There will be if you don't shush," Rigby said through gritted teeth.

It was clear that he had been dreading the patrol more than any of them. His lanky frame crawled inelegantly through the mud, veins protruding from his neck and forehead in concentration. They kept their bodies low to the ground, high enough only to allow enough vision to spot snipers and wire before they did their damage. Butterfield went first; he was light and athletic and darted from sunken cart to shell hole, keeping under cover while his sharp eyes scanned the terrain ahead. Stack and Captain kept either side of Rigby, encouraging him with their presence.

They paused for a moment, looking up at the body of somebody who had felt the metal teeth of the wire too well. He dangled eerily, staring out over the German lines like some sort of tortured god. They tore their eyes away as Butterfield beckoned to them, crouching behind the shell of a murdered tree.

"We split here for now," he said in a low whisper. "Get as close as you can, but don't let them see you. I want reports on everything you can make out; the layout of the trenches, how many soldiers and their ranks, even where they take a piss. Anything could be important."

"Good luck," Stack whispered, patting a white-faced Rigby on the arm as they parted.

After a time surveying the line of German trenches – far superior in design to those waiting for them on the British line – they regrouped in one of the deeper shell holes. Butterfield considered everything they had to tell him and compared their information to notes provided by previous patrols, before deciding on the best point for him to enter the lines. The plan was to be discreet and quick; find anything that may be of use, quietly dispose of any unlucky soul who happened to stumble upon him, and slip back into the night.

"Watch my back," he addressed them all, looking odd in German grey. "And each other's. Keep up surveillance but don't stray too far from the group or this hole – I want you all safe. If you encounter a patrol, take them out, but don't go looking for trouble. With any luck, I won't be long. If I'm not back in 2 hours, get the hell out of here and send my love to my family. If 2 hours haven't passed but it gets too dangerous, get the hell out of here and send my love to my family. Understood?"

They nodded, Collie a little begrudgingly. The corporal pulled himself over the side of the hole and disappeared into the night.

"He's mad," Captain observed.

"Idiot wants a promotion," Collie said bitterly. "It annoys him that the officers never listen, thinks he needs to be more than a corporal."

The blonde man crawled up the muddy incline to ground level, lying silhouetted as a darker black upon the black of the night, beneath the gruesome shape of the twisted corpse the wire had claimed.

"What are you doing?" Captain asked.

"Surveillance," Collie replied. "Like he said."

"From here?" Captain pulled a face. "So we don't even do any patrolling, just sit in a hole? Kent needs to sort out his punishments; this is nothing. You can't even see anything from here."

"Don't complain about it!" Rigby hissed, face still white.

He sat scribbling in the dark, trying to get onto paper the layout of the trenches he had observed. Captain paid him no notice. He was still staring at Collie – or past Collie, at the hanging man in the wire. He tilted his head, studying it intensely and muttering to himself. "You can't see anything from here. But up there…"

In a flash he was off, before anybody had the chance to hold him back. Quickly studying the way the dead man hung, he threw himself onto the twisted barbs, wincing as he imitated the body as best he could.

"What are you doing?" Stack crawled hastily after him, trying to pull him away from the painful spikes, but Captain shook him off.

"They must be used to seeing us hanging up here," he whispered. "They'll never guess I'm a live one."

He winked and Stack almost laughed. It was a very Captain-ish thing to do. Still, even in the dark he could see the dark patches of blood forming on his tunic, his face arranged in a grim expression.

"Wait," he moved instinctively to point, ripping the skin on his arm. "There's someone out there. No, four of them. Jerry patrol; I'm certain of it."

Stack hurried back to warn the others, followed by his friend as soon as he managed to disentangle himself. He was bleeding in multiple places and his uniform was torn but he shrugged it off, wincing at the movement of his punctured shoulders.

"What should we do?" Topper whispered.

"You heard the corporal; take them out," Collie replied.

"How?" Rigby hastily stuffed his paper away and clenched his rifle instead.

"Oh," Collie hesitated. "Shoot at them?"

Captain clapped his hand painfully to his forehead in exasperation. "And bring the whole army down on us?"

"We need to be as quiet as we can," Stack said thoughtfully, Captain nodding in agreement. "If we're lucky we could ambush them. Cap and I could sneak round behind them, Rigby and Johnson to the right and Collie and Topper from the front. Just bayonets and knives if we can help it, and try to take prisoners not lives."

"And what if they have different rules?" Rigby asked irritably. "What if they're quite happy to pick up their rifles and shoot us in the head?"

"We'll be on them before they have the chance," Stack promised. "You trust me don't you?"

"I bloody wish I didn't," Rigby replied, but fixed his bayonet and gritted his teeth.

The first German got a finger to his trigger, but Johnson and Collie bowled him over before he had the chance to pull it, as Stack and Captain jumped on the remaining three, Rigby and Topper approaching from the left to help. Stack got his hand over his opponent's mouth, trying to ignore the sharp pain as teeth bit down hard. The man squirmed and lashed out, catching Captain forcefully in the stomach and knocking him away, winded and coughing.

He released Stack's fingers and in his moment of hesitation managed to get his elbow to the Englishman's jaw. They slid down into a puddled shell hole, hands finding Stack's throat and tightening, keeping their grip as he kicked him hard and they rolled. He pulled away with great effort, having no time to massage his neck as he dodged another lunge. He caught his arm and turned the man over, holding his face into the mud. He struggled and kicked, dislodging Stack's grip and managing to crawl a little way, only to meet the butt of Collie's rifle. Collie struck again and he reeled backwards, blood forming from the gash in his head, and lay still.

"You alright?" Collie asked, but Stack was looking past him.

Two of the enemy patrol were dead, but Rigby and Topper had a hold of a living man each and Rigby's in particular was of interest. Where the other was wriggling and protesting, this figure yielded with dignity, something on his uniform catching Stack's eye in the darkness.

"Silver cord!" he exclaimed, disbelief coursing through him. "We've caught ourselves an officer!"

Rigby's eyes widened in elated shock, but their happiness was short-lived. A deafening crack and a cry from Topper brought their attention to the other prisoner – now lying motionless as Topper cradled a bloodied palm. Whether an accident as he struggled or in a deliberate defiance of his capture, the man had shot himself, taking a good part of Topper's hand with him and no doubt alerting snipers to their position with the noise.

"Brave bastard," Johnson cursed. "They'll all be on us now, what do we do?"

"Get out of here," Rigby replied, needing no excuse.

"Not without the corporal," Collie shook his head.

"We need to get this one back to our lines," Johnson jerked his head at the German officer. "Topper too."

"We have to wait!" Collie protested.

"And what happens if there's more of them?"

"Topper," Stack interrupted. "Can you run?"

"Of course I can," he replied. "It's just my hand."

"Good man," Stack rubbed his brow. "Johnson, Rigby, you take charge of the captive. Get him back behind our lines no matter what. Topper, Cap, get yourselves back okay. I'll wait for Butterfield with Collie."

"Me?" Captain did not look impressed. He also did not look in a fit state for another grapple; their skirmish had in no way improved his gouges from the wire. "What am I leaving for?"

"You're hurt Cap."

"I'm never hurt," Captain scowled at him, but the scowling seemed painful. "I'm staying here."

Stack sighed, fixing Collie with a forceful glare. "Make sure he goes back."

"But-"

"Don't worry about Butterfield; I'll get him. Get Cap back."

To his utter surprise Collie nodded, putting a firm hand on Captain's arm. Stack expected his friend to protest, but he only looked from him to Collie, a great smile forming on his lips.

"If you command it," he cast a knowing eye over his friend's face, enjoying his astonishment, and followed Collie back towards their lines.

Once they were gone, Stack found he could not wait around for long. Now he thought of it, Butterfield had not been gone too long; he could easily still be above ground, and there was no use in him risking his life when they already had an officer for a prisoner. Relying on a mental image of the maps the corporal had considered earlier, he headed in the same direction, keeping an eye open for any sign of him.

It wasn't long before he caught him up. The wire appeared to have been fixed since the date of the notes that promised a path through it, and Butterfield was dutifully hacking away at it, moving silently so as to attract no attention. In that field though, he had failed.

The corporal seemed not to notice, but Stack caught sight of the movement behind him, walking softly to avoid alerting the man cutting the wire. Until he came up behind him, then he was soft no more. Swiftly he raised the butt of his rifle, bringing it down hard on the back of Butterfield's head.

Idiot! Stack thought. *He should have come back for help with the wire.*

There was no time for thinking now though. He held his gun steady, firing into the back of the man before he could reach down and lift the stunned corporal. Butterfield fell back to ground as another German emerged from the night, searching for the shooter who hit his friend, but he fell too before his fingers could find the trigger.

A shout told Stack that the gunshots had not gone unnoticed. Instinct took over and he threw caution to the wind, crawling as fast as he could across uneven ground towards the corporal. One of his would-be captors started to lift himself, blood darkening his front. Stack paused only to pull out his wire cutters, burying them in the flesh at the base of his neck. He twitched and gargled, convulsing in a grotesque way, but Stack had no time to feel bad. He passed him and reached Butterfield, who was lying where he had fallen, blinking back unconsciousness.

"Stack?"

He had no time or spare concentration to reply. Bullets began to fly from the German lines, thankfully blind for now, but if he stayed still too long they would soon find him. He wrenched the cutters back from the dying German, spewing blood, and snapped through a coil that had snaked around Butterfield's wrist. Not waiting to see if he could stand unaided, Stack grasped one of his forearms and draped it over his shoulder, heaving him from the floor. The shooting had thinned now to just one or two guns, but on looking back he was not happy with the reason. More men were climbing from a pockmark in the ground, rifles aimed.

Stack spun around; looking at them would do him no good. He dropped Butterfield's arm and scooped him up completely, throwing him over his shoulder like a sack of potatoes, and ran. His legs moved at zigzags, trying to evade the bullets, but the corporal was heavier than he looked and he could feel the men behind closing the gap, shouting something in German.

A shot flew past his shoulder, but this one was heading the wrong way. Another patrol. He was trapped. Tightening his grip on the man in his arms, he threw himself into the nearest crater, noticing too late that he had thrown himself right at them. He deposited the corporal in the mud and spun to face his fate.

A crack split the air, but he remained standing, and alive. The two at the lip of the hole hadn't turned, still focused intently on the direction from which he had come.

"Two down," Captain's voice came triumphant from under his helmet. "You still here Ben? Get on with it; we can't keep them back all night!"

Stack could have argued – it was him who was supposed to have got out of there – but he couldn't deny that their appearance had probably saved his life. He pulled Butterfield back up again and they ran, tripping their way back across No Man's Land at a crouch. Captain and Collie caught them up as they neared the British lines and they slid over the parapet together, narrowly avoiding being impaled by the bayonet held erect by a wide eyed Tommy Miller.

"Are you alright?" Collie was already attempting to tend to Butterfield's bruises as the other man pushed him away in embarrassment. "We got us an officer, silver cord and everything."

Sandford pushed his way through the gathering crowd, eyes darting from one man to the next, counting silently. The relief was clear on his face when he reached seven. He knelt down beside Butterfield, checking with Collie that everything was alright, before getting back to his feet and addressing Stack.

"Private Stack," he twitched as if the little boy inside him wanted to embrace the man, but he kept himself upright and dignified. "You got them all back."

"I didn't, sir," his breath came sharply after his sprint, and adrenalin coursed through his body, still in flight mode. It was hard to concentrate on anything but the beating of his heart and the earth around him. "If Captain and Collingwood hadn't followed me, we'd both be dead."

"Probably," Sandford agreed, but shrugged as if that simple fact didn't change anything.

Stack looked to Captain for support, expecting his friend to speak up and claim the glory he deserved. The man just met his eyes silently, and grinned.

****

Captain was waiting for him outside the aid post, leaning against a tumbledown stone wall and pulling cheerfully on a cigarette. He had taken the opportunity to wash his hair and spruce up, looking more like a holidaymaker than a soldier. The gashes he sustained from the wire had bled a lot, making them seem more severe than they were, and after a bit of patching up and an extra ration of rum he was fit to return to duty.

"Butterfield's fine," Stack informed him, coming to lean beside him on the cool stone. "They're sending Topper home; he's no use with a rifle unless that hand heals."

"I bet he'll be hoping it falls off," Captain remarked, watching the smoke curl away into the morning. His eyes followed it towards the grubby tents before coming to rest on his friend's grubbier face. A smile twitched around the corners of his mouth.

"What?"

"Are you still going to tell me the boys don't look up to you?" he smirked, stubbing the cigarette out on the wall. "You were a regular officer out there, barking orders and saving people's lives."

"You and Collie saved *my* life," Stack corrected him. "Why aren't you bragging about that to everyone who'll listen?"

"They followed your orders," Captain insisted. "If it was anyone else out there Johnson and Collie would have spent all night bickering and Butterfield would be left to Fritz. You're a leader, Ben. I wish you'd believe me; I could do with a friend at the top." He winked.

"Collie and Butterfield are close; he would have gone after him if I was there or not."

Captain shook his head. "Collie's not as brave as he makes out, or as smart. He might not have gone back without him, but he wouldn't' actively go looking for him, not without someone making the first move. Heck, I wouldn't have risked my neck for Butterfield if it wasn't you out there with him."

"Well if I'm such a great leader," Stack asked. "Why didn't you listen to me when I told you to go back with the others, you cocky idiot?"

"Me?" Captain laughed. "Because I'm your friend, Ben; I wouldn't follow your orders if you were a goddamned field marshal." He paused. "And I'm a cocky idiot."

4.

South-East England, 1915

The grass tickled Harriet's cheek and she enjoyed the feeling, brushing her face against the dew where she laid in the grounds with Eliza, her sister with her pretty nose in a book. She stared at the blank paper again, chewing the inside of her mouth as she attempted to turn thoughts into words.

"You know what, Hattie," Eliza propped herself up on a gloved elbow. "I want you to stay here forever. Please hurry up and get married to a Kentish man."

Harriet rolled her eyes, ready for Eliza's new favourite topic of conversation. "What would father do without me in London?"

"Cheer and be very happy for you?" she smiled sweetly. "Look, I've accepted that you're never going to fall for a rich gentleman, but I want my baby sister nearby. I swear I'll settle for anyone you choose."

"Eliza Redmond," Harriet ignored her sister's correction of her surname. "No matter how much you try you are not going to coerce me into getting married. There's a war on."

"What on earth do you do that affects the war?" Eliza laughed again, her eyes lighting up merrily. "Now you're just finding excuses. I think you're scared."

"Maybe I am," Harriet was silent for a moment, wondering if she actually was.

She was definitely scared of Ben being at war and getting hurt, and scared that she would never see him again, but she managed to get along fine with life while he was gone. According to every source she could think of, if you really loved a person you couldn't go a day without them or you ended up completely miserable. Harriet certainly didn't consider herself any more miserable than the average person. But then, neither was Sylvie. Sylvie loved Edward didn't she? Harriet couldn't work it out and it made her head hurt.

She let the warm morning air push these thoughts back into their box and smiled cheekily at Eliza. "Scared of ending up like you."

"You'll be jealous of me soon enough," Eliza grinned. "When you help to deliver my dozens of children while you're left a barren old maid."

"Trust me," Harriet returned the smile. "I have seen enough women giving birth to make me think twice about having dozens of children."

"Oh, you're awful," Eliza hit her lightly with her book. "I love babies and I'm going to have as many as I can, and they'll grow up to be disgustingly rich and beautiful."

"Better hope they take after their mother then, or they won't be all that beautiful!"

Harriet rolled out of the way and scrambled to her feet, running through the dewy grass with her sister hot on her heels, laughing and demanding she take it back. Not paying attention, she almost ran straight into the old butler.

She stuttered an apology and moved past. The man was almost completely bald and portly, with the air of somebody with extremely high self-worth. Harriet didn't like him much, though she supposed she didn't like very many of the servants anymore; not since the news of Aedan's death. As far as she was concerned, if they couldn't have him they shouldn't need servants at all.

"Come on Liza!" she called, wanting to get away from the butler and her memories of Aedan's dreams to become one himself. "Do you give up?"

"One moment," Eliza held up a hand to silence her, listening to the old man intently.

Harriet wandered back to catch what they were saying. "Why don't you invite him through? I am quite happy to receive a visitor in the garden on a day like this."

"Begging your pardon milady," the butler bowed his head. "He doesn't seem like that sort of visitor."

Eliza shrugged. "I suppose it would do me no harm to go to the door. Hattie, wait here, I'll be back in a minute."

Harriet did what she was told, seating herself and picking at blades of grass to pass the time. It wasn't long before she was interrupted.

A shriek pierced the air, followed by the sound of her sister's voice; loud and angry. Harriet sprung to her feet and hurried up to the house. She turned the corner and hung back, for what reason she wasn't sure.

Eliza stood at the entrance to the great mansion with a letter in her hand, facing a man dressed in a soldier's uniform. He had a face that looked young, but tired and drawn, as if he stood alone against the whole world. Harriet's eyes moved to Eliza and saw that she was crying. She clutched at the brickwork, all breath leaving her – she could guess what this meant.

Eliza threw the letter in the man's face and stormed inside the house before Harriet could persuade her feet to move. The messenger stood for a moment longer, then turned and walked away down the gravel path, limping heavily. Harriet watched him with frozen eyes, still clinging to the wall of the house as if at any minute it would blow away. Perhaps it would. Everything else seemed to blow away these days.

After what felt like years she peeled herself away and walked hesitantly over to the ornate door. The letter lay crumpled where Eliza had thrown it and she bent to pick it up. It shouldn't be left on the floor where the sudden reminder could upset her sister further.

"Eliza?" she made her way into the house and up the grand staircase, calling hesitantly down the corridor.

"Leave me alone," the reply came, thick with tears.

"Are you-?"

"Yes, I'm sure!" she interrupted, not emerging from her room. "I want to be alone!"

Harriet's feet took her back to her room, where she shut the door and drew the curtains. The sunlight seemed intrusive now, like the house had darkened beyond repair. She wished Ben was there. He wouldn't say anything, so there was no chance he would say the wrong thing. He would just hold her and let her cry on her shoulder until she ran out of things to cry about.

She had cried a lot on Ben when she was younger, to the point that she sometimes suspected Eliza was jealous. She leaned her head on the bedpost and tried to imagine it was his arm, but the wood was spiralled and dug in uncomfortably. There was no use pretending; Ben was in France and wasn't coming home in a hurry.

She didn't sleep easily that night, or the nights that followed. She flipped and turned until the bed was a mess, then got up and paced the room, then sat by the window drawing ghosts in the fog. Eliza hadn't spoken to anybody since the news, despite Harriet's repeated attempts to draw her from her room. Gale's lawyer had come one morning, to inform her of the man's will. The butler had told him to come again in a week.

Harriet was left to spend every day finding excuses to escape the house and see Sylvie and the boys, dreading each night when she had to return to the big empty halls. If it had felt too large when she arrived, that was nothing to how it felt now. When Aedan and some others left for war the rooms had doubled in size, and tripled as they filled with ghosts. Now Eliza wouldn't leave her room, the house felt the size of the channel.

She touched the crumpled paper that sat on her window table – after a month she still hadn't been able to throw it away, or even tuck it out of sight. The last letter the footman would ever write. Her shoulders shook, giving away the sob that had lodged itself in her throat.

"Oh Aedan," she cried, laying her fist against the window. "You brave, stupid fool. All of you. Peter Gale, Ben Stack, Aedan O'Connor; you're all stupid, stupid brave men."

She clutched the table with one hand, the other running through her tangled hair as she cried into the night.

"Where are you father?" she sobbed. "You think I'm better off here, but I'm not! I want to be back at the hospital, I want to be useful! I want to help my sister!"

She knew if Aedan were here he would have heard her and come to check she was alright. If she had been home her father would have taken her into his arms, but she wasn't and nobody was coming. And why should they? She was a grown woman now, and the world had much more important things to deal with.

She wasn't sure if the soft footsteps in the corridor were real or just more ghosts, until the door swung open and the thin figure of her sister stepped inside. She was huddled in a shawl, far from the beautiful woman who had boasted about her brave husband weeks ago; her hair had not been combed for days and her face was drained, but at least her eyes were dry. She closed the door quietly behind her and tiptoed over to Harriet, walking with her shoulders bent as if embarrassed.

"Hattie?" she whispered. "Are you crying?"

"I'm fine," Harriet lied, hastily wiping her eyes. "Just a bad dream."

"Oh sweetheart, no you're not," Eliza mopped her sister's cheek with the end of her shawl. "What's the matter? Your Ben's alright isn't he?"

Harriet nodded. "I think so."

She buried her head into Eliza's shoulder and she wrapped the shawl around them both. "We were stupid not to notice it. Mr Gale knew; he bought his factory. You just boasted about it and I ignored it entirely. I named my stupid horse after the archduke, like it was all some big joke."

"That doesn't matter," Eliza said sadly. "There was nothing we could do; we're only people, and women at that. Big men will declare wars and little men will run off to fight in them, it's how the world is. Everything is money and glory, and no thought to what they'll leave behind."

"Mr Gale thought of you," Harriet remembered. "His lawyer called; his business partners get the factories, but you still have the estate and all the tenants. He's left Mr Moore as your advisor."

"Yes, he did think of me," Eliza said, a hint of bitterness in her voice. "He thought of how proud I was to have a brave husband who would fight for his country. If I hadn't been so vain perhaps he wouldn't have gone."

"Little men run off to fight, Liza," Harriet repeated her sister's words. "You couldn't have changed that. It's funny; I didn't once tell Ben not to go either. I wanted to, all the time, but I never did. Aedan neither; I just kept telling people they were brave. We're just as bad as each other."

"You're not bad," Eliza put her arms around her and kissed her hair. "I'm bad for abandoning you. I'm not the only one who's lost somebody over there; I shouldn't act like I am."

"You're quite excused-" Harriet started.

"No I'm not," Eliza said firmly. "Nobody is; we have to be strong now. If those brilliant boys in France can keep going then what right do we have to give up? We keep going, Hattie, for them."

****

Daisy left the kitchen with a grin on her face, casting one last look at Rob before she shut the door behind her. Harriet and Sylvie rolled their eyes at each other, Sylvie kneading dough while Harriet sewed together yet another of Rob's shirts that had managed to rip almost in two. Rob himself sat in the corner cleaning his father's old gun, his face an angry pink.

"I only said I *might* take her," he huffed, not pleased by the look on his mother's face. "What else was I supposed to do?"

"You're supposed to make your mind up, that's what," Sylvie told him. "I don't want my own son becoming the village heartbreaker."

"I won't be, don't worry," he said bitterly. "All the other boys are in uniform. Even Daisy won't like me for much longer."

"That's what I like to hear," Sylvie smiled patronisingly at him and he went back to scrubbing at the gun harder than before. "You're far too young for girls and war." She stopped. "Did anyone hear that?"

94

It came again; somebody knocking at the door. Sylvie wrung her hands in exasperation, looking at the flour covering them. Harriet set down her sewing and got to her feet.

"Don't worry, I'll go."

She left the kitchen and pulled open the creaky front door curiously. The face looking back at her from outside stopped her heart from beating and she let out a yelp. She had only seen him from a distance before, but there was no mistaking him; the messenger of death. She stared at him, half tempted to slam the door in his face, all sensible thoughts fleeing her mind as her blood ran cold.

"Are you the wife of Private Stack?"

"Which one? I mean, no," Harriet croaked, clutching the door frame for support.

"Private Edward James Stack?"

"Sylvie," she called, her voice cracking in her throat, coming out barely louder than a hoarse whisper.

"What is it?" Sylvie emerged from the kitchen, wiping her hands in her apron. The curious look on her face turned to dread as she took in Harriet's white face and trembling lips. "Who's this?"

Harriet fought the urge to run; away from the farm and the wreck Sylvie Stack's life was about to become. What made it worse was that she had felt relief when she heard Edward's name instead of Ben's. How could she face Sylvie after that? Still, she forced her legs to be still and her eyes to focus as the man handed Sylvie a letter, identical to the one given to Eliza months ago.

Comprehension dawned on the woman's face as she took it; an awful shock of acceptance and agony. Harriet would never forget that look as long as she lived.

"What's going on?" Rob stood in the entrance to the kitchen, still holding Edward's gun. Sylvie gulped back a sob and fixed him with the calmest look she could muster.

"Rob, run down the road and make sure Daisy got home alright."

"This is about my father isn't it?" he ignored his mother and glared accusingly at the man in uniform.

"Rob, go on."

"No!" Rob shouted, advancing on the messenger with the gun held out. If he wasn't shaking so much he would have looked incredibly threatening. "He's dead isn't he? My father's dead!"

"Robert Stack!" Sylvie turned on him. "You will go! Now!"

Rob glared at her and punched the wall, but turned on his heel and stormed through the kitchen, slamming the back door behind him. Sylvie watched him go, her eyes welling up but her face composed. She flicked open the letter and scanned it, seeing in writing what she already knew to be true. She took several deep breaths, folded it calmly and put it in the pocket of her apron.

"I'm sorry," the man bowed his head and stepped back from the door.

"It's not your fault love," she said softly. "You have an awful job; I couldn't do it."

"I do my duty," he replied. "Best I can do with this leg."

"Well God bless you," Sylvie took his hand and squeezed it. "Your mother must be thankful you're not out there."

She smiled with dignity as he left and shut the door carefully behind him, before turning and leaning against it, pulling out the letter to clutch it in her shaking hands. The agony in her eyes spread to the rest of her face in an instant and floods fell from her eyes as ill-suppressed wails escaped her mouth. Harriet put her arms around her, wishing she could do something more.

"What's happened?" Matthew's voice sounded small from the shadows. "Violet's crying."

"My boy," Sylvie held out her arms and he ran into them, confusion and fear plain on his young face.

"What's happened?" he asked again, buried in his distraught mother's bosom. When she didn't reply he turned his wide frightened eyes to Harriet, and she burst into tears.

"Matthew," Sylvie breathed, clutching him close as she attempted to speak. "You don't need to worry about your father anymore."

"Why?" he looked up at her, something new filling his eyes that looked heartbreakingly like hope. "Is he coming home?"

"No darling," Sylvie clutched him tighter as another wave of sobs threatened to engulf her. "No he's not coming home. But he's not in those nasty trenches anymore. Your father's in heaven now, and he doesn't have to shoot anything or worry about getting shot at, not anymore."

Matthew's face went grey. "Rob said heaven isn't real."

"Don't you listen to your brother," Sylvie stroked his hair, getting her breathing under control. "There is such a place and he's there laughing at you for believing such silly things."

"What's it like?"

"Well," she gulped and wiped her eyes on her dirty apron. "It's always summer and you never have to do any work. You can eat whatever you like, because you don't need money, so your father will be eating a great big pig every day. It's full of all your favourite things, whatever they are."

"Are you there?" Matthew asked, creasing his little brow as he attempted to work it out.

"No silly, I'm here with you."

"Oh," he chewed his lip. "But you're his favourite thing, and me and Rob and Violet. Don't we need to be there?"

****

Harriet followed the sound of gunshots through the night, stepping through mud and climbing over hedges, paying no attention to the rips in her dress and scratches up her legs. As she had expected, the sounds led her to Rob. He sat silhouetted against the stars on a fence at the top of the field, shooting at nothing. His shoulders drooped and he wasn't bothering to aim, tearing through fences and hedgerows and mud alike. His eyes were fixed on some distant point on the horizon and he didn't so much as look at Harriet as she approached. She pulled herself onto the fence beside him and he kept staring ahead, letting another bullet fly into the trunk of a dead tree.

"Rob," she put a hesitant hand on his arm.

"What?"

He still didn't look at her, wrenching his arm away and wiping it angrily across his face, taking it away a little wetter than before. He had grown a lot since Harriet had first met him. His face was no longer that of a boy, with stubble growing in strength now from his firm chin, and he had shot further up in height. In the dark, with the gun in his hands and the shadow of grief in his eyes, he looked much older than sixteen years.

"Have you come to take me home like a naughty child?"

"No," she dropped her eyes, ashamed that he would think she saw him like that. They sat in silence for a while, before he eventually turned to face her. His eyes were red, but there was no childish wobble in his lips and his voice was deep and stable.

"Sorry," he reloaded the gun and held it out. "Want a go? It's been a while since Uncle Ben's been here to teach you."

She took it and let Rob adjust her arms, but still hit nothing. She noticed then that she was shivering; with cold or shock she couldn't tell. Rob's shock must have been worse and he was sitting in a thin open shirt, but he wasn't shivering. He took the gun back and fired at a gate at the bottom of the field, shattering the latch and making it swing open.

"I think Ben's done a much better job with you than he has with me," Harriet smiled nervously.

"I'm the best shot around here now he's gone," he replied bitterly. "I'm much better than my father, much better than the other farm boys. The blacksmith's boys have never even held a gun, but they get to fight for England and I'm stuck here waiting for them all to die and doing nothing!" He spat.

"You're sixteen, Rob," Harriet reminded him. "It's against the law."

"So is murder," Rob said darkly. "But the Germans get to do that to my father, and Daisy's brother and your Aedan, and we do it right back to them. Real laws count for nothing in war, why should this one?"

"I don't know," Harriet shrugged, hooking her chin over her knees. "But I'm glad it does, and so is your family. You know what it's like saying goodbye and worrying they'll never come back; would you really want to put your mother through that another time?"

He sighed. "I know, I understand, I really do. If Matthew wanted to go I would be telling him the same things you all tell me. But this is war – I don't want to upset anyone, but there are more important things at stake than people's feelings. My father is dead trying to protect this country. What sort of son am I if I do *nothing*?"

Harriet gazed across the field, trying to think of something to say. It was true; he wasn't the young boy that Sylvie saw, and she understood his frustrating need to do something useful – but in reality he was only sixteen, no matter how old he felt in his head.

"You would go too, wouldn't you," he said quietly. "I know you; you don't want to spent the rest of your life helping my mother with the washing."

Harriet laughed. "I don't know if I'd be brave enough, even if that was possible."

"You would," he said confidently. "You understand it better than the other women. You love Uncle Ben don't you, but you never tried to stop him going."

Harriet didn't bother denying it. After how she had felt when she saw that man at the door, she could deny it no longer.

"I should have," she said quietly, hugging her knees and looking Rob in the eyes. "I hate sitting in the big empty house, waiting for letters, not knowing what's going on, doing nothing."

"You understand," Rob said again. "We should be out there, Harriet. But you're just a girl and I'm just sixteen."

He spat again and jumped down from the fence. "But I can stop being sixteen, and when I do you had better not try to stop me, because if you could stop being a girl I wouldn't try to stop you."

He clutched the gun firmly in one hand and strode off across the field.

****

Despite half the village being abroad, the church was fuller now that it ever had been before the war; there was a much larger need for prayer these days. Harriet caught sight of Sylvie standing a few rows ahead with her children at her side, all in mourning clothes. The organist played a bugle now in France, but no organ was needed to accompany the wealth of voices, singing for hope and a safe return.

The hymn drew to a close and the congregation sat, all except two girls standing at the back. Daisy Lane and her older sister Molly were dressed very prettily and each carried a wicker basket filled with something white and fluffy. Molly took her sister's hand and led her into the aisle, pulling a pure white feather from her basket and handing it wordlessly to a young man Harriet recognised as the boy who had run Gale's kennels before he left to care for his sick mother.

Daisy looked hesitantly at the taller girl and received a look of bossy encouragement. She pulled out one of her own feathers and gave it to the man who sat next to Eliza. He took it with confusion, turning it around between his thumb and forefinger.

"May I ask what this is, my dear girl?"

"It's for cowardice," Molly said spitefully, glaring down from beneath her pretty bonnet. "Our brother lies dead in France and you sit in a church – shame on you. Shame on you all!"

She regarded the gathering fiercely, fixing accusing eyes on every man beyond childhood but not yet at his twilight years. "Cowards."

"That's not fair," Harriet spoke up, wanting to explain about the kennel boy's mother, but Eliza silenced her.

"Hear hear," Mrs Gale said coldly, reaching out a hand to shake Molly's. "If all men were as brave as those in France the war would be won by now."

Molly's shared her look. "Your husband needn't have died milady, or my brother, if these cowards had answered the call."

Every man looked uncomfortable now, even those clearly young enough to be free of scorn, and they took their feathers without meeting their eyes. Eliza watched hungrily, no doubt seeing justice for her poor dead husband. Harriet saw only the family and friends of these men, so relieved their loved ones were safe, feeling for them in their shame.

Bold Molly advanced faster than Daisy, thrusting a feather into Rob's hand before her sister could stop her. Sylvie exploded.

"How dare you, you ignorant wench!" she shouted, snatching the feather from her son and throwing it in the girl's face. "He's sixteen years old!"

"Old enough to hold a gun," Molly narrowed her eyes, holding the woman's gaze. Rob sat between them, his face a scarlet picture of anger and disgrace, fists balled in his lap.

"Daisy!" Sylvie turned on the younger girl, swelling with rage. "What do you think you're playing at?"

"Molly," Daisy said timidly. "Rob's not a coward. He-"

"You shut up," Molly looked at her with pure ice. "I thought you actually cared about Joe. Obviously not."

"No, go on Daisy," Sylvie ordered. "You tell her."

Daisy's eyes filled with tears and she said nothing, shaking her head and slowly backing away. She seemed to shrink under the glare from both women, looking to Rob with a desperate apology in her young eyes. He stared back at her, and awful look of betrayal and anger. He got to his feet brusquely and pushed Molly aside, storming down the aisle towards the door.

"Rob!" Daisy called after him, faltering as she tried to pass her sister.

He turned and glared at her. "I am *not* a coward!"

Billy Wayson stood from another pew and followed him out before he too could receive a white feather, leaving a scene of shock behind him. Sylvie practically picked Molly up and looked as if she wanted to throw the girl against a wall, but put her down when Violet started screaming.

"Come on sweetheart," she lifted the crying girl and took Matthew's had firmly, taking them both out of the church.

"Let that be a lesson to you all," Molly shouted, regaining her composure with unnatural ease. "Your families cannot bear the shame you bring upon them if you do not fight!"

Harriet stood now, shaking with rage. She strode towards the insufferable girl and punched her hard in the face, knocking her backwards into her sister's arms as her bonnet slid from her well-groomed hair. Daisy looked up at her with a mix of terror and guilt that almost made Harriet feel sorry for her. But Daisy had known how much shame Rob already felt for not fighting, and how determined he was to find a way. She knew that nobody had the right to let anyone call him a coward.

"I would have thought better of you," she addressed the younger girl, panting slightly. "Coward."

She too turned and exited the church, apologising to the stunned vicar as she passed him. Daisy was left in the middle of the aisle supporting her dizzy sister, her tiny frame trembling as she cried.

Eliza put an arm around the quivering girl's shoulders, apologising softly in her ear.

"No," Daisy shook her head in despair. "No, Harriet's right; Rob isn't a coward, I am!"

She let go of Molly and let her support herself, staring at her older sister as if she were a monster. She clutched at Eliza's hand, the realisation drowning her. "He's never going to love me now."

Harriet knew Eliza would not be happy with her when she eventually returned home that evening. She had wandered the fields, thinking a lot about what Rob had said; that she would go to war if she could. She had never felt brave enough before, but knowing that he thought she could made her want to feel it too, and now she felt she had proven it to herself. Perhaps Rob was right, and if she were a man she would not be afraid at all.

She marched up to the big doors with her head held high, imagining she was as courageous as a soldier. Eliza was waiting for her in the drawing room, sitting back in her chair with daggers in her beautiful eyes.

"Are you angry with me, sister?" she asked defiantly, seating herself opposite.

"You cannot just hit people, Harriet," Eliza replied icily. "Not when you're my sister. I have a reputation to keep, and those girls had a valid point. If we had more men to begin with, less may have died."

"Eliza!" Harriet exclaimed. "Do you really think it would have helped your husband if the *kennel boy* had gone to war?"

"He has the responsibility to fight for his lord."

"Peter Gale was not a lord," she spoke slowly, taking breaths in an attempt to control her anger. It was no use; it bubbled up her throat and exploded as she shot up from her chair. "He was a pompous brat who bought an estate and stole my sister! You used to be kind!"

She ripped a borrowed decoration from her hair and threw it down on the little table between them. "I'm going home!"

****

Rob vaulted the gate and continued through the field, after stopping to pick up his few belongings. He walked with purpose towards the hay barn on the edge of Yates' farm, his bag and his father's gun over his shoulder. He had no intention of walking back the way he came. No matter what the others decided, now was Rob Stack's time to become a man.

His friends were already waiting for him as he pulled open the rotten doors. They sat and lounged in the hay, lit by gaslights they had hung from the rafters. A couple had bottles in their hands and seemed jovial; others sat with more tension in their young shoulders, angered by the incident in the church.

There were six of them in total and their chatter was not kept to a minimum. Once there would be reason to fear the wrath of Farmer Yates, but since the death of his wife his wits had hastily left him and the place was falling into disrepair along with him. His young son had grown bold and reckless, believing he owned the place. The fourteen year old sat with them now, swigging from his bottle like a hardened sailor. Rob admired the boy's spirit, but couldn't help thinking how his own father would turn in his grave if Rob ran Stack's farm like Richie ran Yates'. The white-blonde boy who sat with Richie was older but smaller, and idolised him more than was healthy. They were thick as thieves, mostly staying out of the way of the rest of the village and running wild in the hedgerows.

It was the youth who sat above them, king of the haystack, who Rob headed for, clambering up until they were level. Billy had been Rob's best friend since they attended school together, before both deciding they had better things to be doing than learning. It had been his idea to gather the underage boys together to form 'the Men of England'. They met at night on Yates' land and honed their fighting skills, waiting for the day they had their own chance at the Hun. Well, Rob decided, that day was to come sooner than they had expected.

"Billy," Rob sat himself next to him. "Everyone's here?"

"I'm signing up tomorrow, Rob," he told him, excitement gleaming in his eyes. "My ma's taking me into town and speaking as proof of my age if I need it."

"What?" Rob felt a little hurt. Of course he was happy for his friend, but they were supposed to be in this together. "Why didn't you tell me before?"

"She only gave in today," Billy continued. "Thanks to your Daisy she says she can't bear to keep me here, all shamed against my will."

"She is not my Daisy," Rob bristled. "But good for you Bill. I'm going too, first train tomorrow."

"Your ma give in too?"

"Don't be stupid," he laughed, that determined smile returning to his face. "I've saved up enough money to get me to London. Nobody knows me there; I can disappear and be on a boat to France before you can clap."

"Won't they ask you for proof of age?" Billy asked dubiously.

"They need men; I've heard they're asking for nothing more than a birthday," Rob leaned forward. "Look at me Billy, I'll get in."

"Yeah," Billy grinned, matching the look on his friend's face. "You'll get in. We both will."

"And the others," Rob cast his eyes over their comrades in the hay. "If we sleep on the streets I've got money to get them to London too. We should all go together."

"I don't know if you should be encouraging them too much," Billy frowned. "Half of them are younger than you, and they act it."

Rob looked at him sternly. "Any man has the right to fight for his country. I won't force them – I'm no Molly Lane – but they all have the right to choose. Anyone who wants in, I'm going to help them. Come on Bill, it's you who invited them all in the first place."

"Before I'd seen them trying to shoot straight."

Rob laughed and clapped him on the back. "We've done our best. Just you wait 'til they've been trained up properly. British law will rue the day it decided not to let us fight."

"We're gonna be heroes Rob."

"Yes we are," they shared a look and Rob stood, still holding his old gun. "So boys, Billy and me are off. We got tired of waiting, and we're off to show them there was no need to make us wait at all. Who's coming with us?"

A cheer went up from Riche Yates and his friend.

"How?" Alfie Barnes asked. "It's alright for Vincent and Richie, but everyone around here knows me, and you too Rob."

"I've got money, Alf," Rob said proudly. "It took me a while but I've got it now, and I can get us to London if you're with me. If we catch the early morning cart into town we can be on a train before anyone knows we're gone."

"I'm in," Alfie stood too, raising his empty bottle in the air. "We should have done this months ago."

"Us too!" Richie and Vincent shot to their feet.

Billy didn't look pleased at this. They were the youngest and the least disciplined; a disaster if you put them in a war zone as far as he was concerned.

"Do you have the money to get to London?" he asked. "Rob can't pay for everyone."

"I don't need to go to London," Vincent said animatedly. "Like Alfie said, people don't know us so well, and my father thinks it'd be an honour to go."

"And mine doesn't notice when I'm here anyway," Richie laughed. "But Rob, do you think we'd get in? We don't have any papers, and we're not all tall and built like you."

"They're desperate for men," Rob told them, fire gleaming in his eyes. The more he said it, the more he knew it was true. "They'll take anyone who lies well enough."

"That's you alright then, Richie," Vincent joked. "You haven't told a word of truth in your life."

"We'll catch the cart with you in the morning," Richie said. "We can sign up in town like the others from round here."

"I'll come to London too," George Hill stood. "I should have a few pennies to get by before our first wage."

All six were standing now. Rob looked at each one in turn, seeing his own frustration reflected in their eyes.

"We're going to be heroes, boys!" he lifted his gun in the air, feeling like a general already. "No, not boys – men! Men of England!"

The rest of them cheered and they sang the anthem, though most appeared to be hailing Rob and Billy rather than their king and country. Rob jumped down from the top of the haystack to speak to Alfie and George about London, and Richie Yates rolled a barrel of ale from one of his many hiding places, ordering them all to enjoy their last night as boys. They drank and sang, Rob and Billy with their arms around each other's shoulders. It was fitting, he thought, that they would be the ones to lead their rise to arms, but odd that they would not be marching into battle side by side as they had always pictured.

Billy accompanied them on their walk to the split in the road where the cart would pick them up, though he himself would not be journeying into town until later. They knew the cart driver well; he travelled this way frequently and had given Rob many lifts before when he ran errands for his parents. How long ago that all seemed now. He was no longer Rob the errand boy; he was Rob the man, and would soon be Rob the soldier. How right that sounded.

"Rob!"

He looked up to see a small figure in a white dress running across the field towards them. His eyes narrowed and his pulse quickened; he had not forgiven her yet and doubted he ever would.

It was Billy who spoke to her. "Daisy, what are you doing here?"

"I wanted to apologise," she panted.

Her face was flushed and her hair messy, morning dew soaking the hem of her dress; she had been in a hurry. Rob looked at her but said nothing. Her eyes darted nervously away from him, taking in the rest of the party, tucking into berries Richie had brought from the farm.

"Where are you all going?"

"We're doing what you told us to do," Rob leaned forward against his gun. "We're signing up."

"What?" she panicked. "You can't, you're too young! They'll send you right back home again."

"I told you a few nights ago," he raised his eyebrows at her. "They accepted Gordon Black from Maidstone with nothing but a birthday. We're off."

"No, you can't!" she said again, glancing desperately at the other boys as if pleading for help. They showed her no sympathy. "You're sixteen, you'll get killed!"

"So first I'm a coward, now I'm a baby?" anger was creeping into his voice now, and she took a step backwards. "I thought you understood Daisy, obviously I was wrong. Just get out of here."

"But I love you," she said in a whisper, the words barely escaping the knot in her throat.

Rob's look was hard enough to smash diamond.

"No," he said. "You don't."

"I'm going to tell Sylvie!" she screamed, turning and running back into the field. "You're not going anywhere!"

"Good!" he called after her. "You tell her if you want; I'll be long gone!"

A rattle and a whinny signalled the arrival of the cart as it snaked its way towards them. Billy and Rob got up and embraced.

"Are you sure you don't want me to come to London with you?" Billy asked. "I could enlist there."

"It's fine," Rob told him. "You save your money and take care of those two."

He gestured at Richie and Vincent who were waving at the cart driver. The cart stopped and the other boys piled on, finding space where they could. Rob gave Billy one last smile, before jumping onto the cart, standing up at the back and waving with his gun as the wheels began to turn again.

"Say hi to my uncle for me!"

"Kill lots of Germans!" his friend shouted.

"I'll kill more than you!" Rob replied. "Your aim's lousy!"

****

"Milady, wake up!"

Harriet's eyes finally came into focus and took her from the nightmare, into the servant's hall where a housemaid – Anna – was shaking her gently. Her dreams had not been kind since the war began, but now they ripped her head apart, worse with every day they failed to find Rob. He was always lost, and nobody could find him, and Aedan always died, every night. And Harriet was haunted by a poster calling for nurses at the front, screaming at her that the men were gone and she was doing nothing.

"Anna?" she wiped her brow, realising she was sweating. "Why am I here?"

"You walked in your sleep, miss," Anna told her. "You were calling for Aedan."

"Oh," Harriet looked at the floor. "Sorry."

She knew that the footman had been popular among the servants, particularly Anna if the gossip was to be believed.

"That's alright," the maid smiled kindly at her. "I know you miss him too."

"He was a good friend."

"He was," Anna leaned against the table, looking up to the corner of the low room. "He got very happy when you came, miss. I thank you for that."

"Really?"

She nodded. "Some say it's you he went to war for."

Harriet was horrified. "But I didn't want him to go to war! Why would he do that?"

"Of course you didn't, miss," Anna shook her head hastily, realising what she had said. "Ignore me, it's only idle chatter. Don't you go blaming yourself."

That was it. Whether Anna's words were true or not, the hearing of them left her no choice. Her men had gone to war, to give their lives for their country and friends. She had been one of their friends and she lived in their country, and they gave their lives for her. But she didn't have to sit there and let them. If they could give their lives, then she could save them.

She marched back up the stairs in a hurry, throwing open Eliza's bedroom door without thinking to knock. Her sister woke sharply as she entered, hair tousled and eyes blurry with sleep.

"Liza, I'm leaving," Harriet announced.

"I know," her sister groaned. "Leave then, go back to father."

"No," Harriet shook her head – she had completely forgotten about their quarrel. "I'm leaving the country. I'm going to the front."

"What?" Eliza squinted up at her, confusion plain on her brow. "What are you talking about? You're a woman."

"They need volunteers, nurses to tend the men," she explained hurriedly. "I saw a poster a while ago, and I'm going."

"But won't that be dangerous?" Eliza sat up, alarmed. "Father told me to keep you away from the hospital, not to send you right into the war itself!"

"You can't persuade me not to, not even father can," Harriet told her firmly. "I need to do something useful. I'll take care of myself, I promise."

"No you won't," Eliza shook her head, tears welling in her eyes. "*I'll* take care of you."

It was Harriet's turn to be confused. She moved closer, looking at her curiously.

"I'm coming with you, you idiot!"

5.

The new recruits arrived early, tired from their march. They lined up stiffly, their uniforms straight and clean; no sign of action yet in the fabric. These were Kitchener's men – the second big wave of volunteers – but thankfully trained to the liking of Major General Maxse; relieving to know when there were so many hopeless souls being sent unready across the channel. Kent addressed them together in what was once a town square, curious members of his company gathering to get a first look at them.

"They're babies," Captain flicked his cigarette to the ground in distaste. "Half of them look like they don't even shave."

"Even Miller shaves," Rigby frowned. "How desperate have they got?"

"And with not enough kit for us already," Captain folded his arms grimly. "It'll be a heck of a job looking after this lot."

"They say we've got the best general in the war," Rigby took a thoughtful drag before dropping the butt next to Captain's. "Maybe they won't be so bad."

"They're babies," Captain said again. "The lot of them will be dead before you can say trenchfoot. I'd even bet on it if it wasn't disgusting."

"Whose lives are we betting on this time you morbid bastard?" Stack rounded the corner, his hair damp and his shirt hanging loose about his chest.

"Finally, you had a bath," Captain cheered. "You better suit up sharpish though; we're playing teacher and I don't think Professor Kent will be too pleased with you looking like that."

"Professor Kent?" he joined them in their nosing at the new boys, while hastily buttoning up his shirt. "He been giving you the cane now?"

"He wishes," Captain snorted. "Or maybe The Stork would be a better name; he's delivering us children Benji, look at them."

Stack squinted against the rising sun, taking a better look at the rows of figures listening avidly as Kent spoke glorious nonsense. There were a fair proportion of older men, but the fresh round faces stood out like dozens of plump thumbs, unaware of how sore they were about to become. They were lads of his nephew's age, tall and brave and void of all sense. His stomach clenched to think of Rob standing in these strangers' places, as he doubtless would be soon if hadn't done already.

"You okay Ben?" Captain clicked his fingers in front of his face. "Not scared they'll steal your place in Sandford's heart are you?"

"No I am not," he laughed roughly and gave him a shove. "You're right, that's all; they are bloody young."

"How many do you think are actually nineteen?" Rigby asked.

"In our platoon, ten," Captain held his hand out. "And that's a bet."

"Twenty," Rigby slapped his open palm.

"You're on," Captain grabbed his hand and shook it. "Closest gets the other's rum for a month."

"You're confident."

Rigby jumped and spun at Sandford's voice, seeing him standing behind them.

"Second lieutenant," Captain greeted him. "Just the man I wanted to see. There's been a serious mix-up, sir; they've sent us a school trip. There are some very happy soldiers somewhere looking at castles."

Sandford's lips tightened and they could tell he agreed. Stack had always thought the second lieutenant too young to be there, but he was ancient compared to some of these pups.

"They've sent us brave men who want to help win this war," he replied, his perfect voice slipping as it did when he was unsure of himself.

"They've sent us toddlers," Captain said bluntly. "You need to check their papers, sir; half of them are not nineteen."

"The recruitment posts would have done that," he told him, looking like he believed this just as much as the rest of them. "Anyway, they're here now and it's up to us to make sure they get the hang of things fast. You were just as inexperienced as them once and nobody laughed at you."

Captain looked him straight in the eye; serious for once. "Nobody's laughing, sir."

"A year ago we were saying the same sort of things about him," Stack commented as Sandford walked away.

"Mm," Rigby agreed. "He grew up, mostly. Not sure these nippers will get the chance. You've seen how the officers are these days; we're being herded to the slaughter and it's getting closer."

"The big push," Stack mused.

"Better build up your arm muscles boys," Captain sighed. "Us veterans will be pushing for two."

Captain had changed his tune by the end of the day. He had already adopted a pair of youths – Richie Yates and Vincent Waterman – who shared an enthusiasm for battles and drink that Captain found hilarious. He sat with them now teaching them the platoon's marching songs, enjoying how they laughed at how traditional words were replaced with profanities. Rigby and Miller watched them with a curious eye from their game of cards, Rigby with a hint of sadness, Miller with more than a touch of jealousy.

"How's it feel Tommy?" Stack sat down next to him and picked a card from his hand, placing it on the table.

Rigby scowled. "That's cheating."

Stack ignored him. "You're not the youngest pup in the litter now, hey?"

"I'll be the youngest pup in England soon," he muttered. The boys were now dancing clumsily on a table, Captain and a few others clapping their time. "Those two are idiots; they'll be blown to bits in a day."

"I have never heard you sound so goddamned gloomy," Rigby handed the boy a cigarette. "Don't worry, they won't steal your glory; you're still a pipsqueak."

One of the other new recruits wandered over from Captain's group, shaking his head in disapproval. He was tall enough to be nineteen, but skinny too, as if he had grown upwards at great speed and his proportions hadn't yet had time to catch up. Sand hair shorn short stuck out at odd angles from under the cap he wore like a trophy and he sported a look that reminded Stack of Sandford; tight lips and steady brows that made the boy feel like a man.

"Mind if I join you?" he asked.

They nodded and he scanned their faces, stopping at Stack's with an almost well-hidden look of alarm. His body twitched as if to move on, but he was committed now so he drew up a chair and sat, trying to avoid his gaze. Now Stack came to think of it, there was something familiar in those bony cheeks and brave blue eyes.

"Bored of your friends already?" Rigby asked, collecting up their cards and dealing him in.

They boy regarded them with a look somewhere between pity and disdain. "I should never have let them come; they've been acting like children ever since we got here. They only stop when they're training, and that's just because they like to shoot guns. I only hope they calm down when we get out there."

He jerked his head - in the opposite direction to the front line, but how was he to know. Stack's memory clicked.

"What's your name, boy?"

"Private Wayson, sir," he told him, puffing out his chest in an attempt to look older.

"I knew it, Billy Wayson!" he was leaning across the table now to get a better look at the youth. "When did you arrive? Is Rob with you? Why didn't I see him this morning?"

"It's William Wayson now," the boy corrected him, colour rising in his cheeks. "Billy sounds so childish."

"But you *are* a child!" Rigby had to restrain him now to stop him falling across the table to get to the poor lad. "Where's Rob? Why isn't he here? You joined together, didn't you?"

"I'm not a child," he said stiffly, avoiding his questions again. "You have no proof of my age."

"No proof? I bloody watched you grow up! Where is my nephew?"

"Easy, Ben!" Rigby pulled him sharply back into his seat. "Maybe he doesn't know."

"How could he not know?" Stack turned on him. "They were friends!"

"I don't," Wayson interrupted. "I swear it. Rob was clever; he didn't tell *anyone* where he was signing up, or what his name would be, not even me. He could have a medal already for all I know."

"You really don't know where he is?"

"No sir," Wayson looked down at his cards, guilt on his face. "We practised shooting together and decided together we were joining up, but he had to be sneaky about it and I didn't."

Stack settled down, taking a long swig from his flask. It wasn't Wayson's fault that Rob had signed up; he had been aching to go since before war began and what Rob wanted eventually he would get. He was a determined lad and cleverer than his school career gave him credit for and he would work himself to the bone if he thought it necessary. Stack took another gulp, decided it wasn't helping and offered the rest to Wayson. At least he knew Rob could shoot straight; that was a small comfort.

"Hey Collie!" they heard Captain call across the room, holding a boy in each arm in a friendly headlock. "Look, I'm a father!"

"At least we know they're being looked after by someone just as brainless as them," Rigby commented. "You'll get used to him, Wayson; just part of trench life I'm afraid."

"When do we actually get to the trenches?" he asked, suddenly reminiscent of an excited puppy. If he had a tail it would be wagging furiously. "I want to shoot my first German!"

Stack and Rigby snorted, sharing a look. "You won't be saying that in a few days."

"If you had any sense you'd be writing to your mother and telling her to send in your birth certificate and get you home."

"Sense doesn't win wars," he said proudly. "Bravery does. You're all here aren't you; what sense does that make?"

Stack had to admit he had a point. He still wasn't entirely sure himself why he was here, or why Captain or Mackie or Collie were. Rigby went on that he was fighting for his girl, but under all that there must have been a thousand other reasons.

"It is exciting though," Tommy Miller spoke up. "Killing your first German."

"Don't lie, Miller, you wet your pants," Rigby teased, making the boy go bright red.

"I did not, I fell in the mud," he scowled. "I thought now these youngsters were here you would stop being mean to me."

"What's it like though?" Wayson interrupted, an eager spark still glistening in his eye. "Really."

"Muddy and cold and it stinks," Stack said bluntly. "We're not going to lie to you, Wayson; it's nothing like Kitchener told you."

He shrugged. "I don't mind that. When I get home I'll be a hero and nobody will call me 'boy' again. I'll be a man of England, just like the rest of you."

Miller looked pleased by the thought, but Stack and Rigby just raised their eyebrows, both knowing what the other was thinking – not when, *if*.

****

Waterman and Yates practically ran up the communications trench, so eager to see the front line that they completely forgot about discipline. Stack and Captain had to grab them by their collars and pull them back in line, Wayson glaring as if every foolish thing they did was a personal insult. He had the sense to wrinkle his nose as the smell hit him, glancing at Stack as if to say "you were right" without actually admitting it out loud. It was the sort of thing Rob would do.

"Wayson, please rein in your puppies," Captain said in exasperation as Yates wriggled out of his grip.

"Don't look at me," he pulled a face. "It was Rob who said we should let them come, not me."

"It would be, wouldn't it," Stack rolled his eyes and caught sight of Yates climbing onto the firestep. "Woah, no you don't!"

He managed to get a hand on his head and push it down before it could extend over the parapet to be removed of its brains through a bullet hole.

"What was that for, sir?"

"Yeah, *sir*," Captain repeated, grinning that annoyingly perfect grin of his.

Wayson had started it out of gentlemanly politeness and the boys because they thought his scar was the best thing ever, but it had caught and the new soldiers now addressed Stack as 'sir'; Tristan Holden, Adam Price, even Bobby Watson who was older than he was. Naturally, Captain found this hilarious.

"You don't want to be doing that," he told Yates sternly. "That's the best way to get your head blown off before you get that gun of yours anywhere near a German."

Yates' eyes grew wide in morbid fascination. "Will I actually see someone get their head blown off?"

"Yes," was the simple answer. "Unless it happens to you first."

"Hey, Vince, did you hear that?" It was unnerving how much this seemed to please him. "Have you seen it?"

Stack rubbed his forehead as if trying to erase the memories. "Far too many times, now don't add to that."

Content that the boys wouldn't be poking their heads above the trench any time soon, he continued down the duckboard with Captain. Yates turned to look for Waterman, getting a face full of something sticky instead. He gaped in horror at one of the new recruits from another section, blood gushing from what had been an eye seconds ago. He fell forward, smearing Yates further as he slid down the young boy's rigid body onto the floor. Wayson jumped back in shock, bumping into Bobby Watson who held him upright. Yates stared at the body at his feet, too stunned to move.

"What did I tell you?" Stack called grimly. "Keep your head down!"

Captain chuckled at the look on poor Yates' face, ignoring his friend's orders not to laugh. At least they knew now, Stack thought. With any luck they'd learn the lesson and survive long enough to lose the stupidity that had persuaded them to sign up in the first place.

"Are you alright Richie?" Waterman put an arm around his friend's shoulders and tried to lead him away.

"I'm alright," he shook himself and cleared his throat. Something had become wedged in it that made his voice come small and scared and that would not do. "I guess that answers my question." He attempted a laugh. "We'd better be more careful; don't want us ending up like him before we've taken any of them down with us."

Despite this initial shock, Richie Yates didn't find trench life quite as glamorously dramatic as expected. The idea that the brave men of Britain had to do chores and use holes in the mud as toilets was not one of the best as far as he was concerned, in fact it was darn right insulting. He told the other men this and they laughed, throwing him a shovel and telling him to dig a new latrine if it bothered him so much. Waterman got along a little better, but he followed Yates in everything, so was also found complaining about work more often than not. They spoke together in excited whispers about what their first battle would be like, discussing who would win the first medal.

Wayson much preferred the company of the veterans - particularly Stack - and was obviously trying his hardest to wise up so they would see him as one of their own. Stack wanted to tell him that manhood was not all it was cracked up to be, and he should try to stay young for as long as he possibly could, but fifteen years with Rob had taught him that this was absolutely useless.

"So, Wayson old chap," Captain addressed him over the top of the pump. He and Stack were charged with clearing the small flood lapping at their boots, and the boy was working nearby. "Did you see yourself arranging sandbags when you walked into that recruitment post?"

"Not exactly," he replied, working methodically and without complaint. "But I don't mind; it's useful, and I'd imagine a damn lot better than getting shot at."

"Wise boy," Stack commended him. "Try teaching that to those two."

"Don't blame me." It seemed that Wayson had said this far too much since they arrived, always in regards to Waterman and Yates. "It was your recruiting sergeants who let them through."

"Our recruiting sergeants?" Captain stopped working for a moment, flushed in the face from his labour. "Well listen to that Benji, we own some sergeants. How much do you reckon we could get for them at the market?"

Stack laughed. "I thought you wanted to spend your life killing rats, not selling sergeants."

"Why not both? They'd be equally fun," he flashed his friend a mischievous grin. "You will quickly learn, young Wayson, that rats are the worst thing that ever crawled the earth, but sergeants are the worst thing that ever walked it."

"Not captains?" Stack asked.

Captain thought for a moment. "True, Kent is worse than Bollock. But if I said captains as a whole I would include myself, and I am certainly not the worst thing that walked the earth."

"Debatable," Stack teased.

"Oi," Captain scowled. "You'll be getting one of those sandbags poured over your head if you're not careful."

"Wayson wouldn't let that happen, would you lad?"

"No sir," the boy shook his head vigorously.

"Suit yourself," Captain shrugged and went back to his pumping. "But you have to agree he has such a good aim he deserves to be sandbagged."

"He does," Wayson agreed. "He taught Rob and Miss Harriet to shoot, and Rob taught me."

Captain looked like a child who had just won a pound at the fair. He turned to Stack with an accusing look lighting up his face. "Who's Miss Harriet?"

Stack rolled his eyes. "Why do you get so excited whenever you hear a girl's name?"

"Answer the question," he practically sang. "Is this the girl you got drunk with?"

"Why do you remember that?" he exclaimed.

Captain just winked. He sighed; he hadn't let Rob convince him that she saw anything in him, and he wouldn't let Captain either. It was stupid.

"We're old friends," he answered simply, guarding her from his friend's taunting.

"How descriptive," Captain said sarcastically. "You'll tell me, won't you Wayson?"

"She's the sister of the lady who married our landlord," he said, eager to prove he knew things about the world. "She moved into the big house the summer before the war, but spent most of the time with Rob's family; she knew them before Rob was born."

"You taught the lady of the house to shoot?" Captain looked incredibly impressed. "Good for you, Ben! Is she pretty?"

He didn't want Wayson answering that one. He had no idea why, but something rose in him like a fierce urge to defend…something. What that something was was unclear.

"Yes, she is," he said quickly, ignoring the delight on his friend's face. "But she's not a 'lady of the house.'" He smiled fondly. "She can be a very pretty pain in the neck; you two would get along amazingly."

****

By the end of a relatively quiet week at the front, the new recruits were well on their way to a dangerously false sense of security. Yates and Waterman were bolder than ever, and Marshall was useless at controlling them – something that made everyone really appreciate Wayson and his quieter bravery.

He had settled in well and earned the respect of Second Lieutenant Sandford; expressing his eagerness through careful preparation and questions rather than boyish showing off. Stack saw a lot of Rob in him – they had been best friends after all – but without the temper that so often got his nephew into trouble. He was fixated, to the point of obsession, with an aching thirst to prove himself in the eyes of the men he looked up to. It was an obsession that Rob had displayed all his life.

He snapped out of his thoughts. Why had he been thinking of Rob in the past tense? If Wayson was still alive, it was perfectly feasible that his nephew was well too, if not safe. He rubbed his eyes, itching with exhaustion, and went back to the repairs he worked on.

Voices floated around the corner and he recognised Tommy Miller's squeak, Wayson's calmer tones and the excited babble of Waterman and Yates.

"I'd be happy to die for my country," Waterman was saying boldly, the effect ruined slightly by the fact that his voice was halfway through breaking. "I'd have a medal sent to my father and people everywhere would thank me for saving their lives."

"I'm not saying I'd *mind*," Yates replied, his voice still firmly stuck in the tones of boyhood. "I will have a hero's death, and before I'm too old to be useful too – I'm not ending up like my old man. But I don't plan on dying anytime soon; I'm going to live just long enough for the Germans to learn my name and fear it worse than Death."

"That," Wayson cut over him. "Is never going to happen. The German's don't fear things, not even Death. We're not here to become a German horror story. We're here out of duty because we are men of England and we were born to protect her. Vincent has the right sort of idea; you're just ridiculous."

"What I think is ridiculous is how willing you all are to die," Stack could imagine Tommy's face, trying to look old and wise. "I've been here a year now, and the best thing we've all learned is keep your head down and shoot them before they shoot you. It's *living* that'll make people proud of you."

"Where's the glory in that?" Yates asked indignantly. "If I survive it'll be because I'm good. I'm not here to cower down and only shoot when I'm shot at. Look at what they've done to France, imagine this was England; wouldn't you be angry enough to do anything to stop them?"

Wayson sighed. "Anger is not going to help us. We need to be calm and disciplined; that's what makes a good army."

"When I'm angry I shoot straight," the boy said passionately. "I'm getting those French the revenge they deserve." He sighed loudly. "God, when are we going to do some real fighting?"

"He's a brave one, you've got to give him that," Captain pulled off a boot, sniffed it and pulled a face, throwing it away from him. "I'll get it in a second, my foot's killing me."

"Is it alright?" Stack asked, concerned.

"Don't worry, I'm not rotting, just twisted it earlier."

"So you're not invincible then? The Germans will be pleased."

"It's a twisted foot, I'm not dead," he kicked at something on the ground. "This rat seems to bloody think so though!"

He picked it up, squirming and twisting in an attempt to bite his hand.

"Cheeky bastard tried to eat me." He glared into its beady eyes, letting it know how much he loathed it and its brothers. "If I threw it from here, reckon I could hit Yates?"

****

The bombardment started on 24th June, five days before it was finally due; the big push. The top dogs themselves had come down to barracks to address regiments together, promising glory and an easy win. The war would be over soon. Wayson looked up in awe, taking in every word that was said, as Rob had done when Gale spoke at the estate. Waterman and Yates were practically exploding with excitement, bragging long into the night about how that would be them one day, highly decorated and giving speeches. Even Mackie seemed encouraged by the talk of a quick victory.

Stack wasn't so convinced. He stood at the back of the crowd with a frown and crossed arms, Rigby puffing nervously on a cigarette, his face grey. The extra rations and rallying talks all seemed too much; a bribe to disguise a bloody mess. The offensive may lead to victory or it may not, but how many of these eager men would still be here to see it? They were numbers, statistics; if they had less dead than the enemy it would be called a victory, regardless of how high that number was.

"This is what I call a real war!" Yates' face was lit up as he watched the battering of the German lines.

"Enjoying the fireworks?" Captain asked. "You'll be part of it soon enough."

A great grin spread across the boy's face. "I can't wait." He turned to Waterman and they clapped their hands together. "Men of England!"

The noise was never-ending; a mix of fear, excitement and hope that drove everything else from their heads. The officers tried to keep up routine – drills, training and working parties – but with great difficulty. Corporal Marshall had all but disappeared, only keeping his fragile wits together when Sandford or Kent was near. The captain had become even more of a tyrant than usual, though Stack could see why. He certainly wouldn't want the responsibility of leading a whole company into enemy fire, knowing that all deaths and risks of failure were riding on his shoulders.

The change was clear in Sandford too, as he made regular rounds of his troops with encouraging words and Red Cross packages. He looked at his men with pride for the coming battle, dismissing the openly scared as a disgrace to their comrades. This was their chance to win the war; nobody in his platoon was going to jeopardise that chance by panicking. He kept a special watch on Marshall and his section, something that Collie was quick to pick up on as they received yet another round of rum.

"Hey, sir," he called. "If our NCO was a coward would we get special treatment too?"

"Careful with your accusations Collingwood," Sandford said darkly. "Coward is a strong word."

"You're jealous Collie," Captain waved his flask at him.

"I don't know," Rigby lit up another cigarette. With all the packages coming through and the stress of the oncoming destruction, there was rarely a moment when he wasn't smoking. "If I could swap Marshall for Butterfield I'd gladly give up my rum."

"Butterfield's an idiot," Captain scoffed. "He'd blow his own head off for a bit of glory."

"He wouldn't risk his men though," Stack reminded him. "He'll lead them through alright."

Rigby nodded in agreement. "That man's in love with his men even more than Sandford is."

"I wouldn't trust any of them," Captain watched the second lieutenant's retreating back. "We're numbers and promotions, no matter how they act. As long as they win, what do they care if we die?"

"Sandford cares," Stack told him firmly.

The rain poured down as they approached zero day, falling on apprehensive faces and shaking hands, waiting for the order. They felt the freshness run through their hair for perhaps the last time, watching the bombardment that cleared the way for their attack. The tall figure of Second Lieutenant Sandford swept through the night, drawing the attention of men half paralysed with courage and dread.

"The guns are waterlogged," he shouted over the bombardment and the storm. "Water levels have risen too high, and the forward trenches are flooded. We have to delay the offensive while everything is cleared. We move on the first of July."

Nobody said anything, a wave of dismay passing through them. What if the whole attack was defeated by the weather before they even reached the Germans?

"We can take this as an advantage," he promised them. "This is two extra days of our artillery pounding the enemy lines. Their wire will be pulverised and their morale shattered; every trench will be free for the taking. This is two extra days of your lives, men."

"I am proud to die for my country," Vincent Waterman muttered through gritted teeth, not looking like he meant it anymore.

Nobody breathed a sigh of relief at the news of the delay. What were two days if you were doomed to die anyway? The brave and foolish were impatient for action; the rest just wanted it to be over.

The morning of the 30th June dawned as wet as the last, but no message came from command to halt the advance. They would march into position at 0200 hours that night, ready to face their fate. Stack woke early; not that he had been able to sleep. Captain and Mackie were already awake, watching the boys as they slept curled up together, Yates shaking uncontrollably.

"Poor idiots," Captain said glumly. "I bet they wished they had used their age now. They could have stayed at home without shame."

Stack shook his head. "Not without shame."

"The country doesn't deserve us Benji," he put a hand through his hair. "Not if they're going to scorn boys too young to fight. Let the Germans have them."

Stack stretched, pushing the thought of Rob in a great offensive out of his mind. "You're starting to sound like Rigby."

Captain spat, his usual look returning to his face. "Don't say that, I'm being realistic not goddamned suicidally depressed."

Captain being realistic was not something that put Stack in the easiest of moods.

He improved throughout the day, as everybody else became more and more tense. It was calming somehow, watching him lean back on his chair with a cigarette in his hand and a smile on his face as he attempted to cheer up Tommy Miller who was on the edge of mental collapse.

They sat around a table outside one of the many rough tents pulled up for the men awaiting their move to the front – Stack,

Captain, Miller, Wayson, Pritchard and Collie, with Rigby sitting a few feet away carving a bullet shell into a work of art. His eyes were fixed in concentration, brows almost touching as he squinted at his restless hands, forcing himself to ignore the hours ahead of him. Wayson sat with a determined look on his face, running through for the thousandth time their orders for the following morning.

"We wait until the bombardment stops, then the mines," he recited, Stack nodding in encouragement. "Then when Sandford gives the signal we go over the top, walking pace, capture the lines. No turning back, no stopping. Montauban will be ours by the end of the day."

"That's the idea," Stack nodded, wishing he had as much faith in their abilities as the young private.

"But you leave the capturing of the village to me," Captain told him lightly.

"I'll do as I'm told," Wayson said firmly, the perfect little soldier.

"If there's anyone left to tell you," Captain fixed him with a hard stare. "The poor fools won't know what's hit them. I give Marshall ten minutes."

"I don't envy you him," Collie stubbed out his cigarette on the table. "Our section's lucky we have Sergeant Butterfield."

Captain went to make a comment about the corporal's recent promotion, but was interrupted by Rigby standing up suddenly. His face was pained and he clutched the shell in one hand, his knife in the other – fingers clenched so tight he was drawing blood.

"Bugger this," he said to nobody in particular. "I might die tomorrow, I've got to propose."

"What?" Captain laughed. "How are you meant to get married if you're dead?"

Rigby said nothing, pushing past them with grim determination.

"Well don't send her that!" Captain called. "She'll ditch you in an instant!"

"Leave him alone," Stack told him. "We're all scared to death."

"I'm not," Wayson said automatically, fixing his face to look brave and manly.

"Of course you're not," Stack said kindly. "We'll all be fine tomorrow; the wire will be cut, the Germans destroyed and all we'll have to do is take the ground."

He hoped he was right. Sandford seemed confident in the plans, and Stack trusted his judgement.

Tommy Miller nodded in frightened agreement. "And we'll win the war and I'll marry Cap's sister."

"That you will boy," Captain promised, smiling at him.

"I fight for her," the youth stuck his chin into the air, lifting his flask. "I fight for her."

"For Rob," Wayson met the flask with his own.

"For Butterfield," Collie joined them, Pritchard echoing his call.

"Sandford," Stack added, Wayson copying him and then the others.

They looked to Captain, who sat with arms folded and flask firmly on the table. The man smiled, framed perfectly by the curls that fell over his dark eyes.

"I don't fight for officers," he shook his head, still smiling. "What do they care about me?"

"You have to," Stack told him, brows furrowing in concern. "You know the punishment for desertion."

"I never said I won't fight," he replied, an intense look filling his eyes. "Fair play if Fritz gets me, but I'll be buggered if I'm letting myself get shot down by my own side. I'll fight alright, just not for them. What do you think of all this, Ben? This plan?"

"It doesn't matter what I think, Cap; we fight for our lives."

"And our country," Wayson added.

"Well I don't," Captain sat forward, looking each of them in the eye. "My country is the same as any other patch of grass and stone. I won't fight for Kent; he would spit on my grave sooner than breathe. I won't fight for Sandford; he's a boy who doesn't know what he's talking about. None of us would fight for Marshall; he's a bloody joke. Butterfield's brave but he makes stupid mistakes. I'm not risking my life just because they want me to."

"Then who will you risk your life for?" Collie asked. "Stack's right; it'll be the firing squad if you don't."

He looked at Tommy Miller. "Who's always led us better than Marshall ever could? And Collie, who saved Butterfield's backside on patrol?" He fixed his friend with a serious look. "I fight for Ben."

Stack laughed. "You're doomed then, Cap. Fear's clouding your head."

"I mean it Ben, I keep telling you," he looked at the others. "Who's with me? Don't you think he'd make a better officer than any of them?"

"No," Stack snorted. "Cap, you're mad; I don't want you fighting for me!"

"I'll fight for you, sir," Wayson joined, his face the picture of determined innocence. "You know us better than the officers do, and Tommy says you know how to handle things when it gets tough. What you say goes with me."

"*Sandford* knows how to handle things," Stack insisted. "And he knows us all better than you think."

"Nahh," Pritchard shook his head. "He's got a point. You did bring Butterfield back from the Hun in one piece."

"Captain and Collie brought *me* back!"

"Face it Ben," Captain put an arm around his shoulder. "You're our honorary general."

"To General Stack!" Tommy Miller raised his flask back into the centre of the table.

"Seriously, stop it," Stack tried to frown at them all over the top of his amused smile, but they were not perturbed.

"We fight for Stack!" Wayson echoed, Captain and Pritchard joining him.

"Stack *and* Butterfield," Collie leaned forward.

Stack felt touched. He had no idea what they were talking about, but he appreciated it nevertheless. He watched them clink their flasks and take one last swig; his friends who had been through so much with him since landing at Le Havre a year ago. They were so alive with fear, excitement, anticipation at the prospect of the war's end.

He wondered how many would be left to drink together the day after tomorrow. He looked at every face in turn, his heart breaking at the thought of those faces lying blank in the mud. And here they were saying they would risk it all for him.

He wondered what he would do if it were really up to him. Could he really order these men to give their lives for victory? Yes, he thought grimly, he would have no choice. They were all volunteers; they had known what they were getting into. They had all realised long ago that their own lives were secondary to the prevention of the onslaught.

"Well I fight for the lot of you," he told them. "Rob too, and Sandford and Butterfield and even Kent and Marshall. Edward and Thomas, Charlie Pepper, Aedan O'Connor and all the other poor souls who didn't make it this far. Whoever comes out of this alive, and whoever falls tomorrow, we keep fighting; for them."

"For them," the others echoed in a sombre tone.

****

Richie Yates and Vincent Waterman crouched behind a low wall, clutching their rifles in white-knuckled fists. Their faces were paler than the ghostly mist that hung over the River Somme, floating over

No Man's Land like an ominous cloud. The rain had stopped and the sky was clear, but this gave them no comfort now. They were fifteen, no more men of England than the mothers neither had to cry for them.

"Go together, after three," Richie whispered, seeing his own terror in Vincent's face.

Vincent replied in a tight voice, barely able to move. "We were cleaning our guns. My finger slipped, and you shot me in shock."

Richie nodded, aiming his rifle at his friend's foot, watching Vincent do the same for him. He closed his eyes, taking a gulp of air to steady his inconsolable nerves.

"One," he tried to say, but nothing came out. He cleared his throat and spoke louder.

"One."

He steeled himself, trying not to imagine the pain that would rip through his foot.

"Two."

He tightened his finger, eyes still closed, hoping that Vincent wouldn't back out now.

"Privates!"

Sandford's voice boomed across the night, making him jump so much he almost shot early.

"What are you doing?" he marched over to them, looking very tall and authoritative from where they sat shaking on the floor. "Why aren't you resting before tomorrow?"

"Nobody's resting, sir," Richie squeaked, blinking furiously to stop himself crying. "We're cleaning our rifles."

Sandford looked suspiciously at their white hands on the rifles and the petrified glaze on their faces. His stare hardened. "Do you know the penalty for cowardice?"

Tears broke free from Richie's eyes and his shoulders shook as he regarded the second lieutenant with the eyes of a damned child.

"Please sir," he managed, choking on his own words.

Sandford shook his head in disgust.

"You should have stayed at home." He pulled them roughly to their feet. "I won't say anything this time; losing more men will help nobody. You two will march with the rest of us and you will be proud."

He spun on his heel, leaving the two boys a quivering wreck; thankful to have their lives but knowing they were likely to lose them in just a few hours.

Those few hours later, the platoon lined up to collect their kit, scared faces painted brave as they fell into their units. Sandford stood by to offer encouragement as they passed, knowing that he led each man to his fate. Wayson and Miller stayed close to Stack as they made their way to the second lieutenant, both their faces losing colour as they saw the wire cutters.

"Wire cutters?" Stack asked Sandford in a whisper, not wanting the boy's to hear the answer. "Isn't the wire meant to be cut?"

"Just a precaution, the wire is cut," Sandford said loudly, before leaning closer and lowering his voice. "The patrols haven't seen what we wanted; the wire is cut in places but not fully – 30th Division got lucky with their area but ours is more intact – and the defences aren't half as cleared as we'd like. They have machine gun posts in No Man's Land that haven't been touched and their dugouts are deep and practically unharmed."

He gave Stack a look that begged for help. "Things aren't going to be as simple as planned. I need you to keep your section focussed, lance corporal."

"Lance corporal?" Stack was stunned.

"As of tomorrow," Sandford nodded. "I need somebody to keep them moving if Marshall can't."

"Yes sir, thank you sir."

"You're a good man, Stack," Sandford shook his hand. "Good luck."

"You too sir."

There was no moon that night, no rain and no clouds. Any other men would be looking forward to a warm sunny day, but sun meant nothing to soldiers marching to the reaper. Captain kept them singing as long as he could, but even his voice dried up. The assembly trenches were crowded with those readying themselves to go over the top; saying a final prayer or looking one more time on the face of their sweetheart, kept crumpled in tunic pockets. Yates and Waterman stood hand in hand, staring up at the torn sky, no room for fear now. Sandford pushed through the throng, shouting over the roar of the guns.

"We move forward at a walking pace," he reminded them. "Keep in line, keep moving forward. Whatever happens around you, if you have your life you keep moving forward. Nobody retreats, nobody stops."

"What if someone shoots us?" Captain yelled.

"You keep moving forward!" Sandford ordered.

Mines shook the earth as they were detonated beneath the German lines, throwing mud and whatever else into the air along the Somme valley. The ladders wobbled ahead of them and one man slipped down, Kent instantly forcing him back up again. Stack felt Wayson pressed up against him, staring up like a rabbit caught in a snare.

"Sir," he whispered. "I'm scared."

Stack looked down the line, seeing the same fear in all of them. Sandford speaking strongly, pretending he wasn't a schoolboy; Rigby clutching his girl's picture to his chest; Tommy Miller with his eyes round as his face, lips moving silently as he counted to keep himself calm; Yates and Waterman still as statues and white as marble. Collie stood alongside Butterfield, his bright blue eyes fixed on the backs of the men in front, the sergeant's gaze darting from man to man as if looking at them all could keep them safe.

Mackie kept his stare on his watch, counting down to the half hour when hell would turn its ugly eye away from the shellstruck Germans and face them instead. Captain stood poised to move to the ladders, his eyes narrowed in concentration. He turned his head and called to Stack just as the whistles blew.

"Hey Ben!" he yelled, surging forward with the rest of them. "Happy birthday!"

Stack had completely forgotten.

The next minutes were chaos, happening so fast it was hard to tell if they were happening at all. The first wave were up the ladders, their feet hitting No Man's Land as the bullets hit their chests. Men slumped back down the ladders, getting in the way of those who followed, others flying backwards over the trench and slamming into the back wall among the waiting.

Stack ducked, shielding Wayson from the broken body that crumpled over them, a bloody mess of flesh and bones where a face had been moments before. They threw the corpses aside or stepped over them; there was no time for sympathy now. By the time they were at the ladders no floor was left beside the dead and the dying.

"Go, go, go!" Sandford was shouting over the screams of guns and men.

Yates and Waterman looked at each other, fixing their faces. They gripped each other's hands, screaming "Men of England!" before they joined the others scrambling up the ladders.

Tommy Miller's head emerged over the parapet before he was thrown back onto the shoulders of those behind him, a bullet breaking through his nose and exploding out below his helmet. Wayson faltered, horror twisting his face and forcing him back down the ladder.

"Wayson!" Stack yelled, pulling himself over the edge, not daring to slow down. "With me!"

Pushed from behind, the boy sprinted back up the ladder, falling back into the line already riddled with holes. Bullets ripped through arms and legs, cutting people down as they advanced, watching comrades fall but forcing themselves onwards into the sharp metal bite.

A machine gun tore open Sergeant Pollock and he fell sideways into a shell hole, leaving half his stomach behind. Mud pulled at their boots, then boots were left in the mud along with the feet they held, snapped bones protruding above stained leather.

"Keep moving forward!" Sandford's voice sounded through No Man's Land, urging them onwards past broken figures writhing on the ground and bullets that missed them by inches.

Blood burst from Marshall's shoulder, then his chest then his stomach, finally breaking the bones of his knees as he collapsed in a grotesque mess – more dog meat than man – screaming like nothing Stack had heard before.

Waterman stumbled and panicked, running sideways instead of walking forwards. Stack caught him and spun him around to face the devastation ahead, not daring to look back; it felt like they had made no ground at all.

"Keep together!" he yelled, watching Adam Price go down.

A bullet brushed past Waterman's arm, cutting his tunic and grazing the skin. He stopped dead, staring ahead with mad eyes.

"Waterman!" Stack bellowed. "Keep in line!"

Yates tugged on his arm but he didn't move a muscle, ignoring his friend and continuing to stare straight ahead.

"Come *on* Vince!" he turned his back to the guns.

"Yates, keep moving!" Stack hesitated, unsure whether to hold the line or go to the boys.

"See," Yates shook Waterman desperately. "I'm in front; you won't get shot anymore, I promi-"

His eyes rolled back in their sockets and he vomited blood, his back punctured as the machine gun fire made its way back through them. He fell forwards, crushing Vincent beneath his dead weight; a boy of just fifteen. Stack wrenched his eyes away from them, Wayson beside him, tears pouring down the boy's dirty cheeks.

He almost fell into the crater, paying more attention to the plague flying about him than where his feet trod. He slid down the muddy slope, Wayson following, tripping over the piles of wounded who had pulled their shattered bodies down in search of peace. They reached the bottom, stopping for a second to regain their breath.

A hand closed around Stack's ankle and he looked down to see half a man emptied into the mud. His helmet was cracked in two and with a sickening lurch Stack realised the mess beneath it was his brain. Wayson stared, looking as if he were about to faint. Stack reached down to grip the man's hand as he plunged his bayonet deep into the ruined heart.

The rasping stopped and the head rolled to one side, spilling its contents from the hole in his helmet. Stack tightened his clutch on the hand, the ringing in his ears threatening to drown out even the sounds of battle; to drown him out completely. Sandford's shout of "Keep moving forward!" brought him back to his senses and he jumped away from the dead man, seizing Wayson's arm and pulling him up the other side of the crater towards the German lines.

They were stopped by another man who, after reaching the top and looking out at the bloodbath, had turned back and headed for the centre of the crater. Stack recognised him from the time he had taken supplies to the front in Butterfield's working party; he had been one of those to help Captain and himself with the wounded. He stopped still as they approached him, looking at them but not seeing. His eyes were dead and resigned, all sense of feeling driven from them. He had lost his rifle and his helmet, but stooped to pick up a pistol from the warm hand of a dead officer. Still staring through Stack and Wayson, he raised the pistol to his head and blew his own brains out.

"No!" Stack screamed, catching the man as he fell into the pit, but he was dead before he reached his arms.

He let him drop and continued, tripping over bodies and forcing himself not to hear their wails. They emerged back into the slaughter, crawling at first until they could pull themselves back to their feet. Tristan Holden hung in the wire, bullets still ripping through his body despite him already being dead. Stack pulled Wayson down behind the shell of a cart of some sort and scanned the terrain ahead, finding enough holes cut either by the bombardment or their fellows to get them through.

"Head for the gaps!" he yelled at nobody in particular.

A boy was knelt hacking at the wire with his cutters and stood as he spotted a breach, sent back down again as his chest exploded;

leaving him tangled in the wire he had been trying so hard to break through.

With a jolt of relief, Stack spotted Rigby emerge from a smaller shell hole and make a run through the wire ahead of him. A machine gunner followed his progress, but Stack was in a good position to return fire and the man fell limp upon his gun before he even knew he was being targeted.

He made a dash out from the safety of the cart, Wayson hot on his heels. They were ignoring the orders to walk now, moving and falling faster as the enemy concentrated fire on those near enough to pose a real threat. A bullet grazed him but he hardly felt it, seeing another crack a man's chin and send him reeling backwards nearby. He kept Wayson behind him as he bolted for the scar in the soil, fumbling for a Mills bomb grenade and throwing it hard at the men below him. Before the smoke had cleared he was shooting down on them, Rigby doing the same a few yards away.

"Where's Cap?" he yelled, hesitating at the edge of the trench.

Rigby shook his head. "I don't know!"

A corpse collapsed over the side and they aimed their rifles, gunning down the man's killer. He left a trail of blood on the wall as he slid to his knees, hanging as if praying with his head facing the ground. Limbs littered the floor below them, broken faces staring at the sky from ruined sockets. A boy no older than Wayson clutched at a hole in his torso, crying out in pain and terror. Stack put a bullet between his eyes and he was silent.

"Let's go," Stack jumped down into the trench, reloaded his rifle, straightened his helmet and pushed on.

6.

The screams of the mothers of Britain echoed across the channel. The objectives east of Mametz were reached by the end of the day – Montauban taken by 30th Division – but at a huge price. Both 30th and 18th Division had suffered more than three thousand casualties each, and they had been the successful ones. North of the Albert-Bapaume road the mud was stained with blood spilled in vain as the German defences held; deep dugouts and miles of wire unbroken by the weeklong bombardment.

The stretcher bearers worked hard under fire, joined by survivors of broken regiments, bringing back the endless wounded to wait at clearing stations for ambulance trains that never came. The air itself was heavy with loss, wailing into the ears of blank faces with departed wits, hugging their rifles close and rocking back and forth in the mud. This was not a glorious war; it was a massacre.

Stack wandered among the wounded, hearing their cries only faintly behind the white noise in his ears, walking as if in a dream. Everything was grey and brown and red, and it blurred before his eyes and swum in circles, like wounded souls fighting to escape their ravaged bodies. There was no purpose to his wandering, no sight in blind eyes that met blind eyes, seeing nothing but repetitions of hell.

His gaze passed over Johnny Pritchard, leant up against the wheel of a broken gun, clutching at the bloody mess that used to be his leg and trying not to scream. The man next to him made no sound at all, staring with wide eyes at nothing as life ebbed away from his chest and soaked the ground beneath him.

Some were dead already, lying motionless with open eyes and mouths twisted with pain. He bent to close the lids of a boy Miller's age and wipe the blood from his forehead, paying no attention to the smears over his own face and hands. He wanted to cry but he was numb, walking like a dead man with no right to stand in the midst of the fallen.

"Excuse me." He only half heard, fixing the speaker with an empty stare. "The captain wants to take roll call. The medics can keep up on their own; all infantry to the rendezvous point."

Stack couldn't care less what the captain wanted, but he followed the orders anyway as he had followed orders all day; keep moving forward, keep moving forward. What a useless order it seemed. Looking at the men on the floor, winning objectives didn't seem worth it.

He made his way past Butterfield, who had attempted to gather his section for their own roll call. He looked about in despair at the small group huddled before him, dead on their feet.

"Adams," the call echoed through Stack's exhausted brain. No reply.

"C-Collingwood," his voice cracked. No reply. "Colling...Collingwood?"

Butterfield broke down, his knees hitting the floor as his shoulders shook, chest rising and falling noisily. He slumped on the ground, crying hard, agony – not victory – filling his eyes.

Stack wandered on, passing somebody rolling and screeching on the floor, the sound cutting through his consciousness like a knife.

The man held no visible wounds, but the mind behind those darting eyes was shattered beyond repair. Three men attempted to hold back a fourth, pulling away from them and muttering that they must keep moving forward. They tried to tell him it was over – they could rest now – but it fell on deaf ears.

Kent's voice could be heard now, calling names that received no reply. Weary voices spoke back when they were called, but between them was no reply, no reply, no reply. The silence threatened to split his head. Every non response drove him deeper into despair, eyes scanning the bedraggled crowd for his friends. He almost turned to leave – not wanting to hear Miller's name without the squeaky reply – but somebody was calling him.

"Stack!" Sandford pushed through his men away from Kent, hunched and dirty and looking a lot weaker. His eyes held a pain that nobody back home could understand. "I thought you were gone too."

He reached for the older man's shoulders to hold himself up. He wasn't crying, but he seemed like he could at any moment, looking at Stack again as if begging him for help.

"What have I done?" he shook his head, still holding Stack for support. "What have I done? So many dead, whole villages wiped out. For what? What have I done?"

"You followed orders just like the rest of us," Stack told him, speaking without feeling. He wasn't sure if he would ever feel again.

"I led them to their deaths," he choked. "My poor platoon, I killed so many."

"You kept us moving," Stack remembered. The man shot himself again in slow motion, and Sandford's voice drew Stack and Wayson back out of the hole. "You led us well."

He spotted a familiar curly head a little way away. "Excuse me sir."

Captain sat inelegantly hunched over, legs at odd angles as if he didn't have the energy to arrange them comfortably. He held his head in his hands, shaking heavily. Stack pushed his way over to him, passing somebody retching and vomiting in the mud. Faces blurred as he passed, attempting to recognise them behind the blood and dirt.

"Cap?" he called.

His friend lifted his head from his hands, revealing a face covered in blood and tears. He drew breath heavily as grief wracked his body, worlds away from the carefree man who had laughed and declared Stack general the night before. The sparkle was gone from his eyes and his quivering lips were bleeding; he looked like he had never laughed in his life. He stared at Stack as if he didn't recognise him, unable to stop the tears that washed down his face as his friend sat beside him.

"It's over, Cap," he told him softly. "We made it."

Captain just cried louder.

"I killed a boy," he said, his voice strange and unfamiliar. "Shot him right in the chest."

He prodded his finger into his own bare skin, exposed by a rip in his tunic. "He was so young."

"We all did," Stack looked him in the eye, trying to draw some spark back from behind the tears. "They shot plenty of ours back."

"He wasn't German," Captain said in horror. "One of our own. He was running scared back to our trenches and I shot him. So many guns...dust...I thought he was a German!"

He broke down, burying his face into Stack's chest. His friend didn't know what to say.

"It wasn't your fault," he ventured. "You didn't know."

"It doesn't matter if it's my *fault*," he wailed. "He's one of ours and he's dead and I did it!"

"He would've been shot for cowardice anyway," Stack realised bitterly. "Better he didn't have to see it coming."

Captain didn't seem comforted.

"Did you see Tommy?" he coughed as he choked on his own tears. "He wanted to marry my sister, and they shot him in the face."

Stack nodded. He didn't want to think about it. Tommy Miller wouldn't be collected by the stretchers from a hole in No Man's Land. He would have been trampled into the ground by soldiers pushing forward to climb the ladders, squashed beneath more that fell like him. There would be nothing recognisable to identify his body, Stack realised. He would be buried in an unmarked grave if they found him to bury at all. He had been such an innocent, hopeful child; what would he think of a death like that? All for a village and a few lines of trenches.

"The Scots played their pipes as they walked; did you hear them?"

Stack shook his head. His friend was starting to scare him, crying into his chest and speaking of death. Where were the jokes to shock and cheer the rest of them?

"They got quieter as they got shot down," he continued, his voice breaking on the last word. "They only stopped playing when they were dead."

"It's over, Cap," he said again. "Nobody's getting shot anymore."

"He'll always be getting shot," he looked up with desperate eyes. "You didn't see his face, Ben. He was so young, so scared. Why did I shoot him?"

"What's up with you?" Stack hadn't noticed Rigby approaching. He was drawn and tired; he had been running with the stretchers all afternoon. "Finally realised death isn't funny?"

"Don't," Stack told him. "He's shaken up."

"You haven't seen the worst of it," Rigby said wearily, attempting to light a cigarette but giving up as his fingers failed to find strength. "They found Waterman alive. He hadn't moved an inch, stuck under Yates' body and covered in his blood, shaking like a mad thing. But his eyes were the worst – God, Ben, those eyes. He's a shell; nothing left in there, man or boy. They're sending him to a hospital but there's nothing they can do for him there." He shuddered. "I think I'd rather be dead than live through that."

"Well we have," Stack wiped somebody's blood from his face and sat straighter. "We're still alive and we'd better keep living, because there'll be more like it."

He looked up and down the lines of weary souls and madmen, faces void of feeling and faces twisted with grief and guilt. Sandford pulled at his hair and buried his face in his hands, moaning with every man of his reported missing. Even Kent had none of the usual power in his voice as he read through the names of the damned.

"We haven't won yet."

Captain cried louder.

7.

"Morphine!" Harriet's scream was lost in the clamour.

She was not the only one calling for it. The marquee – and in fact the whole clearing station – was full of the dead and dying, and those charged with caring for them under increasing pressure.

"We need more morphine over here!"

"There is no morphine, we're all out," Emmeline Gray skidded to a halt beside her, carrying a tray laden with bottles of spirits, blonde hair tumbling messily from beneath her nurse's cap. "These are going to have to do."

"There can't be none left!" Harriet exclaimed in shock. "I thought we were prepared for this!"

"Tell that to the trains," Emmeline said dryly. "Supplies are too low; what we have left we need for the serious cases."

"This is a serious case!" Harriet gestured at the man on the bed; writhing like a lost soul, his leg held on by only bone and dirty bandages. He waited in agony for surgery he may die before receiving.

"They all are if you ask me," the other nurse muttered, thrusting a bottle into Harriet's bloodstained hands. "Just give him this, it's better than nothing."

Harriet took it and knelt back down beside the wounded soldier, stroking back his hair and holding the bottle to his pain-contorted lips. "Here, you like a good drink don't you? Just like being back home, no pain at all."

"Only the barmaids back home were none as pretty as you, nor as covered in blood."

He forced a grin despite his pain and took a huge gulp. His hair was matted with sweat and blood, the huge rush of casualties granting no time for washing. She wondered if anyone had even stopped to look at him as the stretchers carried him screaming from the front, if anyone would even remember that face. It could have been a handsome face, if it wasn't so broken. Somebody must be missing it.

"No, no, hold on there private!" she heard Emmeline panicking and hurried over, leaving her patient to drink his fill.

By the time she reached her, the American girl was bent over with a wrist in her hand, searching for a truant pulse.

"He's gone," she stood up sadly, attempting to tuck her hair back under her cap but succeeding only in streaking the blonde with red.

"Can you help me move him?" Emmeline stared at her like she was crazy, stammering something about disrespect. Harriet tried to ignore her. "Somebody alive could use that bed."

No amount of time in her father's pristine London establishment could have prepared her for this. She saw parts of the body that before had only been visible to her in books, hanging exposed from their owners like gruesome adornments, and within her first week more had died on her than she could recall in her entire time in London.

A commotion drew their attention outside the shade of the marquee, to horses' hooves and the orders of the medical officers and quartermaster.

"There's more?" Harriet gasped in exasperation. "We're overcrowded already!"

"God, it must be awful out there," Emmeline breathed, setting down her bottles and making for the exit.

Harriet rushed after her, scanning a desperate eye over the beds as she passed, searching. Men were already laid out beyond the cover of the tent, and those brought by the ambulances were being laid out roughly beside them. These looked as bad as the last, and now with no morphine to ease the pain.

"Where the hell are the trains?" she hissed to Eliza as they lifted a man together, his chest riddled with shrapnel. "We were promised trains to take enough further west and make this manageable!"

"Nobody expected it to be this bad," Eliza murmured, following her sister's gaze as she searched the faces of men being hauled from the carts. "Stop looking for him Hattie."

"I'm not," she snapped, pressure shortening her nerves. "Just counting."

"You are; you've been checking everyone since morning and it isn't helping."

They set down the injured man under the best shade they could find then headed back for the next. Harriet couldn't stop her eyes darting again to the bandaged and bleeding faces, looking and dreading what she might see.

"Stop it!" Eliza caught her face in her hands. "Do you want me to hit you?"

"Hitting people is not ladylike," Harriet fixed her with a hard glare before pulling away and seeing to the next man.

"We're in your world now, Hattie," Eliza bent down to take his legs. "My rules don't matter here."

The wounded came thick and fast as the day wore on, expiring even as they poured brandy down their throats to ease their parting. At least she couldn't see him here, she told herself, nor Rob or anybody familiar. All strangers. She wondered if they had anybody frantically searching for them. Some of these men wouldn't have wives or mothers or families at all; perhaps their brothers and fathers had already died here. Somebody had to remember their bravery and this now fell on Nurse Redmond, the last one to see them writhe in the cruel world of the living.

She took in every crease and freckle that she could as she went about her duties, committing them all to a blood-soaked memory. Here was a boy whose hair could have been auburn under all that blood, with a button nose and protruding ears. He couldn't have been much older than sixteen and his skull had been violently opened. He breathed – loudly and painfully – but would never wake up. Here an older man stared in horror at the bones of his ribcage, opening and closing his weathered mouth as if trying to say something. She held a bucket for a handsome man who coughed and vomited blood, soaked in sweat and painted red by wounds in his torso.

She cut away a mangled boot, trying to keep her face straight as the smell hit her; the ruined foot had been dying long before the bullet hit.

"Reckon it's a Blighty one?" the man whispered.

"If you're lucky," Harriet smiled, fighting the urge to cover her nose.

"Is it coming off?" he said quieter.

"It's likely," she sighed. "You'll just have to cross your fingers and hope."

"Hope I lose the damn thing," he said darkly.

"Why would anybody want to lose their foot?" she dabbed at it gingerly, still keeping an encouraging smile on her face. "It may not be pretty, but it's the only left foot you'll ever have."

"You haven't been out there miss," he stopped watching his foot and lifted his eyes. Green, with straight eyebrows that matched the thick dark hair covering his head. "To get away from that shit any man would blow off his whole leg."

By the end of her elongated shift, Harriet was sure there was no more room in her head for dying faces. They spiralled and merged with each other despite her best efforts to keep them separate, always finding ways to end up looking like him.

She watched Emmeline as she packed away; giving each soldier she passed a quick kiss on the forehead – if his forehead was in one piece. She was an oddity, Nurse Grey, especially to the young Londoner who had never met an American before. Emmeline had been rich in New York – much richer than Mr Gale – the spoilt daughter of a Wall Street wizard who was used to getting what she wanted. Though more skilled in flirting than nursing, she was a novelty and the soldiers loved her.

"Hey nurse," one of them sat up, calling in a hoarse whisper. "You couldn't give me a real one could you?"

"Oh alright then," Emmeline smiled cheekily and doubled back, taking his face in both hands and planting a long kiss on his lips before skipping gaily away. "Now you get some sleep, you brave, brave man."

"Umm, Emmeline," Harriet stared at her with something between disapproval and admiration. "I don't know how you do things in America, but we're not supposed to do that."

She shrugged, pulling off her cap and running her fingers through her hair. "Desperate times, desperate measures. Poor bloke might never get a kiss again, and it's such a shame for a brave man to die lonely. It's sad; I think I've forgotten what men look like without blood on their faces."

"Still, you'll be for it if they see you acting like that," Harriet warned her, glancing about to check for the presence of any of the stricter senior nurses.

Emmeline grinned at her. "I won't tell if you won't."

****

It was a relief to all of them when they were transferred to the city; the general hospital was a lot cleaner and better organised than the chaos that had been the overcrowded casualty clearing station. In fact, certain aspects of the large building reminded Harriet more of the pristine corridors of the Gale manor than a war hospital. She liked to play with the idea of being a servant not a nurse, imagining herself scuttling about the passageways with Aedan as she waited patiently for a day's leave to run down the little road to the Stack farm. There would be no 'milady'-ing from Aedan, and maybe even Ben would see her as something more than a posh old friend. Maybe Aedan wouldn't have felt the need to join the army to impress her, as Anna believed he had. She could have been Anna, and Aedan could have been alive.

She finished rolling the bandage around a soldier's arm and picked up the old dressing – significantly dirtier and smellier. She smiled at the man, who returned the gesture, before walking back down the ward, checking that all the men she passed were comfortable.

All but one. She had avoided the man in the corner bed by east entrance since he had arrived, wearing a very different uniform to those she was used to treating. The grey of Germany. She averted her eyes from the face of the killer, covered in bandages that she had not seen removed. He was regularly surrounded by curtains when dressing changes were required, and it made her blood boil to see the enemy receiving such special treatment.

"It's disgusting," she muttered to Emmeline as they passed. "That German would have shot every man in this room if they met in another situation."

"He's badly wounded," the American replied in a whisper.

"Good, I hope he dies," she said spitefully, glaring at the bed.

"Harriet, I'm ashamed of you," Eliza snapped, carrying a large collection of dirty bedsheets. "Somebody's sitting at home worried sick about him."

"Somebody German," she said darkly, unsure as to why her sister was being so un-patriotic. Hadn't it been her who was adamant that the kennel boy should have gone to war?

"You are such a child," Eliza looked thoroughly appalled. "None of this is his fault; he's just the same as our men."

"No he isn't," Harriet protested. "I'm not going anywhere near him; it would be like spitting in the face of everything our boys have sacrificed! What's the use in them risking their lives to kill Germans if we're just going to patch them back up again?"

"You had better hope that the German nurses don't feel the same about our casualties," Eliza said coldly.

"Of course they do, and they have every right," she scowled. "They wouldn't keep one of ours in such luxury."

"So you think if a German nurse found Ben Stack wounded on their side of the line, she should just leave him to die, for the war effort?"

Harriet faltered, the firm look of hate on her face interrupted by the thought.

"She would have every right," she repeated, her jaw fixed defiantly but unable to deliver the words with the resolve intended. "Doesn't mean I have to like it."

She shouldered angrily past her sister, focusing on the crush of faces in her head to banish the image Eliza had conjured.

"That was cruel," Emmeline commented, watching her go.

"Not as cruel as she was," Eliza said firmly. "She's a child – no matter how grown up she thinks she is – but she can't get away with saying things like that."

"Are you angry at me?" Harriet whispered from under the bed covers that night. Attempts to sleep had been driven back by the bandage-faced German joining the throng of squatters in her mind.

"Only if you're still angry at our patient," her sister replied coolly. "Are you angry at me?"

"Yes," she pulled the blanket back to reveal a stubborn little face. "I'm always angry when you're right."

"You must hate me a lot then," Eliza smiled.

"Not so much," Harriet adjusted her head on the pillow. "I'll look after him if I have to, because I'd want them to look after ours." She paused. "And for his family. But you can't expect me to like him."

"That's fair," Eliza sighed. "I've spent my life actively seeking out the company of people I don't like; I suppose I can't begrudge you that."

"He could have been the one who shot Mr Gale."

"So could the whole German army," she sounded tired, not wanting to dwell on the subject. "I can't blame any of them; they're just people. They fight because their leaders tell them to, not because they want to kill."

"The newspapers said-"

"Hattie, darling!" Eliza interrupted. "Please don't ever believe what the newspapers say! It's all mindless propaganda, to help the big men persuade the little men that their cause is worth fighting for. I should know; my husband was a major shareholder."

"And you really think people only go to fight because of what it says in the newspaper? Because the big men tell them it's for money and glory?"

"I'm sure people have many reasons," Eliza mused. "I shouldn't simplify it to that. Our boys are very brave, though there certainly wouldn't be any wars if it wasn't for money."

"I never thought I would hear you say a bad word about money."

"I have always been a fool, Hattie," Eliza admitted sadly. "You knew that once. Apparently it takes no less than death to make me grow up. But in answer to your question, I think men go to war because they think they have to; it's the picture the world paints."

"Like Molly Lane's feathers," Harriet remembered with significant loathing. "Emmeline said men go to war for women."

"Emmeline is an American," Eliza looked disapproving. "And everybody knows that Americans are insufferable show-offs."

"Anna isn't American," Harriet chewed on the inside of her lip as she tried to think how to phrase it. "She said…Liza…do you think Aedan was in love with me?"

"The footman?" Eliza laughed. "He was certainly fond of you."

Gloom settled on Harriet's face. "Then it was my fault."

"What was your fault?" Eliza propped herself up on one elbow. "Hattie, he was a young man and you're a pretty girl and he enjoyed your company; that doesn't mean he was in love with you. If it did, I would be the biggest heartbreaker in London!"

"But you said a few times when I first came to stay…"

"I was teasing you sweetheart," she said soothingly. "I thought it was funny that a pretty young thing with the perfect connections I had made you would prefer to spend time with servants. Why, did you want him to be in love with you?"

"No, of course not," she assured her. "I never even considered it; I was too excited about finding Ben again, but then Anna said…"

"What did Anna say?"

"Nothing."

Harriet returned her face to its resting place in the folds of the pillow. She didn't want the maid to get in any trouble because of her, and she was beginning to realise how stupid and vain she sounded. Why on earth would Aedan – or anyone for that matter – be in love with her, especially when living in direct comparison with her sister?

"Hattie," Eliza fixed her with her stern big sister gaze. "What did Anna say? You can tell me."

"Mmf mmmf mmf," she mumbled into the pillow.

"I can't hear you when you're trying to gag yourself."

She lifted her head an inch or two from the pillow. "She said he went to war for me."

Eliza laughed. It shocked her so much that she was half in a mind to get up and slap her. This was not a laughing matter.

"Did you tell him to go to war?" she asked, noticing the look on her sister's face and curbing the laughter.

"No," Harriet said indignantly. "Why would I do that?"

"Then he didn't go for you," she smiled. "And that's final."

"You don't think-"

"Hattie," Eliza interrupted again. "There is *nothing* for you to feel guilty about. Wars are all about men; brave men and stupid men fighting for greedy men who will take all the credit when the fighting's over. Whether we like it or not, women are nothing to do with it. Really Hattie, all the men in England went to war; are you saying they're *all* in love with you?"

"So you don't think it's my fault that Aedan's...you know...dead?"

"No sweetheart, I don't, and if he ever heard you saying that he would be most displeased with you."

"I wish he wasn't dead," she said quietly, hugging her pillow.

"Of course you do," Eliza got up from her own bunk and sat on the edge of her sister's, holding out her arms to embrace her. "Come here. I know you'd rather someone with a little more stubble and an infantry uniform, but your big sister will have to do for now."

Harriet laughed, snuggling into her shoulder. "That'll do just fine for me."

****

Harriet woke to the first rays of sunlight breaking over the tormented horizon, ready for another early shift. She relieved the girl on night duty before any of her colleagues arrived, and before many of the soldiers had woken up. It was peaceful at first glance to see them sleeping there, with no pain to trouble them for a while. Then she looked closer, and the shuddering of the dreamers complemented the faces of the shellshocked and she knew pain was there still.

She stroked the hand of one of the sufferers on her way over to the bed in the corner by the east entrance. Having deliberately paid no attention to the German, she was naturally curious about him. It was disappointing to see, on closer inspection, that there really was no way of viewing his face behind the thick bandage wound around it. Even his nose wasn't visible; the bandage must be thicker than the nose was long. If that were the case, he must have a rather flat nose or a small head. She racked her brains for any memory from the newspapers; were Germans known for their small heads? She felt a little ashamed as she realised she really didn't know anything about them. Here she was hating the people and calling for their deaths, but she had no idea what a German was really like.

"Their job is to kill your friends," she told herself quietly. "That's all you need to know."

"Ah, Nurse Redmond."

She could have jumped ten feet in the air. The deep and husky voice of the matron still scared her.

"The bandages need changing for Gefreiter Koopmann," she said sternly, sounding German herself as she pronounced the foreign syllables with ease.

"The German?" Harriet couldn't help asking, wondering inwardly what a 'gefreiter' was.

"Yes, Redmond, the German," she said impatiently. "Though he is simply a patient to you, and you do not discriminate. Do you hear?"

"Yes matron," she nodded obediently, feeling a little silly after her proud outburst the day before.

The man had a ready set of new bandages at his bedside, along with a sizeable pot of water and a sponge. There was also a large bottle of spirit, though the usefulness of this last item was debatable seeing as she had never seen the man awake. Perhaps this bottle was the reason for his peaceful slumber, she thought as she drew the curtains around the bed.

Her line of vision darkened as the thin morning light was shut out, leaving only that bold enough to penetrate from above. It was more than a little spooky, she thought, to be stood in the half light as one of the patients outside began to moan and she drew back the wrappings of the enemy's face. Those she had remembered flickered before her, as if her mind was trying to guess what the man looked like before she saw for herself.

She dropped the end of the bandage in shock, stumbling over her own feet as they tried to take her as far from the bed as possible. This was the face the government should be using in their anti-German posters, for it bore no resemblance to a human. The jaw had been shattered, leaving the right side of the face caved in; a jagged protrusion beneath the stretched skin of the cheek the only evidence of there having been a bone structure. The surgeon had done his best to stitch a covering over areas where the skin was removed altogether, but it was taut and dead-looking. The lines of stitching cut valleys through the already mutilated visage and twisted his mouth hard to the left, where an angry puss told of a losing battle with infection.

She knew now, why his nose had been hard to identify; the pitiful mess through which he drew breath was nothing more than a pair of surgically bridged holes flattened against an empty face. And the eyes. They stared at her; wide, bloodshot and yellowing, until she realised that it wasn't a stare – he was physically unable to close them. The last remnants of an eyelid clung shrivelled and burned to the top of his right eye, no use to him now. She doubted he could even see her.

She fought the impulse to run from this hideous creature, forcing herself back to the bedside. Her hands flinched back as she reached to remove the last piece of bandage, and he felt them. The awful lips creaked open and he tried to speak, but managed only incomprehensible grunts, half a tongue flopping in his mouth. His breath was foul and she had to pull back again, holding her mouth as she fought the urge to be sick. In all her years of nursing, she had never imagined that a human face could look so terrible, so tortured. And worse than any of his wounds, even the burns, was the single tear that swelled below his eye, growing to maturity then flowing down the ruined face. Just a single tear for so much suffering.

She shook, her fingers fumbling with the sponge and dropping it to the floor. She would have to fetch another; the floor wasn't particularly dirty, but the risk of infection was too great. She cursed her clumsiness but was glad all the same to step back through the curtain and into the light. The force of the day hit her and she promptly vomited.

8.

The platoon pushed through the wood, thick foliage and a few remaining fires slowing them as much as the heavy equipment they carried. There had been attempts to torch Bernafay, but the coarse undergrowth had grown dense and unruly in the years of war and it would take more than shells and flamethrowers to convince the trees to let them pass unheeded. Until very recently this had been enemy territory, and the ground was not letting go of its loyalties too soon. The trees were black and charred but still reached out their tortured fingers to snag tunics and scratch the faces of their attackers.

Captain Kent drove them forward, and for many it was a relief to be marching again. Too many faces were missing and too much space was available for sleeping now that their comrades would sleep forever. The tormented minds that replayed death worked better when fixed on a goal, the survival instinct kicking back in to override the sleepless nights. Kent himself seemed happier to be moving again. With Sandford as his new right hand man he stood taller again, barking orders with a familiar sharpness much more comforting than the cracking voice that had read out names that doomed afternoon.

The young lieutenant too had recovered from his shock, taking the new responsibility in his stride as he lead them to the edge of the wood where they would again be thrown into the jaws of the devil. This time felt different though. Any remainder of boyhood had been shattered on the Somme and the man who now pushed through the thorns had a look of strong determination. He was ready for this one.

Patrols had scoured the woods for days, and attempts had been made by others to capture their goal. He and Kent had spent long nights pouring over maps and reports until their eyes screamed, drawing up plans and confirming the strategies sent down from their superiors. His men were not to be slaughtered so easily this time.

He held great confidence also in the NCOs who led them forward with him; brave men the lot of them who had proven themselves that dreadful day and many times before. He walked beside the new platoon sergeant; an ambitious young man by the name of Butterfield who had singlehandedly cleared a machine gun post in a shell hole after the occupants had cut down half of his men. Further to his right he positioned the section he had spent most of the war watching. Though safe in the hands of their new corporal, he had grown incredibly fond of them and saw no reason to stop his vigil now that poor Marshall was gone.

They neared the edge of the wood and he held out a hand to halt them, meeting the eyes of his sergeants and corporals. Stack nodded back at him, sending a similar look to the rest of his section. Wayson and Captain stood either side of him, the boy's blue eyes fixed in a determined stare that attempted to burn down the next wood before they even reached it.

Captain was not so steady, unnerving Stack far more than the prospect of the machine guns and mortars they were soon to face. There had been no bet with Rigby on the outcome of the battle, no teasing about who was likely to die first. He had barely even smiled when Stack told him he had to get over eighty points or he'd be digging the next latrine. He had slept too, far too much. For anybody else this would be normal – seizing the chance while at rest and training – but Dan Captain never slept. He was always there to keep Stack awake when his eyes were begging to close, but the nights had become eerily quiet.

Now the man stood poised like the rest, but those eyes held none of the bravery of Wayson's or the grim determination of Rigby's. Stack knew they didn't even see the field and wood ahead of them; they continued to stare inwards, watching again and again the bullet fly from the rifle that had slain the young Briton.

Sandford gave the first signal and Stack braced himself, feeling his men do the same. He looked down the line once more, really leading them into battle for the first time. It felt strange, but there was no time to contemplate his feelings on the promotion Sandford had thrust upon him. Captain had always believed he could do it; now was the time to prove it.

"Ready?"

They nodded back at him, faces united in courage under the brims of their helmets. All except Captain.

"Cap?" he asked. "You got this?"

His bottom lip started to wobble, speaking in a whisper barely audible behind the sounds of war and the constant white noise in Stack's ears.

"Don't make me shoot anyone Ben."

The whistle blew loud and sharp and they burst from their cover, entering the exposure of the field that separated the two woods; one in British hands, one in German. Other divisions in their area had sent units to capture and hold the second wood, but none had succeeded. The terrain was broken from previous bombardments and they stumbled over fallen trees and fallen men alike, nothing on their minds but reaching the relative shelter of the skeleton trees. When they got there they could face the next challenge. Until then, keep moving forward.

"Stick together men!" Sandford called down the line. "Hard and fast and the wood is ours!"

"Stick together!" Stack echoed him. "Move quickly; the undergrowth is thick but if we cut fast it shouldn't hinder us. What are bushes compared to wire?"

Wayson grinned bravely at him, eyes flashing with the spark of victory that had made him leave his home and enlist in the army. Under all that grime and uniform, he was still just a glory-hungry boy.

"Grenades ready!"

By Sandford's calculations they should be nearing the first set of digs in the wood; nothing elaborate but enough to bite hard if they weren't cleared. Wayson clutched at the weapon like it was his favourite birthday present, but Captain made no change to his stance. He walked forward with his rifle held threateningly but – Stack suspected – with no desire to use it. This was no time for guilt, not now their lives were on the line again.

"Captain!" he growled sideways at him. "Grenade. Ready."

The scouts had been right about the undergrowth. It pulled and ripped at their legs, slowing them for the convenience of the German shooters. A couple went down near Sandford – an unfortunate place to be when the enemy aimed for officers. The lieutenant, however, continued to stand, a marker for the rest of them as they made their way swiftly through the trees. A mortar smashed through the air and Stack ducked to avoid a naked bough that was hurtled towards him, shielding Wayson with his shoulders. Mud and bush and limbs flew into the sky, falling like diseased rain on the advancing troops, but they were not to be stopped. There was something of revenge in the way they walked, bullets screaming the names of their fallen friends. The soul of West Kent was red that day, bloodthirsty for the first chance to prove their fellows had not died in vain.

Stack vaulted down a ditch with Sandford, pulling his bayonet from the body of a German defender to stick it in another before he even felt the blood splattering across his face. He heard the crack of the lieutenant's pistol as he dealt with a third, standing in the remains of a man now strewn across the floor by their efforts. They met each other's eyes and gave encouraging looks as the rest of their men leapt down to join them, Rigby stopping to pull a cigar from the pocket of a dying German before shooting him in the head.

Stack turned back to check his section, wiping the blood roughly from his face with an elbow. All remained who had followed him into the wood. He waved them forward, stopping only to grasp Captain's lapel and speak fiercely into his weary face.

"You pick up that rifle, Cap," he breathed heavily. "And you use it, and you enjoy it. You don't fight for me today and you don't fight for you; you fight for Tommy Miller. You hear me?"

Captain nodded, grasping hold of something real at the sound of the boy's name.

"Good man. Let's blow their bloody heads off."

Stack put a quick hand on his shoulder before scrambling back up the side of the ditch with the others, his friend close behind him. He pushed through the undergrowth, ignoring the cuts that tore into his already interrupted face, slowing only when he was back beside Wayson. Another blast broke the line, bringing ripped up trees with it to rip up more men, but they merely spread further, filling the gap and continuing their onslaught.

A familiar sound drew their attention as spurts of red erupted from torsos and limbs, Bobby Watson's tunic a deep crimson by the time his body hit the floor, crumpling the shrubbery beneath him. Stack cursed, but there was no time to dwell if the rest were to survive.

"Machine gun!" he yelled, passing the warning to those further back.

"Over your way," Sandford called back, leaving Butterfield's side and forcing his way towards Stack. "We'll have to take it out."

"I've got it sir," he replied, sharp eyes already searching the rubble of trunks and brambles for the flash. It came a little to his right, from a thick dark mass of dead leaves and branches.

"There!" Wayson made a run at it with two other boys from the next section but Stack caught him, dragging him back behind a tree as the others were mown down like grass.

"Don't," he snarled, heartbeat racing, "be so stupid boy!"

Wayson frowned back at him, lips pursed in proud determination. "It was a machine gun took down Richie."

"Well they're not taking you too, got it?" Wayson tried to move, but Stack held him. "You run straight at them and you're no use to anybody. You want to take one down?"

Wayson nodded feverishly.

"Then you stick with me and do what I say or I'll make sure you don't get within fifty feet of one again."

"Yes sir."

They left the safety of the tree – and just in time before it was ripped apart.

"Mackie!" Stack called, looking about for the skinny little man in all the chaos.

He found him crouched behind a fallen log, picking off men in the fury ahead one by one. From what Stack could see, he didn't miss once.

"You're quick and small; reckon you can get behind the gun post unseen?"

He replied that he could.

Stack spoke quickly. "I need your cover – Wayson and I are going in. You stay at a distance and keep sniping at them, I trust your aim. Don't bloody hit me."

"Yes sir," he nodded and scuttled off. It was incredibly strange being called 'sir' by Mackie. Wayson was a child, but Mackie had been there just as long and fought just as hard as he had.

The post was a spot well chosen; surrounded on all sides by thick undergrowth, save a few gaps for German entrance and clearer shooting. There were two MG08s – one facing the left and one the right – poised to cut down the attackers in both directions.

Mackie's shot rang and Stack rushed forward, Wayson in tow, feeling the recoil against his shoulder as he released the little pellet of death into the enemy's throat. The gunner clutched at the wound, fingers staining red as he choked and drowned on his own blood, staring about for whoever had made the shot. He looked to the other gun and saw Mackie's target already slumped upon it, his second trying desperately to haul him out of the way and return fire himself. He would be too late.

Sandford was already upon them, forcing his way through the branches and brambles as if they were water. Stack vaulted through, slamming his rifle down on the head of a boy pointing the machine gun at his chest, not waiting to raise it again before he put a bullet through the man behind him.

"Wayson!" he called, watching the boy half stride, half fall into the nest. "You want to get back at the bastards who killed Yates?"

He ducked aside to give him a clear shot at the boy fumbling to get his hands on the warm machine gun. Unfortunately for him, Wayson was faster. His chest erupted scarlet streams and he shuddered, clutching onto the weapon to keep him from falling.

Striding forward with a fierce look welling behind the tears in his eyes, Wayson pushed the barrel into his contorted face.

"He was fifteen, you son of a bitch," he whispered, before pulling the trigger and putting him out of his misery.

He stood for a moment, still mesmerised by the inside of a man's head no matter how many times he saw it. He felt sick, but at the same time he felt strong. No, it was not likely that it was this man who had gunned down his friend, nor was Rob – wherever he was – likely to slay the same artilleryman who fired the shell that buried his father. But this was what they were here for. This man would never murder another Briton again, nor would the others lying about him. He, William Wayson, had saved lives. This was what being a man was all about. He shot, he swore and he saved his country. He stood tall and proud.

So why couldn't he tear himself away from the broken visage slumped upon his gun, who had once laughed and smiled and kept so many memories in that disgusting mess that spilled from his head?

"Forward men," Sandford gave Stack a warm look of encouragement and continued, slicing at the foliage.

The corporal collected his men with his eyes, focussing on his youngest as he stood in the centre of the nest. He bore a similar look to the one Rob had worn the first time he shot a fox – the mix of pride, guilt and confusion.

"Come on," he said, speaking to Wayson in particular. "We haven't won yet."

"Thank you sir," he breathed, blinking away the water that rose behind his lids. This was no time for remorse. He was a man and men fought on.

****

The Germans were not going to give up the wood too easily. Even with trenches cleared and machine gun posts taken, the artillery fought on. There was no chance to rest as they cowered from Howitzer shells while attempting to fortify their newly taken trenches in time for the inevitable enemy reinforcements. Sandford marched up and down the lines, offering words of encouragement and helping at each bay before moving on to the next. Kent too showed his face, checking up on equipment and morale; telling them they had done a good job and all they had to do now was to hold the ground until morning.

"Then the worst will be over," he promised them.

Captain scoffed. "The worst will be over when we're dead."

Stack hit him hard in the face.

"What the hell was that for?" he rubbed his cheek, the expression on his face making it clear that the hurt went deeper than skin.

"Get a grip Cap," he told him firmly. "It's going to be a hard night, thinking like that is not going to help. I've got a whole section to look after, I can't be babysitting you."

"You're stressed Ben," Captain observed, still holding a hand to his face. "You don't think you can do it."

"No, but you do!" he said in exasperation. "You said I could and I'm trying, but goddammit Cap you made me a corporal, don't make me do it without you!"

Captain smiled – a welcome sight. "I didn't make you a corporal, Ben, you made yourself. I just prodded you a little. But you're not my corporal, you're my friend, and from one friend to another I think you're doing a great job."

"Watson's dead already," Stack reminded him, leaning wearily against the trench wall.

"No one can stop a machine gun," Captain took his palm away from his face and prodded it gingerly. "That's going to bruise you know. You've made me as ugly as Rigby."

He met Stack's eyes and they both grinned, relief coursing through Stack's exhausted body. Behind all the seriousness and the guilt, Captain was still in there. One joke though didn't mean he was back for good, and Stack watched him with dull eyes as he shuddered at his watch, clutching his rifle.

"He'll be fine," Rigby told him, flicking a cigarette between his fingers in distraction but lacking the courage to light it in the dark. "He's Captain; he's always fine."

"He'd better be," Stack pressed his thumbs into his eyes to keep them from closing.

"I don't see how you can be sleepy in the middle of all this," Rigby said, another mortar landing further down the line as if to prove his point.

Stack shrugged. "Maybe I'm finally reaching my limit."

He took his fingers away from his face and rested his shovel against the wall; there was no use digging foxholes when no sleep was to be had.

"I'm going to talk to Sandford. The artillery should have died down by now, but it seems like it's getting closer again."

He made his way past the rest of the platoon, a withered fist clutching his heart as he walked through Butterfield's old section, Collie's friendly greeting noticeably absent. He found Sandford easily enough, hunched over a sheet of paper covered in lines and scribbles that absorbed his attention. As he heard the corporal approaching he looked up from his labour and the dark beneath his eyes showed the same tiredness that Stack felt.

"Corporal Stack," he greeted him. "How are your men?"

"Alright sir," he replied. "Ready to move when we're needed."

"And Private Captain?" he asked, making Stack love him all the more for his concern.

"On and off," he admitted. "He fought with the rest of us, which I suppose we can't complain about."

"We need him on, Stack," Sandford's eyes met his, again with the shadow of the look he had given on the morning of the first of July. This time was different though; not a plea for help from a lost schoolboy, more a request of assistance between equals. "Their reinforcements are coming in fast. They'll be on us at dawn if they have any sense. The regiments of both sides are weakened too far and help isn't coming quick enough. They can't hold ground if they're hit with fresh troops; Captain Harropp has warned us already that if they come down too hard he'll have his men retreat. He advises us to do the same, says the wood can't be taken."

"Will we?" Stack asked him, dreading the answer either way.

"The wood *can* be taken," he said with conviction. "I know it can, we just need to hold our ground. I don't want today to all have been for nothing." He sighed. "Do you think I'm being too stubborn? You know I wouldn't risk the men if I didn't think we could win, don't you?"

"I know that," he assured him, following the younger man's gaze towards the hidden army amassing just beyond their view. "What does Captain Kent say?"

"He's determined to stay and fight it out," Sandford told him. "But that's just who he is. If I tried I think I could persuade him otherwise."

"But you don't want to?"

Sandford rubbed his forehead. "I think we can do it, but…"

They were silent for a while, both seeing the same image of the wounded and dead laid out for what seemed like miles, hearing the unanswered names of the roll call echo through time.

"If you think we can do it, we can," Stack said finally.

The sun was starting to surface at last, painting the wood grey and gold; the contrasting colours of their thoughts.

Suddenly a familiar sound rattled Stack's eardrums and he instinctively threw himself to the ground, taking the lieutenant with him. It was as if the sky had erupted, shells falling thick and fast from nowhere. Stack scrambled to his feet, shouting to the lieutenant that he needed to get back to his section. Sandford called for him to wait, fumbling in his pocket. He pulled out a flask, which he thrust into his corporal's hand.

"For Captain!" he shouted over the commotion. "For courage!"

"Thank you sir!" Stack called back to him, holding his helmet tight to his head as he rushed back down the trench, stumbling over bodies without stopping to see if they were crouching or dead. He reached his section with a wave of relief, instinctively holding a shoulder over Wayson as he thrust the flask into Captain's hands, telling him to drink.

"Ready chaps?" he collected his section together. They weren't much, but Sandford believed in them and that was all he needed to know.

"We'll be ready for them," Rigby said through gritted teeth. "Their bloody snipers have stopped me having a smoke for too long and now I'm cranky."

Stack moved an arm in front of his face as an explosion of dirt was sent flying towards them. He moved it away again in an instant, grunting as he pulled the shard of shrapnel from his bicep. He threw it to the ground, forcing himself to ignore the pain. His rifle needed a strong arm right now.

He couldn't tell if it felt like years or seconds before the barrage made way for the infantry, but there was no mistaking it. They clambered onto whatever firestep remained, ready for the onslaught.

"Hold ground!" they heard Sandford shouting as he made his way along the line. "We do not fall back!"

Light had barely broken when the reinforcements were upon them, not bothering to sneak as they brought flamethrowers and high explosives on the exhausted British. They slipped from the crippled firestep but kept up their defence, bloodied faces dropping from the parapet only to be pulled back up again by their comrades. The posts they had taken, now manned by their own machine guns and hastily altered for a fight in the opposite direction, performed commendably as they cut down the approaching horde in waves.

Mackie took each shot with deliberation and care, every bullet hitting home. Rigby and Wayson fired more haphazardly, tripping the attackers as the bones in their feet cracked and their shoulders were punctured. Silent tears ran down Captain's face as he knocked down men and boys alike, the bruise on his cheekbone an angry purple.

Down the barrel of his own rifle, Stack saw what his friend saw. It was a smaller scale, with more trees, but the concept was the same. As they cut down the approaching soldiers it was themselves they were watching fall to the ground; the tables were turned.

Sandford hurtled around the corner of the bay, his path lit by the jet of flame that just missed him. His head was bleeding through a rough bandage made from the cloth used to clean his pistol and he limped heavily on one leg, but didn't falter. He positioned himself beside Stack, taking a shot in the direction of the flamethrower.

"It's happened," he told him, barely audible over the battle and his own heavy breathing. "Both flanks are pushed back. Even if we tried to retreat now we'd be overrun and not one of us would make it back."

"Can we still hold?" Stack ducked another jet of flame, feeling his helmet grow hot with it.

"We can," the lieutenant panted. "But not forever. If they sent the damned reinforcements they promised I wouldn't be so worried."

"Someone needs to get a message out."

"I know that!" The earth before them blew up in their faces and they nearly lost their footing in the shifting soil. "But to go now would be suicide."

"I can make it," Mackie volunteered.

"He's right sir," he told the lieutenant. "He's got the best stamina I've seen."

Sandford pondered for half a second then his eyes set and he gave Mackie the nod of approval. "Fast as you can private."

"Yes sir." In a flash the small man was gone, avoiding the wreckage of the nearest communications trench and sprinting back between the trees.

Flames burst again over their heads, catching the undergrowth and bringing down a feeble bough that spat sparks as it collapsed between men. This marked the end of the initial charge by the German infantry, but no illusion allowed them to believe they had given up. The remaining trees behind them were ablaze now, the wood a furnace on both sides. They sweated in their gutter, pressing faces into the earth in an attempt to cool themselves as they reloaded rifles and tried to organise equipment.

Captain leaned heavily on the wall, glugging deeply from Sandford's flask as if his life depended on it. Stack watched the movement in his throat as the cool liquid passed down it, but he couldn't risk drinking and clouding his head, not now he was an NCO. He wiped his dripping forehead in his sleeve, hair stuck to his head beneath the helmet that burned his scalp.

"They don't even need the infantry," Rigby panted, looking up at the jets of apocalypse with desperate eyes. "This'll pound us to dust and all the rifles will need to do is piss on our ashes. What's Kent playing at keeping us here?"

Sandford looked uncomfortable, opening his mouth to reply before Stack did it for him. "You want to be a Bosch prisoner? We turn our backs on them for one minute and they'll have us."

"Better a prisoner than a bloody campfire," he spat. "Don't tell me you're on his side now Ben? We should have retreated with the others when we had a chance."

"Shut it Rigby," Captain took the flask away from his lips and poured the remaining drops on his face. "If Ben trusts them, we do too. He's our corporal, you bloody coward."

"Oh, and you can talk can you?" Rigby snapped, the heat making his blood boil. "You can't shoot without crying like a girl!"

Captain scrambled to his feet, his bayonet pointed towards him, but they were interrupted by Wayson's voice calling over the sound of charring trees.

"Bombers!" he yelled, eyes fixed on a band of grey uniforms further down the line. "Bombers!"

Sandford was already sprinting back through the fire to their aid, but was stopped by an explosion a corner away. He spun back, falling heavily against the opposite wall before scrambling to his feet and taking a shot at the attacking column. Stack and the others were already back on their crudely reconstructed firestep, no tears on Captain's cheeks this time. The small column retreated sooner than expected, Rigby watching with confusion as they scrambled back to their holes.

"They'll be back," Sandford promised. "They're wearing us down. I need to check on Sergeant Butterfield; he was right in the middle of that."

He got down from the firestep, wincing as his leg wobbled beneath him. Stack caught him and leaned him back against the mud, giving him a stern look.

"You're hurt sir," he said, noticing the dark patch seeping through his trousers.

"So are you," Sandford breathed, nodding at the deep gash in Stack's arm. With all the adrenalin infecting his blood, he had forgotten all about it. Now the lieutenant mentioned it, the pain found its way to his consciousness and he gritted his teeth.

"Just rest it off here for a bit sir," he said firmly. "Butterfield can look after himself."

Rest, however, was not to be found in the wood that day. The bomb attacks continued, each time bringing the enemy closer to the shattered ditched in which they crouched. But if they thought they would break the British spirit they were much mistaken. Every attack strengthened their resolve to hold, to ensure their fellows had not died in vain.

Stack couldn't keep Sandford still for long; he took a drink to dull the pain in his leg before returning to pacing the sections. He was on his way back down the line when he was stopped by a boy with a grubby face and a tunic spattered in dirt, giving the impression that he had fallen more than once in his sprint through the wood. He clutched a piece of paper in his hand and panted heavily.

"Lieutenant Sandford, sir," he straightened up and tried to salute.

"Don't worry about that," he shook his head impatiently. He didn't recognise the boy from his own platoon, or any of the others within the company; he must be a messenger from the main lines, and about time too. "Where are the reinforcements?"

"Relief is coming, sir," he puffed, holding up the letter. "I need to take this to Captain Kent."

But he had lost Sandford's attention, the lieutenant's eyes fixed on the sight of the larger column that now cast its shadow through the flames. They were coming for them now, he knew it.

"Bayonets!" he bellowed, increasing his speed as he pushed past the unlucky messenger.

"They're coming," he panted, falling into line beside Stack. "It's serious this time."

"We can hold them," Stack promised. For all the shells that had fallen and the flames that threatened to burn them alive, the company was still strong.

"Fritz really wants his wood back," Captain commented, a familiar glint returned to his eyes.

"Well he's not going to get it," Stack told him firmly. "We hold this ground like it's England. This bastard earth is your home, men, don't you let them touch it!"

"Men of England!" Wayson screamed, his words drowned out by a blaze of fire and a blast that blew burning men into the air to their left.

Dark shapes flooded down into the trench the instant the flames had cleared, swarming like insects into an unwilling home.

"Bayonets, let's go!" Sandford called urgently, leading the charge towards the breach.

Those left to guard the intact bays moved aside to let them pass; there was plenty of room now that their stolen channels had been blown apart. Sandford's limp was all but gone as he and Stack ran side by side, blades held out in front of them as they smashed into the invaders. Butterfield was fighting already, hitting out in hand to hand combat with decreasing force as he got himself slashed to pieces. Stack and Sandford cut their way over to him, pushing him out of the battle's centre.

"Get out of here sir!" Stack shouted over his shoulder as he opened a German's stomach.

"Like hell," he pulled himself back to his feet, pushing past Stack and shoving his bayonet through another man's throat, screaming "For Jim!"

Stack now had more things to worry about than stopping Butterfield being the brave idiot that he was. He brought up his rifle to block the blade that lunged for his chest, forcing it aside and baring the holder's own torso for piercing. He spun to land a punch in the face of the man approaching from behind, immobilising him long enough to retrieve his bayonet from bleeding lungs and plunge it into his eye.

He retched as he pulled out more than just steel from the ruined socket and the butt of a rifle caught him off guard. He stumbled back, tripping on the body of the man he had just killed. The German blade came for him and he knocked it aside with his own, grabbing onto the barrel of the rifle and wrenching it out of its owner's hands. The man surrendered it, clutching instead onto Stack's upper arm, fingers pressing into his wound. He cried out and dropped the rifle, the other man quick to regain it. Stack brought his fists up to the man's neck but he dodged, right into the path of the blade that sliced through him, spraying blood and leaving his head hanging as he fell forward onto Stack's chest.

"Twenty points," Captain panted, holding his bayonet out like a sword, shoulders heaving. He noticed the stunned look on his friend's face and grinned. "What? Didn't think I'd let you have all the fun did you?"

Stack shook his head, a smile creeping into the corners of his mouth as relief flooded through him, both for his own life and the reappearance of the real Captain. He took his hand and was heaved back to his feet, catching the man in a quick embrace.

"Okay Benji, I'm fine," Captain laughed, pushing him off.

"Right," Stack nodded, pulling himself back together as he remembered where they were. "Behind you."

Captain ducked and Stack drove his bayonet into the man behind him before he had time to open his mouth in shock.

"Shit, your turn."

Captain rolled out from between them, lunging at an ankle and pulling the owner to the floor before he could bury his blade in British flesh. He slit the man's throat and got hastily to his feet, back to back with Stack as more approached.

"Twenty points?" he asked over his shoulder.

"Twenty points," his friend smiled grimly, dirt and blood caking his face. "And more coming."

Even as Sandford shouted that the Hun's strength was weakening and they should take prisoners rather than lives, more shapes dashed through the smoke, foreign voices calling for them to surrender.

"Come and take us!" Captain screamed, punching the air and firing wildly into their midst.

More voices joined him; some shouting insults, others just yelling incomprehensible sounds to add to the noise. Stack heard Wayson screaming his motto as he swung his rifle in an arc, splashing red from the face it collided with. His eyes flickered to meet Stack's, as if checking he was doing it right.

"Ready corporal?" Captain asked, eyeing the approaching column. "Take a few down with us, for Tommy and Collie?"

"You bet."

Stack thought of them sitting around the table on their last night and his vision flashed red. This was the ground they had made because of their sacrifice – they were not going to give it up, not for anything. Blade met blade met flesh and bone as they spilled out further from the shock of earth that had been their shelter. Stack felt a new kind of strength as he forced them away; bashing, slicing and punching at any opportunity. Captain fought beside him and Wayson behind them, keeping the worst away from the boy while still allowing him a part in it. Every stab kept them their dirt, their little piece of England that was to be defended at all costs.

Sandford kept track anxiously, aware of the shells falling around them and the decreasing ratio of West Kents to Germans. There were too many of them, and the relief wasn't coming fast enough. A blow to the back of the head knocked him forwards, spinning instinctively to stick his blade in the one who had dealt it. He threw the body away before it crushed him, catching sight of the messenger boy he had spoken to earlier. He stumbled down into the mud beside him, eyes staring at nothing and blood cascading from his neck. He hadn't even needed to be there, he was only a messenger.

A familiar feeling of deep guilt stirred in his gut. They should have retreated. He had done it again; allowed his men to be led into a bloodbath. He was not fit to lead a platoon. He stayed on his knees, roaring in anguish as he took a shot at another barbarian murdering his men.

"Where's the relief!?" he screamed at the sky. "Where's the bloody relief!?"

"Chin up James, they're falling back."

He felt Captain Kent's hand on his upper arm, pulling him upright before rushing away again. He was right; the column had fallen into disorder as their own shells fell into their midst, killing more Germans than British. Sergeant Butterfield stumbled forward – still attempting to give chase despite his wounds – but Stack caught him and held him back, his own arm starting to give him trouble again.

"Fancy that," Rigby wiped his mouth, his lip bleeding where a tooth had gone through it. "Who needs relief when you've got the German artillery?"

"They'll be back," Wayson said grimly, taking the opportunity to hastily reload his rifle.

"And we'll throw them off again," Rigby looked down at the boy with a sense of pride; he had come a long way since arriving only a few short months ago. "You heard Stack – we fight like it's England, and damn it we'll hold it. I've never seen us so determined."

The day was wearing on when they heard it, like the sound of every dream they'd ever had coming true. The shouts of their comrades were strong and cheerful as the relief battalions cut their way through to the beleaguered lines, pushing the enemy away from both flanks and whooping with eagerness.

"They're here!" Rigby clutched his face as tears of relief pricked in the backs of his eyes. "Thank God, the reinforcements! They're here!"

"So are the Germans," Wayson warned, lying on his stomach ahead of the trench, scorched eyes scanning the graveyard of trees.

"What do you think lads?"

Stack pushed back his dirty sleeves and surveyed the party; his own men and those of Corporal Whitby – whose body had been stretchered away, leaving his arm and half his blood supply behind. They looked back at him – exhausted and bedraggled – but with one final surge of energy lighting up their eyes. They were no longer a trapped battalion on the brink of collapse; they had won and they knew it. What was one more desperate effort from the losing side, after two days of flinging them back?

"Who's up for one last round?"

He smiled at them with confidence, Captain grinning back at him, and they fixed their bayonets one more time.

****

A bathing parade was organised for the last day they were to spend in the training camp, much to Captain's approval – the lice in their clothing had seemed to take on a new ferocity since the taking of the wood. There was even talk that Kent was behind it; a reward for their hard work in the wood, which had granted him a much boasted of promotion. He rode at the front of the column, with such an air of pride that an ill informed country boy could mistake him for the king himself.

They threw off their uniforms and dived into the river, splashing and racing each other like children. It was a welcome relief from the stiff drills of training and the sun had come out to warm the water nicely. After the trials of the wood, it was the perfect opportunity for the men to compare their healing wounds, competing over who had the worst flamethrower burns or the most masculine scars to show off back home.

"You not coming in, sir?" Captain called, spotting the major still fully clothed and astride his horse. "The lieutenant's joined us."

"As your commander I believe it is more appropriate for me to supervise from here, private," Kent replied, stiff as ever.

Something sparkled in Captain's eye and he gave Stack a mischievous look before shouting out again. "You know, Sergeant Pollock never came in to bathe either. Makes people think you officers might have something to hide."

"Oh for God's sake, fine, I'll come in if it means that much to you," Kent snapped, hastily dismounting and making a show of entering the river with the rest of them.

"You are an awful person, Dan Captain," Stack laughed. "He'll be parading his bollocks to us for weeks now just to stop your rumours."

Captain shrugged. "Got to keep these officers on a tight leash, Benji, or they might start thinking they can actually control us."

He flipped and swum away from them, performing a backflip for Wayson's amusement. There was nothing to suggest that he wasn't the happy-go-lucky man he had been on the last day of June. Still, Stack had seen him sleeping, watched every grimace as he fought with his dreams. And there was something about the way he baited Wayson that didn't seem quite heartfelt.

"You need to stop worrying," Rigby called from his perch on the bank, enjoying the sun and a cigarette as he dangled his feet in the water. "He's Captain; he's invincible."

"I don't know," Stack replied. "He still doesn't seem quite right."

He ran a hand through his wet hair. It was getting too long again; Kent would have something to say about that. Since they had been moved for training, the newly promoted major had been determined to act like the hero his superiors were hailing him as, and dress his company accordingly. How Captain had got away with keeping his curls nobody knew, something Rigby enjoyed teasing him about.

Captain fought back with his usual banter and the others considered him cured, but Stack knew him better than that. Despite all the jokes, shadows passed behind his eyes when he thought nobody was looking. And there were the nights too. He still slept too much, often passing up the chance of entering the gambling circles with Rigby to dream his crooked dreams and mutter into his threadbare pillow.

Rigby puffed thoughtfully. "He's not crying anymore, and he still gives me a verbal beating whenever I open my mouth; just be happy with that. He's on the mend, Ben, trust me. And trust him."

"I do, Rig," he sighed. "You just hear things, don't you, about men going mad out here. You were there, you saw them after the offensive. You saw him."

Rigby took a long drag and exhaled slowly, shuddering. "I did. But you didn't see Vincent Waterman. That's madness, Ben, that's bloody madness. His eyes were all wide and starey but they didn't see anything. And there was something behind them too, like there was a demon in there trying to get out, but first it had to eat him up from the inside."

He took another deep draw on his cigarette. "If I live to a hundred years or drop dead tomorrow, I'll never forget that look. Cap's fine, Ben; you be thankful for that." He raised his voice so Captain could hear him. "He's still the most useless fool in the battalion."

"I really hope you drown!" Captain called.

"No you don't," Rigby smiled annoyingly, casting Stack an encouraging look and sliding into the water.

The sun was warm on their bare backs and there wasn't a cloud in sight – even the sounds of gunfire couldn't seem to penetrate the thick air of late summer. It almost felt like they were back home; old friends messing about in the river with nothing but their scars to remind them there had even been a war. Perhaps Rigby was right about Captain. There was that twinkle in his eye that made the French girls swoon and had always drawn the admiration of poor Tommy Miller.

You worry too much, he told himself happily. He fell in beside his friend as he swam against the gentle tide, before pulling harder with his arms and passing him, kicking water in his face.

"One day, Ben," he spat out the waves that filled his mouth. "That'll be me out-swimming you, you bastard."

"Is this the same day you'll shoot straighter than me?" Stack called back, enjoying the feel of the water on his mending arm. "Face it Cap, your pretty boy arms just can't handle it."

"I'll have you know, I have biceps as big as Wayson's neck," he pulled the boy closer as if to prove it. "That's what happens when you spend your life digging holes all over France."

Wayson pulled away and dived under the water, making Captain jump to dodge the splash. Stack burst out laughing.

"I can't believe you; over a year covered in mud and lice and you still jump at a splash of water?"

"I can fix that," Rigby grinned, launching himself onto his back and dunking his head into the river.

It was strange under the water; the sounds of laughter were dulled and sounded like something different entirely. Weeds floated upwards, churned out of slumber by the many feet kicking about in the river, clawing at him like the desperate hands of drowning men. The sound of the water filled his ears, but it wasn't water he heard. It was machine guns and screaming, the thousand footfalls of men walking to their graves. The bagpipes of the Scots played faintly in the distance, getting quieter and quieter as the brave players fell.

And still those fingers reached for him, begging him silently not to let them down. They were so young, they were so scared. Now they had a face; the boy stared up at him from the depths, his mind twisting the terrified look in his bloodshot eyes into a glare of pure accusation. The weed finger pointed like the condemning hand of the reaper as the shot replayed and the face fell backwards, dark blood dribbling from the corners of his mouth.

"I didn't mean to!" he tried to tell the boy before he vanished, but only bubbles came. "I didn't mean to! I thought you were German!"

"Rigby," Stack swum back over, his strong arms making short work of the stretch of water between them. "Rigby, let him up."

"He's just playing, nobody can drown that soon."

"Let him up Rig," he dived down and seized his friend under the armpits, pulling him back above the waterline. He struggled against him, quaking as if cold though both the river and air were perfectly warm.

"I didn't mean to!" he spluttered as soon as his head broke the surface, water running down his face. "I didn't mean to!"

"It's okay, Cap, look at me," Stack held him steady as his struggling subsided. "Cap!"

Captain's eyes met his; scared and confused as if waking from a nightmare and unsure of where he was. He glanced about the others looking on in alarm, shame setting in as his breathing steadied.

"Sorry Ben," he said quietly, shoulders drooping beneath his friend's hands. "I keep seeing his bloody face." He glanced again at the men watching him. "They think I'm crazy."

Stack shook his head. "We've always thought you're crazy, but not because of that. Come on, let's get out of here for a bit."

They made their way back to the bank, sitting themselves down on the resilient grass and watching the others at play, each lost in their own thoughts.

"What are we going to do with you?" Stack said at last, giving his friend a look.

"I don't know," Captain shrugged, his expression lost and hopeless. "Shoot me for cowardice probably, if Kent has his way."

"Don't joke about that, Cap," Stack warned him. "Even Kent can see you're not a coward. You haven't deserted."

"Nope, not me," Captain shook his head. "I'm here 'til the end. I'll die facing the enemy with a German bullet piercing my heart."

"Or in a warm bed wrapped in the arms of some poor girl at the age of seventy," Stack suggested.

"I resent your choice of wording," he looked sideways at him, a smile tugging at the corners of his mouth.

"I resent your choice of death."

Captain barked a laugh, wiping the remnants of tears from his eyelashes with the back of his hand. "Alright. How about a shell instead?"

He grinned cheekily, taking Stack's friendly punch and returning it. He got to his feet, making the decision that it was time to return to the others, and led his friend back into the water.

"You back in the world of the living, ey Cap?" Rigby greeted them. "You've got to snap out of this; having a conscience really doesn't suit you."

"Get stuffed Rigby," Captain splashed him. "Having the ugliest wife in the world suits you perfectly, but you don't see me rubbing it in."

Wayson looked up at Stack in exasperation and the older man rolled his eyes back at him, remembering the look he and Rob used to share when Edward and Thomas were bickering like children. The memory hurt, but he allowed himself to feel it for a while longer. In the sun by the river it was like the shells and rats couldn't touch them, and his nephew smiled back from Wayson's young face.

Captain tired of Rigby baiting and fell back in between them, draping an arm over each of their shoulders and starting them up in a nonsense song that quickly spread to the rest of the company. He was so unpredictable; one minute in tears and the next howling about kissing sergeants goodnight. But, Stack thought, that was what made him Captain.

9.

The light was dimming as the monster crawled up the road, churning up the dirt with her tracks and roaring like the predator she was. Men rested at the side of the road on their long march to nowhere, kicking off their boots and setting down their packs for a glorious few minutes, but got to their feet at the sound of the beast. She rumbled past, slow and majestic with great guns protruding from her armoured sides – the picture of victory. The very sight of her warmed their aching muscles and raised their spirits; a beautiful but cruel titan queen, sent to strike fear into the hearts of their enemies and bring them finally home.

They waved their helmets and cheered as she approached, some of the younger and more energetic lads running up to her flank and walking beside her a little way down the road, revelling in the glory of her existence. Even the sun seemed to be praising her; bowing down behind the fields and laying out a golden carpet in her wake, blessing the ground on which she travelled. None of them had seen a tank in action – most had never seen one at all – but such a specimen could not be doubted by any. With every turn of her tracks she promised victory, and for that she was gorgeous.

For the men inside, their vehicle of victory was seen through less enchanted eyes. Even in the cool dusk the heat was unbearable and fumes were a constant threat, overwhelming many crewmen even with the masks they wore for protection. Conditions were cramped and uncomfortable and vision was poor, especially when the flaps and hatches were shut for battle. And then there was the noise. An angry shout of triumph to the soldiers watching from the road, her voice was magnified tenfold within the confines of her body, deafening the crew who controlled her. There was no real conversation to be had inside a tank; communications must be passed using signals if they were to be understood and even these were carried out in darkness.

But despite all her shortcomings, the men who rode within her loved her with all their hearts. They had christened her 'Naughty Betsy', after Sergeant Carthouse's favourite from the herd of cattle he kept back home, and they treated her like their own prize bull. She was not the spectacle of majesty that people cheered for wherever she went, but she was theirs and each man felt a pride in her that far surpassed anything they had known. They signed up to make a difference in this war, and how much of a difference they would make, just by giving this giant the gift of movement. How they could not wait to take her into her first battle.

None more so than the young gunner Kit Allenby, crouched against the starboard six-pounder that was his charge. Used to the din and the heat, he pressed his eye eagerly to the sight, heaving the gun about using the shaft at his right armpit to get a better view and give the weary infantry a good show.

He had never once complained about conditions in the belly of Betsy – much in contrast with his fellow gunner, Welshman Dafydd Jones – for as far as he was concerned the sheer excitement of his situation was well worth a sore back and a headache. He could still remember the first time they had seen the hulking shape of a landship after what felt like years of training; finally the secret weapon they had been promised. He had not been disappointed. Looking at that great metal machine of destruction, he had been looking at destiny.

The tank bumped over something in the road, jostling its occupants. Though the roar of the engine drowned out any real noise, Kit imagined he heard Dafydd swearing violently from the portside gun. The man had a temper on him to rival his own, and that had been something Kit had been known for back home.

He took after his father in that respect, and many others, though the man had become calmer in the years before he died. It was for him that he sweated in the dark, peering through the sight and dreaming of the day he would use it to aim and fire at the vermin that scuttled over France and Belgium like lice in the trenches. Every one of them was responsible, and they all would pay.

His loader, Ollie Powell, nudged into him as Betsy lurched again, pressing his eye sharply against the sight. He pulled his away, looking around to make out the shape of the boy in the darkness. They shared a barely visible smile, before another jolt in the road threw Kit's head back against the sight.

The two had been inseparable since signing up together at what felt like the beginning of the world; both enthralled by the idea of a secret weapon to end the war. It had been a wrench to allow their friends the glory of crossing the channel first – they had probably already taken down a dozen Germans in the recent offensive – but they had decided that, once their training was complete, the wait would certainly be worth it. To their delight they had been kept in the same unit and, as testament to their luck, even assigned to the same gun.

"Comfortable?" Ollie shouted over the noise of the engine.

"What?" Kit shouted back. "I can't hear you!"

Ollie shook his head and changed into the sign language that Dafydd had invented with his loader, Colm Baker. *Prostitute?*

"What?"

Kit burst out laughing, inhaling a gulp of fumes that made his head swim. Of course for every ordinary word, Dafydd had invented a similar sign for another, more vulgar term. He had no idea what Ollie had meant to say but had no time to ask as Betsy's nose plunged downwards, throwing them against the hard inside of the tank. The engine protested loudly, before the driver shut it off.

"Oh bloody hell Carthorse!" Dafydd shouted from the portside gun. "Learn to drive! I've got Dove's knee up my bloody arse!"

His loader replied in a thick Irish accent. "Don't swear Daffs; you forget there's children on board."

Kit scowled. He and Ollie may have been able to effortlessly fool the recruiting sergeants, but Colm and Dafydd were another story. They were constantly making teasing threats that they would report them to the military police, and called them Whipper and Snapper, despite the fact that neither of them *looked* underage. It was only harmless banter, but Kit couldn't help taking it to heart sometimes. *He* knew he wasn't a little boy anymore; why did nobody else want to accept that? He was part of a tank crew now, in charge of firing a bigger gun than his father had ever seen. Surely that deserved respect.

"Sorry Betsy."

Kit could make out the shape of the driver patting the large steering wheel apologetically. The sergeant was a gentle soul, with a love for machines that had encouraged the peaceful man to answer the call for technologically-minded men needed for the army's great secret. He was broad-shouldered and strong, reminding Kit of an older version of his uncle, and his size had given them cause to dub him 'Carthorse' rather than Carthouse.

His hair was greying and his face frequently lined, making Kit wonder more than once if it wasn't only Ollie and himself who had lied about their age. He would never ask him though; he was their father figure and despite his caring nature that still carried authority in Kit's eyes. Besides, he was sure Dafydd or Colm would venture the question soon enough.

"It's getting dark," Betsy's commander, Lieutenant Cuthbert, concluded.

"How about a kip then?" Dafydd suggested.

"We're nearly there," the lieutenant said firmly, leaving his seat beside Carthorse and pushing his way past Kit towards the door at the rear of the sponson. "And don't try telling me you'll be sleeping when we get there; I know you, Jones."

"A quick breath of fresh air then?" Colm asked, lifting his mask and wiping his sweating forehead. He was usually quite handsome, but the heat made his face red and an angry rash had taken to creeping up his neck after a spell in the tank.

"Come on Cuffs," Dafydd pleaded. "Firetop's expiring back here!"

He had a point. The poor gearsman staggered through the door after the lieutenant, having to hold himself up against the man to stop himself collapsing. Roy Furnace had the unfortunate luck that the colour of both his hair and his face perfectly matched his surname, much to Dafydd and Colm's delight.

It had been their idea to give them all nicknames, after already blessing Kit and Ollie with theirs. Firetop's fellow gearsman, Ethan Heart, was Valentine – mostly because of his name but also due to the ridiculous amount of effort that went into his appearance. The lieutenant had become Cufflinks after the discovery that he had been well-off before the war, living in a country house and hosting dinner parties.

Dafydd had tried to name himself something heroic, but Colm had got their first with Daffodil – the Welsh national flower, so a perfect choice. His friend had not been so pleased with being associated with a flower, no matter whose national emblem it was. In retaliation he altered Colm's nickname (Dozen, after a baker's dozen) to Dove, but disappointingly it didn't catch on so well.

Kit ripped off his mask the instant he left the tank, revealing a well-shaped young face with a strong jaw and deep eyes. He had been a favourite with the village girls once but, unlike Valentine, he had better things to think about now. His hair stuck to his forehead and he pushed it back, enjoying the soft breeze on his skin.

Kit leant against the tank's side, watching the lieutenant as he walked slowly down the road, examining the way carefully. Since the man had taken charge of their little unit, the boy had looked up to him tremendously. He was everything an officer should be; authoritative and powerful with cropped dark hair and a strong moustache, but also kind and clever and sensitive to their needs. Of two things Kit was certain; one day he too would be a tank commander, and he would be just like Lieutenant Cuthbert.

"The ground isn't too bad," he told them on his return, speaking mostly to Carthorse. "A few shell holes but nothing Betsy can't handle." He looked around at the six of them. "Where's Furnace?"

"How did we lose him?" Dafydd asked incredulously. "Fritz could see his hair from Berlin!"

"Leave him alone, he's only having a piss," Colm laughed, emerging from the other side of the tank. "Damn fumes mess him up."

"Language please, Baker," Cufflinks said automatically, though Kit could tell he found it amusing too. The tight-lipped lieutenant had adjusted well to the rowdy bunch he found himself commanding, something else that the young gunner admired about him.

Despite his pride, Kit was glad when Naughty Betsy came to a final halt and he could breathe freely again. The ground was already strewn with infantry by the time they arrived, possibly the same men they had passed on the road; for all their power, tanks were not known for their speed. The men lounged outside in a mass of chattering bodies interjected with tents for the officers. They would be sleeping outside then, not that Kit minded. They were at war after all; he didn't expect the lap of luxury.

"Right, let's get her covered up," Carthorse patted a sponson fondly as Firetop and Valentine fetched the tarpaulin. Keeping Betsy and her fellows invisible, especially from the air, was of top priority.

"Hey mister?" an infantryman approached the sergeant, casting an excited look back at his friends. "Can I have a go inside?"

Carthorse laughed kindly. "You can't I'm afraid, and you wouldn't want to either; Betsy here's damn near suffocated us for our troubles."

"Please sir, only for a little bit?" the young man pleaded, looking past the sergeant in awe. "You lot are going to win us this war; I want to see inside!"

"Oi, you heard him," Dafydd pushed in between them, knowing the soft old man was likely to give in soon. "You can't go inside, this is top secret stuff. Now sod off."

"Sorry son," Carthorse apologised as the soldier retreated, looking incredibly disappointed. "You don't have to be nasty Daffodil, he was only asking. Where's the harm really?"

"You are too soft," the Welshman shook his head. "Cuffs, you wouldn't let an outsider play around with Betsy, would you?"

"I would," Kit spoke up. "Every man wants to be part of the victory, why should we stop them?"

"Same reason we should stop you, young Whipper. He's untrained and you're an infant; you should both go on back home and watch victory in the theatre with your mummies."

"I'll give you something to take home to your mummy!"

Kit jumped at him but Dafydd just turned and caught him, swinging him over his shoulder. He struggled, about to wriggle free when Colm came to his friend's aid and took hold of the boy's legs.

"Right then," Dafydd grinned, gripping Kit's upper body in arms that were a lot stronger than they looked. "Time for a beer I think, 'ey Dove?"

"Lead the way flower-boy," Colm smiled back and they marched through the mass of lounging soldiers to the large stone building at the side of the camp, outside of which sat men with welcome tankards in their hands.

"What are we going to do with them?" Carthorse watched them go with a fatherly look in his eyes.

The lieutenant lit a cigarette and perched it beneath his moustache, smiling at the boy being unceremoniously dumped before the open doorway. "For now, let them be; there's plenty of time to be serious later. They have a big shock headed their way when we get called up to a real battle."

"Think they'll be up to it?" Carthorse asked apprehensively. "Whip and Snap are only young, and Daff and Dozen are even younger in their minds."

"I wouldn't underestimate the boys," Cufflinks mused, blowing a steady stream of smoke into the night air. "They're good at what they do. And" – he chuckled – "you're right to say they're a lot more mature than Jones and Baker."

"Hmm," Carthorse murmured. "Sir, can I ask you something?"

"Of course."

"I don't know if I have a right to be wondering this, but do you think Betsy's ready? I'm no coward, sir, but I've been worrying. There aren't many of us tanks over here yet; don't you think they're being a little hasty?" He looked sideways at the lieutenant, checking that he hadn't crossed the line. The younger man looked back at him with no anger in his unusually green eyes, so he continued. "Sometimes, sir, I don't think we've had enough of a chance to really get to know them; how they work, how we correct things that go wrong. Can I even really drive her?"

"Ted," Cufflinks looked him firmly in the eye. "You are an excellent driver. We're all well trained and when Betsy's time comes Fritz won't know what hit him." He smiled. "Would you really like to be on the wrong side of a six-pounder fired by Dafydd Jones, or Kit Allenby for that matter?"

He held out the roll that still sat in the palm of his hand. "Cigarette?"

"I suppose I wouldn't," Carthorse took one and popped it into his mouth. "We have the angriest gunners in the whole British army."

****

"Oh no you don't," Kit caught the card as it made its way to the edge of the table, flipping it over triumphantly. "I believe this was your original card, wasn't it Daffodil?"

Colm clapped in delight. "Beaten by an amateur; how does that feel, Daffy? I lay my cards at your feet, Whipper, I've been trying to figure out his secret for months."

Kit grinned. He too had spent many a night frustrated by the skill with which Dafydd took the majority of their wages. "After watching the crooks my uncle used to play, I can figure out anyone if you give me long enough."

"Your uncle is a very bad man," Dafydd grumbled, pushing a few coins reluctantly across the table. "Taking a baby like you out gambling."

"You're just sore, Flowers," Colm got to his feet. "Come on Whip, I'll get you a drink."

"*He* should be buying the drinks," Dafydd called after them. "Dirty hustler!"

"That was impressive, lad," the Irishman leaned on the bar, his strong bare arms tapping on the stained wood. "I've never seen him so flustered. You're going up in the world, young Whipper."

Kit copied his stance, leaning casually forward to attract the barman's attention. "Maybe one day I'll have gone up enough for you to stop calling me that."

"Oh no," Colm chuckled and shook his head. "You're stuck with it now; you'll be Whipper when you're seventy."

"Well then, Dove," Kit grinned back. "Maybe I should return the favour."

"You're a bloody cheeky one, for a nipper – two beers please pal," he waved at the barman. "You need to take a leaf out of Snapper's book. He's got manners, respects his elders."

"Yeah, well," Kit shrugged. "You won't be saying that when I'm commander."

"Don't you go doing anything bad to Cuffers," Colm joked. "He's our commander and I quite like him, no matter how funny it would be watching you trying to control a tank."

"You two are tank men?" the barman passed them their drinks, keen interest in his eyes.

"We are," Kit nodded, wanting to beam with pride but settling instead on a look he hoped was strong and manly. "I'm a gunner, he's a loader."

"I'm the one with the muscles," Colm nudged the boy with his elbow, grinning as he signed in their private language: *show off*.

The barman looked impressed.

"These are on me," he pushed the drinks towards them. "It's the likes of you two that will finish this war and get me home to my wife."

"Good man," Colm thanked him, taking a beer in each hand. Kit frowned a little; he was perfectly capable of carrying his own drink.

"Bloody tank coward," somebody hissed, turning to glare Kit in the eye. He could smell the alcohol on his breath as it came at his face in sharp bursts.

"Careful who you're calling coward," he narrowed his eyes, the word ringing in his ears.

"You ever seen your best friend have his head blown off right in front of you?"

Kit didn't move, silence answering the man's question.

"Sit down Bert," somebody from the nearby table pulled at his arm. "Let it go."

He wrenched away, pushing his face into Kit's. "You're a little boy, and a coward." He spat. "Go home."

Kit saw red the instant his saliva hit his cheek. Not bothering to wipe it away first, he swung for him, landing a punch hard against his nose. He rubbed the blood from his knuckles into his shirt while Bert staggered backwards, unprepared for the power the 'little boy' possessed. He recovered quickly though, catching him in a headlock and pulling him down painfully.

"You little bastard," he snarled, twisting Kit's shoulders to the side.

This was a mistake. Kit got his elbow into the man's stomach, making him loose his grip enough to wriggle his head free and push him back into the table behind them. They had gathered a crowd now; men watching in differing states of concern and amusement. Kit almost expected to see his uncle at the front, allowing him his freedom but ready to step in when needed. Only he wasn't needed now – Kit was a man now and could fight his own battles.

He stood triumphantly over his opponent on the table, feeling a little bad for him; he had just lost his best friend after all. He wondered how he would feel if he saw somebody shoot Ollie's head off. Probably just as hungry for a fight, or worse.

Bert wasn't giving up so easily though, and Kit was caught off guard as he lunged back from the table, sending them both crashing to the floor. The back of Kit's head hit the ground hard and he faltered long enough to allow the bigger man to connect his fist with his cheekbone. His face was knocked to the side and he spotted a bottle lying on the floor, within reach of his unrestrained arm.

He ignored it, grasping instead the man's face and forcing it backward, fixing his shoulder against the floor to lever the weight away from his torso. Perhaps one day the situation would require him to forget his pride, but for now he was not a cheat.

Still feeling the sting on both sides of his head, he kicked back against the ground and rolled them over, resisting the momentum that threatened to put Bert back on top. Jamming his knee between his legs to restrict movement, he put a hand on each shoulder and held him to the floor.

"I'm not a coward," he snarled, anger contorting his face. "Got that?"

Bert said nothing, staring at him in confusion. Kit gave him one last triumphant look and stood, happy that he had taught the man a lesson – taught the room a lesson. Underage or not, he was not somebody to be trifled with.

He pulled the man roughly back to his feet before walking calmly back to the table where the others were sitting in stunned silence.

"Whipper," Dafydd said in awe. "I'm bloody impressed. Look at you all grown up and killing people."

Ollie shook his head, the only one unsurprised. "Save it for Fritz. We're on the same side, remember."

"Don't be bitter, Snap," Colm took a gulp of his drink. "Whipper may act like a man, but he's still a baby just like you."

"You be quiet Dozen," Kit smiled proudly. "Unless you want the same treatment as him."

"I've got to say," Colm admitted. "I thought you were a goner."

"He should be," Dafydd commented, still looking at him like he had just told them he was the king. "I think we misjudged you, little Whipper. Who are you really? Who is Kit Allenby?"

He shrugged, avoiding Dafydd's favourite sport of prodding into his life. "I am."

Kit gracefully declined another game, heading outside instead for fresh air. A barrel of water had been left beside the door and he filled his hands, pouring the cold liquid over the back of his head. He rubbed his hair, freeing it from the small amount of blood beginning to congeal there. He splashed some onto his face too, prodding the bruise that was blossoming nicely on his cheek. He could see his uncle now, trying to look disapproving behind the smile that lit up his eyes.

"This time I mean it; next time you want to come out I am not going to fight your father for you," he would say, trying to mop up his face while his nephew attempted to dodge. *"You're just like him, always trying to prove yourself."*

"Not to you though," Kit would grin. *"You know I can hold my own better than anyone else in the village. Except you, of course."*

"Yeah," he would agree. *"I do. Just you remember that, next time you feel like getting your face kicked in. I'm proud of you Rob, and your father is too, even if he doesn't show it so much."*

Kit sat down against the wall, hugging his knees and staring out towards the front line, wondering where his uncle was tonight. They would both certainly be proud of him now; a gunner in the war's greatest machine. If only they knew. His father had died still believing him to be a child, safe and useless at home. He knew his uncle would be impressed, if only he could write to him. But he knew he couldn't write; no matter how impressed he was, his uncle would feel that he had to tell his mother, and she would report him for sure. He could think of nothing more humiliating than being torn from his friends in disgrace and sent back home underage.

The triumphant feeling from the fight was beginning to wear off and he didn't feel much like heading back inside. He splashed himself once more before picking his way back over to where Cufflinks and Carthorse were already asleep.

Thinking about his disconnection from the ones he loved bothered him, and he would rather sleep before his mind started thinking the worst. Uncle Ben would never die, he told himself, he was just too good. But then, he had thought the same about his father. And what about his friends, those who joined the infantry when he joined the tanks? Richie, Vincent, George and Billy; he always wondered what had become of them.

Still, sleep came easier than it had done whilst plagued by guilt and frustration at home. He wasn't sure how long it was until he was woken by Ollie stumbling over him in the dark. His eyes had not adjusted to the dark as well as the rest of the crew's, and Kit sometimes wondered how well he would cope loading the gun in a real battle. He had been fine in training, but under real pressure, who knew?

Don't be stupid, he thought angrily. *You're getting as bad as the others. He has just as much right to be here as anyone else.*

He must have moved, for he heard a voice in the darkness. "Are you awake? Rob?"

"*Kit!*" he hissed, looking about to see if anyone had heard. "You idiot!"

"Don't worry," Ollie rolled onto his front, thankfully speaking quietly. "Everyone's asleep."

"You don't know that," he replied equally quietly.

"They wouldn't even notice if they were; everyone has nicknames. You're too careful Rob."

"Kit!" he corrected him again. "Are you really that stupid that you still don't remember?"

"I'm not stupid," he sounded hurt. "It's just nice to get a little reminder of home."

"I know," Rob propped his head up on his arms to look at him properly. "Just keep your reminders in your head where nobody can find them."

"Don't you ever get lonely?" the boy continued. "I haven't spoken to my family in months; it's like I'm forgetting who I am. It'd be nice to be called by the name they gave me, once in a while."

"It's only a name Ollie," Rob told him. "You're still yourself, just now there's nobody telling you you're too young to be who you are."

"Come on, can't you call me Alfie just this once?" he pleaded. "I swear nobody's listening."

"What difference would it make?" Rob sighed. "We can't risk it. I thought you wanted to prove you could fight, not whine like a homesick child."

"I do," he replied indignantly. "I, Alfie Barnes, can fight; that's what I want to prove. Who's Ollie Powell?"

"You are," Rob said firmly. "You're Ollie Powell and I'm Kit Allenby, and you'd better remember that. Unless you *want* to get sent home?"

"No," Alfie shook his head. "I'm Alfie Barnes and you're Rob Stack and if we forget that, what's the point in us even being here? I'm fighting for my family, *Kit*, and I'm not going to let myself forget them. Are you so ashamed of yours that you'll just throw away their name like a dud? Your father died out here, you can't just forget that."

"I will *never* forget that," Rob snarled, hands curling into fists against the ground. "Never."

He pushed off from the dirt and stormed off into the night, kicking a stray helmet that got in his way. He was sick of other people's opinions. He had been called incompetent and coward too many times, was he now also to endure being called heartless?

"No, Kit, wait!" Alfie called after him, scrambling to his feet and following him towards the field where Betsy was hidden.

"I'm sorry, I didn't mean that," he panted when he caught up with him, already leant against the tank with arms crossed tightly across his chest.

"I really hope you didn't," Rob replied stiffly. "Don't ever accuse me of that again."

"I won't, I swear I didn't mean it." He paused, but Rob said nothing so he continued. "I'm not as strong as you, I miss home a lot."

"You think I don't?" Rob raised his eyebrows, hugging his arms tighter about himself. "Difference is you have a home to go back to. My father's dead and my mother's probably so angry at me she won't even see me. I've left my little brother all on his own to get locked up in case he follows me, and I've given up the chance to know if my uncle's alive. You think that's an easy thing to live with?"

Alfie shook his head. "I'm sorry."

Rob took a deep breath, thinking instead of the tank as he always did when confused or upset. "That's alright. It's all worth it, isn't it? We're here when they all told us we couldn't be, and we're going to show them all they were wrong. Think how much better your family will love you when you come home a hero."

Alfie smiled hopefully.

"We are lucky, aren't we. Whatever I was thinking when we signed up, it wasn't this! The others will be so jealous, especially

Richie. Can you imagine his face when he finds out?" He grinned at Rob. "How do you think they're all doing? Think they've been over the top?"

"Maybe," Rob shrugged, not wanting to think of Billy's face among those they had passed laid out motionless for the gravediggers. "If they did, Richie and Vince will be bragging until the end of the world. They must be driving Billy crazy."

They smiled at the thought, remembering the last night they had spent together in the barn and trying to picture how their comrades would look now after their first taste of real war. Rob wished they could all be together now. He had come to feel almost like their leader, and they certainly treated him so, which made it odd to realise he may never know what would become of them.

He uncrossed his arms and hung his hands loosely from the braces that climbed his broad shoulders, enjoying the cool feel of the night air on his chest. It wouldn't be long, he knew, before he was back in the sweltering heat at the core of the tank, peering down the sight of his big gun, this time to aim and kill. He almost laughed when he thought of how many more Germans he would shoot than Billy, maybe even more than his uncle.

"Do you ever think about Daisy?" Alfie asked, catching Rob off guard.

He spluttered before answering with one word in an odd voice – "No."

Alfie looked at him in interest. "Not at all? She must miss you awfully."

"The war changed a lot of things," Rob said darkly, regaining composure. "She doesn't miss me, and if she does she deserves it."

"Does she really?" Alfie looked sad. "Everyone knows her sister's a menace, what did you expect her to do?"

"I didn't expect anything," he said bluntly. "She's just another girl who doesn't understand the world of men. If you ask me, I had a lucky escape."

He patted the tank. "Our Betsy's the only girl for me."

10.

Boots crunched through the snow, cracking the puddles that matured into ice and leaving their dirty tread to turn crystals into slush. Breath came as mist in the freezing air and they marched with vigour to stay warm. What they wouldn't give for the furnace of Trones Wood now that winter had taken hold. Feet sweated under their layers then froze in their own sweat, clammy and painful until the cold turned them numb. Step, crunch, step, crunch on the freshly fallen blizzard, with little other noise as they funnelled their energy into stopping the shivers.

The town through which they walked was as bare as their spirits, nothing moving but the odd gust of snow that the wind swept up and threw into eerie shapes. They danced along the roofs of abandoned buildings, singing in shrill tongues of a time before soldiers marched their streets, spiralling down alleyways in search of children long departed. The flakes caressed the wounded walls of houses crippled by shellfire, trying to kiss life back with their dead white lips before swirling angrily back at those who invaded their grief. Then they settled upon the cracked headstones of a graveyard half destroyed by some explosion. It was a reminder to all who passed – nobody rests in peace.

Stack could make out the shape of a little girl, tiny and frail, balanced on a stool at the entrance to the church with a skinny dog who sat as if guarding her. He noticed with a lurch that no legs protruded from the hem of her tattered dress, and her left arm was mangled beyond recognition. She must have been freezing, with no coat or blanket or even sleeves to shield her from the elements, but she sat still and rigid, her little face glaring at them from beneath a tangle of dirty hair. Even from this distance, Stack knew that look in her eyes; blame.

The door swung open and her gaze was broken, turning her head to face the old woman who peered suspiciously from behind the tortured wood. She too glared sharply at the soldiers before scooping up the girl in her arms and taking her inside, the dog trotting closely at her heel.

"Did you see her?" Stack sensed Rigby behind him.

"The little girl?" he pulled out what must have been his tenth cigarette of the day. "I saw her."

"Does it make me pathetic that after nearly two years of killing people, things like that still make me sick?"

"No," Rigby shook his head, struggling to create a spark in the cold. "It makes you human. If you're lucky you'll never get used to it. If you do" – the spark finally caught – "that's when you're past saving."

"Thanks," Stack smiled gratefully and let Rigby guide him back to the column. "It's bad enough seeing our own like that, but civilians…they had no choice. At least we signed up for this."

"Not all of us," Private Jackson Weir's voice sounded small and vulnerable. "Not all of us, sir."

****

Wayson kicked off his boots, allowing his toes the chance to move freely, before the cold forced him to ram them hastily back on.

He shifted his weight to sit on his feet, crushing them with what warmth remained in his body. Hearing stories about frostbite was good enough for him; he was not about to try it himself.

He could hear the crackle of the fire from the other side of the wall against which he leant, and the chatter of the older men around it. All seemed quiet now on the front, and there were rumours that the Germans were busy behind their lines, building something ready for the spring. None of them liked the idea of that.

"I'm sorry," Captain whispered, voice shaking from the cold. He had been curled up in a ball against the weather and now stretched, still asleep judging by the vacant look in his eyes.

"Sorry about what?" Wayson asked hesitantly. He had spoken in his sleep before, but never directly to him.

"I'm so sorry," he said again. "I swear I didn't mean to."

"You didn't do anything," Wayson tried to tell him, panicking a little as the man clutched at his arm. "Stop crying, it'll freeze on your face."

"Please," Captain continued to whisper manically. "Please forgive me."

"It's me!" Wayson backed away, trying to stand. "It's me, Wayson. Sir! You didn't do anything to me, it's Wayson. Sir! Sir! Sergeant Stack!"

"Wayson?" he emerged from behind the wall, mouth still full of the hard cake they had been trying to heat. "What is it?"

He swallowed quickly when he saw his friend clutching onto the worried boy, hastily wiping the remaining crumbs from his chapped lips and hurrying over.

"Please believe me," Captain was sobbing, on his knees as he held Wayson's wrists. "I didn't mean to, I didn't mean to."

"Cap," Stack knelt down next to him, seizing his hands gently but firmly.

"One minute he was sleeping, then the next he went all weird," Wayson tried to explain, rubbing his wrists.

"I know, thanks for calling me," Stack gave him a comforting smile. "You go get warm, everything's fine."

He took Captain's head between his hands and turned it away from the boy. "Cap, you can wake up now. It's only me and Wayson; nobody's blaming you for anything."

"I didn't mean to kill him," he panted, heartbeat slowing as he remembered where he was. The fog over his eyes began to break and they swam into focus, catching onto his friend's face.

"Cap?"

"Oh god Ben!" he buried his face in Stack's shoulder. "Every time I think he's gone…"

"You're okay Cap," he hooked an arm beneath his armpit and lifted him to his feet. "Now you're going to stay up tonight, like you always used to. We've got a good fire going and Rigby's missus has made the most god-awful cake, but we're missing the right person to tell him just how lucky he is."

Captain laughed and wiped the trails of salt away from his cheeks, along with the flurry of snow that had attached itself to them. "You need me then. I suppose I'd better oblige."

"Yes," Stack replied. "You'd better."

****

"It must be strange, being here without a reason," Wayson said over breakfast; a meal that seemed to shrink in quality and quantity every day as winter and German blockades took a firmer hold.

Breakfast, of course, was not the only meal to suffer; their main diet now revolved around biscuits as hard as rock and the odd bit of bread that tasted like stale turnips. Thin soup made a regular appearance – foul if not heated – and if you saw meat on two consecutive days you were a lucky man indeed.

"We all have a reason," Captain leaned back against the wall, stretching his feet towards the remains of the fire. "We're here because we're here because we're here because we're here."

He started singing in a jolly fashion, trailing off when nobody joined in.

"That's not a reason," Wayson sipped on cold tea and pulled a face. "I mean, us veterans" – Stack had to smile at the boy's labelling of himself – "we chose to do this. For king and country, for women, for glory…whatever the reason, we all had one. You're just here. I can't imagine how strange that must be."

Weir smiled dryly, fiddling with his unappetising food. "Not so strange; there's plenty of us. For my part, I can't imagine signing up on purpose. You're only a boy, you could've escaped this altogether if you'd stayed put."

"I don't stay put," Wayson replied, the fire of pride ablaze in his bright young eyes. "I couldn't sit at home being called coward while everyone else was off fighting for our freedom."

"Well you're a lot braver than me," Weir admitted, looking at him with a sort of pitying reverence – the sort of look someone might give Jesus on the crucifix. "You all are, even the objectors."

"The objectors?" Wayson scoffed. "They're worthless cowards who won't fight for their country even when they're asked to!"

"I'm not so sure about that," Weir mused. "The way I see it, it takes a lot of courage to be willing to die, and even more to be willing to kill. But to stick by your morals, even when the world hates you for it; that takes the most courage of all. I could never be as brave as any of that."

"You can't be all that bad," Captain pointed out. "You've got four dogs, two children, and a wife on top of it; now that's something I couldn't face."

Weir smiled. "You get used to it. You'll be getting married soon, won't you Rigby?"

Rigby looked up proudly from the picture he was scribbling of a woman far prettier than a real likeness of his fiancé. "If this war ever gives me the time."

"Poor woman," Captain sighed. "Not only does she look like a dog, but she'll have to put up with seeing your ugly face every day."

Rigby flicked a biscuit at him.

"You know I'm joking," Captain caught it in one hand, attempting to break it between his teeth but giving up in seconds. He tapped it against his forehead. "They should make helmets out of these; a bloody tank couldn't crush this."

He pulled his arm back and threw the thing hard, chipping off a piece of wall. "Could be used for bullets too."

"Oh no," Rigby gasped, eyes focussed on something beyond the tent where Kent was pitched in relative luxury.

"Relax, it's only a wall."

"No," Rigby got slowly to his feet, staring at a small figure approaching the large group of soldiers. "What's he doing here?"

Stack also stood and Captain sat up straighter to gain a decent view of the youth walking hesitantly through the resting platoon. He seemed shorter than before, with none of the pride and bounce he had once possessed, but there was no mistaking the white-blonde hair and puppy dog face. He wobbled slightly as he walked, coat drawn tightly around him, and something told Stack he would be shivering like that even on the hottest day of summer.

"I thought you said he was mad," he whispered, making sure Wayson didn't hear – he had sheltered the boy from what Rigby had seen in his friend's eyes.

"He was," Rigby replied, watching with increasing trepidation. "He *is*. I saw his face; nobody can recover from that. What the hell are they thinking sending him back?"

"Maybe they fixed him?" Captain suggested hopefully, though unconvinced.

Rigby shook his head. "You can't fix that."

"Can't fix what?" Wayson looked over in confusion, first at their faces, then at the spot on which their gazes fell.

"Vincent!" he shot to his feet, eyes ablaze with delight, and rushed to embrace his friend. "I thought they sent you home!"

"No home for me," Waterman smiled shakily, his voice sounding as if the shells on the Somme had reversed the hard work puberty had put into breaking it. "I'm a man of England aren't I; not going to abandon our cause."

The sight of him was pitiful, especially coupled with his attempt of a strong speech. Stack wanted nothing more than to throw him over his shoulders and carry him back home himself, swimming the channel if he had to. But young Wayson was oblivious, buying the brave words and seeming nothing other than delighted to see the boy returned to his company. How easy it had been to trick these youths, he thought sadly, to persuade them to give up their lives when they so gladly saw glory in everything.

"You've missed so much," Wayson was babbling happily, an arm around Waterman's shoulders as he led him over. "Stack's a sergeant now, so you have to actually listen to him, and I shot one of those bastard machine gunners who got Richie; right in the face, and up close too. You should've been there Vince; you could have shot one too."

Waterman nodded and Wayson looked pleased, but the older men could see that behind his faint smile he looked like he was going to be sick.

Stack held out a hand to greet him, shaking it warmly as he supposed he should. "Welcome back son."

"Thank you sir," he gulped, then added. "I'm sorry sir, for not moving forward. I won't do it again."

"What?" Half a year ago the boy had frozen in No Man's Land, and he had had every right to. "Don't you worry about that, we're going to take better care of you now. Sandford has Kent's ear now; he won't let anything like that happen again."

"I don't think he has a choice, sir," Waterman said in a very small voice, remembering the look in the second lieutenant's eyes when he caught himself and Richie that night before his best friend was taken from him. Sandford would be doing nothing for him, he was certain of it. Everyone always said the man hated cowards, and he was the biggest coward of them all. If he hadn't been such a coward, Richie would still be alive.

"Oh, the lieutenant can do anything if he puts his mind to it," Wayson promised. "Now, you have to meet the new boys. We're not the new recruits anymore Vince; we're veterans now." He grinned at Weir before pointing at each man in turn. "This is Weir, Dimery, Grant, Penley, Foden and Harper. This, lads, is my pal Vincent Waterman. He fought with us on the Somme, so you had better show him respect."

Captain chuckled. "Look at your boy, Ben, strutting about like an officer. He'll be taking your place soon enough."

"This is wrong," Rigby shook his head, Wayson giving him no mirth. "He should not be here."

"Oh, give him a break Rig," Captain slouched back down and began to fiddle with another biscuit. "If the boy wants back in, who are we to stop him?"

"No, Rigby's right," Stack continued to watch him with concern. "I'm going to talk to Sandford."

The lieutenant was sat inside his tent, taking breakfast with Kent. Stack couldn't help but notice that the major's spread looked a lot more appetising than theirs, but also that his lieutenant had refused the jam and meat and was nibbling unenthusiastically at a biscuit drowned in thin tea. He looked up as Stack entered, grateful for a reason to put the inedible thing down.

"Sergeant Stack," he greeted him, surprised.

"Lieutenant, I need to speak to you about Waterman."

"He is fit, isn't he?" Sandford asked with concern. "They assured me that any wounds he had sustained healed months ago."

"As far as I know, yes, he is physically fit, sir," Stack told him, holding himself still and straight as he felt Kent's critical eyes. "It's his mind I'm worried about. Private Rigby found him in No Man's Land, still laying under the body of his dead friend and shaking like a mad thing. We can't send him back out there, sir, he's too young anyway; you know that."

"All we know," Kent interrupted before Sandford had a chance to speak. "Is that he was declared a clean bill of health and was to return to his regiment after a spell of leave; the regiment, may I add, that he joined aged nineteen. Tell me sergeant, who do you think has more authority on the matter – the doctors or Private Rigby?"

"Begging your pardon sir," Stack continued. "But the medical corps is under a lot of pressure; what if they made a mistake? There's something not right about him. I got to know him before and something's different."

"War changes people, sergeant," Kent leaned forward, fixing him with a firm authoritative stare. "It is the job of the men in the medical corps to operate under pressure, as it is yours. They do not make mistakes, and I do not expect them from you either. If you are concerned with Waterman's attitude then I suggest you correct it."

"Not his attitude, sir," Stack returned his look as calmly as he could. "There's something wrong with his mind-"

"Correct it."

His tone was final, bearing such little compassion that Stack was tempted to disregard sense and argue further. Thankfully, Sandford spoke first.

"I believe it was me the sergeant wished to speak to, major," he said bravely, looking Kent straight in the eye like an equal. "And I am interested to hear what Private Rigby has to say."

"You do not have the authority to dismiss a man from my company, lieutenant," Kent said icily.

"Nor do I plan to," Sandford replied, getting to his feet. "But this man is in my platoon and therefore it is my place to ensure he is fit and ready for whatever those with authority throw at him. Morale is key, major, you must know that."

He wished he believed that he did. It wasn't the major's fault that the boy had been returned, yet he knew the men would see it that way. He wished Kent would open up a little more, show them he was no monster; just another man who wanted to die in a trench just as little as the rest of them. But there was too much pride beneath that perfect uniform, and too much fear. Until his promotion had brought him closer to the man, Sandford hadn't realised just how much fear.

"Thank you sir," Stack followed him outside. "I'm sorry if I've got you in trouble."

"No," Sandford sighed. "I'm not in trouble. I've never been in trouble, even as a boy; sometimes I wish I was. It feels like I should be after everything I've put you men through."

"Not you sir," Stack assured him. "Just the war."

"Yes, war," the lieutenant mused. He stopped a little way from the tent, within earshot of only Stack. "It ruins the best of us. I'm not sure if you know – I would assume they didn't mention it – but I caught Waterman and Yates the night before Yates died, with their rifles aimed at each other's feet. I always thought I would have any man shot, if I ever caught him being such a shameless coward. I spared them for the sake of manpower and they ran into the bullets as bravely as the rest of us. That was when I realise, there's no such thing as cowardice and bravery; just sense and those who lack it. Where's the sense in any of this, Stack? As far as I can see, the only men with sense are shot for it."

"If Rigby's right, Vincent Waterman has no sense left, sir. He won't be giving you any more trouble of that sort."

"Poor boy," Sandford shook his head. "I should have left them behind, made some excuse. I'm only just realising how little sense I had myself."

"Wayson said to me once," Stack remembered. "Sense doesn't win wars; bravery does. You've got enough of that to keep the rest of us going."

He smiled bashfully. "Thank you sergeant. I would say the same about you."

"I don't know," Stack shrugged, shivering slightly in the snow. "I'm like the rest; just enough sense to know we're better off taking our chances with Fritz than following instinct and trying to run."

"That's not your instinct," the lieutenant said confidently. "You'd only run if every last one of your men was safe first."

"Then that's something we have in common, sir."

"I suppose it is," he adjusted his cap uneasily. "Look, Stack, I know what people think about Major Kent, but I know him better than that now. He feels like the rest of us, it just shows itself differently for him. He's scared too, you know – scared of dying and equally scared of people knowing he's scared. What I'm trying to say is it isn't only you and I who are trying our best for this company."

Stack had to smile; typical Sandford wanting to look out for everybody, even the man to whom he reported. "Why are you telling me this?"

"Because I trust you Stack," he replied. "And because if the men decide to make a fuss about Waterman, it will be him that they blame. Unless you tell them otherwise, if you make them see he's human too. You must know he can do nothing for the boy; it's out of all of our hands."

"I'm afraid I can't do that sir, he apologised, scratching the back of his neck awkwardly. "I can tell them anything you like, but they'll believe what they believe and that'll be based on evidence, not what I say."

"And what do you believe?"

Stack thought for a while about his answer. Sandford may speak to him like an equal, but he was still his superior and an officer.

"I believe that you're the commander of my platoon, and you're a damn good one," he said finally. "I answer to you, and anybody above that is up to you. If you believe in them, I trust your judgement."

Sandford sighed. "Which is a diplomatic way of saying you share their view."

"I'm not going to lie to you, sir."

"No, it's alright, I appreciate it," he shrugged and they began to walk again, heavy boots leaving dents in the whitened ground. "But I do believe in the major; he's a good strategist and he's taught me a lot."

Stack looked up at the officer who only a year ago had been a boy. "Then I trust your judgement."

****

The little Jack Russell padded through freshly fallen snow, its jaws tightly clasped around the dark body of a rat almost as big as it was, leaving a trail along the duckboard. The dog trotted up to where Jackson Weir was readying his bayonet for stand-to and deposited the rodent proudly in his lap before splattering him with the droplets of snow it shook from its fur.

"Thanks for that Toby," he laughed, rubbing the dog fondly behind the ears. "Never wanted anything more than a giant rat in the morning."

"Hey, look, it's Monty!" Harper called excitedly, leaning over to poke the rat. "Your dog finally pulled through."

"Seriously?" Captain stopped in his tracks. "I've been trying to catch that bastard for days."

"Looks like the dog got him after all. Or the cold." Harper pulled a face as he lifted the rat by its tail. "He's frozen solid! Your dog's still useless."

"Leave Toby alone," Weir ruffled the fur on the dog's back as it licked his face happily. "He's still learning, aren't you boy?"

"You'd better stop fussing over him and get up on the firestep," Captain warned him. "According to Kent, even frozen Germans can attack at dawn."

He pulled his elbows into his chest for warmth and exaggerated his shivering. Stack let him get on with it, making Wayson laugh and Rigby roll his eyes. He had improved in the long months since July, as Rigby had promised he would, but behind the jokes and curses Stack was sure the ghost of that young boy still ran towards him through No Man's Land.

"Quiet," Butterfield barked, checking along the line that everybody was in position.

Captain rolled his eyes. "Oh hark at you; you used to be one of us. I remember you and Collie chattering in the cold this time last year."

A flicker of pain shot across the platoon sergeant's face for a second, but he kept it under control. His brows lowered over serious eyes and he lowered his voice along with them. "If you're quiet for me, you won't need the major to come along and give you an earful."

Something moved behind them and Waterman let out a whimper.

"I don't want to go Billy," he said quietly, breathing sharply as he attempted to control the tidal wave of panic bearing down on him from the German lines. "Don't make me go out there."

"You don't have to go anywhere," Wayson took a hand from his rifle to put it warily on his friend's arm – not a great deal younger than him but so much more vulnerable than he could ever remember being. "It's only stand-to."

"I can't go over there!" His hands dropped the gun and he jerked away, Wayson catching him just in time and holding him firmly against the wall.

"You're not going anywhere," he hissed. "You just need to look at it. Look! Nothing there."

"I'm not a coward," Waterman squeezed his eyes tight shut, muttering to himself as his fists clenched and unclenched. "I'm not a coward. Keep moving forward."

"He's going to get us all killed," Rigby said later, watching Waterman forcing his shovel into the frosty mud.

Captain had finished his work early, as usual, and lay back against the wall with his helmet pulled over his eyes to shield them from the glare of the winter sun. The odd snowflake fluttered through the air and settled on his chin, making him twitch as it melted into water against his warm skin. Rigby left the rest of the small frosty mound to Stack and dropped himself down next to Captain, stretching out his back with a loud click.

"I don't know what the doctors were thinking," Stack flung a sandbag onto the parapet. "Just one diagnosis of shellshock and he'd be safe at home and no danger to anyone."

"It's not shellshock," Captain muttered from under his helmet. "He can control his limbs."

"Sometimes," Stack added.

"They're not allowed," Rigby told them gloomily.

"What?" Captain pushed up his helmet and stared at him. "What do you mean, they're not allowed?"

"Shellshock," Rigby continued. "It's not allowed to exist anymore."

"That's bollocks," Captain scowled. "You can't just forbid an illness to exist."

"I know that," Rigby shrugged, stretching out his limbs irritatingly. "But that's what they're doing. There's a shortage of men isn't there? We're losing enough to shells and frostbite; can't afford to lose even more to 'malingering'. At least that's the way they see it. They're sending as many back here as they can, and apparently in a few months it'll be completely illegal to diagnose it at all."

"Nope, no more shellshock." He shook his head. "It's got a different name now, and one that doesn't come with any honours or Blighty leave – NYDN; Not Yet Diagnosed, Nervous. You want to know what the lads in fourth are calling it? Not Yet Dead, Nearly."

"Don't be so bloody morbid Rigby," Captain's face had been growing darker with anger at every word the man spoke and now he shot to his feet, knocking a stack of rifles to the floor with a clatter as he stomped away down the duckboard.

"What's the matter with him?" Rigby asked, annoyance clear in his voice. "I was only telling the truth."

"Not yet dead, nearly?" Stack replied incredulously. "And you wonder why he's bothered? It's like a death sentence, for Waterman and for him."

"It's a joke. The amount of times he's told me to get shot, and I take it. Hasn't he realised by now that not everything's trumpets and glory in this stupid country?"

****

"Poor boy," Butterfield commented, joining Stack as he crunched down the duckboard to his watch post. "I got promoted to change things like this; I guess even platoon sergeant isn't enough."

"I don't think it's as simple as that," Stack replied. "Sandford would have already done something if it was."

"I doubt it happens everywhere," Butterfield shook his head. "Just our bloody major is an idiot."

Stack was taken aback; he was quite sure that platoon sergeants were not supposed to talk about their superiors in such a way.

"You don't have to pretend to like him with me," he read the look on the older man's face. "Lieutenant Sandford may be a soft young boy who wants to see good in everyone, but he doesn't fool me. I know what it's like to be lower down the ranks, remember. I still know what an unreasonable bastard he can be."

"The lieutenant said he was scared."

"He is, very much so," Butterfield shrugged, no sympathy on his face. "He's the most paranoid man I've ever met; jumps at his own shadow every time a soldier puts a toe out of line. The trouble is he's scared of the wrong things. He'd gladly lead us all to our deaths if it would prevent a mutiny. His bloody pride is all he cares about. But you know what they say – pride comes before a fall – well sometimes I think I wouldn't mind being that fall. Imagine his face if he was transferred to make way for me as company commander."

Stack highly doubted it would work that way, but he kept his thoughts to himself and Butterfield continued.

"There was a machine gun bunker hidden in a shell hole." He didn't have to elaborate; both men knew exactly what he was talking about. "It massacred my men and a fair few of yours if I remember correctly. He had patrols, he knew it was there, just like he knew the wire wasn't cut as well as we'd like, but did he warn anybody? I'm certain Sandford didn't know or he would have rearranged the line to deal with it, and none of us had a bloody clue. He did everything properly – he couldn't risk a panic or he'd lose his precious discipline. He couldn't bring himself to stray from his higher orders and because of that people died who shouldn't have. I can't forgive him for that."

"Collie," Stack murmured.

"I loved that whole section like they were my brothers."

"You're not the only one who's lost a brother out here, sir," Stack said heavily.

He tried not to think about it – and the responsibility of being a sergeant helped a great deal – but every now and then he still felt the earth pressing down on him, and the shock when he realised that Edward had not been pulled out with him.

"But I honestly don't think Kent could have done anything about it," he continued. "You'd be better off if you didn't try to blame anyone."

"But you see, I can't do that Stack," his strong face crumpled slightly, a quiver in his throat giving away the grief that crushed him every day. "Because if there's no one else to blame, that leaves only me."

"Then blame the Germans; it's safer that way."

"Oh trust me, I do. Before I go down I'll take every German I can lay my hands on and I'll laugh doing it. But when it comes to it, the Germans are just the same as us; they're not killers, not naturally. It's bad leadership that gets people killed, Stack." He looked fiercely down the trench. "I used to throw myself at every opportunity possible just for the glory of it, Jim thought I was mad. I realise now there are more important things than just glory. I need more responsibility, to stop things like this. I know Sandford tries, but he's just a child. If this company was mine, I wouldn't let any of you get hurt again."

Stack thought over what the man had said while on watch. Butterfield had never been the most realistic of people, but at least it was only his own abilities he overestimated – he would throw himself into the lion's jaws but never risk the men with more than a cub. Stack wasn't sure if he would make a good commander overall, but he would certainly be a lot fairer than Kent.

It was his emotions that got in the way; where Sandford had grown into a sensible, intelligent lieutenant, he could see Butterfield throwing all strategy to the wind if something rattled his grief. It was something Stack tried to learn from, not allowing himself to mourn for the likes of Edward and little Tommy Miller, letting Captain's jokes divert him. It was what they would have wanted, and Collie too, if only Butterfield could see that. The young man wouldn't have liked to see the look of pain that crossed his friend's face every time he was remembered.

The sound of movement snapped him into alertness, but it was only Toby the dog sniffing for rats. The ditches on the other side of No Man's Land were too quiet these days. From what he could gather from those previously on the front line, there hadn't been a small raid or even sniper activity for weeks, despite the men becoming more and more careless with fires and cigarette as the cold lingered on.

Most saw this as a welcome relief – a chance to endure the snow without having to deal with shellfire on top of that – but Sandford was obviously disturbed by the silence and this feeling rubbed off onto Stack, especially after the lieutenant had shared with him worrying sightings reported by the reconnaissance planes.

"Hey Ben," a familiar voice made him jump. "Want some tea?"

"Jesus Cap, don't sneak up on me like that. I'm supposed to be keeping an eye on our Jerry friends."

"No point in doing that pal," Captain sprung up beside him, perching precariously while holding out a tin filled with something that looked vaguely like tea. "They're long gone. Bloody cowards. Now have some tea; Rigby made it so it tastes like toenails, but at least it hasn't frozen yet."

The 'tea' tasted more like dirty water than toenails – not that he knew what those tasted like – and ice had already begun to form around the rim, but it felt good to hold something warm in his chilblained hands.

"Would be nice if the planes got it wrong and they were just running away."

"They are running away," Captain said certainly. "No matter how fortified their new lines are, they're still behind the current one so they're giving us free ground. That's called running away as far as I'm concerned."

He smiled and patted his friend on the arm. "You worry too much."

"Says you," Stack raised an eyebrow.

"I know, I know," Captain took a swig from a flask that definitely did not contain watery tea. "You don't have to mock me for it. Besides, I'm making a real effort now, if you hadn't noticed. Since poor Waterman came back I think more about him than anything else. I look at him and think, 'bugger, I really must seem pathetic'. That's how everyone sees him, isn't it, and there's no way I want that for me." He looked his friend in the eye. "Sorry Ben, I must have been a real drag."

Stack shook his head. "Do you think Waterman is a drag?"

"No," he moved his foot, watching the unsettled snow floating down from the firestep. "No, I don't. I think he's a bloody brave little boy and I want to see him rewarded for that. His mate died all over him and he still tries; I don't think I could do that."

"Well I've got to say," Stack smiled. "It's good to see you not sleeping again. I was starting to worry I might actually get my six hours a night."

Captain laughed. "Don't lie Benji; even without the snow, the rats, the risk of imminent death, you still would've been awake all night worrying."

He pulled a face, mocking himself, but there was sincerity in his eyes when he spoke. "Seriously though, thanks. It means a lot."

11.

"They never tell you, do they," Rigby complained, breaths fogging up the air in front of his face. "The amount of bloody digging we have to do. They're full of honour and glory and shooting Huns, but they never say before you sign up that you'll be nothing more than a glorified rabbit."

"You know what I thought," Captain said irritably as he forced his shovel further into the frosty ground. "I thought they were meant to be retreating."

"They are," Stack told him for what felt like the thousandth time. "That's why we're digging."

"If they've got such a great line to fall back to, why are they stopping off at every outpost from here to Berlin? Do they want us to wipe them out before they even get there?"

"Except we won't have time to wipe them out," Rigby grumbled. "Because we're too busy digging stupid holes."

"These stupid holes give you a place to sleep," Weir reminded him, still with little Toby whose paws were now furrowing into the ground with gusto in an attempt to help his human companions.

"If we stopped digging and killed the buggers, we could sleep in there." Rigby swung his shovel to point at the village atop the hill.

"Unfortunately, private, no 'buggers' can be killed until we receive the orders," Lieutenant Sandford appeared out of nowhere, causing Rigby to quickly return to work. "And at present, orders are to dig in and wait, so I suggest you dig in."

"What do you think we're doing?" Captain retorted, flinging a shovelful of dirt a little higher than necessary before quickly adding "Sir."

"I don't mind digging sir," Wayson spoke up, stretching himself to full height. "Better a sore back than a bullet through the head from no cover."

"Good man Wayson," Sandford nodded to him and continued on his way.

"Why don't you do it all yourself if you love it so much?" Rigby hissed when he was out of earshot.

Wayson paid him no attention, too busy beaming to himself at the word the lieutenant used to describe him; 'man'. With that word in his ears he would gladly dig a trench all the way to Russia.

However, poor Wayson's burst of pride would be short-lived. It was with a sense of gladness that the battalion finally received the command to advance on the outpost – anything was better than sitting in the cold, and the relative quiet of winter was unnerving – and the preparations were quick and efficient. The artillery had already begun their shelling of the target, and Wayson was particularly excited to know that the cavalry too would be part of the assault.

He had had his first real taste of victory in the wood and was eager to repeat the feeling, the boredom of winter having dulled any sense of danger he may have fostered in the summer. His helmet was straight, his uniform flawless and his rifle ready.

"What?" the boy could not believe what he was hearing.

"I need you and Waterman to guard the trench," Stack repeated.

He had made his decision a long time ago; Waterman should not fight, and having Wayson behind the lines to look after him would also serve to take a load off his mind.

"But I can fight, you know I can!" he protested. "Vincent can guard the trench himself. If you give me a shot at the Jerries I won't let you down."

"I never said you'd let anyone down," Stack said patiently. "There are always people left to guard the trench, and today one of those people is you."

"But there's nothing in it!" This was beyond cruel. If he had just wanted to guard something useless he could have applied to the estate; he wanted to do something important. "We only dug it a few days ago!"

The sergeant lowered his voice and bent forward.

"For God's sake Wayson," he said in a harsh whisper. "Vincent Waterman can't fight, and who knows what he'd do if we left him here alone? I need you; you're the one who knows him best. Don't make this difficult for me."

"Yes sir."

He watched as they climbed the shallow trench walls and scuttled away, attempting to control the bitterness he felt towards the boy beside him. He was nothing more than a child and Wayson had never wanted him there in the first place. If only Rob hadn't been so intent on being so goddamned fair. Yes, he and his best friend certainly did have the right to go to war; they had the skills and the stomach for it, and in all evidence but their birth certificates were no more underage than Kitchener himself.

Richie and Vincent had never had the skills for war and, though they were brave lads, war had broken them. Rob was the one who had allowed them to think they could do it, and now Rob was swanning around somewhere along the front shooting Germans left, right and centre and carrying none of the responsibility for their fates. He had that knack of getting away with anything and always coming out on top in the end; something Wayson had always admired and envied.

He turned to the whimpering boy at his side, fidgeting unnaturally, and wished he could say something inspirational like Rob, to stop him shivering.

The horses of the cavalry looked glorious as they charged, heads held high and muscles rippling, hair flying out behind them like their own equine banner that announced to the world the superiority of their race. Hooves thundered up the hill towards the outpost, throwing up gales of snow in their wake that danced in the face of the infantry like swirling confetti; the elements celebrating the wonder of these courageous animals.

Then they began to fall, one by one crashing to the ground like great wounded battleships, the snow sent into the air by their tumbling bodies now flecked with crimson. The infantry stepped over them, boots accustomed to navigating bodies, faces stained by dirt and the bite of the cold. It was these men who walked forward as the horses wheeled around, the commanding voice of the big guns ordering them back to the past where they belonged. There was no place here for beauty and pride; this was a war of grit.

Snowflakes were falling heavily as they approached a dip in the earth, where the artillery had prepared a rubble of shelter for the advancing soldiers. Stack threw himself temporarily out of the sights of the defenders, pressing his back against a crumble of stone and dirt next to Sandford. Ice was already thick on the broken walls but nobody felt it anymore with the heat of attack coursing through their veins.

"I want you up front," Sandford ordered, barely pausing for breath after his sprint between holes and debris. "It isn't only artillery; there's a hoard of machine guns that'll cause us trouble on all sides. Stack, MacDonald, can I trust you to deal with the right flank?"

"Yes sir."

"Good," he lifted his head to peer over the wall, pulling it down again with haste. "Corporal Green's men will be behind you. If all goes well, we'll advance. If not, get yourselves out – don't wait for orders. I want living men more than obedient ones, understand?"

"Yes sir," Stack said again, holding in an amused smile. The lieutenant made his dash back to Butterfield's side and Captain caught his friend's eye.

"Imagine if Kent heard him talking like that; he'd be court-martialled for sure!"

"So would we if he caught us running away, no matter who had told us to," Rigby said dubiously, hoisting his rifle to a better position.

"We'd better not run then," Stack grunted, readying his own gun. "Come on lads, let's go."

The big guns Sandford spoke of were on top form, guarding the inconsequential village as if it were Berlin itself, pounding the ground around it as the attackers scurried forward only to be pushed back again. Their own flanks of artillery seemed nothing in comparison; creating an impressive mess but doing little to put the enemy off. They crouched in the holes it provided, making dash after dash towards the outpost only to be halted again by a barrage of machine gun fire.

It was certainly not the triumphant charge they had hoped for, as Wayson could see from his post. He had become excited for a while – perhaps he would in fact be needed if the Germans broke out to chase the failing attackers back – but he soon realised they were not going anywhere. After all, the Germans were retreating; what good would it do them to take trenches in the wrong direction? He sat firmly planted on their icy mound of a firestep, eyes almost as icy as he stared out at his fellows.

"I should be out there," he muttered, picking at the buttons on his tunic. "I should have gone to London with Rob; we could be out there together, not babysitting you. Why are you even here, Vince? You obviously don't want to be. Why don't you just tell them your real age and go home?"

"I don't want to be a coward," he replied, wincing at the sound of a shell.

"You wouldn't be," Wayson remained as he was, unmoved by the noises that held Waterman captive. "You'd just be being sensible."

"But what about you?"

"What about me?"

"If I hand myself in, what if they look into you too? I don't want to be the reason you get sent home."

Wayson felt his chest drop as the anger subsided, filling instead with guilt. He wrenched his eyes from the scene around the village and fixed them instead on the face of his friend. His true friend, who had joined this adventure with him and stuck it out even when everything had gone wrong.

"Vince," he choked on a lump in his throat, incredibly touched. "You don't have to worry about me. I don't think they'd deliberately go out of their way to lose a soldier. If you want to go home, go. I'd be happier if you were safe."

Waterman smiled nervously.

"Rob should've listened to you, shouldn't he? You always knew Richie and me couldn't do it. Did you know, we tried?" His voice broke and his shoulders started to shake. "We tried to get home the night before the push, Richie and me. If Sandford hadn't found us first we would've shot each other's feet and never had to walk into those machine guns."

"But Vince," Wayson gasped. "They would have you for the firing squad. You would never have got away with that."

"We used to think we were invincible," he said sadly, staring down at his boots. "Rob did too. He believed in us, and that's what we kept telling each other after Sandford found us and that's what we were thinking when we went over the top. Rob thought we could do it, and at the end I think Richie did too. He tried to keep me moving because he thought I could make it; he thought I could be a true man of England like Rob always said we would be. How could I go home now? I don't mind what the rest of the world thinks, but I can't live with myself thinking that Richie and Rob are ashamed of me."

"They're not, Vince," Wayson slid himself down from the mound to sit beside his friend. "They're proud of you; prouder of you than they are of me. After what happened to you, you still came back. Your head plays tricks on you and you're still here; that makes you braver than any of us."

"Really?" he continued to look at his boots. "I know you're trying Billy, but you could never understand what goes on in my head. I don't understand it myself."

Stack and Mackie crouched either side of a head of bricks, holding their rifles steady as they attempted to silence the machine gunners as a sniper would. The others were less precise, firing in bursts and hoping they hit at least something German. The runner slid in behind them so quickly that Rigby spun and almost put a bullet through his head before he realised he was one of their own.

"It's no good," he panted, trying to ignore the fact he had nearly been shot. "Orders are we pull back."

"Right, Stack needed no further persuasion. "Pack up, you heard the man, let's get out of here."

They did as he ordered, removing their eyes from the sights and turning to sprint – or at least run as fast as their packs allowed them – back towards the scrapes from which they came. Stack caught sight of Butterfield taking one last longing glance up at the village before he also turned his back on it and followed them down the hill. The projector of the field guns followed them back to their holes, but calmed after a long enough battering to encourage them to stay put.

They had been quiet for a while when night fell; the dark bringing a welcome relief for soldiers who had spent the last part of the day crouched in whichever part of the trench they had found themselves returning to. Under cover of darkness, Lieutenant Sandford's platoon fell back into place, their leader swiftly counting the heap of tired bodies and assigning watches before calling for one of his sergeants.

"Sergeant Stack." The older man got to his feet, his head above the parapet of the hastily-dug trench. "Can I talk to you?"

Captain sat up straighter, fixing the lieutenant with curious eyes. He whispered a quick "good luck" to his friend as he passed, following Sandford along the bay and around a corner. They kept walking until they found a stretch that was relatively empty, where they stopped, Sandford seating his tall frame in the mud to keep his head out of view of snipers.

"Do you not have an office, sir?" Stack asked. Nothing should shock him by now, but the sight of Kent's second sitting in the dirt didn't seem right.

"The major has a place behind the lines," he told him. "But the problem with that is the great distance between here and there. I am the commander of this platoon and I'd like to be on hand if I'm needed. But enough about my sleeping arrangements; you set Wayson and Waterman to watch the trench earlier."

"I did sir."

"I didn't tell you to assign anybody to guard duty," the lieutenant's tone was authoritative, but the look in his eyes gave away that he wasn't really angry, just interested. "I had enough good men to keep our humble scratchings safe. Were you really that concerned about this stretch of dirt?"

"No sir," Stack admitted. Sandford patted the ground beside him, offering a seat, and he took it. "I was concerned about Waterman."

"As are we all," he sighed, a thick mist rising from his mouth. "He's rattled and a liability to everyone, including himself. I only wish there was something we could do for him."

"There is," the sergeant said gruffly. "We don't send him out. We don't leave him on watch by himself and the only time he leaves the line is when we're all going behind it. We'll make him last until the end, whether he likes it or not."

"That's all well and good," Sandford said heavily. "But how long until somebody queries why he never does anything? And even if we could make it work, do you really think a boy in his condition could last until the end? When is the end, Stack? They said it would be before Christmas, then they said July; we're still here. No, we can't just put our faith in ends anymore, we have to do something more."

"What though?" Stack let his head drop back against the wall, frustration making it heavy. "What have we got that can get him out of here? We know he's ill, but the doctors don't believe it. We know he's underage, but we have no proof. We don't even have a birthday."

"The twelfth of August, 1900."

A small voice attracted their attention to the end of the bay, where Wayson stood in the shadows, half obscured by the corner. There was a startled look about his face that evening; more the face of a guilty schoolboy than the gallant soldier mask he wore so well, reminding Stack that he too was too young to be there. His skinny limbs were pulled inwards as if to protect himself and he seemed unable to raise his eyes to any point above their chins.

It was the ultimate betrayal, Stack realised. The twitches in his legs gave away the urge to turn back and pretend he hadn't said anything, but it had had to be done for his friend's sake. The boy was certainly brave.

"Private Wayson," Sandford greeted him. "Shouldn't you be on watch?"

"MacDonald relieved me," he said quietly, avoiding their eyes. "The twelfth of August, 1900; that's Vincent Waterman's birthday. He's sixteen, fifteen when he joined. I can give you his address too. His father's really proud of him but you might be able to persuade him to send a birth certificate if you do it right. Don't let him think his son's a coward or he'd kill him himself."

Sandford stared at him like he was a gift from the heavens, the hardened battle commander's composition slipping for a brief moment back to the youth he had been when he first received his commission.

"It's worth a shot." He was a lieutenant again, out of his trance and already getting to his feet. "Wayson, can you tell Major Kent what you just told me?"

"Major Kent?"

The boy's eyes widened. The major had always held some kind of awe with him, no matter how much Captain belittled him. When he had joined the company, he had seen their moustached and hard-faced commander as a role model; an inspiring and courageous leader whom he should follow to the end.

As time went on this golden image tarnished, but instead of becoming a figure of ridicule the major began to scare him instead. He was unstable, Wayson thought – perhaps almost as much as Vincent though in a different way – and instability was a dangerous trait for a leader. He would much have preferred to take his information to the strength of Sandford and Stack and let them deal with it.

But he was a man of England, he reminded himself, and if he was too afraid of his own major to help his friend how on earth could he hold his head high against the enemy?

"Yes sir," he nodded decidedly. "I can."

"Don't worry," Sandford said reassuringly. "We'll be with you. I have a mind to take you there now. Stack, can your men spare you a little longer?"

"Yes sir," Stack nodded, also getting to his feet but ensuring his head still bent below the sandbags. He stopped as they approached the skinny boy with his dirty face and unevenly cropped hair, looking him in the eye. "Thank you Wayson. You did the right thing."

"I know sir," he attempted a smile before following them through a communications trench that lead back behind the lines to Kent's quarters.

The company commander was pouring over maps and messages when they arrived, squinting in the dim gaslight as he attempted to find an acceptable explanation for their failure that day. His batman was nowhere to be seen, banished so as to avoid distractions as the wiry man worked his nerves to breaking point. The addition of three more bodies to his working space was not, therefore, a welcome sight.

"Yes?" he spoke irritably as they entered. Sandford seated himself opposite, while his companions hovered more nervously in the doorway. "What is it lieutenant?"

"This is Private Wayson, sir."

"What has he done?"

He looked Wayson up and down with scrutinising eyes. Stack had been sure to straighten the boy's cap and brush off the excess dirt from his uniform before they arrived, and he stood as tidily as he could.

"He hasn't done anything wrong," Sandford quickly corrected him. "He has information you need to hear."

"Information?" the major's ears pricked at this and he sat forward in his chair, suddenly interested. "You were on a patrol? Well spit it out then."

"No sir, it's not information about Germans, I've never been on a patrol sir." Kent slouched back again. "It's about Private Waterman, sir."

Kent listened reluctantly to what Wayson had to say, and even more reluctantly as Sandford quizzed him further and began a discussion about how best to address the issue. Eventually he agreed that the matter should be reported, and he would do so himself first thing in the morning. That ought to keep them happy. In fact, he would be glad to see him go; one less excuse for the men to bear ill feelings towards their commander.

"You may go," he told them after making his promise, waving a hand at the exit. "Except you, Stack. I'd like a word with you alone."

Wayson thanked Kent, before turning to the sergeant. "Please get him out of here."

"What about you?" he replied quietly.

"I'm a man, sir," he said proudly. "I am quite fine."

"You are," Stack agreed, patting Wayson's arm. "I'll see you back at the line."

He returned to his seat as Sandford led Wayson past. He could think of nothing the major would need to speak to him about, especially not alone. Unless… What if they had found Rob? The first time he had entered the major's office, his brother had been beside him. The second time, he had lost both brothers and his guilt at Sylvie's distress had made him refuse the offer of compassionate leave. His hands shook as he forced himself to look the major in the eye, trying to read his expression. How could he ever go home if they had lost Rob too? It was too much, too much for one family to take.

Captain was waiting for him as he stepped back out into the night, lounging on the ground and pulling cheerfully on a cigarette. He sprung to his feet as he saw his friend emerge, excited curiosity lighting up his face.

"So," he greeted him with a heavy pat on the back. "You a general yet?"

"What are you doing here Cap?" Stack chuckled. "You could have been asleep by now if you're not needed for work."

"I don't sleep, remember," he flashed a grin and skipped ahead a little. "And it isn't every day that your best friend gets called off to speak to the major alone is it? So, what did he want? If you get promoted again can I have the section?"

"Lay off, Cap, I'm not promoted and I don't want to be," he pulled his arms about himself as the wind reminded him that winter was still going strong. "He's going to try to get Waterman home though. And apparently the French are going to mutiny."

"Bugger," the smile slid a little behind the smoke. "They're not pulling out are they?"

"I don't know," he shrugged. "It's only rumours for now."

"If they do, we're finished," Captain frowned. "The whole front to hold and no reinforcements. What's it got to do with you though?"

"He's worried we'll do the same, wants me to look out for him and report back anything suspicious."

"Nice." For some reason, Captain looked impressed. "You're really in there with the officers now, aren't you. You'll have Sandford to thank for that."

"Thank?" Stack pulled a face. "He wants me to spy on my friends."

"Yeah, but you won't." Captain flicked the cigarette to the ground and pushed his hands into his pockets. "What is there to spy on; bad dreams and complaints about the tea? It's a compliment, that's all it is Ben; you make sure you take it as one."

"I guess." He hadn't seen it as a compliment, but now he thought about it Kent had said that Sandford had suggested him. If the lieutenant thought it a good idea, perhaps he was getting stressed for nothing. It was good to know he was trusted, in any case.

"What if it goes to my head?" he joked. "How many things could I tell him about you, hey?"

"None," his friend replied. "Because I'd box your face in before you could open your mouth."

"Really?" he raised an eyebrow. "You think you'd be up to it? I hope you're not forgetting all those times you lost to me before."

They reached the rough slope in the mud that would take them back beneath the parapet and onwards to the main trench and sprung down, landing with a soft crunch in the snow.

"Who in the company would you most want to take on one to one?" Captain asked. "Friendly, not trying to bash their brains out."

"That's easy," Stack replied. "Butterfield. You?"

"Waterman?"

"Waterman?" Stack repeated. "Even you would be too much for him. It'd be over in a few seconds."

"No," Captain held out a hand to stop him, creeping forward towards a huddled shape laying in a bundle on the firestep. "Is that Waterman?"

Only a face protruded from the coat he clutched tightly about himself, moonlight reflecting off snow to make it look eerily white. He was still – no dreams troubling him tonight – with eyes shut to the world.

"Why is he not with the others?" Captain whispered. "Should we move him?"

Stack shook his head. "He can sleep where he likes; he's going home tomorrow."

"He doesn't look very warm," Captain frowned. "We should get him somewhere more sheltered."

He reached out to touch the boy's cheek. "Shit Ben, he's freezing."

"Vince," the sergeant gently put a hand on each shoulder and squeezed. "Time to get up."

The frost on his eyelashes was undisturbed by lids that stayed closed. He didn't move, not even to breathe.

"He's too cold Ben," he could hear the panic entering Captain's voice. "Get up Vince, God why is he so cold? Get up Vince, you're going home!"

Stack put a shaking hand against the boy's icy neck. No pulse, only the flutter of snow.

"No," he choked, seizing a pale wrist. "No, no, no, you're going home."

He thrust a hand beneath the blanket to pull the boy into his arms, and it touched cold metal. He pulled his arm out and the blanket fell away, revealing a dark stain in the frost where Vincent Waterman's knife had found flesh.

"Oh God!" Captain backed away, his voice and face contorted into something ugly as hot tears burned through the snow on his cheeks. He sunk to the ground, quivering fingers gripping the mud of the firestep where the sixteen year old had taken his life in this frozen corner of hell.

Stack couldn't find words, or tears. He was numb as the boy that lay in front of him, separate from the world where men killed and died and they called it right. Snowflakes settled on his eyelids but he didn't feel them. He stared helplessly at the frozen face on the firestep, the ringing in his ears drowning out the gulping sounds that came from where his friend had fallen to his knees, until there was nothing left but him and the boy and the cold. One more day and he could have been going home.

****

"No more digging, Vince."

Rigby lay down his shovel and joined the circle around the little wooden cross. They stared solemnly for a few moments, each lost in their own thoughts, remembering the boy who had danced on tables less than a year ago. Then they turned away. The platoon joined the column of D Company in their march onwards, boots crunching dolefully through the snow, wind biting their faces, eyes fixed ahead. There was nothing they could do for him now.

12.

Rob scrubbed the button brush along his teeth in a hurry – the army issue toothbrush was still unused and ready for inspections. He spat on the ground, quickly running a comb through his hair and ignoring the dirt behind his ears; he would only be ten times dirtier soon enough. He pulled on his shirt and checked his reflection in a shattered shaving mirror, pleased with what he saw. Even his mother couldn't mistake him for a child today. He was a grown man through and through; taller and broader than half his crewmates and proudly sporting a dash of hair across his jaw and lip. He lowered his eyebrows fiercely as he set the silvery pieces back down, adrenaline flooding his body.

They were all already congregated around the tank by the time Lieutenant Cuthbert emerged from the darkness; Rob and Alfie impatient to get moving while Valentine and Firetop seemed less keen, the latter the colour of sour milk. Carthorse was the only one truly calm, leaning back against Betsy and watching the heavy clouds trudge across the early autumn sky.

There was likely to be more rain, he could tell, and heavy mud to navigate the tank through as well as the network of trenches and craters already anticipated. He breathed slowly, the cogs of his mind turning as he visualised the terrain and the actions he would need to take to carry the younger men to their goal. He could feel their anxiety like a buzz in the air – even the lieutenant's – but he had no need for such feelings. Killing and dying was not what he was here to think about; he was only the driver.

"Alright chaps," Cufflinks greeted them curtly. Rob couldn't help but notice the faint lines below his eyes that gave away a lack of sleep, but there was nothing about his expression that suggested fatigue or fear, and his moustache was just as splendid as ever. "Who wants another crack at the Bosch?"

"We do, sir," Rob replied fiercely. "We'll have Passchendaele by lunchtime."

"Aye," Colm nodded. "We'll make that bloody Kaizer think twice about messing with us."

"We'll make him think twice about bloody breathing," Dafydd added, making the lieutenant smile.

"I've got myself a good unit," he regarded them fondly. "Chin up Furnace; the cowards will turn and run at just one look at Betsy, we won't be out there long."

"We've never fought in a battle as big as this before," the gearsman muttered anxiously.

"Then we've never seen quite so many Germans running away before," the lieutenant smiled reassuringly. "You just concentrate on your gears and you'll be fine. Allenby, Jones." He turned to the gunners. "I don't need to tell you to blast as many as you can before they run."

"No you don't sir," Dafydd assured him, nudging Rob with his elbow. "Me and Whipper have it sorted."

"Good," he nodded. "Baker, Powell; you make sure you keep the ammunition coming."

"Yes sir," they said together.

"Then what are we waiting for?"

He clapped his hands and they scurried into the tank, Rob attempting to enter first but being pushed back by Dafydd.

"Sergeant," the lieutenant tapped Carthorse discreetly on the arm. "Could I have a word?"

"Of course sir."

"I'm going to need you on top form today," Cufflinks said in a low whisper. "The battle is fierce and the mud is fiercer. They've had to abandon field guns that sank and countless men have been lost already. It's only going to get worse if the rain doesn't ease; they need us to finish this before the whole salient becomes a swamp. Driving is not going to be easy for you."

"Don't you think we should tell the others?" Carthorse asked.

"They know all they need to," the lieutenant told him decidedly. "There's no need to worry them unnecessarily."

"You think this is unnecessary?"

"The infantry have dealt with more than a bit of mud for years; we don't need to be worried, just cautious. Terrain is for you and I to think about, let the others focus on driving Fritz back."

"Don't you worry about that sir," Rob called from the sponson, where he had hung back to listen. "You two concentrate on your mud, leave the bastards to us."

Carthorse smiled. "You've been spending too much time with our Daffodil; he's a bad influence on your language."

Rob pulled a face. "You sound like my father."

All flaps were pulled shut long before they reached the battlefield – the gunners and driver using only periscopes to view the outside world – and vision was almost impossible within the tank. Each man was left with only his own thoughts as the sounds of war grew closer and the mud grew thicker, throwing them about as the tank lurched through it, pulling hard to avoid being grounded. Rob kept his eyes on the periscope, peering out at the devastation; each broken horse and abandoned vehicle spurring him further in his eagerness to punish those who had caused this. He gripped the gun, hands shaking with adrenalin, ready to use it.

His pulse quickened as the front line came nearer and nearer, until the shells fell close enough to shake the ground they moved on. He watched the thickening stream of men as they passed – vast amounts of wounded retreating from battle and their replacements moving forward with as much haste as they could muster in the mud. Some, he noticed, were waist deep and he realised just how true the lieutenant's words had been earlier; the whole place was practically a swamp already.

Betsy's pace slowed as she slogged her way through churned ground, but they were starting to leave the wounded behind and reach the flooded gouges from which those men had emerged that morning. Rob steadied his grip on the six-pounder, swinging it heavily to face the lines.

Smack. He tripped forward, eye pressed hard against the sight – he still hadn't learned to avoid that one. He pushed himself back up angrily, resisting the urge to take his hands from the gun to rub his sore face. The Germans must have found their target, and hit dangerously close.

A thin shaft of light broke through the darkness as Carthorse opened the driver's flap, stinging his eyes with its suddenness. The sergeant leant forward in his hard seat to peer out at the ground ahead, Lieutenant Cufflinks leaning over his shoulder to share the view. As his eyes reacquainted themselves with the light, Rob could make out the words he signed to his driver in the half-light.

Just mud – I'll find a path, the lieutenant was saying, attempting to slide past Carthorse to the door. *Follow me.*

No, the sergeant replied, shaking his head firmly. *Too dangerous. I'll see through the flap.*

I'm fine, Cufflinks dismissed him, looking very brave and commanding and making Rob incredibly proud to be in his unit. *Have to hurry.*

He made for the door, just as a large explosion from outside knocked the tank's side and forced Rob's face back into the sight. He pulled it away again to see the sergeant's gloved hand clasped firmly around the lieutenant's arm.

No, he repeated with his free hand.

Angrily, Cufflinks abandoned the crew's sign language and pulled the sergeant close by his shirt to shout in his ear.

"For God's sake sergeant, I am your commander!"

"And I am your driver!" Carthorse shouted back, keeping his grip tight. "And this tank isn't going anywhere without you in it!"

Cufflinks glared at him, but dropped his collar and reverted back to signing before sitting down again. *Fine, I'll deal with you later.*

The tank began to move again, Firetop and Valentine working furiously with the gears as her engine strained against the heavy mud around her. Silhouetted against the line of day that penetrated through the open flap, Rob could see Carthorse expertly working the clutch and throttle, slowly driving Betsy free of her sticky constraints. Another shell burst ahead of her, but served only to clear the way for her escape from the hole. Carthorse's shoulders relaxed as her nose emerged back onto more level ground and thudded back to earth as the tank straightened.

Rob pulled himself back into a suitable position, glancing at Cufflinks for approval before eagerly firing a return shot. True aim was impossible with the vibrations the tank suffered when moving, but he had been trained well in estimations and confidence shone in the intense smile that broke across the face beneath the mask.

Alfie lost no time in reloading and Rob fired again, the blood of vengeance surging through his veins. Naughty Betsy crawled forwards, looming on the German lines like creeping death, bearing down on his father's murderers. His clothes were soaked with sweat, and the splash of molten lead from the core of German bullets was starting to find its way through gaps in Betsy's armour, but he had never felt better. He was a war hero. Billy would be so jealous.

Not everybody in the belly of Betsy was doing so well, however. Alfie was slowing with every round he loaded, and as the heat and fumes took hold Valentine was left manning the gears alone as

Firetop's consciousness gave way. And they were not advancing anywhere near as fast as they had hoped.

Not the fastest vehicle at the best of times, the pull of the mud and the interruption of shellfire had slowed the tank to a snail's pace, the stricken infantry walking and falling behind her. Lieutenant Cufflinks was obviously aggravated, leaving the currently useless brakes and stumbling about the tank, checking up on Dafydd and Rob and attempting to revive poor Firetop. Another near miss rocked the tank, Rob noticing to his horror the carcass of another lying on her side in the mud as they passed.

"Hurry up Ollie!" he yelled, shock telling him to fire faster before Betsy fell victim to the same fate.

How could a tank be defeated so easily? They were the pride of the army, the terror of German nightmares, the machine that would win them the war.

A sharp pain burned through Rob's arm as a hot splash of lead found its way through his sleeve and he swung the gun to survey the scene while awaiting Alfie's ammunition.

"We're drawing the fire!" he shouted, unsure if the others could even hear him. "We're saving the men; they're only shooting the tanks!"

"Bloody shoot them back then!" he heard the lieutenant faintly over the racket.

With a sickening lurch, Betsy's nose sank into another pool of quagmire, squelching her to a halt. Rob jumped at the opportunity, aiming carefully and smashing a machine gun into the faces of its users. He clenched his fist in victory, wincing slightly as the muscles tensed around his burn. They were close enough now, they could still win this.

A direct hit blinded the starboard gun's periscope, showering Rob and Alfie with molten lead and knocking Lieutenant Cufflinks back. His head violently struck a pipe and he dropped to the floor, limp limbs crumpling beneath him.

"Cuffs!" Rob read Dafydd's lips as he broke away from his gun to examine the fallen lieutenant. The Welshman had removed his mask when the heat became too much, and had been punished for this by a fierce burn on his cheek.

"Get back to your gun!" Rob screamed at him, all too aware that the tank remained stationary.

Defence was their only hope now until they got moving again. Dafydd squinted at him, unable to make out his words and Rob growled angrily, taking his hands away from the vision slit he was struggling to open and signing to him.

The engine spluttered and howled, fumes pouring into their small container as she struggled against the muck. The gunner looked anxiously to his loader, who was spluttering almost as badly. A glance back at the gears told him that Valentine was worse, slumped against the side and holding himself up weakly with a shaking arm. Even Colm's strong body was doubled over and Rob himself felt his eyes rolling back as his vision swum around him.

Dafydd left the lieutenant but did not return to his gun, picking his way instead to stand beside Carthorse, who was trying furiously to pull his beloved Betsy out of the mud, her usual driving team of four reduced to only him.

Get out! Dafydd signed hurriedly to him. *Stuck, no use!*

How? The sergeant replied, gripping the clutch as something smacked against the bottom of his viewing flap and bounced off, narrowly avoiding entering. *Not leaving her.*

"Sod your stupid tank! And close the flap, that was a bloody grenade!" Dafydd yelled, but Carthorse couldn't hear. *I said sod Betsy! Close the flap!*

Need to see, Carthorse insisted, still fumbling hastily with the throttle, clutch, primary gearbox – anything he could think of to give her that extra burst of power to break free. The tank rocked again as the ground beside them exploded and Dafydd returned hastily to his weapon.

Alfie was ready and Rob turned back to his gun, firing into a group of approaching Germans who seemed to grow bolder as they saw the predicament of the stranded tank. The mud sucked at their boots and swallowed those who fell from Rob's blow, but his aim was off through the crude vision slit and he only caught their flank, and the living kept advancing. Soldiers had no tracks – bad terrain couldn't stop them.

The air was now unbearable, waves from the overheating engine scorching his back and making him wish he could tear the mask from his sweating face. The core of another bullet found its way into his leg, reminding him why he couldn't.

"Keep shooting Whipper!" he caught Carthorse's voice only from lip-reading, the dying bellows of the engine threatening to blow his eardrums. "We can still hold them!"

The tank driver turned his head back to the front flap, a look of determination on his weathered face. His head fell backwards at the same time as the engine died, steam billowing from the pipes as blood flowed from the hole in his forehead.

"I told you to close the flap!" Dafydd cried in anguish, his voice clear now the sounds of Betsy's life were extinguished along with her loving driver.

Rob felt hot tears pricking in his eyes and he blinked furiously, trying to look through them to aim again at whoever had killed their sergeant. His fingers tensed but were pulled away, Dafydd wrenching him from their only form of protection.

"What are you doing?" he shouted, wriggling against his grasp. "Carthorse wanted us to stay! We can still fire from here, the infantry need us!"

"To hell with the infantry!" Dafydd yelled back, pulling his fellow gunner further from his weapon. "Look at your loader!" He forced Rob's face around to look at Alfie, coughing into his forearm. "Betsy's spent; we've got to get out!"

He couldn't argue. The sight of his struggling friend, along with the motionless bodies of Cufflinks and the two gearsmen, was enough to tell him that he was wrong on this one. He nodded reluctantly to Dafydd and the Welshman let him go, hurrying to lift the lieutenant over his shoulder. Colm cradled Firetop in his strong arms and Rob doubled back for Valentine. Alfie wrenched open the door and they staggered out into fresh air, the shock of it threatening Rob's consciousness all over again.

They didn't have much time to accustom their smothered lungs to the sudden surge of oxygen as bullets flew past their heads and shells continued to explode dangerously close to the lifeless tank. Valentine began to splutter, regaining control of his body, and Rob dumped him unceremoniously in a puddle, turning back for Carthorse's body. His foot caught in the mud and he fell forward, his face hitting something sharp.

But it was the blast above his head that struck his senses. He remained on the ground, glad of his legs for wobbling and keeping him from reaching the shattered corpse that was only a few moments ago his glorious tank. He thought of Carthorse still inside; there would be no body to rescue now.

"I'm sorry Betsy," he raised his head, blinking back more hot pricks of water. Grown men didn't cry. "I'm sorry Carthorse."

He scrambled back to his feet, catching Valentine again as the young man staggered aimlessly through the mud, wide eyes fixed on Betsy's death. They leant on each other's shoulders and their pace quickened, following Dafydd as he beckoned and bellowed at them through the bullets, dragging Cufflinks with him. The new air wasn't working fast enough for Rob, his mind fogging with every step, and Valentine was in a worse state than he was.

The ground behind them exploded and they fell forward again.

"Whip! Val!"

Colm swung about with Firetop in his arms, fighting the urge to keep running without them. Rob got to his knees, but a shower of bullets had him back on the floor, shakily thanking his reactions for keeping him alive. The Irishman had not been so lucky. A shot to the thigh brought him crashing to his knees, still cradling the bullet-ridden body of the gearsman and crying out in anger and pain.

"Roy!" Valentine screamed, crawling forwards through the sludge and attempting to shake his friend back to life.

It was too much for Rob to take in. Eyes swimming in and out of focus, he stumbled forward, held up by somebody's arm, though whose he could not tell. He didn't understand how it had all gone so wrong. They were the crew of Naughty Betsy, specially trained and equipped for victory. Now two of their number were gone and the rest on their way, slogging through the mud for their lives. He wondered if this was how his father had felt when the ground swallowed him; dazed and unable to comprehend the situation he was in.

Death by mud. Both his father and his uncle Thomas had suffered this way, and perhaps he was soon to follow.

"No, I can't die," he told himself, his voice coming out slurred and uneven.

Whoever he was leaning on said something back, but it didn't penetrate his groggy mind. He kept himself walking, forcing all remaining energy to his feet. His mouth spoke words he didn't hear and he felt the passing of bullets and debris like in a dream. He walked like this, in and out of consciousness for what could have been minutes or could have been days, until he woke on his back with the stars in his eyes and the blissful taste of rum on his tongue. He closed his eyes again and slept.

****

Rob took a drink and set the glass back on the table, along with his feet. After all, the mud had followed them everywhere else so why not the tabletop? Since Carthorse's death the crew had become like sons without a father; slovenly and disorganised. Even Lieutenant Cufflinks seemed to shrink a little without his confidante, his splendid moustache slightly lost atop an unshaved chin. They would recover, Rob knew, but they deserved their time to grieve at least until they received their new tank. And their new driver and gearsman – now that was an odd thought.

"Some heroes we turned out to be," Valentine said darkly, looking melancholically out from under hair uncharacteristically unkempt. "Couldn't even save our own crew."

"We all knew what we were getting into," Rob sighed. "Firetop and Carthorse too. We should have been ready for something like this."

"Don't beat yourself up about it, Whip," Dafydd finished his food and leant forward on his elbows. "Nobody likes to see people die."

"Well you're a solemn lot today."

Rob turned in his seat, hastily pulling his feet down from the table as Cufflinks approached. He had finally shaved and perhaps had washed his uniform too. It was straight and tidy again, looking more like the commanding lieutenant the young gunner so admired than the sad man who had lost a friend.

"What are you so damn pleased about?" Dafydd asked him, studying the lieutenant's face.

"Language please, Jones. A little bird told me we have a lance-corporal in our midst."

Of course, Rob had forgotten that with their sergeant gone, one of them was likely up for promotion. After all, Cufflinks needed a second command in case anything happened to him. It was probably Dafydd – he was the oldest other than Colm, and nobody knew how long the Irishman would take to patch up – though imagining the fiery gunner as their superior was amusing at best.

The lieutenant continued, looking right at him. "Isn't that right, Allenby?"

"Me, sir?"

It was like a lightning bolt to his system. Everything from the last few days was obliterated and replaced with shocked pride, and a keen awareness of the untidiness of his chin. He realised too late that he was gaping, shutting his mouth hurriedly.

"Hold on Cuffs," Dafydd looked almost as shocked as he felt. His dark eyes were round as saucers as he leaned over the table closer to the lieutenant. "Are you telling me that little Whipper is in charge of the rest of us? Who the bloody hell thought that was a good idea?"

"Language Jones." A grin crept up the side of Rob's mouth, putting on an authoritative voice and enjoying the look on his friend's face.

"Now don't you start," Dafydd held up a finger. "This is all some joke and you're just making yourself look silly."

"No joke, Daffodil," Cufflinks smiled, a glint in his eye. Rob and Alfie laughed; the lieutenant didn't usually use their nicknames. "Kit Allenby has been named lance-corporal, and you will do best to respect your superiors."

"Well I'll be damned," Dafydd sat back in his seat, a mix of indignity and admiration plastered across his face. "Who are you, Kit Allenby? You never stop surprising us."

"I'm not surprised," Alfie said proudly. "We're not as useless as you like to think."

"Thank you sir," Rob breathed, slowly being hit by the full weight of the lieutenant's words. "I won't let you down, I swear it."

"I don't expect you to," Cufflinks patted him on the back with a kind look in his eyes. "You were chosen for a reason Allenby; don't let these jokers get you down son."

"I won't sir, don't worry," he smiled determinedly.

The word 'son' stuck in his mind. He hoped his father could see him now; surely now he would be proud to have him as a son. Rob had been angry when he died, and he had told Matthew there was no life after death. It had seemed stupid and babyish to imagine such a thing; when so much was wrong with the world how could anybody with sense believe there was a God? Still, he wanted to believe that now more than anything. He wanted his father to see him, he wanted Carthorse to see him, he wanted to write a letter to his uncle and his mother and Billy Wayson.

"Well done Kit," Valentine congratulated him, and he was glad to see the first look of true feeling on his face since the failed advance.

He guessed that this news was hope to all of them – Valentine was only a few years older than himself and Alfie, so he stood for all of them in proving that age didn't matter. He could see Alfie's ambition shining in his face, and he was glad that he had accompanied him to London. After the mess of poor Betsy, he had begun to wonder if his self-confidence had been misplaced. Alfie had never doubted him. And now he would never doubt himself again.

13.

The men heading past in the opposite direction walked like they were already dead. No, not walked; their legs moved but they had no conscious control of them. Feet trudged, stumbled, fell, empty eyes unseeing in their sockets even before the lids could close over them. Those without feet rode wagons pulled by beasts so dirty and dejected nobody could recognise them as horses, or they were carried by companions so exhausted they were unrecognisable as men.

The unlucky fell and had nobody to pick them back up again. Proper graves were a luxury abandoned for the dead of the Ypres salient; claimed by mud and neglected by manpower unavailable to fetch them. The rain had not relented and the ground refused to stay beneath their feet, rising up above their waists in some areas where an ill-placed step could see a man sucked away forever from the sounds of artillery fire, too tired to fight it.

D Company marched with increasing dread. Every face they passed seemed more terrible than the last, each man a possibility of what the watcher himself may soon become. Many turned their gaze away, unwilling to look upon the ghastly face of the future. Others met the eyes of every one of the walking wounded, caught up in their sorrow and delirium, unable to look away.

A rickety wagon struggled past, piled high with the unseeing victims of gas, their eyes a blind mess in their sockets. Rigby gulped, clutching the army issue mask that hung about his neck. This was a weapon nobody ever wanted to face.

Stack slowed his pace, blue-grey eyes following the progress of the wagon and the stragglers that came behind it, holding onto the unsteady structure for support as they walked. These men – as far as he could tell – had not been the victim of chemical warfare, but were simply exhausted past the point of comprehension. A young lad blundered past, half carried by a man who did not look well enough to stand himself.

"ROB!"

He broke from the line, lurching at the boy like a drowned man gasping for air, pushing Captain and Rigby aside. Weary eyes looked up at the noise; the eyes of his nephew staring at him from the stranger's face.

"Rob!" he pulled him into his arms. "You're alive! Are you alright, what happened to you?"

The boy continued to stare, eyelids drooping even as he tried to make sense of the blur attempting to communicate with him.

"Come on, you're going home."

He took a hold of Rob's arm and started to pull him away from the trail of wounded. He had no plan, no idea what he was doing, just the strongest urge to get him away, to safety.

"Sorry mate," Rob's companion interrupted, placing a protective arm on his shoulder. The boy pulled out of Stack's grasp and leaned instead on this man. "You're got the wrong man. His name's not Rob."

"It is!" Stack insisted, trying to catch a gleam of recognition in the drooping eyes. "I know my nephew. I have to get him home."

"My name's Whipper," a murmured voice escaped the cracked lips; definitely Rob's voice. "Twenty-one years old, starboard gunner."

"Come on Ben," he felt Captain's hand on his shoulder as he and Rigby stood behind him. "It's not him."

"I know my own nephew Cap!"

The wagon was moving again, and the boy and his companion moving with it. He made to reach again for Rob, but Rigby held him back.

"Let me go, that's my boy!"

"It isn't him, Ben," Captain said again, helping Rigby restrain him as he continued to pull towards the retreating wagon, screaming his nephew's name.

"Hey mister," the boy turned, voice stronger than before and with a hint of pride behind the delirium. "Does your nephew ride a tank?"

He stooped struggling and just stood, watching as Rob moved further and further away.

"Yes," he replied, more to himself than the shrinking boy. He had always been strong back home, and now he realised that war hadn't changed that. Trust Rob to find his way into a tank. He was okay. He had made it this far and he had people looking out for him, and he was as strong as ever. A smile broke onto his face despite himself, and he thought he saw it returned by the boy looking back at him. "Yes, he does."

****

Stack wiped his face, only managing to smear it further. Rain ran off the rim of his helmet and dripped from his hair, finding its way past his overcoat and down his back. There was no firestep to watch from – the previous one having been defeated by the weather – so he simply lay up the side of the trench, already so saturated the mud could bother him no further. He let off a few rounds, more in frustration than anything else.

"Can't sleep?" Captain asked.

It was a joke, of course; nobody could sleep with the amount of constant work needed to keep the rain from bringing down the trench around them. Captain himself was supposed to be working with the pump but he crouched instead, ankle-deep in sludge, lit occasionally by the flicker of a match as he attempted to burn lice out of the seams of his tunic.

Stack shook his head, kicking at the puddle forming at his feet. He could see now why the wounded they had passed on the road were so filthy and downtrodden; Passchendaele was nothing but a quagmire. And men were giving their lives, for this.

"Too dirty for you, hey Cap?"

"By far," he replied, scowling at a particularly large cluster of parasites. His head jerked unnaturally; a twitch he had developed recently that concerned Stack more than he let him know. "I can't enjoy sleep anyway. I close my eyes for a minute and I'm right back to the first of July. I'm better suited to being awake."

"You are okay, aren't you?" Stack asked, concern clear in his eyes.

Since Vincent's death the months had not been kind to Captain's nightmares. Though he dismissed them as best he could while awake, Stack could see them taking their toll.

"It's me," Captain reminded him reassuringly. "I'm fine. I've had these dreams for over a year now; it's nothing new."

He let out a long sigh and gave up with the infested tunic, pulling it back over his shoulders. Grubby arms pulled him up the side of the trench to lie beside the sergeant. "No, you're not rid of me yet, not by a long shot."

"Good," Stack said gruffly. "'Cause I'm going to need you. Seeing Rob…what am I going to do if I get home? I can't face Sylvie anyway, if anything happens to that boy…well, what's the point in going home at all? Who's going to be there to understand?"

"True," Captain looked thoughtful. "Don't worry Benji, I'll be there, God knows you've been there for me. Me and Rigby can help you on the farm, and I can help you catch that girl of yours."

Stack smiled. "Poor Harriet."

"Poor me," Captain grinned. "I've got my work cut out. Really, you can run into bullets but you can't tell a girl how you feel."

Stack punched him on the shoulder.

"We'll be alright, the three of us," he continued. "I suppose Rigby could marry my sister, now that poor Tommy can't – we'll just have to dispose of his dog first. As for me, I guess it's time I settled down too. Harriet doesn't have a sister does she?"

"She does actually," Stack chuckled, amused. "Widowed with a huge estate."

Captain winked. "Just my type."

****

Any amusement the sergeant could muster was short-lived. Even Sandford's attentions could do nothing to save them from the rain that flooded their trench day and night. They slept standing to avoid drowning – those who slept at all – and morning could only get worse.

"Keep together!" Stack shouted over the sound of shellfire. "Rigby, how's your rifle?"

"It'll do!" he replied, getting a mouthful of mud as the ground flew up a few feet away. Mud was not kind to guns, and Rigby's had been showing threatening signs of jamming.

Out of the flood and above ground conditions were not much better as they moved forward to relieve the battalion ahead. Thick mud still rose up their calves and pulled on their boots as they tried their best to keep a decent pace. Wooden planks had been placed in areas to aid movement, but many of these were now splinters, or else half eaten by the gluttonous mud.

They skidded into positions, adrenaline hiding the uncomfortable squelch of mud seeping into their sodden trousers.

"Thanks," a man rushed in a New Zealand accent, before signalling to his men and falling back.

The Anzac battalion were off in a flash, so grateful to be leaving that they carried no regard for duckboards or the aim of the enemy. The commander went down almost immediately, blood converging with bog as one of his men dodged the blow only to take a wrong step and disappear into the quagmire of souls beneath their feet.

"Watch that hole!" Stack bellowed, making them look at the mouth that gasped for breath, arms floundering uselessly as the mud took him. "We're not ending up like that!"

"We have to do something!"

Wayson broke from the small crater of sludge they crouched in, wide eyes anxiously scanning for danger as he reached for the flailing arms. He seized a slippery finger and tightened his grip, just to find himself flattened, face forced into the mud as a hit ended the drowning Anzac's suffering.

"Ben!" Captain was there in a second, heaving the sergeant's heavy body off the private's. "You alright?"

Stack seemed more interested in the blackened boy beneath him than his own wellbeing.

"You bloody idiot!" he screamed. "Don't-"

"No," Captain spun him roughly. "*You're* the bloody idiot. What are we meant to do without you!? You do know that risking your stupid neck for Wayson is *not* going to save your nephew?"

"Get back here," Stack pulled Wayson back to cover, where the boy crouched shaken by his side. His heart beat quicker than it should have, and not only from the shock of the blast. Captain's words rang in his ears like the white noise he knew so well. "Eyes front, watch the enemy, avoid the mud."

"Easier said than bloody done!" Rigby retorted, tensed to breaking point. "We just get used to bloody Fritz and now the ground's trying to kill us too!"

"Stay calm Rig!" Stack ordered, squinting against the rain.

"Easier said than bloody done!"

Weir called that they were being signalled forward and they splashed back into the firing line, crouched low to the ground with heads down, helmets protecting them from both bullets and rain. They barely had time to find a foothold before becoming engaged in a shooting match with the darkened figures that slugged through the mud ahead of them, like an army of the undead. Round after round flung across No Man's Land, Rigby's face white behind his rifle and Wayson's contorted in concentration.

"We're not going to hold them!" Sandford yelled, keeping his eyes on the approaching hoard. "Bayonets ready!"

The lieutenant was the first to make the dash out from their flooded hole to bury his blade in flesh, Butterfield hot on his heels a few yards away. The rest followed suit, screaming ferociously to propel themselves forward into the fray.

After a bout of grappling, Stack forced back his enemy's wrist to impale him below the armpit, and was impressed to see Wayson jumping forward to save Rigby from a similar fate. Despite his moments of idiot youth, the boy really had grown into a very good soldier. To his left Weir guarded Mackie's flank as the athletic little man was caught up in fists with a German junior officer. Harper and

Dimery fought around Sandford while Grant, Penley and Foden were forced back a little way away, Penley missing his helmet.

"Cap?"

He scoured the battlefield, vision blocked by desperate men and showers of mud as hell rained down. He found him as a cloud cleared between them, knocking back a burly man twice his size. He got his rifle and bayonet up under the man's chin, piercing him with the blade and blowing out the back of his skull as his fingers found the trigger.

The recoil sent him falling in the opposite direction, landing hard on his back in the mud and struggling to keep the weapon in his grip. He twisted his body to push himself back to his feet, turning his head to face the thing that lay almost beneath him.

The Canadian he had spoken to in the theatre stared back at him with eyes that bled mud. He must have been there a while; only his face was visible above the mud and it had started to decompose, leaving sagging discoloured skin to hang from cheekbones that had once risen in a smile. If it wasn't for the distinguishable shape of his jaw, he might not have even recognised him.

Captain yelped and jerked backwards, staggering to his feet and lifting trembling arms to defend himself against the figure running towards him. His stature said he was young, and the dirt that covered him made his uniform hard to see. He got closer and still Captain didn't act; just stared, all life seeming to drain from his face. Stack caught Rigby's eye and they shared a worried look – they knew exactly what he was seeing.

Still he did not move and Stack made a dash for it, bundling into the German and bringing them both splashing down in the mud. The Englishman got up first, sending his boot hard into his adversary's skull and pummelling him deeper into the mud until his legs stopped twitching.

"What were you doing!?" he panted. "That one's German; you're meant to shoot him!"

"I can't shoot," he said, panic clear in his voice.

"Yes you can!"

"I can't move my arms!" he stared desperately at the limbs that protruded from his shoulders, real effort apparent just to hold them there.

"Yes you can," Stack replied, wading over to shake his shoulders. "You're invincible, remember!"

His words mingled with Sandford's hurried cries of "HOLD THE LINE!" and he turned his attention back to the advancing line of tired bodies driving more tired bodies before them. A bayonet broke through Penley's unprotected forehead and he fell sideways into the abyss. Before he could even reach the ground, an ill-aimed mortar ripped his limbs from his body – along with a couple of Germans – and they were left with only a shattered pile of flesh and bones and a blood-spattered face screaming out from the mud.

****

Major Kent was not happy with his company, but none of them cared. The land that had been gained that morning was lost again, at the cost of too many lives for a few feet. They could barely walk as far without seeing a dead or wounded Anzac, and the British were in no better shape. Stack sat back in the wine cellar they had been posted to for rest barracks, eyes growing accustomed to the dark and ears attempting to block out the sounds of the dying.

"I'm sorry Ben," Captain broke the silence. "I don't know what happened. I couldn't move. I wasn't even scared…I don't think."

Stack looked at Rigby, Captain's own words playing in their heads; *it's not shellshock, he can control his limbs.*

****

A wine cellar was a bad place to position Private Dan Captain at the best of times. All he had ever had was laughter – and how many times had his friends told him that was what kept them going too? But even the greatest comedians could find no humour in the shit that was Passchendaele, and he was finding it harder with every second. He had told Ben countless times to just forget it when things got too much, but he had never foreseen how difficult it would be to follow his own advice. The barrel he had found hidden in a wall of the cellar provided the only answer he could think of.

He would not be Vincent Waterman. He refused.

"Hold still!" Rigby ordered through gritted teeth.

He bit the end of his tongue as his fingers guided lead over paper, creating the grin they knew so well. He looked up and the man had moved again.

"For God's sake, Cap," he threw down the drawing irritably, an unfinished Stack and Captain smiling up from the page. "Are you physically incapable of staying still?"

"I've got everyone's mail," Weir announced, breaking up the inevitable scuffle. "We're not doing too badly today, looks like two food parcels at least!"

"Anything from Lydia?" Mackie asked from his corner, a shyly pleased smile lighting up his face as he received a package.

"Like I said, we're doing well," Weir dispensed the rest of the bundle. "Our ladies haven't forgotten us yet."

"Cap's will only be his sister," Rigby snorted. "Only woman who could ever love him."

Surprisingly, Captain didn't rise to the bait. He was more interested in the contents of Stack's hand.

"Is it Miss Harriet?" he asked excitedly, attempting to sneak the letter away from him.

"Don't call her that, it's weird," Stack chuckled and moved out of reach. "This is why I don't open my letters around you!"

"Whyever not?" Captain smirked. "What are you hiding, ey? Come on, she can't be worse than Rigby's dog."

Stack grinned despite himself, looking up for Rigby's reaction. He hadn't even noticed. His head remained down, stony-faced as he attempted to digest the stale words that slid uncomfortably past the lump in his throat.

"Rig, is everything alright?"

He raised his eyes in slow motion, extending an arm to offer them the paper.

"She's left me," he said in a hoarse voice.

Captain took the letter and skimmed the first two paragraphs, the smile slipping from his face. He folded it neatly and tucked it into his tunic.

"She wasn't good enough for you," he held out a hand and pulled him to his feet. "Where's her picture?"

Rigby reached a numb hand into his pocket and pulled out the crumpled photograph he carried everywhere, smoothing it with a gentle thumb.

"Enough of that."

Captain snatched it from him and threw it to the ground. It landed face up, displaying the visage that his friend found so beautiful. He put it under his foot and stamped hard, crushing it against the stone floor and causing a tear along the fold. Rigby stared at it.

"I'm not getting married," he said blankly.

"You'll get more than married tonight," Captain grinned, a familiar glint in his eye. "What do you say Benji; the three musketeers hit the town? Or what's left of it anyway." His gaze flickered to the letter still in Stack's hand and his grin widened. "Don't worry lover-boy, you don't have to do anything untoward."

"Permission for leave tonight, sir?" Sandford looked up as the three of them climbed the steps from the cellar. His hair was dirty and messier than usual and his face lined beyond its years. "Just a few hours."

"A few hours? Take as long as you like; we'll be back out there soon enough and there'll be no leave then. I'll answer to Major Kent."

There would have been a lot of answering for the poor lieutenant to do had they met the major that night. Sympathies were high and drinks were cheap in the stricken town, and even Captain's tolerance couldn't hold against the torrent he poured down his throat. Evidence of the front was everywhere and those based nearby parted gladly with their wages to forget how they had been earned. The town itself was mostly abandoned and what remained was there purely for the troops; bars and establishments that made enough money or gave enough support to make the danger worth it.

By the time they left the bar, Rigby had to be carried. He had spent all night in a state of confusion, halfway between agreeing with everything Captain said and angrily mourning his failed engagement. As for Captain…where was Captain? Stack blinked his eyes forcefully, attempting to clear the impending headache, and looked groggily about himself. He had been caught between sleep and oblivion when Rigby had decided they needed to leave, so had assumed they were all together.

"Rig?" he heaved him up as he started to slide down his arm. "Where's Cap?"

"Getting someone pregnant," he shrugged, sliding down further.

"What?"

"Leave him to it," he shook his head clumsily. "I don't want those girls, I want mine."

"No, you don't, she's ugly," Stack corrected him. "You want to find Cap."

"He doesn't want to get found," Rigby pulled a face. "Who wants to be found like that?"

"I don't think-"

"He's fine. He's better off than either of us right now."

The corridor was dark and damp; it wasn't the classiest of establishments that Stack turned into, trailing a grumbling Rigby. The woman on the door was old and gnarled with a temper to match, and though she answered their queries she insisted they pay their way in as any other man would.

"You know he wouldn't go looking for me," Rigby complained, holding his head with a grimace. "Let's just go to bed."

Stack held a finger to his lips. He could hear something coming from the other end of the corridor, and not the sort of noise one would expect to hear in a brothel – crying. Rigby looked a little guilty as they hurried forward; both had heard him enough at night to recognise those sobs.

"…And there he was," Captain took a gulp of breath, tears running freely down his cheeks as he clutched at the skirt of the baffled half-naked girl. "In the mud…skin and bones and so much blood…Not as bad as the gas though, men go blind and throw up their insides…God, I've seen so many insides…There was a man with hollow eyes, and no chest, just ribs…ribs and a machine gun…Machine guns got Yates and he didn't even shave, and we found Waterman dead in the snow by his own bayonet…God, they were so young!...Tommy Miller was in love with my sister, I watched the bullet go through his skull like it was paper and then he was gone, just like that…just gone…"

The door opened and the girl squeaked as footsteps entered the room, warm hands on Captain's shoulders.

"Cap, it's okay."

"And that poor boy!" he sank back onto his heels, head falling back against the friend crouched behind him. "He was so scared…so scared…I've never seen someone so scared and I shot him!"

"Cap!"

He felt himself being lifted, but his legs wouldn't hold his weight. They were so disobedient these days, as if they didn't really belong to him anymore. They belonged to the war and it did with them as it pleased. Everything belonged to the war.

"They don't understand, Ben," he stared at him with desperate eyes. "Nobody understands but us. They have no idea what it's like out there."

"That's a good thing Cap, you don't need to tell them." He heaved him to his feet, but they crumpled and both men returned to the ground, Captain clutching Stack's neck for support as he mumbled into his shoulder.

"I can't go back," he choked. "I'm not strong like you. You're a rock. I'm just the mud."

"All rocks need mud to stand on," Stack wrapped his arms tighter around his torso and pulled him back up again. "I need you, Cap, now get up! You're just drunk, okay? You'll be fine later."

He wished he believed it. Rigby had managed to pull himself together and the two of them carried Captain back out to the street, trying to interrupt his strangled apologies with happier talk. They passed the bar they had visited earlier, an Anzac soldier now crouched outside crying into his sleeve. Stack shared a sympathetic glance with the man's companion, looking as tired as he felt.

"I'm sorry," Captain shook his head again.

"He can't hear you."

"Not him," he lifted his heavy head to look Stack in the eyes. "You, and Rigby. You're the only real friends I've ever had. No-one else would look for me; they all think I'm a bastard."

"You are a bastard," he replied with a half-smile.

"We know it, instead of just thinking it," Rigby added. "That's the difference."

"Get shelled Rigby," Captain rolled his head to the side. "No, I don't mean that, and I'm really sad you're not getting married, but I'm glad you can do better now. And Benji, you're the best sergeant in the regiment, like I always said you would be."

"You just like the extra rum rations."

"No," he said firmly. "You're a good man and a better friend and I stick by what I said before half the world got their heads blown off. I fight for you, and you too Rig. I FIGHT FOR YOU!"

The Anzac looked up from his sleeve startled by the shouting Englishman in the middle of the street. He was much louder than he had been on the last night of June 1916 and his eyes held a fierce desperation. He had clung to those words in the battle that followed and they had carried him forward through Trones Wood, through the winter and even now in the Ypres salient. They were all he had.

****

Another stint at the front had just about killed them all. The rain came down to drench any hopes that remained beneath the sodden uniforms that crouched in puddles. Retreat followed gain followed retreat followed gain and the stalemate continued, adding more corpses to the mud. Rigby's cigarettes wouldn't be lit by any variation of lighter he could create in the swamp and even plucky Wayson had lost the light of adventure from his eyes. Craters continued to form as shells splashed down into the mud, covering the lucky in dirt, the unlucky in worse.

Stack had not slept for days – even when spared from the fatigues, something about the salient wouldn't let him close his eyes. The flooding worsened with each bout of rain, washing away mud from the wall to reveal buried limbs, but it was the living who really bothered him. He kept a frequent watch on Wayson and the conscripts, and stayed with Captain when work was done, keeping him from the dreams that rattled his sleep.

Every time his consciousness slipped, there was the British boy, squelching towards him across No Man's Land. Every time he would wake, screaming and sweating, only to assure the others he was fine and it wouldn't happen again. In the end, he had forbidden himself to sleep.

Stack sat with him now, legs protruding from water that rose past their boots, ignoring how they shivered and ached. Neither had shaved in over a week, and Captain's curls were matted with the same filth that filled his fingernails. Nevertheless, they kept each other cheery, Captain filling Stack's head with talk of women and home, allowing him to hope for a while.

The rest of the section were dotted about the trench, some attempting to pump the flood by cover of darkness, while others passed out where they stood, faces pressed into the sludge for support. They could hear Rigby sneezing a little way away, his lungs not having taken well to the constant damp. Wayson huddled in a foxhole he had dug himself in the wall above the waterline and Weir was on watch, his faithful dog curled protectively around his feet.

"Thanks Ben," Captain mumbled. The sky was beginning to get lighter, stand-to wouldn't be far off. They had managed another night.

"What for?"

"For everything," he breathed heavily, eyelids drooping. "Whatever happens, I'm glad I fought with you."

"Me too Cap."

"I'm not scared of dying, you know," he continued, his voice beginning to slur as exhaustion took hold. "Not anymore. I used to think I couldn't die, then I thought I was going to Hell." He sighed. "I realise now, I'm not going to Hell when I die. Hell is Passchendaele, Hell is the Somme. We're not going to Hell, Ben; we've already been."

"What are you talking about? Cap?"

A soft thud on his shoulder told him that Captain had finally fallen asleep. His head rested against Stack's arm and his chest rose and fell peacefully. No nightmares furrowed his brow and Stack allowed his own eyes to close and his head to fall sideways onto that of his friend. His consciousness departed, taking with it all memory of the past few years. They were simply men, asleep at night, no rifles in their hands or words of feud on their lips. Soft grey light fell on their exhausted faces, smoothing away lines and scars and taking them back in time; two men laughing as they entered their first day of training, having never shot a human. For a short time, sleep was peace.

14.

However long their sleep was, it was not enough. It seemed as though Stack had shut his eyes for little more than a second before they were open again, responding to the orders for stand-to.

"Cap," he nudged his friend awake. "Rise and shine sleepyhead."

He shuddered and blinked dull eyes, looking as exhausted as Stack felt. They pulled themselves together and got into position, Stack checking that the rest of the section followed suit. Rigby breathed uneasily against the wall, face grey with a combination of dirt and illness. His weary eyes followed Weir's dog as it threw itself into the water after a rat.

"Face the enemy, private," Kent barked, making them all jump. Rigby gulped and hastily turned his gaze to the dystopia ahead of them.

"Nice of you to show up, major," Captain said darkly, noticing how clean and well-rested he appeared compared to the rest of them.

Kent gave him a look that could curdle their watery tea. "You too Captain, eyes forward."

There was a time when hearing the major use his name would have caused him a great deal of mirth. Not anymore.

"What if I can't," he replied, his arm giving an involuntary twitch. "What if I'm sick of looking out at that mess?"

"You will do as I say, private," the major snarled.

Captain ignored him. Lack of sleep and the feeling of despair that had engulfed the company since their arrival on the salient didn't allow him obedience.

"I can't," he repeated, attempting to control the shaking of his hands. "My head won't move."

"That is nonsense." Kent's face was so close now that he could feel the spittle hit his cheek. "You will do your bit like everyone else."

"I've done my bit ten times over!" he spat back. "We all have! What have you done, *sir*?"

Kent didn't grace him with an answer. He took the private's chin in his hand and twisted his head, forcing his eyes to look over the parapet.

"Face the enemy," he hissed in his ear, before giving them all a long glare and stalking away with a splash.

"You can stop looking now," Stack said lowly, as soon as the major was out of earshot.

Captain was shaking uncontrollably, his eyes unearthly as they stared, fixed on a point in No Man's Land.

"Cap," Rigby touched a quivering shoulder, alarm clear on his pale face. "He's right, you need to stop looking."

But he wouldn't. He continued to stare as if he hadn't heard either of them, the ghost of the young boy squelching through the muck towards him. Then his limbs started to climb, frantically clawing at the mud as they tried to pull him over the top.

"Woah!" Stack and Rigby were on him in an instant, dragging him back as he struggled, landing the three of them on the flooded duckboard.

"What the hell do you think you're doing?" Stack demanded.

"I have to face him."

Captain's helmet was askew, hair dripping with filthy water, confusion more dominant on his face than any other emotion.

"I killed him Ben; I can't just forget that. I have to face him."

He made to get up again, but Stack kept a hold of his arm, his own face contorted with alarm.

"No you didn't!" he panicked. "It wasn't you Cap, it was the war! Just the war!"

He looked at him with wretched eyes, bloodshot from lack of sleep.

"The war can't have me anymore Ben. I'm through. I'll die by a German bullet and take a few of them down with me, now let me go!"

With those last few words he wriggled free of Stack's grasp, seized his rifle and made a break for the parapet. It was Wayson who caught him this time, holding him back long enough for Stack and Rigby to get to their feet.

"Let me go!" He tried to shake them off, their heads now protruding dangerously above cover. A bullet shot past him and he attempted to lift his rifle to fire a return, but the three of them had him pinned. All he could do was yell across No Man's Land – "I can take you bastards!"

"What's going on?"

The commotion was bound to attract attention and it was Kent who rounded the corner first, enraged shock stopping him in his tracks. He shouted for him to get down immediately – he was endangering the other men – but nobody paid him any attention. A second bullet narrowly missed Wayson and he ducked, startled, losing his grip on Captain's tunic. That was all he needed – he wrenched away from Stack and Rigby and pulled his torso over the parapet.

His knees had just reached the ground above when a sharp pain tore through his chest and he fell forward, clutching at the place where blood now flowed. The scene around him blurred and twisted like a kaleidoscope. He heard Stack's scream of "NO!" as if in slow motion, realising with a start that the bullet had hit him from behind. The German lines were ahead of him. He screwed his eyes shut tightly, blinking back the spinning sickness from his head.

Hands were on his legs, pulling him back, and he turned, searching for the source of the bullet. His hazy line of vision swung past his friends' agonised faces to the point that Stack was shouting at. There was Major Kent, pistol raised, arm steady. He ordered him back, or warned him, or something, but all Captain could hear was the sound of his own heartbeat.

Not his own side, he thought desperately. Anything but his own side.

He pushed himself up again, twisting his shoulders to carry him back across No Man's Land to the real foe. Before he had the chance to turn he was ripped open again, falling back into Stack's arms. His wide, startled eyes met those of the major for the briefest of moments; looking just as stunned and framed by sweat.

"CAP!" Stack bellowed, catching his armpits as he slid down the wall. He stared at him, no fear behind those widened eyes, no sadness, just shock. Confusion and shock. That look would stay with him forever. He had tried to shield him, screamed at the major not to shoot, but still he had pulled the trigger. The first time may have been an accident, a panic, but the second – that was murder. The scene replayed behind his eyes; Kent's hand had been perfectly steady.

Stack saw red. Leaving Rigby to support Captain, he flew at the major, catching his throat in his hands and forcing him back into the wall.

"Why!?" he demanded, voice thick with rage. "Why did you do that!?"

The major spluttered, struggling against the fingers that tightened around his neck. "I trusted you Stack!"

"You killed him!" he screamed into his face. Wayson was trying to pull him back now, but he shrugged him off violently. "He was sick, you bastard!"

He dropped the man with one hand and drew it back for a punch, but grief overtook him before it hit and his arm dropped. He let his fingers slip and the major slid free, massaging his throat. Stack's fist collided with the wall before he collapsed to his knees in the water.

"You bastard."

****

"He attacked me!" Kent fumed. He had been storming his way down the trench, on his way to secure the sergeant the punishment he deserved, but stopped to face his lieutenant.

"You shot his friend," Sandford said sternly.

"He was endangering the men, it was mutiny, it was-"

Kent rushed through reasons and Sandford knew he was trying to justify it to himself as much as the lieutenant. As angry as he was, he couldn't blame him. After all, he had seen a critical situation and what did all good soldiers do in critical situations? Shoot. But there was a difference between split-second thinking and death in cold blood, for pride's sake, and Sandford was not going to allow him to waste any more lives.

"You panicked, I know; you don't need to explain yourself to me. We all make mistakes. But I am trying to tell you it will not help you now to court-martial Ben Stack."

"James, you do not understand!" he balled up a fist and shook it in anger. "I need to make an example of him or the whole company will think they can rise up against me!"

"Look," Sandford stood in his way, forcing him to look him in the eye. "For once on this subject will you listen to me? I know the company. And I promise you that if you harm that man you will have worse than a mutiny on your hands."

"If he is dealt with, there will be nobody to lead a mutiny."

"I wouldn't count on that," Sandford said sharply.

"Oh, wouldn't you?" Kent fixed him with an odd look. "It's you, isn't it? You're one of them. All this time I trusted you, but you've been against me the whole time. All I wanted was to be a good commander, James. How can I do that surrounded by people like you?"

He shoved past him, continuing down the trench to a quieter place behind the lines, where he could write his report and calm his nerves.

"Wait!" Sandford hurried after him. "There is no them and us! We're on the same side! Come back!"

His words were drowned out by a telltale *eeeee*, followed by an explosion too close for comfort.

Kent did come back, or at least he fell back. Sandford rolled him over to see the six inch shard of metal protruding from the skull between his eyes. A sniper couldn't have aimed it better.

Poor man, he thought. *Terrified to the end.* But the time to pity him would come later; now he had to act for his platoon.

"Butterfield!" he straightened up, calling for the sergeant. "Tell the men today didn't happen. Private Daniel Captain was killed by a sniper. There was no reason for anybody to attack Major Kent, and nobody did. Do you understand me?"

****

Sandford found Stack a little way behind the lines, sat in a patch of poppies with his back to him. He stared emptily at the rectangle of newly turned-over mud, shovel in hand, wishing he could feel something. He knew that the proper thing to do would have been to stay put in his trench and let the stretchers carry away his best friend, but he couldn't bring himself to care. It didn't matter what he did now, he was for it. He had assaulted an officer. He might as well have climbed the parapet with Captain; he would be dead by firing squad at dawn.

"I would have stopped him," he said numbly, sensing the lieutenant's approach but not turning.

"It was a suicide run," Sandford said gently. "It wasn't your fault."

"I know it wasn't my fault; I would have stopped him," Stack repeated. "He wasn't supposed to die. He just wanted a crack at the Germans to clear his head, then he would come straight back, invincible as ever."

"Nobody's invincible," he tried to tell him. "Captain knew that."

"But he was," Stack took a deep breath that stuck in his windpipe. "Don't think I'll keep quiet about this, lieutenant. Don't think I won't tell them, when he says his bit to have me shot. Don't think I won't tell them *why*. That bastard has something coming to him."

"Nobody will be telling anybody anything," Sandford said stiffly. "Major Kent is dead."

"What?" Stack finally turned his head. "How?"

"Shrapnel," Sandford replied. "I think you understand the importance of keeping quiet about the actions of both of you this morning."

"Nobody's reporting it?" Stack asked incredulously.

"I have made sure of it," the lieutenant nodded firmly.

Stack had to be amazed by him, standing in his long coat with arms crossed and stern face, looking completely in control. He had certainly come a long way from the naively gallant boy who led them from the ships at Le Havre.

"Thank you sir," he breathed a sigh of disbelief.

"There is one price for my efforts," Sandford continued, crouching so they were level. "I'm leading a patrol tonight. There is no man here I trust more than you, and I daresay it'll be a welcome distraction. I want you with me Stack."

The sergeant nodded, his throat still choked with a mixture of grief, shock and relief. "Thank you sir."

****

Nightfall found Stack back in the centre of No Man's Land, exhausted but glad of something useful to do. It was a large patrol and must be of some importance, though he wondered if perhaps Sandford had assigned himself unnecessarily. Unlike Kent, he felt his platoon's losses keenly and was likely to want a distraction almost as much as Stack did.

They spread out across the area, moving close to the ground. Stack stayed at the lieutenant's side as they split off into smaller groups, each vanishing into the night until it was just the two of them. As they moved forward together the terrain was not only mud and wire; the carcasses of ambulance carts and big guns protruded from their graves, interspersed with duckboard previously thrown up by shells.

They were close enough to one of these beasts to make a dive behind it for shelter when a flare went up, illuminating the sweat on their faces. The heavy wheel wobbled precariously as Sandford's back hit it, seemingly just balanced rather than securely attached to the martyred structure.

A movement caught their attention as the flare began to wane, and the thud of something falling into heavy mud. Stack barely had time to swear before the world lit up again, a flaming sword slicing though his mind and knocking him to the ground as he ducked. It was over in an instant, he knew, but somehow it didn't seem that way. Bright spots of light danced before his eyes, dazing him over and over again as they flirted with the deafening noise that spiralled about his head. He couldn't remember why he was here, or indeed where he was at all, the grey world swimming behind those blinding lights.

It was the pain that returned first. It forced its way through the daze – slowly to start, then with force. He drew a fierce breath as his eyes snapped back into focus, alarmed at the sight of the stake protruding from beneath his left collarbone. The wire it had carried had mostly been swallowed by mud, but there still remained an amount to rip its way through his tunic and claw into skin.

He tore it off, bloodying his hands and causing further lacerations before the stubborn line would come away. He found the movement of his arms inhibited by the shaft buried in his flesh; that would have to be removed too.

"Don't!" A voice sounded nearby, caught somewhere between authority and agony. In his shock, he had forgotten the lieutenant was there. "You don't want to bleed to death."

"Sir?" he paused, scanning the debris. "Where are you?"

"Down here."

The pained voice came again and this time Stack found its owner. The unsteady wheel had been blasted from its axle and was now settled over Sandford's legs, crushing them into the bog at an unnatural angle. His face was beyond pale, mouth twisted as he forced himself to remain composed.

"We need to get that off you sir," Stack crouched to grasp the wheel, only to be painfully halted as his muscles tensed around the stake. He gritted his teeth. "I've got to take this out."

"Don't be stupid, man, it's too risky," the lieutenant looked at him sternly behind the blood trickling down from his blonde hair. "Somebody will be along soon; I can wait. Get yourself back to the lines if you can."

He stared at him incredulously. "I'm not leaving you here. I'll wait too."

Sandford looked relieved. "Thank you. Let's hope they come soon."

No sign, however, came from the blackened depths of No Man's Land to suggest that the rest of the patrol were even alive, let alone coming to find them. The night dragged on for what felt like years, the young lieutenant's face becoming greyer with each passing breath. Stack tried again to move the wheel, but the pain in his shoulder would not let him, coupling with the exhaustion of the past few sleepless nights in an attempt to wipe him out completely. He leant against the wreckage, sharing apprehensive looks with the moon.

"I'm really sorry," Sandford spoke in a hoarse whisper.

"What for?" his companion tore his eyes from the sky. "None of this is your fault sir."

"Enough of the 'sir'," he shook his head, smearing mud further into his hair. "I'm no 'sir', look at me. I'm just plain James Sandford, no better than the rest of you."

"You're the best officer I've ever known," Stack shrugged, wincing at the movement.

The lieutenant smiled weakly. "You haven't known very many. A lot of people have died, Stack, where perhaps a more senior officer could have saved them."

"Kent was a senior officer," he said before he could stop himself. "He didn't save anyone; he shot them."

"Major Kent is dead…" Sandford started.

"That doesn't make him forgiven."

"I know," Sandford stared guiltily at the wheel that held him captive.

Here, lying on his back with his brow furrowed in pain, no coat billowing or gun firing, he looked a lot more vulnerable than the strong leader Stack was now used to. He was only young, he remembered, too young for such responsibility. And yet he carried it so well, even now.

"I'm sorry, that's all. I wish things could have turned out differently. We both lost a friend today, you know. For all his flaws, the major was still my friend."

Stack bowed his head. He could never again bring himself to speak well of the man, but he hoped this gesture was enough respect to give Sandford peace.

"I don't think they're coming sir," he said at length, pushing himself up.

"Don't you dare touch that wheel, Stack," the lieutenant warned. "I can wait."

"I'm losing strength, sir," Stack hesitated. "If I don't lift it now I might never be able to."

"I can wait," he repeated firmly. "That's an order. They will come and we will both be alright."

"What if they don't?"

"Don't worry," Sandford smiled again. "I don't plan on dying."

He reached into his pocket, groaning as the movement put strain on his legs, and pulled out a photograph.

"Lily, her name is," he said, handing the picture to Stack. "Soon to be Lily Sandford if all goes as planned. Even officers have hearts, Stack, but something tells me I won't be such an appealing choice if I'm dead."

Stack would have laughed if he wasn't so exhausted. "I think you're right there."

"She took the picture especially, when I received my commission," his eyes lit up fondly behind the dried blood. "She said that she was sure I would be so happy playing soldier that I would forget her if she didn't. It's odd to think of simple things like that, after everything that's happened."

Stack nodded. "I know what you mean."

"Do you have a woman waiting for you back home?" Sandford asked, taking back the picture and folding it carefully.

"No," he lowered his eyes bashfully. "Maybe. Captain seemed to think I do."

He smiled sadly, remembering the countless times his friend had teased him and the odd feeling of hope it had created.

"Only she's not at home, she's out here with us. She joined up with her sister to be a nurse."

"Admirable woman," the lieutenant looked impressed. "Well, Stack, I suggest you keep yourself alive long enough to prove Captain right. He would want that."

He was right of course, and the thought kept Stack going for the next couple of hours as they waited patiently for somebody to come. They talked infrequently, not wanting to attract the wrong attention but needing the distraction to stop themselves falling asleep. The left side of Stack's upper body had numbed to the point where he could barely feel it at all, and the soft ringing in his ears dulled his senses and lowered his lids over bloodshot eyes.

He snapped them open, furious with himself. He had avoided dozing off, just. One minute of sleep at the wrong time and he could kill them both. The sky was past its darkest now; nobody was coming to rescue them. He glanced across at the lieutenant, eyes closed and breathing uneasily, his face the colour of sour milk. They couldn't wait any longer.

Looking about for snipers, he stood warily; his senses were not at their most alert but they would have to do. He took a deep breath and gritted his teeth, closing both fists around the stake in his flesh and pulling hard. The pain came flooding back in a suffocating wave, doubling him over as blood ran freely from the open wound. But he couldn't worry himself with that now.

He blotted it from his mind as best he could and steadied himself, wiping his hands in his trousers and securing them under one side of the wheel. Bracing his shoulders and causing further strain on the wound, he pushed the infernal thing into the air and managed to heave it over to one side. It took all he had to pull the lieutenant onto his back, almost unable to move his shaking legs under the dead weight.

Still, somehow he managed to drag them both through the sludge, forcing himself to move faster with every hint of morning that broke through the cloud. He didn't know where he was going – his mind was too shattered for that – but it was enough to keep walking, staggering somewhere. He didn't know how long he had been struggling for, or at what point his legs gave way. He didn't feel his eyes closing, or the Passchendaele mud that supported his head like a pillow; his mind had been asleep long before his body stopped walking.

15.

The little girl made her way down the bridle-path, the tiny face behind those wild curls screwed up tight as she lashed out with a stick at the surrounding bushes. She was dressed as if she should belong up at the big house, but her frock was torn and she had an angry gash on her knee; something the estate would certainly not tolerate.

"Are you alright?" Ben called, approaching curiously.

"No," she said shortly, glaring at the stick in her hand.

"What are you doing with that?"

"Fighting," she stuck her chin in the air defiantly. "My mother says I'll never be a lady, so I might as well be a man and men do fighting."

"Well you're doing that all wrong," he looked at her sword with a critical eye.

Edward had spent enough time teaching his little brother how to use a stick properly, when he wasn't busy with Thomas of course. He reached out a hand and she reluctantly dropped the stretch of wood into it.

"Look, you hold it like this."

The girl let out a frustrated growl. "So I can't even fight right? I'll never be better than my sister at anything!"

"Why would you want to?" he asked, shrugging beneath the baggy shoulders of Edward's old shirt. "My brothers are always being better than each other, but they're never happy."

He put the stick back into her hand, folding her fingers to correct the grip.

"Come on, I'll show you how to fight if you want," he paused. "But you have to do it for fun, no trying to be better than your sister."

****

His chest rose and fell and eyes moved rapidly behind his eyelids, but still he wouldn't wake. She stared at him as if in a dream, the candlelight waning in the shadows. Its orange glow danced across the bedsheets, illuminating the curve of his chin and darkening the ugly scar that cut his face in two. She wanted to reach out and touch it, as if somehow her fingertips could erase it and bring him home, but she remained as still as him, watching and breathing.

Now she thought about it, she wasn't really sure what use she was to him at all. They had cleaned him up and stitched the damage beneath his collarbone, only the faintest specks of blood now leaking through the bandages that wound their way around his chest. All she could do now was watch.

"How is he?" her sister's voice spoke from the darkness and soft hands lifted her hair back over her shoulder.

"Still sleeping," she replied, trying to hide how much Eliza had startled her. "Which I suppose I should be too."

"You should be allowed to sleep here," Eliza whispered, resting her chin on her sister's shoulder. "You'll never get any rest if you're worrying."

"You know the rules," Harriet sighed, not taking her eyes off his poor face. "Matron's warned Emmeline enough times that anybody she deems too close to a patient will be moved on."

"Damn the rules," Eliza scowled. "You're my sister; you can do whatever you like."

Harriet smiled. "I don't think being your sister counts for too much here."

****

Ben spat on the window and rubbed it with his sleeve, though it didn't make much of a difference to the pristine glass. The two of them peered through into the grand room beyond, the head of the sickly lordling just invisible behind the back of an embroidered chair.

"I think I want to live in a house like George," Harriet whispered.

"George is ill," Ben pointed out.

"I know, I never said I wanted to be *George," she gave him a look. "I just want a house like his, and horses, and servants to do everything boring like playing the piano and getting dressed."*

"I don't," he shrugged.

"I suppose it's alright for you; nobody tries to make you dress up and play the piano," she sighed. "I'm so jealous. But wouldn't you want servants for some things? And a big house, and power too?"

"Not really," he turned away from the window, looking out across the trees and fields instead. "I'm fine how I am, don't need anything fancy. Let's go somewhere else."

They slipped back into the neatly trimmed bushes, pelting out across the grass and screaming with exhilaration as they outran the fat dog that was supposed to keep guard. Ben helped Harriet clamber up the tree whose branches curved in an arch over the great gate and almost touched the ground on the other side, allowing them to enter and leave the estate unnoticed.

They continued to run until the big house was far behind them and they entered the sparse woods that lolled along the side of the stream. The banks were shallow here, but carried enough water for a good splash to ease the summer heat, and if Ben tipped his hand at just the right angle a stone could skim for a good few beats. A small bridge crossed where the road cut through the trees and they threw twigs from the side, spinning to see whose would emerge the fastest.

Harriet leaned her arms on the rickety barrier, resting her chin on them as she watched the twigs continue to race downstream.

"I hate Edward," she said finally. "And Thomas too."

Ben looked up in surprise. "Why? What have they done?"

"Nothing really," she admitted, chewing her lip. "But everyone's always saying how good Edward is at one thing and how good Thomas is at something else. You don't ever get a chance do you?"

He laughed. "I don't want a chance. They can keep being good at things, I have more fun."

"I guess," she continued to stare downstream, her mind running away with the current to a time when people would see her like they saw her sister. "But I still hate them for it."

"That's stupid," he leaned next to her and nudged her arm. "What if I said I hated Eliza?"

"Well that would be stupid," she replied. "She never asked to be beautiful, it just happened."

Ben shrugged. "Edward and Thomas never asked to be better than me."

"They're not," Harriet scowled. "That's the difference."

****

"You know what Benji," Captain leaned against the wall of the barracks, arms folded and hair falling across his forehead. "I think you won't even try for promotion because you think Edward should get it first." He gave him a look, daring him to contradict. "And don't you tell me I'm wrong."

"He is the oldest in the section, and the best soldier."

"Nah," Captain shook his curly head, the fever in his eyes as it always was when he caught onto a silly idea. "He follows the rules best, that doesn't make him the best soldier or any good at leading a section. Can you really see me and Rigby doing what he tells us to?"

Stack laughed. "I can't see you doing what I tell you to either!"

"I would you know," he sparked up a cigarette and held it suspended in front of his mouth. "Everyone would, I reckon. And Sandford likes you; that's got to stand for something."

"Stop it Cap," Stack leaned back in his seat, laughing it off. "You're messing with my head. Why aren't you an NCO if you're so keen? Anyone would be better than poor Marshall."

"I'm not right for it," he took a long drag. *"No, one day Benji, you'll be in charge of this rabble, Edward included. One condition though; you'd better let me be your second."*

"I don't think I could stop you if I wanted to," he grinned, *dodging a kick.*

****

Where are you now Cap? His eyes moved behind his eyelids but he felt as if they would never open again. Every now and then he caught faint sounds of people moving about him, but mostly it was just the white noise. He had given up trying to move his limbs when he realised they were no longer attached to Lieutenant Sandford, letting the exhaustion take hold and keep him still. His chest hurt with every breath he took, but he didn't care. Everyone was dead; he might as well be too.

Captain had been wrong on so many things. He hadn't been able to save Edward, or Tommy Miller or Vincent Waterman or any of the others. He hadn't been able to stop Rob leaving home, or keep track of what had become of him. He hadn't been able to stay awake long enough to get Sandford to safety, and he suspected his failure had killed the man. And he hadn't even been able to save his best friend, the man he had once deemed invincible, who had kept him going through so much and told him he could do all these things.

"It's war mate," he heard him as clearly as if he was standing right next to him. *"People die; it's nobody's fault. Just forget it."*

But he could never forget it. He half wished that shrapnel hadn't killed Major Kent, that the knowledge of shooting his own man would stay in his living memory and break him down until he too was perched on the parapet screaming at No Man's Land. Though, he thought bitterly, Kent wasn't the type of man to let matters of conscience bother him.

"*Forget it Ben,*" the voice said sternly. He closed his inner eyes and went back to sleep.

****

"*I don't want to go outside,*" *she whispered, her voice catching in her throat.*

The thunder clapped again and she jumped backwards, hiding her face in his shoulder. They were both soaked through from the sudden storm, hiding out in the hay barn in the hope that it would pass as quickly as it began. It hadn't.

"*We can't stay in here forever; what if Holler finds us?*"

"*I'll take Holler over the dead horse!*"

He fell back into the hay, unable to hold himself up with laughter.

"*What?*" *she asked indignantly, looking very comical with her wet hair and irritated expression.*

"*You know I made that up, right?*"

"*It could easily be true,*" *she shivered as the rainfall increased outside.* "*You don't know everything.*"

"*I know some things,*" *he grinned cheekily.* "*I know something about Edward that even Thomas doesn't know.*"

"*What?*" *she lay down next to him, distracted for the moment from the thought of ghosts wandering the storm.*

"You can't tell him I know," he told her. "I found out by accident."

"I won't."

"Edward's got a girl," he whispered.

Harriet giggled. "Eliza won't be pleased. She told me once that mother wants her to marry a rich man, but she would prefer Edward because he has nice arms."

"Marrying a rich man wouldn't be bad either," he commented. "You'd be able to live in a big house like George and have servants play the piano for you."

She grinned. "You still remember that? I'll have you know I'm not too bad at piano now, though I still hate it just as much. I don't want to get married though. Eliza's always talking about it, but I can't think of anything worse than signing up to spend your whole life with someone. I hardly like anyone except you and Eliza and father."

She rolled over and propped her head up on her fists. "I suppose I wouldn't mind marrying you; I spend my whole life with you anyway."

"I guess I wouldn't mind that either," he turned his head so the hay tickled his eyebrows. "I'm not kissing you though; I've seen Edward doing it and it's disgusting."

"Definitely," she agreed. "I'd be no good at it anyway."

She reached out a hand and he clasped it, as if shaking on a deal.

"I wish George wasn't dying," she whispered, squeezing his hand tighter. "I don't know how much longer he'll be here for father to treat, and then...I don't know."

"Will you go back to London?"

"I won't," she said firmly. "I hate London. I just know my mother will try to make me."

"Maybe George won't die," he said comfortingly. "Dr Redmond is really good at his job."

"Maybe."

A great thunderclap sounded and lightning illuminated the barn, making her shriek and dive forward into the hay, getting it tangled into her slowly drying hair. He laughed and threw more over her head, a gesture she returned fervently. Farmer Holler found them the next morning; two children curled up together, asleep in the hay.

****

There was something wet on his face. It slithered across his brow then down to his neck, leaving a trail of liquid on his skin. He reached up to touch it, forgetting for a moment that his arms were chained with sleep. To his surprise, just as he remembered he couldn't move, the hand raised itself and hit him in the face, control abandoned in his shock.

Somebody laughed; a woman, certainly not a German prison guard. He blinked, finding that his eyes too were now willing to open.

Harriet couldn't control herself. Nothing was really that funny, but still she clutched her stomach, tears pricking in the corner of her eyes with laughter. It must have been relief, coupled with the hysteria brought on by an inability to sleep well ever since her encounter with the ruined face of the gefreiter. He looked up at her, brows furrowed in total confusion, and it was as if the scar was melting away – this was his face, his expressions and he was really here, and for some reason she couldn't stop laughing.

"Nice to have a man who amuses you," Emmeline commented, pulling up beside her. "You'd better stop cackling though – the old hag's looking at you. Best keep working and come back when she's done with her snooping."

"Harriet?" the sergeant pushed himself up onto his elbows, dismayed at how weak his arms felt.

She nodded, too giddy to know what else to do. Emmeline had her hand and she let her lead her away, promising in a jumble of words and sentences that she would be back to talk as soon as she could. He sat up groggily, no less confused.

"She is pretty," Captain leaned against the bed, bottle in hand. *"I'm impressed Benji."*

Stack screwed up his eyes painfully. *You're not real, Cap.*

"True," he took a swig. *"But she is. And if you don't do something with that I am going to hurt you."*

Emmeline had been right of course, and he looked forward to the times between Harriet's shifts when her superiors were out of the way. He had worried at first that they would send him home – Harriet had even suggested it – but he was healing well and since he had refused the offer presented to him it had not been spoken of since. He knew it was probably crazy, but all he wanted was to return as soon as possible to his men. Rigby had no Harriet to comfort him, and Stack felt uneasy leaving Wayson to face Ypres on his own. They wouldn't even have Sandford to turn to; the lieutenant had already been shipped back to England.

But whenever his worries tightened their hold, Nurse Redmond would appear at his bedside with a bottle of spirits and a headful of memories to ease both their minds. It was good to know that he hadn't been entirely right when he had spoken to Captain that first night in the salient; it wasn't only the army who understood the horrors of the front. Though she had never been in a trench or killed anybody directly, she had seen plenty die in equally agonising ways, believing many of them could have been saved by quicker thinking on her part.

She had the same sorts of dreams, had also lost friends, and reminded him strongly of Captain with the amount of alcohol she now consumed when she had a day off. Perhaps going home would not be so unbearable, not if she was there.

"Were you there when Aedan died?" she asked nervously, hands fidgeting as if she wasn't sure if she wanted to know the answer. "Did it hurt him badly?"

"We were working," he remembered. He had felt so young then, with no responsibility and having experienced the smallest fraction of what he had now. Thomas and Edward had been alive, and his face was yet to be disfigured by the scar that now cut it in half.

"Digging a latrine in fact." The thought of it almost made him chuckle. "Only as fast as we were digging, Captain was refilling the damned thing with dead rats and God knows what else. I guess Aedan's head was just a little too high and a sniper got him. He was laughing when it happened though, and it was quick. I doubt he even knew it happened."

"Thank you," Harriet smiled weakly, blinking back the water in her eyes. "The time I've seen it take for men to die…"

"Not Aedan," he squeezed her hand.

"And not Captain," she returned the gesture. "At least they have that."

Stack nodded. He hadn't thought of it like that before. Nothing could make him forget that look of desperate confusion in his friend's eyes, but at least it had been confusion, not agony.

"You're right," he told her.

"He'd want you to remember that, not the bad parts."

"He'd want me to remember that he's always right and I still owe him a week's worth of rum." He couldn't help but smile at the thought.

She smiled too, sniffing back the last of her tears. "And Aedan would want me to remember where I hid Mr Gale's best cufflinks, and not to run in the servants' hall."

"You're awful," Stack laughed.

She nodded. "He'd want me to remember that too."

"You have a shift tomorrow morning don't you?" Emmeline caught her as she made her way out of the ward. She nodded. "And then the next one isn't until afternoon the next day?" – She nodded again – "There's an Irish battalion on leave in town. I've heard they have a band that's going to play tomorrow night. Gilbey and Ruddock are feeling up to going; a lot of the patients are. The old hag has always said it's a good idea to let them get out and about, for morale and exercise."

Harriet smiled knowingly. "I can cover you, don't worry."

"No!" the American giggled. "That's not what I meant – for once. No, I think you should go."

"Why would I want to?" she looked at her in confusion. "I'm not the one in love with half the British army."

"Don't forget the French and Belgians and Canadians and the Anzacs too," Emmeline told her indignantly. "I do not discriminate. But that's not the point."

A scheming smile crossed her face and apprehension stirred in Harriet's stomach.

"What are you up to?"

"Oh, I'm just on my way to persuade a certain sergeant to take you into town tomorrow night."

"No you're not!"

She flashed a white grin and danced past Harriet as she attempted to block her path.

"Emmeline!"

"You British are so scared," Emmeline shook her head disapprovingly. "Don't you worry yourself; I'm a master at this sort of thing."

****

"I can't believe I let you talk me into this," Harriet scowled at the window as Emmeline and Eliza tried to decide what to do with her hair. "I can't believe *Ben* let you talk him into this! He should be resting."

"Do stop fussing," Eliza shook her head fondly. "I don't see what you're so worried about; you talk to him quite happily in the ward."

"That's different," she tried to explain. "We've been through too much, it isn't *right* to have fun. We're friends here; we can talk about things and try to deal with it. But this is a war Liza; his best friend has just been shot! He doesn't want to go out dancing with some hussy. What right do I have?"

"Harriet," Emmeline seated herself on the bed in front of her and looked her in the eyes. "If somebody shot Eliza, who is the only person who could cheer you up?"

Harriet didn't reply, biting her lip nervously.

"Would you want to sit there moping, or would you want to see as much of him as possible?"

"Okay, fine," she hopped off the bed, out of the way of Eliza's fussing hands. "But you do not need to do anything to my hair and you can put that make-up away right now. I am a *nurse*, not a prostitute!"

She managed to wriggle out of her sister's grasp, nerves almost combated by the desire to get away from these silly females and have company that made sense. Emmeline insisted on frogmarching her out of the hospital and down the road and Eliza followed, laughing prettily like she always had done before war had made her a widow.

They spotted the group of soldiers waiting for them at the turn towards the centre of town and Harriet felt excitement stirring in her stomach. She hadn't been dancing in a long, long time.

"Have fun!" Emmeline beamed, practically throwing her at Ben, who had to catch her as she tripped on uneven ground. "Don't do anything I wouldn't!"

"That would mean I could do anything at all!" she retorted, clutching his arm to steady herself.

The American pulled a face and marched Eliza back up the road, leaving Harriet shaking her head fondly at their retreating backs.

"I apologise for her existence," she smiled coyly, curls bouncing.

"I like her," Ben chuckled. "Captain would like her even more."

"I'd imagine he would, and she would like him just as well!"

She rolled her eyes and they began to walk, following the other four soldiers and one nurse. Tilly Norwich had also been lucky with her shift pattern, looking very pleased with all the attention she was receiving from Corporal Gilbey now that Emmeline wasn't around.

"I do wish I could have met him."

"You two together would be the death of me," he teased. It was a bittersweet thought, but with Harriet on his arm and Captain's mirage striding contently beside them he couldn't feel sad. "I was going to bring him back to the farm after the war. He would be the worst influence on Rob and the three of you would get me into no end of trouble."

"That sounds like fun," she grinned, eyes gleaming with the spark that had led them to misadventure so often in their youth.

The hall wasn't as big as she had imagined. Tables and chairs were pushed to one side to make room for the band and the dancers, thrown together in a happy sweaty jumble as they tangled between each other. A bar was situated along the far wall and it was Harriet's first instinct to head straight there, but Tilly caught her hand and gave her a firm look – of course Emmeline would have sent somebody to keep her in check.

Harriet smiled at her friend's persistence and conceded, letting Tilly and Gilbey lead her and Ben into the throng. It was a jolly tune and the close air caught her, filling her body with energy and clearing her head of everything but the jig and the warm hand holding her own.

The pace of the Irishmen was impressive and it wasn't long before the English couldn't keep up, Harriet falling gratefully onto the bar at the finish of a song. She rummaged in her bag for francs, before hearing Ben ordering for her, coins in hand. He must have read the quizzical look on her face, because he laughed and nudged her.

"A sergeant's wage isn't bad; I'm the rich one out here."

She liked the idea of that. Being the Lady's sister had always felt more like a boundary than a blessing, separating her from normal people. Here she was a person, and Ben was a person, and he was paying for her. She threw the drink down her throat happily and pulled him back for the next energetic dance.

Captain leaned against the bar, drink in hand and foot tapping, watching them proudly as if it were his son, not his friend, dancing with the prettiest woman in the room.

After more songs and more drink even the Irish were beginning to lag, and the band obliged by breaking from the lively ditties for a gentler refrain – an old ballad they all seemed to know by heart. The dancers slowed and those without partners cleared the floor, Harriet finding herself pressed against Ben's torso in a closed hold more like an embrace. Despite the blissful fuzz the drink brought to her head, she felt her heartbeat quicken, and when she raised her eyes to meet his he looked just as she felt. Something tightened in her chest as her lips moved in a whisper without her permission.

"I love you."

"What?" he leaned closer, unable to hear over the music.

"Nothing," she shook her head hastily, glad of his strong arms around her as her legs threatened to turn to jelly. "I…"

She cast about for something to say. Her eyes settled on the thick raised line, unmissable as it cut through his face. She had thought it ugly at first, but the thing had grown on her, so much that he seemed to look more like himself now than he did before.

"Did that hurt?"

"No," he tried to remember. "I don't think so, not at first anyway."

"Shock I guess," she looked at it with interest, the nurse in her coming out.

"Or my face was so used to Rob whacking it before he decided guns are better than swords."

Harriet let out a burst of laughter, her legs steadying with the familiarity of it. She missed Rob, and Matthew, and the way Ben always humoured their games. She pulled her hand out its dancing position to wrap her arms around him, breathing in the smell of his neck and imagining for a moment that they were home. It came easier than she could have hoped for and when she opened her eyes they were wet.

"Hey," Ben brushed a tear from her cheek. "Don't be sad, silly. I'm fine."

She shook her head, wiping her eyes with the back of her hand. "I'm really happy."

"You don't look it."

"I am, I promise," she smiled, making him wince as she pressed her head back into his chest near the healing wound. "I didn't think I could feel this happy ever again, but if I close my eyes it feels like nothing's changed at all. You're here and there is no war. We're dancing at one of Eliza's parties. I've convinced Aedan to smuggle you and Rob in, and Liza's laughing and trying to pretend she hasn't noticed, while Rob's dancing with all the gentry's daughters and Aedan's wishing he never agreed to it. Can't you just see it?"

He didn't need to close his eyes. Captain already saluted him from the bar, and when he looked closer that was Aedan next to him, trying to convince him to go easy on the drink. Rob spun two girls in turn in the centre of the hall, tall and bold and alive as ever, and

Edward sat at the side giving him disapproving looks. Even little Tommy Miller danced bashfully with a young nurse, heckled by Collie and Yates.

It felt like home. After years of meticulously avoiding the opportunity to think too much of those he missed, now she made him do it in just one night. And it didn't hurt him like he thought it should. Remembering wasn't such a bad thing; it kept his friends alive, it kept home alive. He held Harriet tighter, squeezing her shoulder.

"Of course I can see it," he whispered in her ear. "It's real. Everybody's here and Eliza will be furious at you for letting them all in."

She giggled. "Probably. I'd better not go home tonight, or she'll skin me alive. Can we sleep in Holler's barn?"

"I don't know if that would be a good idea," he smiled. "Wouldn't your matron wonder where we were?"

"What matron?" she looked up at him, mischief playing on her face. "There are no matrons in Kent, only father."

"Okay you," he lifted her off the ground, ignoring the pull on his injury. "If you're so determined to get in trouble, let's go find us a Holler's barn."

"One more drink first?" she asked, blinking at him as she had seen Eliza do a thousand times to men in London.

"She is definitely a keeper," Captain clapped him on the back, and for a second he almost felt it.

Stack grinned modestly, replying in his head. *Get out of here, Cap.*

"Gladly," he raised his glass. *"I'll leave you two to it."*

Harriet found the old schoolhouse with only a few wrong turns along the way. It had burnt down shortly before the Germans entered Belgium, but its barren half-walls still acted as a reminder of the destruction of war. Somebody had filled a corner with hay and horses were occasionally stabled there, presumably for the cavalry. There were no horses when they arrived, flushed from drink and their walk, but the corner had not been cleared and the smell of the beasts was thick in the air. It was comforting to their noses; a country smell, a proof of living things and a reminder of home.

Stack stretched his arms and fell back into the hay, enjoying the feel of it tickling his cheek as he had done since childhood. Harriet followed suit, laying her head back against his shoulder so she could look at the stars peeping down through charred beams.

"Ben?" she asked, playing with the straw at his side. "Can Eliza and I stay at the farm, just until we find somewhere else? I don't think she could stand that huge empty house, and I know I couldn't. And...I do miss you, and I'd like to see you more. You're the best friend I've ever had."

"You won't be saying that when I'm waking the whole house up, thinking I'm back in Wipers in my sleep. There are things I've seen I won't be forgetting for a long time." It was only half a joke.

"That makes two of us," she said quietly. "Ben...I know I'm no substitute for your brothers and your friends – they've been with you through everything, nothing can replace that…But I have seen some things, and I know some of what you're going through. So just know that I'm here, whenever you need me."

Stack was surprised to see that she looked guilty, scared almost, as if suggesting herself for help was somehow disrespectful. He smiled teasingly at her. "I guess you'll do."

"Oh good!" she laughed, relief flooding her face. "And you'll do too, I suppose."

"I should hope so, after everything I've put up with from you."

She giggled and hit him on the shoulder, burrowing her head into his neck.

"We should have had years," she murmured. "Climbing trees and swimming in the stream and annoying the life out of Edward and our parents. I wasted so much time in London; I owe you so much time. It's my turn to look after you now." Her hand brushed lightly over the wound beneath his collar bone and she added, "You bloody idiot."

Harriet hadn't slept so well in months, despite the night's chill and the rain that fell through the remnants of the roof to matt her hair beneath his fingers. There were no dying faces to trouble her dreams, nobody shrieking as they lost their legs first to gangrene then to the surgeon's knife. Nothing had changed, not really. She was back in the hay, back with Ben, and they were both going to be in so much trouble when they woke.

****

"Hattie," someone was shaking her and slowly she came back to the nurses' dormitory; warmer and drier but so disappointing to wake up to. Still, she couldn't help but smile, knowing that it wasn't just a dream. She hugged the pillow to her cheek, reluctant to open her eyes.

"What?" she asked groggily.

"Ben's leaving, with the others who are fit for duty. The wagon's at the bottom of the road; if you hurry you might catch them."

"Now!?"

Her eyes snapped open and she shot upright, making Eliza jump backwards. She left her hair and nightdress as they were, snatching only a coat as she sprinted from the room. She hadn't thought they would be discharged until the end of the week, or she wouldn't have slept in so late. She threw herself through the door into the street, practically spinning Emmeline who stood in her way, waving goodbye to Private Ruddock at the back of the retreating group.

"Ben!"

She pulled the coat about her, bare feet splashing through puddles. She caught up to the men marching slowly under their heavy packs, calling again. He turned and she caught his arm, pulling him out of formation. She couldn't allow herself time to breathe, or explain, or her breath would stop and she would never do anything. There was a war on; even Eliza couldn't expect her to be ladylike.

Her hands found his lapels and she pulled herself onto her toes, her mouth clutching at his. It didn't take him long to reply, arms moving up to cradle her shoulders as the adrenaline shook them beneath the heavy coat.

"I love you," she stammered, pulling back to look him in the eyes. Trembling hands stroked his face, roughly shaven skin soothing her palms as her thumbs brushed the line of scar tissue.

"Come on sergeant!" the driver called and her stomach tightened.

"You come back, you hear me?" she pleaded, one hand still on his cheek. "You come back."

He took her fingers from his face and squeezed them between his own, pausing for a moment to hold her gaze. "I will."

"You'd better, Ben Stack."

She let him go and backed away, pulling the coat tighter about her. Her toes wriggled into the mud between them as she watched him shrink into the distance, her heart thumping so hard it could crack her ribs. Emmeline came up behind her, slipping an arm through the crook in her elbow and giving her a supportive smile.

"Oh Em," she dropped her face onto her shoulder, head reeling. "I am going to be in so much trouble."

The American grinned. "I won't tell if you won't."

There was a new energy in Stack's steps as he hopped up with the others, ready for their journey back to dystopia. There would soon be lice in his clothing and mud in his boots, but why should he care about silly things like that?

The man beside him caught his eye, puffing on a cigarette and beaming knowingly. Captain didn't have to say anything; he could read that smile like a book. Life certainly could be surprisingly good.

****

Sergeant Stack's mood darkened with the scenery, the reality of war forcing its way back into his dream-saturated mind. The figure of Captain grew fainter in the thickening air, the teasing smile that played about his lips giving way to the man's more recent expression; one of shock, and such confusion. Stack was dropped off to walk the final stretch, but when they reached the edge of the pile of rubble town where the platoon was barracked, Captain wouldn't walk with him.

"Come on Cap."

"No way," he shook his head, eyes widening in madness. *"I'm not going back out there."*

"Come on," he pleaded, not wanting to face the guns without him.

"Ben!" Rigby jogged out to greet him. "Welcome back old boy!" He looked about. "Who are you talking to?"

"Nobody."

It had been a dream, he realised with a sinking stomach, spirits falling with each step he took, away from Captain and away from Harriet. He had been a fool to believe it could last, that they would always be there; his best friend and the woman he loved. His best friend was dead. And the woman...She loved him. That was something.

"Weir!" he barked. "Weir! Where is he, Rig? I need to talk to him about women."

Rigby played with his hands, guilt crossing his face.

"Weir's dead, Ben. Something took him down – shrapnel or bullets I don't know – and that dog of his rushed to his side, poor runt, trying to get him up again. I tried to get to him, next thing I know I'm on the floor covered in pieces of him. Whizzbang, direct hit."

"Shit," Stack dropped his head to his hands.

"Poor bloody things," Rigby said sadly. "The conscript and his pet. Neither of them belonged here."

"That's it Rigby," he looked at him desperately. "We're not losing any more. Nobody else in my section is allowed to die."

16.

"Aedan O'Connor…"

Wayson turned in his bed, adjusting so the light from his small candle could fall on the grubby trench newspaper in his hands. The winter of 1917 was coming to an end, and the Germans were preparing their strength for the predicted flood of fresh American troops across the Atlantic. There would be a good fight then – likely even earlier, in Fritz's frail hope that he could defeat them before their allies arrived – but until then there was nothing to do but wait and shiver and read the newspaper.

"Thomas Stack…Charlie Pepper…Edward Stack…"

A blast harassed the ground above the dugout – a large assembly of underground rooms and bunks, dugouts having moved on a lot since the crude holes of 1915 – and Wayson ducked. He lay still until the noise ceased and he could sit back up and shake the dust from his hair. Ducking, that was something else to do while he waited for the fight; a lot of ducking and scurrying about in holes.

Here in the dugout beneath something that no more resembled a village than he did, it was harder to hold onto his and Rob's dream; his identity as a man of England. There was too much time to think here. And this winter there had been no Captain to pass the time with jokes and profanities.

"Tommy Miller…Andrew Marshall…Adam Price…Richie Yates…"

Wayson exhaled sadly at the boy's name. No number of months, or years, could ever make him forget seeing him go down, or feel any less guilty about it. He folded up the newspaper and slipped out of his bunk. The sergeant had to be woken; he couldn't take his goddamn roll-call of the dead any longer.

The poor man's sleep had been tortured ever since he returned from hospital. When he was not listing out the names of every fallen man he had known, he was replaying scenes from the front, always waking up looking more exhausted than he had been before he dozed off. Wayson supposed that was what happened when you saw your best friend die; poor Waterman had been worse. For the first time, he was glad the war had separated him from Rob – neither of them would have to go through such a thing.

"Tristan Holden…Jim Collingwood…Bobby Watson…"

"Sir," Wayson whispered. "Wake up sir, you're dreaming again."

"What the hell do you think you're doing?" His eyes snapped open, but the boy could tell he was still asleep. Wayson had heard this too many times before.

"Sergeant Stack, sir," he tried to stay calm. It made his hairs stand on end to hear it again and again, knowing the man wouldn't even remember when he woke. "It's okay, you can wake up."

"No you didn't!" he called to nobody, face contorted in pain. "It wasn't you Cap, it was the war! Just the war!"

"Sir!"

Stack quietened, eyelids shutting again and head falling back to the side. Wayson stood over him for a moment more, concern staying his feet. He had watched Vincent writhing in his sleep many a night, and Captain's dreams hadn't been too pleasant either. Surely not the sergeant too? The man was a rock; things happened and he just kept going, always there for Wayson, always there for everyone. The dreams couldn't take him too.

He scuttled out into the neighbouring bunkroom, where newly-promoted Rigby's section was situated. The tall auburn man was awake, sitting on his bed with a cigarette smouldering in his mouth as he scribbled away at a sketchpad.

"Wayson?" he looked up. "Whizzbangs keeping you up?"

He shook his head. "I can sleep through those by now. It's Sergeant Stack I'm worried about."

"He been dreaming again?" Wayson went to reply, but Rigby fixed him with a firm look. "*Everyone* dreams, Wayson. I'm sure you've had plenty of your own. He's no different when he's awake, is he?"

He gave the boy a reassuring smile. "I know Ben; it's just his way of mourning. Can't keep it all inside forever, but too stubborn to act upset in front of you lads. When Cap died, I blubbed for days. I haven't seen him cry once, not once in all the time I've known him. Of course he's going to let it out somehow. Chin up, you're a man now, and men don't worry about stupid things."

He offered Wayson a cigarette and he took it. Once, smoking had made him feel powerful and grown-up. Now it was just puffing, just a way to make time pass.

"I am, aren't I?" he mused, not sure if he was glad of the fact. "It was my birthday, three days ago now."

"You kept that quiet," Rigby commented. "Happy birthday."

"Nineteen years old," he let out a heavy breath of smoke. "Isn't that strange? I've been here nearly two years already, and I'm only just old enough."

Looking back, with two years more experience, he had to wonder if they hadn't been idiots. Glorious idiots, that was for sure, and the world would thank them for it later, but idiots all the same.

"Can I use some paper?" he asked, motioning at the pad on Rigby's knees.

Rigby nodded.

"Thanks."

Kit Allenby, he scribbled. *Birthday 6 December 1895. Signed up in London.*

He put the paper into the sergeant's hands, waking him from a quieter dream than before.

"It's everything I know," he told him hoarsely. "Along with the knowledge he's in a tank, you might be able to find him."

****

Spring of 1918 dawned red, a crimson smear as the brush of the German advance painted the Western Front with blood. High command was in a panic as they forced retreat after retreat; at this rate, the allies would be broken before the Americans had a chance even to get off their boats. They had taken back the land around the Somme river – ground gained at the cost of Collie, Yates and Tommy Miller, and thousands of men like them. Gone in a few days. It was a bitter waste.

But there was no time to consider that now. Crouched in rubble-filled shallow trenches, they sheltered from the hellish conversation that played out between the Germans and their own artillery. Mackie crouched at the highest point they had, taking careful shots at the storm troopers who seemed to sprint through land it had taken them months to gain. Machine gun fire opened up and Stack replied as best he could in the turmoil. He kept Wayson at his side, and a close eye on the rest of his charges, Corporal Rigby doing the same further down.

"They're coming," Rigby gritted his teeth, wishing he could think of something inspirational to say as Stack had at Trones Wood.

"We will *not* fall back!" Second Lieutenant Butterfield roared. "They will *not* be allowed to trample the graves of our fallen! We won this land, and we'll bloody well keep it!"

"What he said," the corporal breathed tightly, feeling his face whitening.

"What are we fighting for this for?" Private Castle looked about desperately. "It's a bloody wreck of a village; I don't want to die for this!"

Rigby had no time to reply before the man's head was blown backwards and he could fear no more, his last wish ignored. He cursed under his breath, forcing himself to look back towards the enemy.

Fire came thick and fast from both sides, but Butterfield's troops were tired and many expected defeat, so fate kindly handed it to them. Reluctantly, the second lieutenant shouted for runners to carry the message along; retreat. They scattered to the lengths of the line, one falling only moments after leaving Butterfield's side. He tripped backwards, landing helmetless against his commander's chest.

Butterfield bellowed with rage, letting the man drop as he got to his feet and fired fearlessly into the face of the oncoming victors, bullets missing him by inches.

"Sir! We have to retreat with the others!" his batman tried to pull him back down behind the rubble.

"I can't retreat!" he screamed, tears running freely down his cheeks. "They can't take what we lost so many for! They can't have our men for free!"

"If we don't fall back, the others won't follow," the young lad insisted. "We would lose more."

Boots stumbled through the wreckage in disarray, unsure whether to keep shooting or run like hell. They stopped at intervals to duck back down and return fire on their pursuers, or to heave the wounded to their feet, only for the wretched souls to be shot down again in agony. Shrapnel from a blast took the legs from Butterfield's young batman, and the second lieutenant ran with him in his arms, refusing to leave him with the rest of the dying.

"Foden! Dimery!" Stack called, stopping to send off a few shots. "Stop panicking! Follow Wayson, he knows where to go. Where's Mackie?"

He scoured the battlefield for the last of his section, the little man scuttling through the barrage to join them. A hit behind him knocked more men off their feet, Stack's gut tightening as he watched.

"Mackie," he panted. "Get them out of here. Keep them safe, keep them together. I'll catch up."

Mackie nodded.

"Thanks," Stack breathed, before vaulting over a pile of rubble and bodies towards the man on the floor.

"Rig!" he heaved him up, feeling the sickening warmth of blood against his chest. "You" – his eye caught one of Rigby's section, standing by hesitantly – "be a corporal. The rest of you, follow him!"

Rigby groaned, his face screwed up in anguish. "Put me down Ben, you idiot. I'm done for."

"Captain always said you're bloody pessimistic!" Stack adjusted his hold and started forwards, causing the other man to cry out in pain. "*Nobody* else is allowed to die, you included."

"I'm not in your section anymore Ben," he gritted his teeth, his chest, stomach and legs feeling like they were on fire. "I can die if I want. God, this bloody hurts, put me down!"

A blast further along the trench unsettled the debris, causing Stack to trip, smashing his shin. He turned his head to face Rigby's greying complexion, interrupted with crimson, and scrambled back to his feet, wobbling as his leg tried to give way.

Rigby chuckled weakly. "You'll just get yourself killed too. Go on, Wayson needs you."

"Wayson is a good soldier," Stack grunted, putting his weight on the other leg to lift Rigby's shoulders. "He'll be fine."

"Really?" Rigby gasped, crying out again as his friend began to drag him backwards. The wounds on his front stretched and stung as his back was battered and cut by the wood, stone and shrapnel shattered beneath him. "You should tell him that some time. Ahhh shit!"

"Tell him yourself!" Stack shouted over the noise of another shell and Rigby's screams.

A stray piece of wire had caught in his thigh and was pulling at the gaping wound, slicing further into flesh and tangling with the flap of skin that hung sickeningly through his shredded tunic. Stack would have liked to remove it properly, but there was no time.

"Hold your breath," he told him, taking a quick gulp himself before giving a forceful tug.

Rigby shrieked as the wire tore through flesh, his consciousness swimming with pain. But at least he was freed, to be hauled further through fractured boards and shattered bodies, too agonised to reply to Stack's shouts of encouragement. His mouth filled with blood, threatening to drown him, but he knew if he opened it he would never stop screaming.

****

Rob clutched the letter in both hands, his uncle's handwriting giving him a sort of strength and vulnerability he hadn't felt in a long time. It reminded him that he wasn't really Lance-Corporal Kit Allenby; he was just Rob Stack, and he was a long way from home. He couldn't remember seeing him on the road, and he should have been furious at Billy for giving him away, but he was glad he did. At least he knew they were alive, or had been when the letter was written at least. That was a blessing. And Ben had said he was proud of him. His uncle's pride gave him a lot more strength than a fake name and a promotion ever could.

"You haven't had a letter before have you?" Cufflinks asked good-naturedly. "I'm glad the folks back home haven't forgotten you."

"Maybe he's finally nineteen now," Dafydd teased. "He can risk letters now they can't drag him back home."

"Watch it Daffodil," Rob snarled, his voice sounding angrier than he had intended. His nerves weren't exactly stable at the moment. "I'm your superior; I could put you on watch all night."

"You wouldn't," the Welshman stretched confidently.

"Perhaps, but I would," Cufflinks leaned forward in a manner that told them he meant it. "Be a good man and relieve Turner; he's been up there long enough."

With a lot of grumbling, the gunner obeyed, leaving them in the half-collapsed cellar to take the watch from the man who had replaced Carthorse. They shared the cellar with the remnants of a battalion of Anzacs, the tank being their final hope in a bloody retreat. The Germans were close behind them, they knew, and it was here they would meet them for one last stand. They had arrived a battered bunch, asleep on their feet, many carrying the possessions of companions they had lost as they ran. Somehow they held their nerve as they waited, their captain Stevie Allen keeping up a cheery charade, helped by Dafydd and Colm's promises of victory.

Rob hoped they were right. His confidence had taken a knock after the shock of seeing Betsy floundering at Passchendaele, but their new tank had proven her worth since. Though he could not be quite as enthusiastic as the portside duo, the magnificence of their advance at Cambrai had certainly done nothing to harm his spirits in the months that followed.

He closed his eyes and tried to remember that now, yearning to fill his bones with all the pride and assurance he had felt that day. The sound of his and Dafydd's guns scattering the enemy as Turner guided them towards the great Hindenburg Line, before crushing the impenetrable barbed wire defences beneath their tracks.

They had said the Hindenburg Line could never be taken – all year they had been saying it. The Germans had fallen back when blizzards were still frequenting the front, back to the line specifically built to be impassable by their foes. And so it had been, until Rob and his tanks had their way. There had been hundreds of them; the greatest sight he had ever seen, and he had only been seeing it through a periscope. He couldn't imagine how fantastic it must have looked to the infantry following behind, or how gloriously terrifying it must have been for the enemy. An infinite line of great metal beasts, tearing through the thickest of their wire like it was simply grass.

The terrain had rocked them and the anti-tank defences were unkind to their comrades, but they could not be stopped. They rumbled on up the hill, from the shelter of a sunken road and into the guns, then over the guns as they shattered them. Even the fumes couldn't blunt their vigour, Rob and Dafydd shrugging off the pain of the molten splash as they kept up their bombardment, each trying to better the other in aim and speed.

They had climbed onto the tank afterwards – imaginatively dubbed 'Betsy II' – and posed for a photograph, exhausted and triumphant. Cufflinks had bought them all drinks and they had dared to believe the war would soon be over, and everybody would know the vital part they had played in the glorious conclusion.

They dropped off one by one until it was only Rob and the lieutenant awake, each unwilling to put an end to such a day. Rob was a true man that night, talking to his commander like an equal. They shared their hopes and dreams of home, and their aching wish that Carthorse and Firetop could have been with them, driving Naughty Betsy into the history books. He even thought he could forgive Daisy that day; after all, she had been the one to give him the last push to become a hero. He would return home to her and she would never think him a coward again.

Rob had felt like a king that day, or even better – an officer.

But from every dream, one must wake up. Those who followed the path carved by the tanks had not gone far enough and the advance was halted. And here they were, barely four months later, quaking in their boots at an enemy advancing faster than anybody believed possible. Such was the way of war.

Still, he had to believe that they could do it. It had been all he could think about for so long, what did he have left if he didn't keep fighting? He looked about at the shattered Anzacs, Captain Allen holding a picture of his little daughter. That could have been his father, holding a picture of baby Violet. What would he think of him if he started doubting now?

******

"I wasn't disobedient," he said.

Rob had climbed the old bell-tower to sit with Dafydd as he watched out for the approaching horde. The artillery had done their job well, leaving the sturdy church surrounded by rubble. Of course, they hadn't counted on there being a tank hidden in the churchyard. There was still a chance.

"Not really. I just wanted more. Is that so bad?"

Dafydd shook his head. "Of course not, Whip. Not bad, just dangerous."

The Welshman shifted his position, the serious look on his face reminding Rob that despite his antics the man was actually closer to his uncle's age than his own. He surveyed the wreckage, anticipating the inevitable attack following the artillery bombardment.

"Perhaps you should've listened to your father though. He'd only say what was best for you."

Rob felt his chest tighten as he thought back on every conversation they had ever had.

"No," he said heavily. "He knew what was best for him, maybe, when he was my age, but not for me. My mother thought I was a baby and my father wished I'd never been born. Oh, he loved me alright, and I loved him more than anything, but he always knew deep down that if I hadn't come along he could have done more with his life. He thought I was a foolish show-off. What he didn't understand was I never wanted to be the best – just good enough for him."

"I'm sure you are, Whip," Dafydd told him. "You're certainly the best youngster I've ever met. Better than I was at your age and that's a fact. I never knew my father, and because of that I really never have been more than a foolish show-off."

"And now look at us," Rob hugged his knees, trying to forget the past for now and look to the future. "They'd both be proud of us now."

Dafydd made a noise of agreement but said nothing, staring thoughtfully out across the ruins.

"You wanted to know who Kit Allenby is?" Rob said at length. "Allenby was a major in the Boer war and commanded the first cavalry division at the front in 1914. Kit was the name of the first man in our area to die. That's all."

****

"Here they come!" Cufflinks bellowed, his strong voice drowned out by the roar of Death and the engine sent out to halt him. "Fire!"

Rob gritted his teeth and brought the six-pounder to life, his heart a hurricane in his chest. The tank stood alone ahead of the Anzacs' street barricade, a last noble reminder of the hope these great beasts had brought with them in 1916. They had brought the image of attack and victory, rolling over trenches and shell holes alike, driving the fleeing Hun before them. Now the Hun drove them. Now the tank stood alone.

At a signal from Cufflinks, the gunners halted their firing and Turner took them forward, rolling down the flattened street over unmoved ruins and unburied dead. They couldn't let courtesy stop them now; the men behind were depending on them. The lieutenant gave a second signal and the guns opened fire, booming an angry warning at the enemy who sought to silence them. The warning was not heeded.

Rob struggled against the bumps and jolts of movement over rubble, but there was no real need to aim. The attackers advanced like ants swarming over the hillside; unending and therefore unmissable. Rob and Dafydd took them down and more just climbed over them. It was as if they weren't human, with no need for sleep and no feeling of fear, each soul creeping out of its fallen host and amassing again at the back of the crowd.

It was all Rob could do to keep up his firing, frustration mounting as they continued to press on, his speed no match for theirs. He could sense Alfie moving behind him, feel his sweat as their arms brushed, and he tried not to blame him for loading too slow. This was not Cambrai. They were not in control here. They were working beyond their limits already and still making no progress.

A clatter sounded behind him and Alfie slipped, falling hard into Rob's back.

"Get a grip!" he snapped, throwing him roughly off.

"I'm trying!" Alfie replied angrily, red in the face and obviously working as hard as he could.

An explosion sent dust into the air as something ricocheted off the starboard sponson and Rob fired through the haze, not daring to blink his fume filled eyes. The enemy couldn't keep coming forever, he forced himself to believe. They would shoot them to pieces as they had at Cambrai and the tide of the war would be turned. The Anzacs would return home to their little daughters and Kit Allenby and Ollie Powell would return home with medals on their chests. If they would only stop advancing!

"We need the machine guns!" Rob yelled, signing at the same time in the hope that somebody was looking at him. "They'll be faster, and they're getting too close!"

Before he had the chance to move to the other gun, something hissed within the belly of the tank and a jet of steam scorched his shoulder. He wasn't sure what happened – the fumes were too strong and all the concentration he had was focussed on the enemy. Suddenly the gearsmen were stumbling past him, Cufflinks fumbling with the door and shouting at them to hurry. Rob heard Dafydd fire from the machine gun at his sponson and followed suit. Let the others leave first; they would need people to cover them.

The lieutenant got the door open and held out a hand to pause the gearsmen, checking their position before allowing them to leave. He checked, then he crumpled, falling unceremoniously from the tank to the floor. Rob kept his eyes firmly on the progress of his gun, oblivious, until Alfie's hands shaking his shoulder brought his gaze around.

"Cuffs is dead!" the loader shouted, his bottom lip wobbling. "You're in charge now!"

Rob stared, his muscles frozen with shock. Lieutenant Cuthbert could not be dead, he just couldn't. He was their commander, the best commander Rob could imagine. And this magnificent man had entrusted the unit to him.

"Go! Go! Go!" he snapped out of his trance, pushing Alfie towards the door with the others. "We'll give you cover as long as we can!"

He sprayed fire almost blindly, red rage guiding his aim as he screamed out revenge and inhaled toxic fumes. His mind was void of anything else until Dafydd was behind him, telling him that the others had reached the barricade and reminding him of the living. As much as he wanted to let his temper take over, he was supposed to be leading them now, not mindlessly shooting Germans.

"They're with the Anzacs?" he shouted. "That's safe enough, let's go."

He swept bullets once more across the line for good measure then signalled to Dafydd for them to leave. Seizing one of the rifles Cufflinks had the foresight to carry, Rob sprung from the tank, pausing at the sight of the lieutenant on the floor.

"Leave him," the Welshman shook his head sadly.

Rob ignored him.

"Get to the barricade!" he ordered, lifting his rifle to return fire as a bullet shot past his cheek. Dafydd turned and Rob bent to heave their commander into his arms.

Before his fingertips reached the body, he was halted, pulled back by a force in his abdomen that threatened to bring him down completely. Confused, he put a hand to his stomach. Something flowed over it; something warm and sticky. He pulled his hand away to see it covered in blood, and that was when the pain set in. He burned as if it had been a flamethrower, not a bullet, that had hit him and he doubled over, fighting to stay on his feet.

He stared at Lieutenant Cuthbert, his face the picture of shock. This was not what he had pictured; their heroic last stand.

"Come on!" Dafydd called, halfway to the barricade.

Rob closed his mind to the pain and ran towards him, skidding in beside Alfie and Colm.

"Are you alright Whip?" the Irishman asked, concerned.

Rob moved his arm to cover the dark stain seeping through his clothes. "I'm fine. Are you?"

"We're holding up," Colm replied. "Are you hurt?"

"No," Rob told him firmly.

He kept his head down, not wanting the agony on his face to attract attention. He aimed and shot his rifle as best he could, shouting encouragement to the others but always shielding his face and abdomen. He heard every shot that sought them out, felt every bead of sweat that dripped from their brows, drip-drip-dripping from his stomach. He had thought that pain should dull all other senses, but he found his now enhanced, every sound ringing in his ears, every sight crisper and clearer.

The attackers had reached the edge of the destruction now, finding ruins and rubble to hide behind as they crept ever closer to the barricade. The Anzacs' machine gun team did their best to halt them, Rob's eyes picking up every burst of blood even from this distance. He almost felt every hit, his stomach clenching and threatening to send its contents up into his mouth.

Colm yelled for ammunition and he threw it at him without turning, keeping his eyes on the man who made a run for it from behind the shell of the tank. He felt the metal of Rob's bullet in his throat and advanced no more. Volleys of shots crossed the street, their enemies creeping forward as they stayed struggling behind their last defences.

A grenade shook the barricade, shunting a panel of wood hard into Rob's wound. His eyes pricked and he retched, dribbling blood, and the round he fired went wide. He wiped his mouth quickly in his shoulder and reloaded – he was their commander, he couldn't show weakness.

The machine gunners were taken down and he scrambled across the wreckage to take their place, more comfortable with the faster firing weapon in their desperate situation. It also couldn't hurt to put a bit of distance between himself and his unit, now that his front was a dark scarlet. They didn't need to see that.

A shout brought his attention to another grenade, this one having found its way over the barrier. He watched it fall as if in slow motion, before diving to the ground as it blasted the structure apart, thrusting men into the sky. He fell heavily onto his front, showered with broken bits of wood, metal and flesh, the feeling in his stomach threatening to tear his mind from his body.

"Retreat!"

The Anzac captain gave the order, screaming at the men as bullets rained from the heavens to pierce through his bedraggled bunch. Rob pushed himself up onto his elbows, groaning as he tried to pull himself back to the gun. He caught sight of Alfie clambering towards him, the rest of the unit looking ready to follow him.

"Stick with them!" Rob called, clutching at a fallen rifle and painfully firing it through a hole in the barricade. "Follow Captain Allen!"

His focus waned as he caught the look of hurt and surprise on Alfie's face, gaping down at the red flowing from two places in his chest. His legs gave way and he tumbled down the blockade, landing on his back beside Rob. His friend met his eye and turned, showing him the mess of his own stomach. They stared at each other for a moment, no words needing to be said. They knew what this meant.

"GO!" Rob broke the gaze and shouted at Dafydd and the others, spitting blood.

"You too, boss," Dafydd said hesitantly, his boisterous face dropping as he took in the state of the boy.

"We'll hold them back," Rob told him, a lump rising in his throat. "Now go! That's an order Jones!"

Dafydd looked at him a moment longer – a look of such respect that Rob thought he was going to cry. Then he was gathering up the others to join the retreating Anzacs, following his order. Following *his* order. For a short moment in his short life, Rob had been a commander; a commander just like Cufflinks. His father would be proud. His uncle would be proud. He was proud of himself.

His veins filling with honour even as the life drained out of them, he offered Alfie his hand, pulling him back to his feet and handing him a rifle. He readjusted his own gun, getting a firmer grip beneath sweat and blood to fire again through gaps in the barricade.

Seeing the defenders fleeing, the attackers became bold, stepping out from behind their shelters just to be cut down by the fierce bullets fired by the man who remained. Rob glared down the sight of his rifle, firing and reloading faster than he had done in his life, despite the sweat dripping down his forehead and the blood dripping down his chin from the corners of his mouth. He felt Alfie shaking beside him, barely able to hold his gun.

"What's your name?" he fixed him with determined eyes. "How old are you?"

"Ollie Powell," he replied obediently, in a weak voice. "Twenty-two years old."

"No," Rob shook his head, pausing to fire more shots before continuing. "What's your name!? How old are you!?"

"Ollie Powell-"

"Alfie Barnes," Rob snarled, drooling more blood as he fired again. "Who are you!?"

"Alfie Barnes," he replied, finally managing to lift his rifle. "Nineteen years old."

"Who am I?"

"Rob Stack," he pulled himself up and shot through the destroyed blockade. "Nineteen years old."

"That's right," Rob grinned darkly, hot tears pricking at his eyes. "Alfie Barnes" – he shot again – "and Rob Stack. Nineteen years old. MEN! OF! ENGLAND!"

"Men of England!" Alfie chanted, crying freely.

They reloaded their rifles and climbed the barricade, feet stumbling on the loosened rubble, stumbling but not falling. They sprayed the remainder of their lives into the broken street, taking down as many as they could, slowing the advance. A bullet tore through Rob's shoulder but he clutched onto their perch, continuing to hinder the enemy as their friends fell back to better ground. The need to duck encumbered them no longer; fears and obligations and fantasies of glory no more than a memory. For every man they hit, that was another man saved. For every man they hit, three hit them.

Dafydd faltered at the back of his comrades, watching the two boys he had come to love as they were shot down, bodies slumping down the barricade as they could fire no more. They had never had the chance to grow up as boys should, yet they were more men now than he would ever be.

"Brave lads," Colm said solemnly, reaching for his arm to lead him back.

Dafydd shook him off. He ran forward, ignoring his friend's shouts that they needed to go. He remembered the letter Whipper had been reading the night before; it needed to be retrieved. Somebody needed to know their boy had been a hero to the end.

Harry Old. Not Yet Dead Nearly.

17.

The letter trembled in Stack's hands, no strength remaining in his fingers. His heart was broken but his eyes were dry; he felt like he would never be human again. The boy had been his life. He had loved him as if he were his own son, taken him everywhere with him, taught him how to be a man. And now the boy had died like a man. The war had taken everything.

He had been obsessed with it since the rumours started; he had always been obsessed with anything that would make him seem stronger. Helping on the farm, swordplay, shooting, gambling, and then war. He had said once that if he joined the forces he would finally deserve his father. Stack had given him a friendly cuff and told him to stop being silly – he had always deserved his father. Rob had just laughed, saying that he had always deserved Harriet, but if he wouldn't listen to Rob, why should Rob listen to him?

He took a deep breath and went to get to his feet, finding no strength in his legs. He slumped again and took another breath, dropping his head to his hands and crumpling the ill-fated letter. Never again would his nephew laugh at him, or anything at all.

Footsteps sounded but he didn't look up.

"Are you alright sir?" Wayson's voice asked.

Wayson. What had Captain said about Wayson? *You do know that risking your stupid neck for Wayson is* not *going to save your nephew!* They had been best friends, the same age, they had signed up together. So why was this boy alive when Rob was not? He could have hated him. But he didn't. They had been best friends, the same age, they had signed up together. This boy was the last link he had to the boy he had lost.

The feeling returned to his limbs and he shot to his feet. Shoving the letter into his pocket, he seized his rifle, hastily loaded it and clicked the safety off, aiming at Wayson's foot.

"You're going home, boy."

"What?" Wayson startled and jumped back, but Stack caught him and forced him against the wall, trying to get a safe shot at the boy's foot as he struggled.

"You're going home!" he howled desperately. "You shouldn't even be here! Hold *still!*"

"No!" Wayson fought back, panic making him stronger. He pushed and the gun went off but it hit nothing, only slightly grazing the shine on his boot. "What's going on!?"

Stack let him go, the adrenaline fading from grieving muscles. He dropped his rifle and brought a hand to his head.

"I'm sorry," he muttered. "I'm so sorry."

"Sir?" Wayson asked in alarm. "What's happened?"

"Nothing," he stormed out of the dugout, too ashamed of himself to look him in the eye. He was supposed to be protecting him, not making him lame. If his friends had been there they would have held him back, but Captain was dead and Rigby was recovering from his wounds in England. Wayson had lost his friends too; Yates in front of his eyes and Waterman near enough. But Rob...he knew nothing of Rob – this at least was something Stack could still protect him from.

****

"You know I am offering compassionate leave, sergeant," Butterfield shuffled through some papers on his desk.

"I know," he replied unenthusiastically. Rob died and he got to go home; it was hardly fair. "I don't intend taking it."

The lieutenant looked at him curiously. "You could do with a break from all this."

"I'm a sergeant, sir," he said firmly. "My place is with the men. Besides, what do I have to go home to now?"

Butterfield shifted uncomfortably.

"You should take it instead," he told him. "Isn't Collie's little brother living with your sister? Go home for a while and give the poor boy a father figure."

"You know it doesn't work like that," Butterfield said sadly. "I have my duties too, sergeant." He fixed him with determined eyes. "I could have given up when Jim died. God, every day I feel like I could. But instead I have tried even harder, for the men who could have gone like him. Nobody in my platoon will suffer or die unnecessarily and I plan on killing every bastard German I possibly can. It's all I can do. If you won't go home, I suggest you do the same. Remember only the men, Stack – the living ones. You keep them living, and you've got something to live for yourself."

He returned to the dugout, wishing he had one of Captain's silly games to occupy his mind. The spring advance had been crushed – due to the Germans outrunning their supply chain more than any victory on the allies' part – and summer was dawning on stalemate in 1918 just as it had every other year. At least these dugouts were deep and comfort had improved greatly from the dirty holes they had slept in three years ago. Wayson was there with Mackie and Dimery when he arrived – finished with fatigues for the day and settling down for an attempt at sleep – and he stood immediately when he heard his boots on the steps.

"Sergeant Stack, sir," he greeted him somewhat more formerly than usual, even by Wayson's standards. "Is everything alright?"

"Yes, thank you Wayson," he replied, choking back a lump in his throat and trying to look cheery.

"So, earlier…?" he trailed off, not really sure what he wanted to ask.

"I'm sorry, I really am," he shook his head in shame. "You're a brave lad and you have every right to be here. In fact, I'll find you extra rum rations this week if you'll forgive me."

Dimery cheered and clapped Wayson on the back, but the boy didn't look satisfied.

"But are you okay sir? You seemed…distressed."

"I'm fine," he smiled as best he could and headed for his bunk. "I just need some sleep."

Wayson accepted that he would get no explanation at the moment, turning back to the others and leaving the sergeant to get into bed in peace. Still, the incident had greatly shaken him and he sat awake once again as the others drifted off, more returning from work parties for a rest before the real work of night could commence. He looked about the room, accustoming his eyes to the dark and wondering when Corporal Rigby would return. He might know what was up, and what to do about it.

A rigid voice from the corner alerted him to Sergeant Stack's usual roll-call. He let his ears tune into the names; it was familiar now and the monotony of it may help him drift off and get some much needed rest.

"Vincent Waterman…George Penley…"

He swung his legs onto the bunk, stretching out and resting his head on the pillow.

"Daniel Captain…Jackson Weir…"

He felt his body getting comfortable, but still his eyes wouldn't close. He stared across the room, seeing the face of each man as he was called. It was a comfort somehow.

"Harry Nailey…Bert Stockdale…Rob Stack."

The last name caught in Wayson's chest and interrupted his breathing. He blinked in shock, then his eyes released and spilled silent tears down both cheeks. He continued to stare for a moment, salty droplets dripping from the tip of his nose, before he turned his head into the pillow and sobbed.

****

With the arrival of the Americans in force on the Western Front, it was clear that the enemy was fast losing morale. They chased them back from Amiens and once again from the recaptured Trones Wood with remarkably few losses, tipping their hats to those who had died taking the very same spots two years previous. It was an odd and nauseating feeling, walking through places they had once all walked together.

They trod through the wreckage of the old theatre where they had danced on tables for Rigby's birthday in 1916. Now it was dust and rubble, tables overturned or destroyed entirely. Stack stared up at the half-collapsed ceiling, eyes open but not as alert as perhaps they should have been. The battering this place had taken over the past few days couldn't possibly have left anybody alive. A late summer breeze whistled through the corpses of rooms, a warm thing that could have been pleasant if it didn't rustle the blood-soaked hair of dead men on its journey. They had cleared this place alright; now it was Lieutenant Butterfield's for the taking.

Butterfield had been there too that night, and Stack was sure he remembered. Perhaps that was why he searched a different street; perhaps the memory was too painful for him. For Stack, it didn't feel real enough to be painful. In the months following his nephew's death, no memory felt real anymore. He was only a soldier, living and thinking and breathing for his men, with no capacity for memories and hopes and dreams.

Rigby ran a finger through the grime covering what remained of the bar.

"It's so strange," he shook his head, wiping his finger in his tunic. "Seeing this old place so dead. We were so alive here, before anything really happened."

"We were," Stack agreed, running his hand along the side of an overturned table.

"I was hoping it would still be open, that we could have another night like that..." he trailed off. "Not without Cap."

Stack murmured, but said nothing. Truth was, he wasn't sure what he hoped for anymore.

"They're saying it's almost over," Rigby brushed the dust from the bar with his arm. "Got all the propaganda out at home already. It's the Americans that did it; bloody Yankees. We've been here nearly four years and they come over and rout them in less than one. Whatever happened to Great British glory?"

"The Yankees can have their glory," Stack replied, staring up at the ruins of the hall. "I'm not complaining."

"You never do," Rigby breathed out thoughtfully. "Problem is, I've been home. I've seen what it's like for one of us returning after all this and I'm not sure I want to go back. Soldiers are in the street already and the war's not even over; lacking limbs and begging for bread.

People stare at you, Ben, like they've never seen a man before, and they ask you all these questions and pretend they know how you're feeling when they *don't*. They couldn't possibly. And it's so quiet. I thought I couldn't wait for the day when there were no shells whizzing over my head, but God, I couldn't stand how quiet it was back home. I couldn't sleep at night; my head kept telling me there must be a raid coming, have to stay alert. I started thinking, maybe I'm better off out here after all."

"Not if a whizzbang hits you, you're not," Stack pointed out.

"No," Rigby mused. "But what was I back home? A failed inventor and artist with a bad taste in women. Out here, I've got a job and a purpose, and friends who know exactly what I've been through 'cause we've been through it together."

He paused. "I…feel closer to people out here – people who've died. Sometimes I look over into No Man's Land and I almost expect them to come back, like they've only been on patrol. I can't do that at home."

Stack looked at him in sympathy. "Cap's not coming back."

"I know," he shook his head. "It's stupid, but it gets me through. God, he must be laughing. He'd have a field day if he knew how much I miss him." He smiled nostalgically. "I guess Captain always wins in the end. It's just his way."

They continued to walk, reaching a pile of bodies at the end of the hall, where the gambling table had been two years ago. The figure lying on the top was small and fragile looking, a pointed face staring unseeing back at them. True, he wore a German uniform, but he couldn't be any older than Rob.

Rigby shook his head. "What's happened to us, Ben? We're not men anymore."

"We're whatever we need to be," Stack put a hand on his shoulder.

"And what's that?" Rigby looked at him with concerned eyes. "What will we be when this is all over?"

****

10:45am, November 11th 1918. The reserve camp at Le Cateau was a bustle of nervous energy; men standing and sitting and standing again, unsure how to spend their last minutes before peace was declared and the war officially over. After what seemed like hours of Butterfield screaming down the telephone – demanding they not waste more lives for the sake of a romantic time to end on – his office was now silent. The lieutenant stood instead at the edge of the camp, loading and reloading a rifle, firing at nothing to relieve his frustration.

"He has a point," Dimery commented, standing with Mackie who was fiddling frantically with a letter from his girl. "If they've already surrendered, why are we waiting?"

Stack sat in a stupor, resting on a crate of ammunition now never to be used, not bothering to hide the flask of rum in his hand. He drank for Captain and he drank because he didn't know what else to do. In a few minutes time he would no longer be a soldier. He would not be Sergeant Stack, just Ben, with no responsibility for the men around him and no need to shoot anyone ever again. It was all they had wanted for so long, but now it was happening none of them knew how to deal with it. He found himself almost hoping the hour would never come and they could go on fighting.

Perhaps Rigby had been right. Perhaps they were better off sticking with the hell they knew, than trying their hands at a world now alien to all of them. But Rigby wasn't with him now; he had been sent back with wounds just a few weeks before, wounds that did not look good. He had almost made it – just a few weeks.

He could hear hundreds of voices wondering what to do, those more optimistic choosing instead to babble about their families over the noise of Butterfield's shooting. Then the hour hit, and the church bells sounded; whether a celebratory peal or the chimes of doom they weren't quite sure. At the sound of the bells the men fell silent, even Butterfield putting down his rifle. 11 o'clock, on the 11th day of the 11th month. The war was over. Still, the men were silent.

"What do we do now, sir?" Wayson broke the stillness of the air, even now the perfect soldier looking for orders.

"I don't know," Stack replied, his voice catching in his throat.

"Captain would have known what to do," Stack was surprised to hear Mackie speak. "He would have had us celebrating alright."

"Yes," Stack smiled, a thick wave of emotion rising up his gullet and breaching his voice and eyes. "He would, wouldn't he."

With that he broke, tears streaming down his cheeks and noisy sobs erupting from his chest as he held his head in his hands. He wasn't a soldier anymore. He didn't need to be strong, or a good influence on anybody else. They came flooding out; years of watching people die, making people die, losing friends and family and always listening to Captain's words – *the young ones look up to you, Ben*. Nobody needed to look up to him now. There was nobody to save, nobody to tell him he needed to be strong for them. For the first time in years he let it all go, and cried as if he would never stop.

The war was over.

18/Epilogue.

Wayson's anticipation became harder to conceal the closer they came to the shores of England. He wasn't quite an excitable child again – he had finally grown into his height and a thick layer of stubble covered his strengthened chin – but the shadows of war were certainly fading from his eyes, replaced by the spark of glory he had always longed for. So many times he had imagined the moment he would return, both in the trenches and with Rob before they had even left. It was this moment he had signed up for; the proof that he was indeed a man and worthy of every drop of praise thrown at him by a grateful nation. He had made it. He had won the war.

Stack watched him with a suffocating feeling of guilt. He would be looking forward to seeing Rob, he thought, wanting to compare war stories and boast about who was the bravest. Perhaps he should have prepared him after all.

"Wayson," he caught his attention. "I need to tell you something."

The boy looked at him expectantly as he attempted to get the words out. None came.

"You don't have to," Wayson said quietly, realising what he was trying to say. "I know."

"You do?"

"Rob?" he asked. Stack nodded. "I've known since the day you found out. You talk in your sleep; big long lists of dead people."

"God," Stack looked away. "I'm sorry, I should have told you properly. I kept thinking I needed to protect you from it, but…I'm sorry."

"Don't be," Wayson put a hand on his arm. "I *did* need protecting, sir. Rob and I, we were stupid. Brave, but stupid. It was luck that decided I could come home when he couldn't – luck and you. You saved my life more times than I can count. Thank you sergeant, thank you very much."

****

They had trickled out of the station one by one, the returning soldiers and their well-wishers, some on trains and some on foot. Stack had bid farewell to Wayson and the others as they left with ecstatic mothers, fathers, siblings and girlfriends, and now he lay his head down on the bench; the closest thing he could find to duckboard or a firestep.

He didn't belong here, in this world of delighted youngsters. When he left this station he would have to return home, to face a house full of ghosts. He wasn't sure what would be worse; the empty spaces once filled by Rob and Edward or the false smiles of Sylvie, forced to pretend she was pleased he returned in the place of her husband and son. What right did he have to this world?

While it had always been a comfort against a backdrop of shells and gunfire, the humming in his ears was deafening in the quiet British night. He screwed his eyes shut, trying to hear beyond it to shots between patrols in No Man's Land, or Captain's laughter as he cooked up another plot with Tommy Miller. That was where he belonged – he was a soldier, only a soldier.

"Sergeant Stack?"

He must have fallen asleep; here was Sandford, waking him up for the morning stand-to. He fumbled for his rifle and helmet, hitting his hand against the hard bench where he had expected soft mud.

"I thought I might find you here."

He blinked, the lieutenant's face coming into focus in the brightness of the morning. He was shorter than Stack remembered, but he would know that face anywhere. He straightened up out of habit when talking to a superior, and it was then he noticed that the young man was in a wheelchair. His blonde hair was smartly brushed and his face looked flushed and well, but his trousers sagged beyond the two stumps that reminded the onlooker that this man was a survivor of the war.

"Don't pity me," Sandford caught him staring. "I came out of this well."

"Your legs…"

"Would still be lying in No Man's Land under a cart if it wasn't for you," Sandford reminded him. "Come on, I will not have my best sergeant sleeping on a bench. Have you eaten since you arrived?"

"No sir," Stack shook his head, suddenly realising just how hungry he was.

"It's not 'sir' anymore," Sandford smiled. "Luckily, there is a very nice café not half a minute from here; my treat. On my exit from hospital the war office were kind enough to find me a desk job with a very comfortable wage packet."

Stack picked up his bag and followed his former commander from the station, blinking and jumping at the bustle of everyday life going on outside. The lieutenant chose his favourite seat by the window and the waitress removed a chair to make room for him as he cheerfully ordered them tea.

"And I promise you," he added to Stack as an afterthought. "This is worlds apart from the saturated mud we called tea on the front."

"I'm glad," Stack chuckled. His eyes darted about the room, taking in every colour and every movement, so different from the rundown taverns they had deemed luxury before. "How are you sir?"

"Good, thank you," the younger man smiled. "I've landed on my feet, so to speak. My job has allowed me to keep track of the platoon – I haven't stopped watching you all since I regained consciousness. You will be pleased to know that Corporal Rigby is still hanging on." He noticed Stack twitch as if to stand and added: "He is, however, being kept in a hospital near Croydon for the time being, so you will have to wait to see him. I have been keeping a special eye on him for you; I know you were close."

"Thank you, sir," Stack smiled, relieved. "I appreciate it. What about your girl; Lily, was it?"

A grin broke across his face and he held up his left hand to display the band of gold around his finger.

"She was waiting, bless her heart, and I am about to be a father!" He chuckled. "My legs may be gone but there are parts of me still working. I pray every night that she will be a girl and never have to see what we've seen." He breathed deeply. "And what about you? Was Captain right?"

"Yes," it was Stack's turn to smile. In his fears of returning to Sylvie, he hadn't considered that Harriet too would be coming home. "I'd have to say he was."

Their conversation was halted as the tea was delivered to their table and food was ordered; real food, with no tins of bully beef in sight.

"So," Sandford leant on the table when the waitress left. "I cannot believe that a man like you has nowhere better to sleep than a station. And yet, I knew you would be there. It's your brother's wife, isn't it?"

Stack nodded. "My nephew, Rob, he died after you were wounded. My arrival would just remind Sylvie that neither of them are coming back."

Sandford looked at him sternly, the hint of officer still in his face. "Don't feel like that, Stack. It's hard, I know – Lily's brother was killed and I had the same worries – but you have to face her one day."

A train whistled as it pulled into the nearby station, the sudden noise shocking Stack's trench-born instincts into action. His chair skidded across the floor as he ducked under the table, emerging embarrassedly to see Sandford cowering lower in his wheelchair, fists clenched. They shared an awkward laugh, Stack feeling eyes boring into the back of his head as he fetched the chair and sat back down.

"I won't pretend it gets better," Sandford told him, hands still shaking. "If it wasn't for my legs, I'd be under there with you. But it does become bearable, and you learn to ignore the stares – after years of having people shoot at you, what's staring really? The main thing, Stack, is you're not alone. We shared a platoon; that makes us family. If you ever need anything, anything at all, you let me know. That's an order, sergeant."

Stack smiled. "The same goes for you, lieutenant."

A full stomach and Sandford's encouragement left Stack feeling braver than he had when he had lain down to sleep at the station. In truth, he felt braver now than he had since that tragic stand-to at Passchendaele. The morning was crisp and bright and he decided he would walk from Maidstone. The road was long, but years spent marching across France and Belgium made it trivial to trained legs.

His boots found a familiar rhythm and he fumbled in his pocket, pulling out the drawing of himself and Captain, signed with Rigby's scrawl. He had thought he had lost them both, but if Sandford spoke the truth there was still hope for Rigby. And Captain…

"I always said you were his favourite," the handsome man beamed teasingly, falling into step at his right.

"Cap!" Stack would have thrown his arms around him, if he hadn't thought they would go straight through him.

Captain laughed, his hair bouncing. *"That's me. Didn't think I'd let you have all the fun did you?"*

"No," he grinned. "I didn't."

"Sandford's not the only one who's here for you Benji, don't you forget that."

He tipped his helmet to somebody on Stack's left, and he turned to see Rob marching in time with them, his father's arm wrapped proudly around his shoulders. Captain struck up a chorus of "Kiss me goodnight sergeant major" and he heard the rest of the platoon join in; the living and the dead. He marched among them – his men, his friends, his memories – and their company spurred him on towards the hardest battle yet: life after war.

Printed in Great Britain
by Amazon